The Resilient Thistle

Allan Paterson.

10th July 2018

The Resilient Thistle

The Incomprehensible Journey of Daniel MacDhughill

By Pat Gemmiti

This is a story of fiction and any references to historical events, actual people, or real places are used fictitiously. Other names, places, and events are products of the author's imagination, and any similarity to actual events or places or persons living or deceased is purely coincidental.

Copyright © 2018 by Pat Gemmiti. All rights reserved.
First Printing

Produced by
Sea Hill Press Inc.

www.seahillpress.com

Produced and Printed in the United States of America

To Catherine, the dearest and best.

Without your help and encouragement, I never would have known about Daniel, much less have written his story.

Thee I love.

In Memory

of the thousands of Scotland's soldiers

who were captured by Cromwell's Roundheads

at the battles of

Dunbar [September 3, 1650]

and Worcester [September 3, 1651].

Gone but not Forgotten.

The cruel inhumanity of abuse

can never be condoned or truly understood.

May the best ye hae ivver seen be the warst ye'll ivver see,
May the moose ne'er lea' yer girnal wi a tear-drap in its ee,
May aye keep hail an hertie till ye'r auld eneuch tae dee,
May ye aye juist be sae happie as I wuss ye aye tae be.

TRANSLATION

May the best you have ever seen be the worst you will ever see.
May the mouse never leave your grain store with a tear drop in its eye.
May you always stay hale and hearty until you are old enough to die.
May you still be as happy as I always wish you to be.

PROLOGUE

NOT MANY thought much of it when the British Empire's King Charles Stuart the First introduced his new prayer book around the year 1639. Many accepted it and considered it a fine idea, but not Scotland.

At a reading of the prayer book in Edinburgh, Scotsmen rioted in defiance of the English style prayers. They soon united to sign a National Covenant that challenged the book and proceeded to recruit an army against King Charles, who was infuriated and threatened to punish the Scots, going as far as to say that he would rather die than yield to their impertinent and damnable demands.

So the stage was set for the English Civil War, a bloody fight that went on for over ten years. In spite of the seemingly pious affirmations of all factions, this extended horror goaded them until Christian virtues of mercy and forgiveness were replaced with deeply embedded bitterness and hatred.

Clan rivalries flared; viciousness and revenge seethed relentlessly and often boiled over in response to the slightest provocation. Scots were constantly changing sides; the country was confused.

This all climaxed in 1649 after King Charles the First was defeated at the Battle of Preston in the summer of 1648, and was ordered beheaded by Parliament, which was by then overwhelmingly influenced by Oliver Cromwell. The monarchy was abolished and a puritanical Council of State took over.

Scotland's Kirks chose to support the exiled Prince Charles Stuart, son of the late King Charles the First. They offered to bring him back from the Netherlands and proclaim him king of Great Britain, France, and Ireland, under the condition that he accept the Scots' Presbyterian Covenant. Prince Charles, then nineteen years of age, accepted and returned to Scotland in 1650, hoping that by doing so he would in time regain his father's throne.

Once word of the return was received, the English, well aware of Prince Charles's obvious motives, were wary. It didn't take much for Oliver Cromwell to convince the Council of State to take the offensive. They took up the cause and declared war on Scotland on July 19, 1650. Only days after the declaration, Lord-General Cromwell led his English army over the border into Scotland.

If he had expected to take the country by surprise and have easy going, he was mistaken. He found that the Scots had stripped the land bare, driven off the cattle, and confiscated any food they could find.

The English *New Model Army* was coldly welcomed by only women and children who reported that all of their men between the ages of sixteen and sixty had been taken off to fight for General Leslie.

Cromwell groaned but decided to move on. The unusually cold, wet summer soon took its toll on his forces and left many of his soldiers lost to sickness and death along the way.

Scotland's General David Leslie, who once fought on a wounded Cromwell's side at the battle of Marsdon Moor, had strategized and maneuvered shrewdly to keep his *Scottish Army of the Covenant* out of Cromwell's reach. On September second, believing an easy victory over Cromwell was within his grasp, he made camp on the high ground of Doon Hill just above the coastal town of Dunbar, a small village located where the Firth of Forth runs into the North Sea at the base of the Lammermiur Hills.

Upon observing this, Cromwell and his sick, discouraged, and hungry soldiers felt themselves in a seemingly hopeless situation, one both Leslie and Cromwell were well aware of.

Indeed it seemed that the Scots' protected location and greater manpower placed them in a perfect position for victory. Leslie and his commanders were on the same page regarding their advantage; however, there was a big disagreement as to how the attack should be carried out.

General Leslie's superiors were Presbyterian ministers whose fanatical views were inflexible. These Kirks were adamant that things be done their way, and in a *Godly manner*. Their radical judgments went as far as to decide what soldiers should be acceptable in the *Scots' Army of the Covenant*. Their *purging* committee dismissed many experienced, professional officers and militia, mostly for petty reasons like cursing or not honoring the Sabbath. Their *Articles and Ordinances of War* specified the correct behavior for the military, and every soldier was required to swear an oath to obey these edicts. Many failed to live up to the ministers' standards and were dismissed, some even on the day before the eminent battle.

First the Kirks commanded General Leslie to delay the attack in honor of the Sabbath, then, on Monday, they ordered him to get it done quickly and pushed him to abandon the safe position on Doon Hill, attack Cromwell, and claim the Lord's victory straight away.

It took until late in the afternoon of that Monday, September second, for General Leslie, against his better judgment to give in to their whims, finally accept their orders, and send his army of twenty-three thousand men and lads down the hill with their battle flag proudly flaunting their motto *For Christ's Crown and Covenant*.

Once the Scots left their impregnable position and started down from Doon hill, it was all over. Cromwell recognized at once that he now had the opportunity of a lifetime and cried out, "God is delivering them into our hands. They are coming down to us."

Even then the Scots did not attack. Under orders to wait for morning, the soldiers hunkered down in a cornfield. To make matters worse, a thunder storm arose and soaked them with cold, hard rain.

Cromwell, excited and eager to take advantage of the circumstances, ordered his eleven thousand *New Model Army* soldiers, that only hours before were ready to beat a hasty retreat out of Scotland for England, to attack the sleeping Scots. They snuck up and caught the *Scottish Army of the Covenant* completely by surprise at about four o'clock in the morning. The battle was vicious and basically over by sunrise.

It was reported that Cromwell was so elated by this overwhelming English victory, that he acted drunk, danced, laughed, and recited Bible psalms among the slaughtered. More than three thousand soldiers of the *Scottish Army of the Covenant* ended up dead and over ten thousand captured in this bloody battle, while Cromwell claimed only thirty or forty casualties.

Thus the stage was set once more, and over five thousand disparaged prisoners-of-war started out on the infamous *march of shame*, a profound disgrace that placed a black stain on England and Scotland's military and social history.

 Chapter 1

**SEPTEMBER 3, 1650
DUNBAR, SCOTLAND**

THE MORNING was fittingly black. Freezing rain drizzled down from the dark clouds onto Daniel, adding to the pain and aches already invading every muscle and bone in his young, strong body.

He felt a strange heaviness on him. As he looked down, all he could see was blood, and amidst it all, something, or someone, was laying much too still on top of him. He moved his hand up through the sticky mess and felt a shoulder, as he groped more he recognized a cloak with a brooch fastened to it. His heart sank as he realized that the brooch was William's; he knew it well by its custom shape; he had watched him with a smile as he had lovingly formed and forged it. His face had beamed with pride when he pinned it onto his handsome brown cloak.

Daniel was certain now that the blood he saw and felt must have come from his dear brother—but why? What? Under his breath he prayed, *Oh Willy, no, no, please be well.* The scratchy whisper caught in his throat; he retched and nearly lost it.

A sharp pain passed through his head, and as he pushed his brother's still body off to the side, a horror more gross than he had ever known gripped him. Staring back at him was William's severed head, his usually lively, mischievous eyes glazed over and staring frozen in a strangely surprised expression. His blue woolen brimmed hat was lying beside it, untouched.

Daniel vomited uncontrollably as loss and sorrow overcame him. Somehow he turned, straightened his brother's body, and carefully laid the beloved head in place above it. He gently closed the empty eyes and fell sobbing on top of the bloody cloak until blackness engulfed him once more.

When he came around this time the horror engulfed him all over again as he fought to regain his senses. His clenched fist clutched William's brooch to his heart as he painfully maneuvered until he could sit up.

Gagging and filled with regret, he realized that he had no idea who had slain his brother, or where the blow had come from; neither of them had seen it coming.

He hazily recalled being shaken from sleep; hearing the ocean, then horses, gunfire, and the screaming. Suddenly he and William had been thrown into the frenzy of battle; an order was yelled at them to cover the rearguard position.

They fought their way to the rear of the Scots' fan-shaped lines that stretched from the coast to Broxburn Brook and were fighting on the fringe when Cromwell's cavalry broke through and the Scots' line collapsed.

The cacophony—he remembered the thunderous noise and the metallic taste of blood that gusted about them then fluttered softly like raindrops in a sun shower.

The battle had dissolved into a vicious slaughter. He and William had been holding their ground, fighting back to back as they had done before; when out of the blue he had been shoved off balance and hurled to the ground where his head met up with something hard—then nothing.

The brain fog started to clear now, surely it was William's falling body that had knocked him down, and in doing so had saved his life—again. How he wished he had been able to deflect that deadly blow and send the monster who had delivered it to hell.

He moved a weary hand through hair sticky with matted, clotted blood. Fiery jolts once more attacked his head as he discovered a huge welt.

His confused mind immediately flew to Mora; captured sunlight, that's what she called his blonde hair. She loved to run her fingers through it and hold his face softly while her tongue caressed his ear as she whispered, "Sure an' I love ye, Danny MacDhughill. Ye capture the sunshine and wrap it about me. Yer my heart, and it tickles me beyond belief that I will always be that twinkle in yer sky blue eyes."

He smiled to himself, *I'll tickle ye fer sure, my bonnie lass.* She had been so right about being the twinkle, and more. He would surely love her forever. She had a way with fancy words and she murmured them often, so quietly and gently; especially when he held her close and dear. He could feel her warm breath as her soft hands cupped his face. His back relaxed as they moved down over his shoulders, then slid back up into his hair.

Dreamily, his tongue slipped over his lips, but he stiffened as his mood abruptly changed and left him frozen in place—he tasted blood, not love. He felt cold and heard strange sounds.

They must have thought me dead, he rationalized as he glanced about and noticed that his basket hilt sword and carbine were missing. It was a struggle to keep from tumbling over. *Whoa, 'tis more than a wee bit a'doin' this may take,* he thought as he strove to compose himself.

A sharp prod in the back startled him. The flash of a red coat told him that the blur over his shoulder was an English guard, and a mulish, ornery one at that. The infantryman poked his musket at him again and yelled contemptuously for him to get up and get in line. Stunned and weak, Daniel struggled slowly to his feet. He was shaky and wobbled but he bit his lip and forced himself to follow the order.

He had convinced himself that he was in the midst of a nightmare, but as his vision began to clear, reality sunk in. He managed a quick glance to the rear and witnessed hordes of downtrodden Scottish soldiers being goaded toward him; their hands in the air and heads hung low. There were far too many miserable souls to count. He lowered his eyes and wondered if this was the end of the *Scottish Army of the Covenant.*

When he finally looked up, he noticed that the ocean was still visible through the rain; but he could no longer hear it roar, that sound had been obliterated by screams of the wounded and dying; some groaned in agony, while others cried out for mothers they would never see again. The usually green golf course outside the harbor village of Dunbar was soggy with rainwater and blood. In addition to the wounded, it was strewn with the battered and dismembered bodies of Scotsmen lying where they had fallen; many of them piled three and four deep.

Daniel strained to look closer and assess the situation. He couldn't count one red coat among the ignored remains; rather, very much alive English Roundheads seemed to be everywhere.

He couldn't comprehend how this battle could have been lost, especially since the Kirks had told them all many times over that the *Army of the Covenant* had the *RIGHT* on its side, and that would protect them and ensure an easy, great victory over Cromwell, an enemy they considered a hardheaded, extreme Puritan who hated Catholicism and any faith other than his own.

So much for that, he chided himself. *Let's face it, this was a disaster. We got our arses whipped and by the looks, most of us were caught up in the midst of it.*

Head throbbing, with his stomach in knots, he pressed William's brooch to his heart, closed his eyes and clung to it in heartfelt grief. Eventually he pulled it to his lips, kissed it, and held it long and hard while he softly murmured a prayer and a final farewell. After one more tormented glance back at his brother's broken body; he numbly fell in with the seemingly endless throng that had closed in around him.

While the unhappy soldiers Cromwell had assigned to guard his prisoners continued to force the Scotsmen to line up, Daniel painstakingly managed to search the haggard faces around him in a vain attempt to seek out someone he knew. He had known most of the men in his brigade, but wasn't acquainted with many of the newly recruited green soldiers. In addition to the dismissals made by Leslie's overzealous religious commanders, troop losses over the summer had been heavy; some had died in fights and skirmishes, but more often illness had been the culprit. His Dragoon brigade had been hit so badly that it now was almost entirely made up of replacements.

General Leslie's latest army had been hastily thrown together and his remaining forty regiments had been broken into ten brigades. Each brigade was now composed of the remains of three, four, or more regiments. Thousands of men, young and old, had been collected from all over Scotland for this glorious battle. Sanctimonious recruiters had promised them that, with their help, England would be brought to its knees and vengeance for their beloved King Charles celebrated.

The sons and servants of ministers, clerks, tailors, farmers, and others had been offered up by their earls, clergy, or their own families. Most of these clansmen were immature, undisciplined, and had never been trained in warfare. Needless to say, many of them had been among the first to run or be cut down in the furious battle.

Daniel shook his head, *Dearest God, what a mess. What happens now?*

 Chapter 2

SEPTEMBER 3, 1650
A FRIENDLY FACE

SUDDENLY, DANIEL'S heart jumped and he did a double take—even from a distance, there was no mistaking the broad shoulders nor the blustered wild auburn hair and beard of John MacKinney. The ginger curls were a trademark that constantly irritated him. He tried in vain to straighten and keep them parted in the middle, but the locks only stuck out more and he got teased by his friends for the effort.

Their eyes locked in recognition and Daniel immediately relaxed. John looked downcast and battle weary, sharp briny mist and stinging wind lashed at him and caused his huge kilt to flap about. *Thanks be ta God, he looks fit,* Dan thought, then—as John took a few steps nearer he cringed—*Nay, it kenna be—but, ay—'tis a hitch in his gait, fer sure.*

Relieved, a smile clung to tight lips as they carefully crouched and plowed their way toward each other—grateful that no guard took notice as they managed to weave around discouraged and disgruntled fellow prisoners.

"'Tis certain that ye've heard of me. Ay, 'tis me indeed, John MacKinney—from Tobermorey by the sea—just over the peaks it be." He never failed to puff himself up and gesture as he introduced himself that way, and he did so now along with a shitty grin; his way to break the tension. "And there she sits, perched on the hills—'tis the jewel of Scotland, ta be sure." He'd go on and on about his home if anyone would let him. Even those who had never been to Tobermorey agreed that it must be fine, John obviously loved it so.

"I kenna stand yer wild blabberin' right now, John MacKinney, but I must say the sight of ye on this foul day fills my heart all the same."

"As ye do mine, my dreary lookin' friend."

• • •

John MacKinney, Daniel, and his brother, William MacDhughill, were comrades. They considered it a great honor to be in General David Leslie's highly mobile, mounted infantry Dragoons—an elite force that was usually in the vanguard when the army advanced—but could be ordered to hold rearguard positions if ever retreat was called—as happened at Dunbar.

It had been great fun at first. Although they were trained to fight as infantry or cavalry, they considered themselves blessed to be in the cavalry and never forgot it for a moment. "Ridin' 'tis grand," Daniel declared, "but I kenna say the same fer marchin', just ask my feet."

Daniel and his brother, William MacDhughill, had been Dragoons for just under a year, whereas John MacKinney was a seasoned soldier. He had been with *Baillie's Engagers* when Cromwell defeated King Charles *the First* and all but wiped out the *Highlanders* at the Battle of Preston in the summer of 1648. John was taken prisoner at Warrington Bridge and had been incarcerated in a church, but, along with two others, he had barely managed to escape before the church was set ablaze.

Born in Fife, General David Leslie knew every inch of the hilly landscape he called home. His strength was guerrilla warfare, and he used these tactics well. An expert at the cat and mouse game; he ambushed and antagonized Cromwell's *New Model Army* in as many mountain passes and glens as made military sense. After each strike the Dragoons would melt away just out of reach into the hills, while the English were left with nothing but wounds to treat and bodies to bury. The passes were so abundant and immense that these relentless hits had gradually pushed the English to the coast and Dunbar.

• • •

The time-honored Tobermorey spiel behind them—the friends hugged and thumped each other on the back. "John, dang yer hide, thanks be ta God yer here. 'Twas nary a way we ever reckoned things could end so wrong side up. Yer leg seems a bit off—be ye wounded?"

"Nary a thing ta worry yer head about—'tis just fine—my ornery friend. I'll tell ye more a bit later." John was a born storyteller, so even this horrible day caused him no pause.

"There we were, overwhelmed from every side. Ye recall how General Leslie assured us that we were twenty-three thousand strong and invincible, eh? Well, we were chopped down by the thousands, Dan. The ones that dinna run, and plenty that did, were surrounded and captured. I fought like hell, but they got me anyway. 'Twas there my leg got dinged. I was still strugglin' with the bastards when I saw the blow that took William—and my heart stopped as I watched ye both fall."

He choked up, grabbed his forehead, closed his eyes, rocked his head from side to side—and almost couldn't go on—almost! But—he managed to get a second wind and carried on. "Cromwell's shrewd attack under the cover of night was so effective—we were like sheep lined up fer the slaughter. Many of our comrades were killed before they ken what 'twas in the wind. 'Twas nary a doubt in my mind—til now that both ye and Willy were dead. Praise be ta God 'twas nary so."

"Well, I wish with all my heart 'twas nary so, but yer only half right—it pains me ta tell ye that my dear Willy—'tis dead he be—back there alone—cold and forsaken—and 'twas nary a thing ta be done fer the bonny lad."

John's heart sank and he sadly rubbed Daniel's shoulder as he shook his head, "What a loss, Danny—Zounds—such a damn shame—'tis sorry indeed that I be."

The friends fell into a deep silence that lasted until John decided to try to get Daniel's mind on other things. The guards' ears were up and they were on the alert for anything suspicious, but he pressed on with his tale, guardedly, "How grisly ta be caught so bald-facedly with our defenses down; the folly of leaving Doon Hill cost us the lot.

"'Tis nary a way in hell ta imagine what drove our General Leslie ta accept an order ta leave the hill's protection—I kenna grasp it. Ye ken be sure 'twas nary thrilled he be—and who's ta pay fer it? Ye ken be sure 'tis us.

"We both know that we had those Roundheads boxed in, we just had ta wait it out and the battle would have been an easy win. Gave it all away, they did—thought they knew more than General David Leslie; tied his military genius in knots. Blasted Kirks. The only interest they had was ta get Prince Charles Stuart on the British throne in his father's place, and get control of the altar of Westminster Abbey and Canterbury Cathedral."

Visions of William's empty eyes haunted Daniel—the loss of his brother crushed his soul. Everything and everyone about him seemed wild and crazy. He was grateful and happy to have found his friend, but exhausted and in no mood for talk; he just wanted to wipe the whole bloody mess from his mind. But then he caught himself, paused and acknowledged how fortunate he was to have even seen John in the midst of all the turmoil. He realized that they were both frustrated beyond words. He also knew that talking was the best medicine for his friend so, as long as he didn't arouse the guards, he'd listen.

"Oh, ay," he affirmed as he set his jaw, sucked in a deep breath, and took time to exhale before he said, "Oh, I recall it, John, most especially what sittin' ducks we were."

John perked up and welcomed the chance to retell the catastrophe and at the same time search his thoughts for some way he might have altered the downfall, "'Twas the most miserable, cold rain that I ken recollect, and us hunkered down like rats in that cornfield. Nary even the moon showed itself. 'Twas shaken out of me wits I be when the bastards swarmed over us from out of the dark.

"Our torches were out, most weapons stacked, and the horses unsaddled. Like ghosts they were all over us; they thundered out of the murk and struck us from all sides. As everyone scurried about I heard the order yelled fer us ta cover the rear."

Dan interrupted, "'Twas lucky that Willy and I had the sense ta keep our swords and carbines close, we grabbed them and tried fer our horses, but the Roundheads had cut them loose and 'twas nary time ta round them up."

John nodded, "Cromwell, that wily arsehole, took advantage of our foolish move inta the open. 'Twas his top *Ironsides* that got us just as dawn snuck through the sheaves. I thought 'twas a chance ta turn the tables when our lads rallied, but once those *Ironsides* broke through, the line collapsed and 'twas over fer us."

"Ay—ugly, John—but true. 'Twas cornered like rats in a trap we were."

Reliving the chaos had made Daniel more depressed. His mouth tasted foul and, when he clenched his fists, he felt William's brooch bite into his left palm. Wooziness assaulted him, but he forced himself to stay erect. Convinced that he was a dead man, his only hope was that he would have the courage to die well. In spite of his troubled mind, he decided that he could handle whatever was to come now, thanks to his comrade. He looked over at the burly man and smiled—John glanced back and quietly chuckled, then shrugged—finally out of words.

A strange eerie stillness fell over the prisoners and apprehension hung heavy in air that was rank with the stench of blood, sweat, and urine.

 Chapter 3

**SEPTEMBER 3, 1650
RULES OF THE ROAD**

THE DEFEATED Scots were doggedly lined up and stood as steady as they could for what seemed like an eternity. Finally, an English officer trotted his fine horse back and forth in front of his new charges a few times; halted, turned the animal and confronted the wary prisoners. They soon found out that the rider was Major Hugh Leighton. It was clear that he was cavalry, but not one of Cromwell's elite *Ironsides*. In addition to being seated on a magnificent mount, his uniform was enviable. Rather than the traditional red coat most of his comrades wore, he was garbed in a black wool overcoat, which on its own spoke volumes of his family's position and wealth. Black dye was much too expensive for an average soldier to even think of.

He was armed with a carbine and claymore sword, the detailed grip covered by his gloved hand. Heavy set with a full face that ended in a bulldog chin, his build appeared to be more on the soft side than the average combatant.

The aloof cavalry man leered down at them, his small beady eyes full of a hate that seemed to reek from him. It was obvious that he considered the captives less than human; something he would love to crush under his feet. He looked unkempt in spite of his meticulous uniform, and wore a constant scowl.

"Eyes front," he abruptly started out. "If any of you dogs think you will be leaving here today, let me set you straight right now. There is no way that will you be as lucky as those sissies we clobbered and chopped so badly that they couldn't walk or slither away like the snakes they were. It seems that there were about five thousand of those left behind wailing and sniffling on this battle ground in the company of your dead.

"Rather than put them out of their misery, Lord-General Cromwell chose to parole the buggers and let them die on their own or crawl back to whatever dung heap they came from so we wouldn't have to bother with them.

"Those that had any semblance of arms or legs crept off, but no one will ever have to worry that they will ever fight again."

He stiffened his body, let a strange guffaw escape from his thin tight lips, and went on, "As for you obnoxious gutless bastards, let me be clear. Every one of you will do exactly as I or Lieutenant Wilbur Barlow here tell you, at all times, no excuses.

"Oh—and you all look like you're burning up in those silly skirts. How's about we cool you down—GET THEM OFF."

"Git naked? In this arse freezin' weather? Who the hell do ye think ye aire? We got rights. We be honorable prisoners-of-war and we will nary be treat . . ."

The Highlander never got to finish his sentence. His life was taken in an instant by two shots that rang out simultaneously from separate guards.

The captives stared at the Major in disbelief. "You heard right, exactly right," he snarled. "Get 'em off."

Outraged, insulted, and furious, several prisoners lost control and lunged at him. They never stood a chance. The guards had been readied for just such an incident, so at the first move they simply shot the attackers in their tracks. The rest of the shocked Scotsmen stood motionless.

The rain that had prevailed throughout the night had quieted, but it was still cold and stormy. The prisoners already felt frozen to the core, even in their warm wool clothing.

John nudged Daniel, "Somethin's a do—I ken smell it—and—'tis nary a good thing about it," he mumbled quietly. "Ken ye spot how those guards are lined up? Some of them even have those new English shooters."

The Foote guards did indeed seem to be on a mission, but were trying to look calm and at ease. Casual or not, they all had their spears, muskets, or carbines pointed at the prisoners while the cavalry guards kept a close watch from behind.

"Going to be like that, are we?" Leighton snapped. "Just hate to part with those ridiculous skirts, eh? Well, you Scottish scum, we'll just see about that." He nudged his horse and doggedly rode down the line of his section, swung his sword high and gave the order for his soldiers to deliberately shoot every tenth man.

The husky soldier standing on Daniel's right was a ten. He was straight, tall, and strong, undeniably a pike man whose height towered well over Daniel's six feet.

"'Tis a pike ye be, eh?" Daniel whispered.

"Ay sir," the lad replied with pride.

Those were the last words he ever spoke. He never heard the sound of the musket shot that blew out the left side of his neck and spurted blood on Daniel's face before it gushed down to join William's on the soiled cloak.

The young pike landed at Daniel's feet like a log, choked in agony, then was still.

It was too much. The smell and taste of blood caught in Dan's throat as he felt his knees go weak. A sick feeling crept up, prickled in his chest and under his tongue. "Zounds—again?" He heard himself gasp.

He could feel John grab his arm, but couldn't seem to stop the black that was closing in, and he really didn't care much, just waited to be swallowed up.

Laughter saved him. Further up the line of Scots, Micum MacIntyre had been designated as a tenth man also. He was a tiny lad with nervous brown eyes that seemed far too big for his face.

He stood, almost lost, between his two lofty older brothers who had been captured with him.

They became quickly aware of what was planned for Micum, pushed him forward and yelled, "Run fer it, *bráthair*—'Tis yer only chance."

Micum didn't hesitate, he took off like a chicken with its head cut off. He was small, but tough and very fast. Wiry legs dug in and carried him strongly as he bobbed in and out of prisoners and guards alike. First he slipped among them like a wild weasel, then turned suddenly and started zigzagging toward the sea.

In spite of the dire situation both sides broke into an uncontrolled edgy laughter that got louder and louder. For a second it looked as though all was lost when he slipped on the wet grass and his body flayed out of control. English and Scots alike sucked in and held their breaths, but Micum hung on by sheer will, pressed down with all his might on his scrawny left leg, righted himself, and sprung off faster than before.

The lad dodged, wiggled, and was so squirmy that it took two guards to finally take him down. Once they wrestled and got a good hold on him, they handed the speedy Micum kicking and screaming, up by one foot to Lieutenant Wilbur Barlow who had been closely following the wild race, but had not quite decided what action he should take. Without further thought, the cavalry man reached down from his horse, grabbed the runaway by his skinny ankle, and trotted him back to the prisoners' line where he threw the frantic lad, none too gently, down near two Scots, not knowing that they were Micum's brothers.

"He can thank his lucky stars this day, that one. Keep the little shit quiet and in line or I'll blast his head off myself," Barlow said emphatically, as he struggled to smother a chuckle that had tried to sneak out of the corner of his mouth.

That disappeared in a blink when he caught a menacing glance of disgust from the Major. Barlow, head down, urged his mount back toward his position in front of the cavalry where he stayed put and wished he was invisible.

The guards continued to joke and laugh, until a foreboding silence fell over all. Breaths were held once again while Micum's fate was awaited.

The brothers grabbed Micum off the ground, up ended him, tucked him in between them and held him close. White as a sheet, scared stiff and shaky, nothing moved on him but his wild saucer sized eyes which shifted fretfully from face to face while he tried not to think of what might happen next. He couldn't believe that he was still alive, and neither could anyone else.

A great cheer went up but was quickly stifled by a heavy, sinister growl that drew all eyes to Major Leighton. He would have gladly split the rebellious brat in two, but the annoying Wilbur was his sister's only son, and although he considered him a softhearted weakling, he loved his sister dearly and so, totally contrary to his will, he had vowed to guard and protect the little twit. That promise was the only reason he chose not to call him out for saving the irksome lad.

Leighton chewed on his lip and thought for a moment before he decided to take advantage of the lull and seize the chance to reassert himself.

"Oh, . . . Funny, eh?" He sneered, "Well, let's see how funny this is. For the last time, GET THAT GEAR OFF." He hissed the command out in his cold voice as he eyeballed the prisoners and retook control of the situation.

Veins pulsated on his thick neck as he spat on the ground and once more raised his sword high over his head, then strutted his horse up and down the line ready to order more deaths. No one on either side doubted his seriousness, or how much he would love to do it.

Not another word of dissent was heard, and the clothes started to come off.

Daniel let out a deep breath as his senses slowly returned; a stubborn fury roared in his throat and flashes of murder formed in his mind.

 Chapter 4

**SEPTEMBER 3, 1650
HUMBLED AND BENT**

THEY HAD seen more than their share of death, but neither of them could get over the alarming spectacle of unarmed men being killed so indifferently, for no reason. John poked his friend sharply, "Buck up, Dan, ferget those thoughts," he muttered as he choked back his own rage.

"'Tis nary a chance right now; dinna even think of messin' with Leighton—he may be a poor excuse fer one of Cromwell's *New Model Army* soldiers and he's fer sure nary an *Ironside*, but I heard that 'twas some of his friends in that cavalry patrol our Scots captured near Glasgow a couple of weeks ago. Those Roundheads were tortured ta death and their mutilated bodies were sent back ta Cromwell as a warnin'.

"Think ye—just how bitterly did that savage gesture infuriate the English ranks and stiffen their army's resolve? 'Tis nary a way they'll warm up ta us."

Daniel recognized the seriousness in his voice, although he had only heard that tone a few times. John was a bear of a man and the bravest he had ever known. Beneath the corkscrew ginger hair and thick brows, gold eyes were sheltered by long, thick lashes; envied, so he said, by many a fair lass. His kind face boasted full cheeks and a strong nose and no amount of shaggy beard could hide his easy smile—a gentle giant—usually.

There was no easy smile now; the golden eyes had turned to narrow slits, black and cold, full of resentment. Daniel could see that his friend was struggling fiercely with himself, and he realized that he must do the same.

Amidst the ruckus of clothes being cast off, he and John faded back into the horde as far as they could. Barely composed, Daniel dropped his bloody cloak on the ground and removed his simple fighting kilt. Carbines, swords, and muskets had been taken earlier, but John noticed a water skin that dangled from Daniel's waist.

"As much as I hate ta, I fear we'll have ta part with our stockin's—the white—'tis much too visible—but—yer brogs—well, try ta keep yer foot gear on, there be so many of us, we might get by with it."

They had not worn their sporrans into battle, but John asked, "By chance, be there water in that fancy hipflask?" he gruffly whispered. Daniel tenderly stroked the skin and nodded in agreement.

"'Tis a beauty, eh?" he remarked as he gave it another pat, "'Twas a gift from my Da—eighteenth birthday. I think of him every time I take a drink—'twas his plan—fer sure."

John threw out his hands and motioned impatiently for his friend to get on with it.

Daniel kept on the trews his mother had lovingly sewn for him long ago. She had made both of the brown homespun cloaks as well—William's and the now blood-soaked one he had removed. They were warmer than anything the army might have issued, and the brothers had refused to part with them.

The leggings clung to him, stuck to his skin by his brother's and the murdered pike's blood. His trews were, or at least had been, flesh colored, which was always the idea since he did not want to stick out among his fellow soldiers, most of whom preferred to be bare and free. Growing up in the mountains had instilled in Daniel a great respect for his trews. They reached to his ankles and tucked into his stockings. He had taken the chance of being ridiculed because of them, but they had always proven well worth it. Many of his comrades from the Highlands had taken the risk as well.

John moved closer and spoke softly again, "See if ye ken tuck the water flask in yer trews without bein' noticed, and if ye ken, guard it well. I have a feelin' we're gonna need all the help we ken get. Our sad battle may be over, but our survival, 'tis another thing. We'll need God's help and all of our wits about us. Fer one thing, how in heaven's name will the guards be able ta move and feed the lot of us when they ken hardly feed themselves?"

Daniel could see the pain in John's face as he parted with his larger than life kilt that he folded carefully, even now. The thing was a work of art and was big enough to cover the whole body. He had thought it looked like a bunch of old curtains tied around John's waist until he had seen him throw it over his head and watched as it turned into a neat tent that he could snuggle about him to keep out the damp and cold.

He had also learned that things were stuffed in the kilt, even while fighting. A dirk or two was always hidden away along with dried beef, maybe oat cakes, and some kind of dumpling that he loved, but looked like a rock to Daniel. All was stored somewhere within the multitude of folds. In a rare quiet moment, John had once rubbed the kilt gently and mentioned that his late wife had made it for him.

After John had removed the beloved kilt, Daniel couldn't help but wonder where the dirks might have ended up; he could see no sign of them.

His unique goatskin flagon had a small pocket stitched into the cover, made to hold coins or small things—he managed to slip William's brooch into it before he tucked the flask away without being noticed, thanks to the protection of his friend's big body.

He hadn't missed the fact that John had kept on some knitted sort of trews as well, although his were shorter and stopped just above the knees, Daniel grinned to himself, pleased that they both might have some cover.

Humbled and humiliated by their nakedness the captured masses slumped and took on a disheartened demeanor. Their cockiness had taken a beating, but underlying bitterness and resentment were stronger than ever. They hankered for revenge, but for the moment they mostly felt trapped, helpless, and very cold.

Daniel and John tried in vain to see where the line ended. "'Tis thousands of us fer sure," they decided, "Over five thousand of us are prisoners and at least that many be left behind—dead —or nearly so."

Just out of ear shot the guards carelessly piled murdered Scotsmen out of their way. Daniel looked up at the ominous sky, tried to ignore an involuntary lump in his throat, and pondered his fate. "I kenna even fathom what we're gonna eat," he rambled, "but the guards certainly had nary a bit of trouble packin' up all the rations we had stashed in the cornfield. They're probably just plannin' ta kill us all."

"I doubt that, my friend," John replied softly, "I hear that Cromwell already has taken flack from the Parliament fer his cruel ways. If they killed us outright they'd get a lot more, and Scotland's nationalism would rile up more support fer Prince Charles.

"Suppose he sold us fer ransom or paroled some of us, that wouldna work fer him either. The bastard's shrewd; he knows we would return ta our clans ta fight again.

"They might want ta recruit us inta the Parliamentary army, but they're damn right in thinkin' that they could nary trust us Highlanders ta fight against our own."

John scratched his beard and glanced about as a guard stomped by before going on, "Right—Cromwell will want ta look the hero, clean, pious, and upright when he appears back in London. He'll find another way ta deal with us. If word preceded him that he had made a bad slaughter worse by killin' hoards of unarmed prisoners-of-war, his peers would turn on him in a minute.

"The scuttle butt 'tis that he has big plans fer himself. Ay, he frantically wants ta look good; but nary fear, he kenna wait ta get us out of his hair, especially us Highlanders; ye know the particular hate he holds fer us. Rest assured, he'll come up with some scheme that we willna like ta be rid of us."

"Surely yer right, John. Besides they may nary have ta kill us outright. The sickness may take care of that; 'twas on the creep even before the attack. Cast yer eyes on Alan Grey over there. Just look at him, sick as a dog fer a week he's been already. He's grayer than his name; I wonder how much longer he ken hang on.

"Well—we'd best stay strong and sane if we're ta stand a chance of survivin'."

John untied the small cloth that held the last of his rock-like dumpling, pushed half of it into his friend's hand and insisted, "Eat that; who knows when we'll get more food."

Daniel placed it gingerly in his mouth and gratefully forced the strangely textured thing down. Surprised, he nodded his head and had to admit that it tasted really good.

His belly felt better, but he couldn't keep his eyes away from the growing pile of dead comrades and moaned, "God, I miss William. I kenna stand the thought of him lyin' out there; it bothers my heart. Do ye think someone will care fer him?"

Although he had his doubts, John responded, "'Tis sure of it, I be, Dan. Same as always, there will be enough followers after the battle ta see that all the dead get proper burials once the army has moved out."

They shut up and ducked as an order roared out and echoed along the line, "Get down on your arses, you creeps. You look tired you whiny little wimps. Better take a nap, or just shut up and be quiet—otherwise, we can help you with that."

Outraged voices rang out despite the warning. Fortunately, it was not Leighton giving the order this time, so shots were fired into the air and the command repeated, "You think this is a game? Just test me—now, down on your arses and shut your traps."

Chapter 5

**INTO BONDAGE
THE MARCH BEGINS**

AT FIRST light, the Scots were ordered back on their feet. They stood shivering just below the battlefield. They all wondered whether they would live or die, and knew that expectations for life were not in their favor. Aware of their circumstances, they had resigned themselves to their fate, but hopes of escape still lived and loomed foremost in their minds.

Suddenly and methodically Roundhead soldiers, with heavy backup, descended in force and proceeded to bind the prisoners. Strong ropes were securely wound about their wrists and tied very tautly. Other guards tethered the prisoners together in groups of four. Just enough space was left between each man to let him maintain his balance.

Leighton had wanted to hobble their feet too, but he realized that would prevent them from being able to move as fast as he would require.

John and Daniel were tied to each other and made up the center of their row. They heard someone grumble and turned to see their comrade, Alexander Maxwell, dragged into position and tied to John.

As soon as the guards moved on, John broke the stunned silence, "Sweet Jesus, Alex, yer bollaky bare arsed. Dinna ye have the brain of a flea? Why dinna ye keep somethin' on? Damn. Well, 'tis surprised I be that yer feet at least be covered."

"And, 'tis surprised I am that yer still in this army, John MacKinney, with all the carryin' on and swearin' yer always up ta. Dinna ye sign the *Articles and Ordinances of War* old man?"

"Oh, ay, I did indeed sign the damn thing—and I also kept me distance from those batty Kirks. 'Tis mighty good at play actin' I be, in case ye might have noticed at all. If by chance I did find meself even the least bit near one of those bastards, I'd just put me head down and act like one of those unsullied *bairn* clerks they bullied inta their fold. What think ye of that, Mr. Righteous?"

Alexander shook his head, "Nary a surprise—still incorrigible, I see." With a flourish he reached back as far as his tether would allow, patted himself on the behind, and went on, "Well, ye know me—I love ta go bare and free."

"Bare and freeze 'tis likely gonna be," John muttered.

To close that subject Alex quickly turned his attention down the line, "And ye, Daniel MacDhughill, are ye well? What brings ye ta this delightful gatherin'? Methinks 'tis the sunshiny weather, eh?"

"Oh, 'tis well enough I be, I thank ye, Alexander." Daniel tried to make a deep bow, but his restraints put a stop to that. "I must say 'tis grand ta see another friend in any sort of weather, and I kenna think of one I would rather take my last breath beside."

John scowled, "Shut yer hole. 'Tis nary one of us will be callin' it quits if I ken help it," then he joshed, "Truth 'tis, I be honored ta be *hitched* ta ye both!"

More guards appeared—with another tug on the tether their line of four was filled. Daniel and John glanced at each other and at their addition. They were glad to have Alexander by their side; they knew him and what they could expect from him. His strikingly handsome, tall aristocratic appearance made him look stand offish as did the chip he seemed to carry on his shoulder that sent out a *don't mess with me* message. Once they got to know him better his comrades realized that he was a strong, smart, dependable soldier and friend.

Even less aggressive comrades widely admired him, but not just for his military prowess. It was no secret that he had a weakness for the fairer sex and a roving eye that left a bevy of broken hearts wherever he went. One look at Alex and his conquests went weak in the knees and could deny him nothing. He knew it and used it, but was quick to make it known that he loved his freedom.

Standing doggedly on the far end of the tether with a wide brown banged-up scarf barely hanging about his waist and looking most uncomfortable was Robert Jonkings. He stared at them defiantly, told them his name, and met their gaze warily.

Born in 1620, he was the oldest of the group, but no one would have guessed it. Even as under the weather as he was, he carried his slender build well and his sweet round baby face, which he tried in vain to age with pork chop whiskers, only added to his youthful appearance. The close-clipped brown hair and quiet eyes completed a very mild look that made him seem reserved, withdrawn, and distant. None of the other three had known him before, so Daniel smiled and asked, *"Ciamar a tha sibh?* How be ye and how did ye end up here, Robert Jonkings?"

"Careston, Angus, 'tis where I hail from—since yer obviously wonderin'," he said in response to Daniel's inquiry. "And I am fine," he asserted, a bit too firmly. "Just fine," he stubbornly claimed again, although it was quite obvious that he was not.

He stuck out a proud chin, bent his head a bit to the side, and summed them up before he went on, "When they hit I rummaged around like everyone else, but found nary a light fer my musket. When that failed I threw the gun down and noticed that the pike men were trying ta get organized and form ranks, so when they offered, I grabbed a Spanish pike and joined up with them.

"The pike, along with its iron spearhead, was sixteen feet long and heavy; as ye know—and I must say—I managed it very well.

"'Tis rugged I am, and much tougher than I look—although I admit 'twas tricky fer all of us ta keep a firm footin' amongst the wet grass and mud. I heard commands bein' shouted, but nary a-one could make them out above the clamor. 'Twas mad chaos."

"Chaos indeed," Daniel agreed. "By any chance did ye get a look at Cromwell?"

Robert Jonkings shook his head, "'Tis nary a sight I caught of that menace—or Leslie either, fer that matter. Did any of ye get a gander at them?"

Alexander muttered that he thought he had vaguely glimpsed Leslie, but never laid eyes on Cromwell. "I heard though, that those who saw him later on the battlefield said that he was wearin' his breast plate and tunic—but nary any head gear—and his hair fell almost ta his shoulders."

Jonkings grunted and acknowledged that when his post had collapsed, it had been very bloody indeed. It was clear to his three new teammates that Robert had fought bravely, and obviously had battled a bad bout of flux along with the enemy.

Once the rows of prisoners had been hogtied, each group of four was forced to the ground. They found it hard, cold, and uncomfortable, especially Alexander with his bare and free bottom exposed. The reluctant foursome tried as best they could to adjust to their tether and settle in. Overall, they were at least warmer than they had been while they stood.

There they were—Alexander Maxwell tied next to John MacKinney on the ocean side and a weak Robert Jonkings hitched to Daniel MacDhughill on the far end. Being so close to each other had a benefit that John was delighted to embellish on. "Dinna be afraid ta cuddle up. Squeeze together now—any warmth 'tis better than none! Feign that we're in one of yer brothels, Alex."

"Ay, and dinna ye just wish it, ye old fart," he grumbled, but he shifted in closer.

Many of the prisoners just sat bitterly while others gazed into nothing while their brains struggled to manifest some way to outwit the English and escape. Some collapsed into a nauseous, restless sleep. Before they knew it, the Roundheads abruptly snapped into action—roughly rousted them up and yanked the rows of four into a seemingly endless column.

"All right, you mealy mouthed vermin, on your feet, let's move it out—double time and keep your traps shut. I think you know by now that none of us will make a habit of repeating ourselves to such rotten rabble."

The sullen mass of humanity, most of them without a shred of clothing to even cover their manhood, started to budge. Behind them, scattered on the cold, wet ground, plaids full of stories were pelted by the rain and tossed about by the wind.

Chapter 6

DESIGN FOR DISASTER

DANIEL, JOHN, Alexander, and Robert were part of at least five thousand defeated battle-weary men. The mile-long human chain was brutally prodded and goaded forward by Cavalry and Foote soldiers.

Cromwell could not stomach the remotest thought of a counter attack that might free and re-arm his prisoners. To avoid even the vaguest possibility of such an embarrassment he had ordered that they be moved south, and as speedily as possible.

• • •

The Cavalry guards paid no mind to the cold as they rode alongside the naked trussed men. Seated comfortably on their mounts, they roughly pushed the herd to go faster. The many warmly dressed Foote guards did the same.

The prisoners, who were sharply aware of how well armed their captors were with horses, carbines, spears, and swords, snuck fitful glances at each other. They reluctantly moved forward, eyes on the ground, unable to see anything but the muddy mess stirred up by the shuffle of men and horses.

According to plan they appeared docile, but they were strong, and their ears were honed acutely. They listened for any sound that they might take advantage of; although for the moment they heard only broken breaths, choked back by fierce emotions that simmered close to the brim.

• • •

Just days ago, before the Scots had come down from their impregnable position on Doon Hill, Cromwell had sent a dispatch to Sir Arthur Haselrigge, his commander stationed in Newcastle, England. He had begged him for reinforcements and went on to add that his men were falling sick beyond imagination; that the way to Berwick was blocked at the pass with no way through without a miracle. He then firmly instructed Haselrigge to keep this dire predicament secret from Parliament in London.

Now haughty from the unexpected victory, he dispatched quite a different order to Haselrigge that instructed him to have Durham Cathedral and Castle converted into a prison to confine his five thousand *Scottish Rebel Prisoners-of-War*, as he called them. To his credit, Cromwell also ordered him to acquire the supplies necessary to sustain them.

The prisoners-of-war were told nothing of this plan and were given no inkling as to what the future might hold for them.

• • •

Daniel looked around the sorry lot and searched for familiar faces. Despite John's advice, his thoughts were on escape. He knew that secretly, John's were too, and that Alexander and Robert hoped for the same. He twisted and turned in his ropes trying to seek out like-minded comrades with the same intent. Perhaps together they could pull something off, or at least help others slip away, but he found that communication on the trail was all but impossible; the guards' sharp eyes seemed glued to them from every angle.

He noticed John was also observing their comrades. He turned and tried to say something. Daniel strained to hear him over the din, "I know damn well ye'd like ta take the whole English army on. So would I, but 'tis nary a way in hell that would do the least bit a good. 'Twill be one of the hardest things we've ever done, but we must stay as calm and lowly as we ken and keep movin' at all costs.

"Before we found each other, Dan, I saw many of our wounded and mulish lads coldly killed—same as those men that the monster ordered murdered."

Robert recoiled in disgust, "Think ye that this bunch of guards just might have been a part of Cromwell's army that drenched Ireland in blood nary so long ago? About half of the people on that island were tortured and murdered in the months they were there. The evils they committed were a nightmare. 'Tis said that their favorite pastime was thrustin' red hot irons through the breasts of Irish women—and my God—they even hacked and sliced those of nursin' *máthairs* and murdered their *bairns*."

"Ay," Dan confirmed, "'Twas worse than rotten—'tis nary a word ta explain or forgive such acts—and Cromwell's army was surely cold-blooded and merciless over there. It just boils down ta more of the same old thing—everybody tryin' ta be fouler and nastier than the next lad. All the same, we hav'na exactly been angels ourselves, ye know. Ye would think that everybody would have had enough of this bloody war by now."

They all grunted in agreement. "But I must admit, I felt my own belly churn in rage over the slaughter of me dear brother, Willy." Dan recalled, "And I fear that, in my gut, that storm still holds sway." That said he glanced over at John and received the no nonsense look he knew was coming and shut up. He was fully aware of where they stood, and how closely they were strained to the edge.

"'Tis so sorry I am about William, Daniel—'twas a good lad he was—fun and kind ta all." Alexander, who had managed to hear from the other end, affirmed. "But, hold firm we must—the more of us that stay alive, the more soldiers the English will be forced ta invest in us, and the fewer resources they will have ta fight against our army."

Somehow they all managed to smother their exasperation. Although the bile still rose from their depths, they breathed in deeply and lowered their heads. They knew that if they made eye contact with the Foote or Calvary guards, it could be all over for them.

". . . and Daniel, fer the love of God, slump down those shoulders, that tall straight body, full of yerself head and light hair of yers stick up temptin' targets. Same ta ye Alex—the snooty head, I mean."

Alexander gave John a dirty look, but he hung his head. He was used to John's rough chiding, and although he would never admit it to his friend, he knew that he had been walking defiantly. Sad eyes dimmed and Robert mumbled, "Whatever happened ta that easy, great victory we were promised?"

They all stood stiff and quiet while a Foote soldier glowered at them as he passed, then John snapped, "General Leslie fouled up, 'tis what. Once he ordered us ta leave our safe vantage point on Doon Hill, 'twas finished we be. Somebody yelled out that every piece of our artillery and Leslie's whole baggage train was captured. Seems that our General got away, although nary a lad seemed sure which way he headed. We ken only hope that he will defend Edinburgh, but I'd bet he be off ta Stirlin' meself."

Daniel was curious, "Do ye think that the rumble 'tis true—that after the battle Cromwell laughed out loud, sang psalms, and danced like a madman among our wounded and dead?"

John nodded in the affirmative and cringed. "Ay, and 'tis said that very soon after that he moved his army out at full speed toward Edinburgh. 'Tis my bet that he plans ta take control of Scotland, at least the part south of the Highlands."

"'Tis a weird one he be, alright," Robert offered, "I've heard that his face 'tis covered with pimples and warts. What's more, did ye know that he banned Christmas, mince pie and Christmas puddin'?"

"Nay, Robert Jonkings, I've nary heard of such a damnable thing. Ye must be larkin' about."

"Oh, he did indeed." Robert asserted, "'Tis been that way fer four years now. He declared such celebrations immoral, and he called that servin' God. He's just plain daft, I have nary a doubt about that—and 'tis here we are at his mercy."

John couldn't help but think of his own small village and was thankful that it was far enough away to escape Cromwell's wrath. However, the recruitment quotas had been high in his parish near Tobermorey due to the radical minister who sang the praises of young Prince Charles and how it was the duty of every man, woman, and child to help him succeed. Immature vulnerable lads and older men too, rallied in huge numbers and off they went. He wondered how many of them had been killed at Dunbar.

Although Robert's brigade had never trekked this far south, his three companions had. They recognized the well-trodden trail and glanced knowingly at each other. Daniel growled, "'Tis more of our beautiful coast we'll be travelin' along, it seems. The Lammermiur hills are behind us, so 'tis certain that we're headed toward Berwick on Tweed. If I recall—'tis about twenty-eight miles from Dunbar."

"Nary much food ta be found on this route, eh?" Alexander chided, "One of Leslie's regiments really did a good job with the scorched earth policy, 'tis surely been left bare of anythin' that could be of any use ta Cromwell. How quickly the tide has turned, and now 'tis nary a bite fer us either."

"Well," Robert commented, "our stomachs ken vouch fer the fact that the English have nary shared any of our own supplies with us, and 'tis nary an inklin' that they ever aim ta, as much as I loathe ta say it."

They had been force-marched all day. The sun's rays were starting to fade over the beautiful countryside, and they could barely see where to walk. Bound together as they were, the mud made it even more difficult to avoid twigs, dips, rocks, or other jagged obstacles. They constantly bumped into each other, even stumbled over their own feet. If one man in a line of four staggered or fell, the rest had to really hustle to get him back on his feet fast, if that failed they would all be pulled down and slain. Merely being able to remain on their feet had become a matter of life and death.

Chapter 7

SEPTEMBER 4, 1650
BEYOND REASON

THE DREARY cold weather combined with the lack of clothing, breaks, and food magnified discomfort from complaining muscles and feet. They had been on the trail for less than a day, but the prisoners already felt as though they had been marched along the coast forever.

A lad Daniel recognized as a very young Tommy MacDowell begged the nearest guard to let him rest for a while. The guard had given him a wink and a sly grin, cut him free and helped him to the side of the trail where the grateful lad sunk into the bushes.

Daniel remembered Tommy—he had shaken his hand just before they were tied up, and he hadn't been able to put out of his mind how weak and soft it was. Now it was obvious that the rest of him was the same. His exposed pale skin confirmed that he had never spent much time outside.

"Where do ye hail from lad?" He had asked when they met.

The frightened boy had answered, "From Fife sir."

Curious, Daniel pursued, "Do ye come from a family of soldiers?"

"Oh—nay sir. 'Tis a clerk my Da be, and I was studyin' with him so I could someday take his place. He dinna want me in the army and hated ta see me go, but the Earl volunteered me along with seven others ta help meet the quota the Kirks had demanded. He tried ta get the Earl ta let me stay and finish my learnin', but he pointed out that the country must come first—so here I am, the only one of the eight left.

The other seven were cut down in the battle—friends I had grown up with. 'Tis nary what I had thought it would be, and certainly nary the life my Da and I had planned.

"I kenna say that my Da would be very proud of me. I must confess that when I was captured I was fleein' fer my life. A whole bunch of us were caught just north of Broxburn Brook. 'Tis bad ashamed that I am."

Daniel sensed the lad's regrets and comforted him, "Dinna be ashamed lad, many a good man ran from this battle, and because of it some of them will live ta fight another day."

Tommy's row had been only two in front of Daniel's. He had watched him try to keep up the pace, but anyone within sight of him couldn't help but notice that he had been struggling from the start.

The three prisoners he had been attached to had made every effort to help him along, even though his heavy weight was a hindrance. He had not been clever enough to keep his shoes, and sharp rocks along the way had taken their toll on his feet. Nasty scrapes, bruises, and an especially deep cut under his right foot made it impossible for him to walk normally, so he had given up and asked for help.

With his bare, swollen, and bloody feet stuck out before him, Tommy cried pitifully from his bed in the heather and pleaded for a sip of water. Daniel forgot his fetters, let out a cry and bolted straight out in an attempt to dash to the lad's side. The balance of the four comrades was flown out of kilter and they almost lost it. Pure instinct kicked in and John grabbed Dan's left wrist in a flash while Robert latched on to his right without even thinking. They held on as tightly as their bound hands would let them—leaving Alexander leaning on one leg in fear of his life. "Zonkers, Daniel MacDhughill—give it up—ye kenna help."

The friends had barely gotten their grips on Daniel when Leighton, the monster, rode by, spotted the whimpering boy and, without a second's hesitation, ran Tommy through with his sword. He then held the gory thing up and gloatingly looked around, hoping for some resistance and a reason to kill more.

The comrades watched helplessly as the youngster's blood added a red blush to the base of the flattened heather. Daniel sagged between John and Robert, closed his eyes, and thought, *Ye were nary cut out ta be a soldier, dear lad, but 'tis sure ye would have made a truly good clerk.*

"Keep sharp, keep sharp." Alex forced words from his dry throat, "Fer God's sake, Dan—ye know there was nothin' ta be done fer the poor lad. I'm afraid there will be more like him, so many are barefoot."

With a nod of their heads, the friends gave Daniel a jerk on his tether and released their hold just as a guard motioned for them to move along. Dan nodded back—gave a powerless gesture and stayed put in his place in line.

• • •

Tommy's fate had enraged and inflamed the Scots. Despite the sharp vigilance of the edgy guards, their angry protests were quietly muttered and passed along from row to row. The word spread and tensions mounted.

A starless night started to settle in and the English lit their torches. At first the Scots thought that they could benefit from the flickering glow; but it only blinded them, and shadows that danced boldly about made it harder to know where to place their feet.

"Be on guard around that curve ahead, Dan. Word has it that a group of the feisty, younger prisoners plan ta take advantage of the dark and make a run fer it. Nay, they dinna include us, but this might be our only chance."

They all yearned to go, bidden or not, but Alex took a good look at the vigilant guards, the strong rope that bound them, then at John's ugly wound and declared, "We simply kenna do this without wreckin' their chances. Look over the edge of the bank—'tis really rugged and slimy. I dinna think ye could make it with that leg, John, and with Robert still fightin' the flux—I see nary a way he's up ta it either."

He couldn't see how Robert or John could even stand up and continue to march much longer without rest, though they would never admit it. As the oncoming night blurred the trail in front of him, he told them flatly, "The message was quite clear that the lads want none but the youngest, fastest, and most fit ta go—they think that any others might endanger them and—let's face it—they could be right."

"Ta hell with that," John furiously growled. "What right do they have ta decide fer us? We be damn good soldiers and ken make up our own minds. When the lads go, we go—eh, Robert?"

Alexander was right, Robert felt pretty sick, but he pulled back his shoulders, stiffened his spine, and affirmed anyway, "Ye've got that right, we sure ken do it—let's join 'em and get off this trail ta nowhere!"

John felt empowered—he started to work his painful leg and visualized himself dashing about as he usually did. He felt sure that once he got out there, he could easily outwit his captors.

So, the deal was sealed. The four placed themselves on high alert and waited for their chance. Something felt off and it bothered them, but they dismissed it as the call of freedom. In any case, at this point there was no way to change the escape plan.

John softly but firmly ordered, "Be ready—when the lads go for it—run like hell fer the ridge." Years of instincts rose up and raised an eerie feeling at the back of his neck that caused him to mutter under his breath, "I awta feel good about this; what be the matter with me?"

The inkling was well founded. Within minutes, from seemingly out of nowhere, a cold musket was pressed against Alexander's head. "One little twitch and you are gone and your friends here sliced up as well," Lieutenant Wilbur Barlow hissed in his ear.

Somewhere, somehow there had been a leak, the lads' plan had been bared—they didn't stand a chance—and since Highlanders were considered the more dangerous prisoners, Barlow had quietly surrounded and mired them down.

Alex froze, but managed a sharp glance at his teammates and followed their eyes as they zeroed in on a group of Lieutenant Barlow's guardsmen that had suddenly emerged from the shadows. He felt nauseous and powerless as he snuck another quick glance at the distraught faces of John, Daniel, and Robert—they shrugged and nodded. A thwarted Alex lowered his head, bit his tongue, and acknowledged Barlow's upper hand with a reluctant nod of his own.

The lieutenant smugly asserted, "I think you might want to think twice before you decide to go off half-cocked like that again."

He lowered his weapon and assertively walked back to his mount and, after making sure the Scots could see that he had left his guards in place, rode off.

Hearts sank as the four and those around them realized that it would be impossible for them to break through the English to join or even warn the escapees.

About twenty-six hopefuls made a brilliant run for it as the column rounded the bend. They had thought that the cloak of night would give them an advantage, but it turned out to be their worst enemy. Down the line, Scots did their best to distract the guards, but the English were not so easily sidetracked—they were more on the ball than they appeared. Sharp sentry eyes spotted the movement they had been waiting for, and their torches exposed the bare backs of runaways as the lads scattered for cover.

The brunt of the group took direct hits and sprawled on their faces—mowed down from behind before they could reach the embankment. Some had freed themselves of their ropes while others died tied to their comrades. It seemed to Alexander, who could make out part of the ridge from over his shoulder, that about seven had made it to a spot where they could spring over the edge.

Once the gunfire ceased, the English searched systematically for survivors. They felt confident that they had cut down most, if not all, of the runners. It seemed foolish to believe anyone could survive for any length of time among the half frozen slime and mud, so not willing to risk more manpower, Lieutenant Barlow posted two guards to stay and continue the search, then ordered the rest of his men to move on.

The collaborators were devastated by the failed attempt and its sad losses. They hoped that some of the lads had been able to hide and wait until they could slip away unnoticed. They all wished they could have been with them, each one thinking he might have done it better. Some prayed that at least a few of the young Scotts could make contact with Leslie's army and report the prisoners' location. Surely their esteemed leader would come to their rescue. Daniel's row, along with most of the more seasoned soldiers, didn't see much chance of that happening, great as it sounded.

It was Robert who summed it up, "We've been on the move nonstop since mornin' and the pace has been wild and daft—it dinna seem ta me that our army could catch up with us, even if they wanted ta. I dinna believe that General Leslie will be as concerned about us as he'll be about gettin' even with Cromwell."

Still, hope died hard, and each man secretly held on to a sliver of hope—every sound or turn in the road gave them pause as they visualized their salvation. Weary, but still strong, they were eager to fight. At the first hint of support, they would be ready.

As the prisoners marched on into the murky night, each step dragged them down a bit more. Daniel tried to feel his tongue. It was parched and swollen, like an old shoe, he thought as he attempted to prevent it from sticking to the roof of his mouth. At least the vulgar taste made him less hungry.

Chapter 8

BERWICK UPON TWEED

TIRED HEADS snapped at the sound of a snorting horse bearing down from the north. As the animal came into sight it was obvious that it was being pushed hard by its rider who was gasping for breath himself. The proud but exhausted creature came to a halt beside Major Hugh Leighton, who had just come back from enacting his routine scare tactics. He made it a precedent to keep the prisoners aware of his presence by parading his stallion up and down the line at odd times.

John and Alex stared at the soldiers and took advantage of a lax moment between guards' movements to vent their curiosity. "Whoa—'tis an outstandin' animal that officer has there—equal ta Leighton's I'd say. Makes us miss our steeds, fer sure, eh? What say ye, John? Arabian?"

"Ay—and I reckon 'tis a costly beauty at that. That bloke seems ta be well acquainted with Leighton—he's probably wealthy as well. Wonder what's afoot."

Alexander's thoughts had wandered, "The bastards killed my *Star*, shot him right out from under me. I loved that horse—he would've made those two look like ponies.

"'Tis how they got me, ye know. When Star went down, I was knocked ta the ground, and they grabbed me before I could re-arm or get back ta my feet."

The spent rider was winded, but managed to salute the Major as he slipped from his horse, barely able to stand. He had no more than dismounted when a flask of water was placed in his hand. He drank thirstily and then splashed the rest over his face while the Major motioned for food to be prepared.

"This is a tremendous surprise, Richard. By God, I'm glad to see you."

"Great to see you too, Hugh," he spit out, "We got news at my post that I knew you would like to hear firsthand. Leslie has already made for the north with his tail between his legs. He and what was left of his whipped army hightailed it out of Dunbar, left Edinburgh wide open for us and ran straight for Stirling. There's not even a jack rabbit following you. It seems this bunch of rubbish has been written off by the *Army of the Covenant*. They really take care of their own, don't they?"

"Not one of their best points. I really appreciate that you've gone out of your way for me; it helps to know what that swine's up to. You've run yourself ragged, but you've given me a boost I've badly needed.

"Every one of us here wants to join the fray alongside Cromwell—but if we are to be saddled with this duty, at least this news eases the burden. It will be a lot more comfortable now that we can stop looking over our shoulders.

"You're a sight for sore eyes, Richard—even worn out you look as chipper as ever. Wilbur, see to his horse."

"Give him a good rub down and a sack of prime oats," the officer ordered. "And, fix a place for me to bed down. I'll be headed back as soon as we're both rested up."

Surprised and taken aback, Wilbur stood with his mouth agape holding the reins while Leighton dismounted, placed his hand on his friend's shoulder, and guided him off to the side.

"I wish you could stay longer so we could relax and shoot the breeze, but let's make the most of what we have." He motioned and said, "Over this way. Let's catch up while we eat. The supplies we captured from the Scots aren't too bad. Some of it's actually quite edible, much better than those stone biscuits Lord-General Cromwell is so fond of. It's a real pain to have to drag those heavy ovens along so we can bake them ourselves. They have to be the most horrible things I've ever tasted."

They shared a good laugh and shook their heads, "There's a nice spot over there—let's go sit on those rocks. I happen to have a bit of Leslie's Scotch whiskey and that stuff can wash down just about anything. What do you think Cromwell will do?" They continued to enjoy their visit while they waited for their food.

Lieutenant Wilbur Barlow was left standing with his mouth ajar and his ego badly bruised; he had expected to be treated as an equal and be invited to join them. "My esteemed uncle is a real pain in the ass," he muttered under his breath. He was infuriated, but tightened his jaw and said nothing. He called a Foote soldier over, threw him the horse's reins, and roughly ordered him to rub down and feed the animal.

Barlow just happened to have a bottle of that Scotch whiskey himself. He'd have his own party and treat himself to a few sips to sooth his ruffled feathers.

Hopeful that they might catch the gist of the rider's news, some of the prisoners tried to get within earshot as they trudged by, but there was no chance. They didn't have to wait long to figure it out though; within an hour after the friends had finished their visit, Leighton decided to call a halt.

"Moving those wasters is hard enough in the daylight—no need to ride in the dark if it's not necessary," he had grumbled to Richard before he sent two scouts on ahead to set up his tent and locate an area big enough to corral the prisoners.

• • •

With eyes squinted into tiny slits, Daniel searched for landmarks. "As ye expected, John, 'tis Berwick on Tweed—I recognize those wide rollin' hills sittin' against the night sky ta our right. Look down the cliff toward the North Sea and tell me if ye ken make out Bass Rock or North Berwick Law. If ye ken, once we cross their bridge we'll be in England."

"Well, I ken barely make out anythin', but I think I see Bass Rock, 'tis much too dark ta see the other though."

"I'm afraid then, 'tis goodbye ta Scotland. *Soraidh. Ha til mir tullidh.* A sad day indeed. As fer Berwick, it has always held a mixed allegiance—who knows how it will go fer us there. I doubt that Cromwell plans ta billet us around here, 'tis too far north."

They soon found out about allegiances in the area. Residents, who had been alerted by Leighton's bragging scouts, lined the streets even on this dark, wet night. They shouted, jeered, and threw rotten vegetables, horse manure, and other filth at the captives who tried to pay them no heed as they just kept moving.

Robert gagged and then piped up between shots, "I nary thought horse shite could taste so good. Did ye all get a bit of that?"

"Bad shots, they missed me, Robby," Alex quipped, "and I dinna intend ta hang around fer seconds. Those folks dinna even give us a chance ta get friendly!"

Dan nudged John and wise cracked, "It must have been yer distractin' sweet smile that made them miss yer sour puss."

"Very funny," John said, shaking his head after he spat on the ground. "I sorely wish they had missed me, ye jackarse. Ugh, bleck—that tastes ungodly—yuk."

"Kenna ye just feel the love, John?"

"Nay, but I ken taste the shite. Dang ye, Rob—ye might have kept it all fer yerself!"

• • •

Guards herded the prisoners onto the town's magnificent fifteen-arch stone bridge. Just about any other time most of the Scots might have stopped to enjoy this brilliant architectural work, but as the cold wind blew over it and gnawed at them, they only thought it lengthy and drawn out.

When they finally reached the other side, each prisoner was handed one of Cromwell's rock-hard biscuits and was derided with, "Welcome to England, you vermin," and worse. The snide remarks cut the captives to the core and they bitterly resented them, but not one refused his biscuit.

Disgruntled, the sorry lot was rushed on until they stumbled into a field of rough grass near the moors, between the trail and the sea where they were ordered to halt.

Relieved to be past the mob and grateful for any scrap of food, most of the prisoners just collapsed in their tracks and gnawed frantically on the rock-hard biscuits while they huddled together and tried to get warm. A few fed-up Scots took off toward the marsh in an unfortunate attempt to escape—they were given no quarter and were slaughtered in their tracks.

Distressed by the murder of more comrades, some captives made futile efforts to object, but they were too tired to do much more than swear at the guards, call them *blood thirsty bastards* and say a short prayer for the lost souls.

The four friends bunched together as tightly as they could in the coarse grass. The guards' attention was focused on the attempted escapees and that gave the friends a chance to speak guardedly. John heaved a sigh, "Thanks be ta God. I must say 'tis a good feelin' ta stop, I figured they were just gonna run us til we all dropped dead."

"That was one long miserable day," Daniel agreed, "but if the English are confident enough ta interrupt the march, they must be damn sure they are nary bein' followed, and that confirms that 'tis nary a chance in hell of anyone comin' fer us."

"Ay," John added sadly, "'Tis sure I be that we agree with that rotten bit. Bein' forced ta leave our beloved Scotland like some kind of scum was about the most mortifyin' and painful thing that could ever be."

That off his chest, John shifted his weight until he felt the pressure leave his throbbing leg. He took a deep breath and complained, "*Zounds*, what a stinkin' fix we're in. Seemed like it took ferever ta get across that damn bridge."

Daniel tried to change the subject, "'Tis good that we ate heartily before the battle and I thank ye fer sharin' yer dumplin'. It helped me get through the day. As ghastly as that biscuit was, I was glad ta get that too, but if I am still starvin', which I be—*famished*—those who fasted fer two or three days before we came down from Doon Hill must be even hungrier. I could care less fer that ritual. Contrary to battle folklore, I fight better on a full stomach."

A pale, exhausted Robert gulped, bit at a dry lip, and confessed, "Unfortunately, I bought inta the fastin' deal. 'Tis hungry as hell I am."

Not wanting to think of his own growling stomach, Alexander

feigned disgust at the hell word, and John couldn't resist the opening, "Ah, ha—ye'd better watch yer mouth, Robert, if the Kirks ever catch ye cussin' like that they will kick yer arse and throw ye out of this man's army. I wonder now, how would that frost yer pumpkin?"

Too hungry to be in the mood for humor, Robert moaned, "'Tis well and good fer the great John MacKinney ta blatha' on, eh? Yer always cussin'—ye bossy old bloke. I'd say *hell* a million times, if it would get us out of here, but 'tis a bit late fer that."

There was not a Scotsman in the massive bunch whose mouth wasn't watering for food, but neither that nor the steady rain could keep any of them awake.

The next morning came abruptly with a nagging reminder from rumbling stomachs. The hungry men were soon rounded up and forced back on the trail.

The rain had slowed and the wind shifted into a feisty breeze that swirled the dying leaves and gently swayed the bushes and trees. Robert looked up at the gray, gloomy, overcast sky. "We could do with a bit of sun," he remarked, "I wish some of this mud would dry up. My back feels like 'tis carryin' two horses."

"Keep wishin', Robert. I wish we were on the backs of the two horses!"

They could dream, but their reality was unchanged. The brief rest had helped and had given Daniel a chance to refill his goatskin while others sucked up water from puddles that had snuggled in between the marsh grasses.

Chapter 9

BITTER REGRETS

MAJOR HUGH Leighton had been relieved that his friend had given him confirmation that the *Army of the Covenant* was not a threat and part of him was thankful, but the rest of him bristled and was disappointed. He had actually been itching for a fight so that he could showcase his true capabilities as the brilliant leader he just knew he was. *If only*, he thought, *If only I could have been instrumental in defeating Leslie or his cronies, the scales would have tipped in my favor and the promotion I've always known I deserve would have fallen in my lap. I'd have shown them—all I needed was the chance.*

Embittered and resentful, he realized that his fate had been sealed—he saw no escape from the lowly duty that he felt was so far beneath his ambitions and capabilities. He placed the blame squarely on the loathsome prisoners for the ruin of his career and the loss of friends—he vowed he would make them pay. He badgered them relentlessly and hounded his subordinates constantly to bump up the pace.

The increased gait distressed Lieutenant Wilbur Barlow so much that, at the first opportunity for privacy, he pulled his horse up beside his mammoth uncle and blurted out, "This is ridiculous, you're pressing too hard, Uncle Hugh, my men and I are exhausted—and for what?"

Before responding, the monster took a moment to look down his nose at the intruder, "Well now—pooped out are you, eh? Now isn't that just too bad—and you will call me Major Leighton, Lieutenant. Army life too much for you? Worn out already? Huh, and we're just getting started! Your problem is that you're weak and always knackered in one way or another. That makes it harder and harder for me to keep my promise to your dear mother—I can't depend on you; you always come up complaining or lacking. You don't have the gumption or guts to be anything but a thorn in my side."

Humiliated, Wilbur sat like a statue. He realized that he had made a futile attempt, wasted his time and over stepped, so he swallowed his pride and tried to look contrite, "I'm sorry, unc . . . ah . . . I mean . . . Major, I'll try to do better," he stammered.

"I should hope so—you've only one way to go." But as Wilbur turned to leave, he added, "Sonny, hold on a minute, for your mother's sake, I may have a surprise for you soon. In the meantime buck-up and get your sorry ass back to your duties—get those slackers to churn out some headway."

Tail between his legs, Barlow bit his tongue, heaved a sigh, and returned to his post to carry out the harsh orders.

However, after four long days on the trail from Dunbar, no matter how hard Leighton pushed, the column became more sluggish as the weary men grew weaker. Exhaustion, sickness, and starvation were taking their toll and the nasty weather never let their naked bodies dry off or warm up. Casualties had increased significantly, especially among the young innocents like Tommy MacDowell, who had never really wanted to be in the military and were not cut out for it.

Tongues hung out and tried to catch icy cold rain that drenched them from one downpour to another. Freezing shaky hands made it a challenge to lap the trickles from their ropes and arms as they had done earlier. The rainstorm served only to make mud, cause more misery, and entertain the guards as they watched the prisoners struggle.

"I know that those bastards dinna give a rat's arse about us, but 'tis gettin' me pissed. How I'd love ta wring that son-of-a-bitch Leighton's neck."

"Watch yer mouth, John. Remember what ye told me."

"Git outa here, Robert, *rat's arse* 'tis nary cussin'—and *pissin'* —well—'tis a natural thing—and—ah—the others are—well—only family jargons."

"Ya, ya, ya—Well, while yer at it, jargon yerself out of this trek, smart arse," Rob good naturedly wise cracked back, but then stopped suddenly and tugged at the tether, "Oh, oh, trouble ahead. Bide a wee—somethin's up."

Big trouble, the row ahead of theirs was wobbling about, off balance and distressed. Alan Grey, whose gray face had worried Daniel earlier, was the reason.

His team thought at first that he had fainted and tried to drag him along. It soon became obvious that Alan was dead and they wouldn't be able to deal with his heavy body much longer. Once his weight became unmanageable, nothing could keep them upright—the row would collapse and they would all be doomed.

Out of the blue they were blessed. A very young Cavalry guardsman happened to be riding slowly by—he didn't stop or hesitate, but simply slid his sword down and in a very surprising and compassionate gesture, cut through the tether that tied Alan to his comrades. Then he rode coolly away as if nothing had happened. Grey's body slipped off toward the ditch, but not before it flew back and slammed into Robert. The dead weight hit him full on, knocked the wind out of him, pushed him off his feet, and left him to dangle by his tether.

His companions instinctively dug in and braced themselves. Daniel yanked the tether hard on his right and pulled Robert as close to him as his bound wrists would let him. John grabbed the tether on Dan's left side and quickly pushed it toward the ground which forced it taunt. The rope on Alexander's end then tried to drag him down, but he drew back on it and yanked it toward him in order to stabilize himself while he struggled to maintain his balance and keep them all upright; which he somehow managed to do while John and Daniel held firm.

To say that they were lucky was an understatement. Amazingly Robert remained conscious, although he certainly was loopy and out of it. His inherent reaction dodged disaster—he twisted, turned, and executed some tricky footwork until both feet finally touched the ground so he could steady himself.

"Rob, Robert—fer God's sake, be ye fit?"

Choked up, he tried to answer but could only move his head in a slight nod. He finally managed a crooked smile and heaved a giant sigh—still grateful to have the support of Dan's arm. He was a sorry-looking sight—his hair stood on end and scratches and bruises covered his body, but nothing appeared to be broken.

It was a great opportunity, but everyone, even Alexander, passed on the chance to poke fun at Robert's lifesaving dance—they were just thankful and relieved that they and their friend had survived.

Several rows had been discombobulated by the misadventure, but they had hastily shuffled, adjusted their positions, and remained upright.

"Zounds, poor Alan, what a sad endin' fer such a good man," Alexander noted. "His buddies are safe though, thanks be ta that quick-witted guard."

John added, "Good thing the monster dinna see him cut Alan's body loose or ye ken bet the bastard would have had that fine lad's arse in a sling or worse."

"'Tis senseless ta try ta get ye ta watch yer language, John MacKinney."

"Good, 'tis damn glad I be ta hear ye've given up on that." Alex gave up, and the three comrades peered down the row to scrutinize Robert.

"Well," Alex heaved a sigh and groaned, "I fer one have had enough excitement fer a while. Thank the good Lord, yer alive, Rob. That was quick thinkin' on yer part, and I must say the rest of us dinna do so shabby either," he boasted.

Dan smothered a grin, gave John a friendly tap on the arm, and released his hold on Robert, who slowly fell back into the monotonous shuffling rhythm and finally stopped gagging enough to squeak out, "'Twas weird indeed. I dinna know what hit me at first—who would ever expect a body ta come flyin' out of the blue like that? 'Tis most grateful ta all of ye I be—'twas a wild zany bit, eh?"

"*Zookers*, aaaayee—ye ken well say that, Rob!"

Chapter 10

**ALNWICK CASTLE,
NORTHUMBERLAND, ENGLAND**

THEIR MINDS were rattled and all were unusually silent, especially Robert who was still shaky from his wild encounter with Alan Grey's body. The humdrum tedium calmed him, and he doggedly managed to hold his own as they scuffled on—then suddenly, the column was forced off the trail—strange—since the day was still young.

"Zonkers, what in God's good name 'tis goin' on?" They were all curious until the reason became apparent. Alnwick Castle sat handsomely off to the left side of the trail, and they were being coxswained straight to it.

"Ahh," John ventured, "'Tis mayhap we good ole blokes ken find a roof over our heads fer a change. Think ye—could it be anythin' but?"

The castle was conveniently located for the English. It was situated twenty-eight miles south of Berwick upon Tweed and thirty-five miles north of Newcastle. The first Lord Percy of Alnwick had restored it, primarily as a fortress. It boasted a formidable constable's tower with a middle gateway. The enormous stone mass sprawled out over a gently sloping hillside and enjoyed a panoramic view of the surrounding region.

The captives were ordered in through the center gateway and were forced directly to the middle bailey of the castle where they were literally packed in. The great gate was slammed—then chained up behind them. The earsplitting jolt was followed by dead silence. Startled, the prisoners gawked at each other in utter dismay. "'Tis a creepy place," . . . "and dank ta boot," someone stammered from the back.

Scots shuffled and wiggled about as they maneuvered for a place to sit. With no site obvious where they could stretch out or lie down, the four friends hunkered in and did the best they could to get somewhat comfortable in a spot they had wangled out of the overcrowded space. Still struggling with remnants of the flux, Robert scrunched himself up into a tight ball and was soon sound asleep.

Time passed in morbid silence—a few stooped elderly peasants eventually appeared and brought some water that was gratefully received. They hauled in their buckets and set them just outside the gate so the captives could reach the dippers from between the bars and share the water. The aged ones then moved on without making contact of any kind. All prisoners hoped that food would follow, but not a scrap came—nor did Leighton or any of his men.

The captives were simply baffled at first but serious concern soon spread that they had been crudely abandoned. The place remained as quiet as a tomb—which was exactly what it was turning into. The Scots checked and rechecked every inch of the dungeon in search of a possible weak point that might offer a hope of escape.

Before long, raw and bloody fingers frantically scratched at the walls as they sought out that one crack or crevice that might lead to a way out. This part of the fortress was huge and strong—it had been built for the sole purpose of keeping prisoners in, and was well suited for the job.

Alex was always full of surprises, but they were all startled when he began doing some serious praying. John cussed a lot, and Daniel and Robert were inclined to go along with John, whose leg was swollen, hot, and ugly. His friends kept the wound as clean as possible but were frustrated by their helplessness—there was no way they could relieve the pain that constantly gnawed at him. It became apparent just how bad it was when the big man groaned aloud in his sleep.

By the fifth day a desperate Alex had gathered up some like-minded comrades who had squirmed close enough to unite with him in prayer, and it seemed they were going at it constantly. He tried nonstop to get his buddies to join them, and Robert sometimes did, but there was no way he could coax John or Daniel into the group.

Dan sat quietly brooding and feigned that he preferred to stay put and just enjoy his leisure at their host's expense—no one laughed. John alleged that he was much too busy planning to stay alive to oblige them.

"Ye clodhoppers ken hang around and sit on yer bahookies if ye want ta, but me and Alex here are callin' out fer any help we ken get. Since 'tis nary a sign of earthly aid pitchin' in, we are urgin' the Lord ta lend a hand—and at the very least fergive us and grant us peace," Robert declared.

"Now, now—Robby, dinna wear yerself ta a frazzle—go fer it— 'tis pretty clear that we ken use any help we ken get." Daniel voiced, and followed with, "I be *prayin'* that ye will just do it quietly, 'tis all."

"Dan's right, Rob," John conceded, "Ye and Alex carry on—ye may yet have somethin' there, I hope 'tis so. We be behind ye—ye know that—fuddy-duddy pains that ye both may be."

"Ay, indeed we know that," Robert softened, "and 'tis dear ta us. More than ever now that we're rottin' in this stinkin' hell hole. Ye mean a lot ta us ta boot—ugly old grouches that ye be."

John couldn't quit, "And, how be ye holdin' up anyhow, Jonkings? Yer lookin' a bit green about the gills."

Robert feigned a crushed look, "And, yer lookin' like the pain in the arse that ye as ever were, John MacKinney—and we all know 'tis nary a cure fer that."

Alexander and Daniel looked at each other and burst out laughing—and before long John gave in and joined them while Robert chuckled to himself.

As the days went on there were very few who were not convinced that they had been intentionally left to starve to death. Most just sat, stared, and waited for the inevitable. Some desperately shook and rattled the bars—others pounded and scraped at the walls. Bloody screams rang out to no avail, echoing horrors that raged inside dying minds.

Their cries and hopes rumbled down empty halls then flew out and up into the sky where they searched for the ears of a God who seemed to be busy elsewhere.

"Dearest God, please help me."

"I kenna grasp this, ye bastards, git out here and fight like men."

"Kill me, ye cowards—bring it on—face me and get it over with. Come on."

"I kenna do this. Somebody—anybody—get me out of this hell hole."

"Ma, Oh Ma . . . Fer God's sake, help me."

"Suck it up lads, get yer courage up."

"If depart this life we must—ken we at least go out with some honor?"

"Honor? Who the hell be ye joshin'?"

By the end of the week, dead bodies were everywhere. The dreadful stenches of death and feces permeated everything and everyone. Still, not a soul showed—to bring nourishment, clean the filth, or carry away the dead.

Those who could did their best to give some solace to the sick and dying. They didn't have much to offer aside from some kind words and a few sips of water. The prayers continued, but they were now quieter, less hopeful—more pleas for forgiveness.

■ ■ ■

Finally, a huge ruckus shook the bulwarks—seemingly from out of nowhere—the huge gate swung open at last and voices were heard as English guards shouted for the prisoners to get their asses in gear and turn out.

Barely able to stand themselves, many Scots tried to help carry those who could not move on their own. The guards had been ordered not to bother with the dying or immobile. They tore the limp bodies away from their comrades, threw them back in the dungeon, and clanked the gate shut behind them.

Exactly one week from the day the Scots had entered Alnwick Castle, Major Hugh Leighton and his subordinates waited for them just outside the middle gate. They all looked rested, refreshed, and cocky. The monster's hair had been trimmed and his face shaved clean. His immaculate uniform stood out and he made quite a dashing figure on his great horse. Lieutenant Wilbur Barlow looked a bit shamefaced, but he had enjoyed his uncle's surprise and seemed a new man too—even the Foote soldiers looked rested—the break had done wonders for them.

It soon leaked back to the prisoners that the guards had spent the week in a small village that was nestled merely a few hundred feet behind the castle. The inhabitants had treated them as conquering heroes, and they had lacked for nothing.

Their merriment was over now though, and it didn't take long for them to get back into the humdrum routine they had been dealt, and loathed. If it bothered any of them that they had locked away fellow human beings without food or basic comforts, there was no evidence of it.

The Scots were anything but refreshed—sunken eyes stared back at Leighton and his guardsmen, irate, disgusted, and livid. The monster on the other hand, was disappointed that so many had walked out. Obviously, he had not received any communication from Cromwell or Parliament as to their schemes for the captives.

Daniel MacDhughill, John MacKinney, Alexander Maxwell, and Robert Jonkings had made it, although noticeably wasted and distressed. For each other's sakes, they tried to put on an air of confidence but failed wretchedly, all they could do was look powerlessly at each other. They had left too much horror behind—there was no way to cheer up the dead.

"Onward, *bráthairs*. Let's get on now—one step at a time, eh? Come on, ye Scots. Bend yer backs, lads—show these arseholes some guts. Much as they wished it—they dinna see the last of us yet."

Chapter 11

MORPETH

THE DECEIVINGLY beautiful fortress faded from view into the picturesque terrain as the wretched looking survivors continued the degrading march to the south. With false bravado they staunchly attempted to hold their heads up in spite of being forced to leave their dead, frail, and dying comrades behind.

Careful to be out of the guards' hearing range, Dan irrupted into a rant, "Dead and done nary says it, me *bráthairs*. How we ken even keep movin' has me stumped. I tried ta fight it, but they win—that dungeon filched me mettle—I feel as though me heart and soul have been ripped out. Any bit left of me—'tis useless. The cold air nary pestered me afore, but now the slightest gust rips through me. 'Tis frozen ta the core I be—I think me very blood has turned ta slush. I feel about as useful as a teat on a bull—and I kenna see how 'twill ever get any better."

"Low an' behold now—did ye hear that? 'Tis fer certain helpful as hell, 'tis—an' a mouthful at that, Dan." John disgustedly grunted, "What a surprise! We all be low—an' who ever had any freakin' use fer bleak frigid air even when clad fer it? What good 'twill it do us ta moan about bein' in the buff, starvin', and all tuckered ta hell out? 'Tis plain sense that nary amount of wretched bitchin' will help—so—'tis an end we must put ta it. 'Tis nary a way we ken afford ta be down in the dumps if we expect ta keep our heads on straight—let's git on with it an' let the sulky guards do the damn grumblin.'"

Robert coughed and forced some slurred words to work their way out, "And, just who died and made ye God—O, Mighty John? Eh? I reckon we all be owed a bit of bitchin'. What have we got ta look forward ta, anyway? Maybe those left behind be the lucky ones. Ye may have some guts and gumption left, John MacKinney, but Dan's nary the only one who had his sucked out back there."

"Enough, lads" John came back, "How's about we cut each other some slack eh? There be nary a reason ta be so hard on ourselves. *Zookers,* naught even the strongest Scot could leave off eatin' fer as long as we have and expect ta be frisky."

That put an end to it. Alexander sheepishly nodded his head but did not utter a word, and neither Dan nor Rob ventured to point out more of the obvious.

They sullenly pushed forward and, albeit their stiff and sore muscles made any kind of movement a challenge, the sharp cold air helped revive them a bit. In spite of the rough days on the trail most of the prisoners had gone into Alnwick still fairly strong. They had come out dehumanized—sullen and mere shells of themselves.

Two more days down the trail, still haunted by death and mayhem, they drifted on, dazed, and barely conscious. Daniel's eyes were puffed, swollen, and sunken in all at the same time. His usually shiny fly-away blonde hair was a stinky slimy foul mess. He was trying to size up the other three when Robert startled him with, "Yer a scary lookin' sight, Daniel MacDhughill, and the worst of 'tis, ye look the best of the lot. What a pathetic bunch we are, matted and covered with everythin' from vomit ta piss and worse. Zounds—we be dung bags."

John just grimaced, but Alex acknowledged, "Ye've got that right, Robert Jonkings, nary even our dear *máthairs* would recognize us, but the lice seem ta know us well enough. I've nary been so itchy in my life."

Dan rubbed his sticky eyes and said, "I kenna see much, but it seems ta me that ye take the *cèic,* John. Yer wild hair has grown so fast and furious that yer big mouth has disappeared completely, and who would ever think that could happen?" He cracked himself up before he playfully went on and weakly spit out, "And ah, if ye ever plan ta part that quirky mop of ginger down the middle again, I reckon ye'd best ferget it and just shave the whole danged thing off."

Alex and Robert looked down the row at each other and suppressed a laugh as John glowered, "That will be the day and 'tis nary a wee bit funny, Dan."

It had become obvious, even to Leighton, that the column was getting nowhere, so he reluctantly ordered that a biscuit be doled out to each prisoner. "One biscuit each," he bellowed. "Wouldn't want those dogs to get too fat and lazy, now would we?"

They weren't allowed the luxury of a break—the infamous biscuits were tossed out to the captives while they labored to move forward. They staggered, grabbed for them, and gobbled them up like they were Christmas dinner. The stone like things went down hard and didn't settle very well on empty stomachs, but most managed to keep at least some of their biscuit down.

About an hour later John couldn't resist drawing attention to some weird hullabaloos, "Ken ye hear yer bellies, lads? They be hootin' louder than bagpipes on Sunday. Who would have thought that one biscuit could make us all gurgle so?"

They all tuned in, and Dan affirmed, "Ye got that right, we're louder than the horses, and dinna John's farts just add a tangy touch, eh lads?"

That did it. They were so beyond caring that at first the sounds amused them and they chuckled—next sniggers slipped out and all hell broke loose—the four of them broke into a devil-may-care laughing fit. More burbles and escaping gases rang out and egged them on—the harder they tried to shut up, the more the laughs came roaring out. Their stomachs ached and their ribs hurt until tears mopped their way down filthy faces and vanished into grubby beards.

The men in the row in front glanced back and wondered if their comrades had gone completely daft. Expecting Leighton or one of the guards to blow some heads off, the row in back slowed down also, but by the time a guard rode by the four had lost the humor of it and fallen into a dead silence that lingered as they stomped on quietly for hours until Alexander felt sermonic, "I kenna help but discern that, as bad off as we are, we're better off than a lot around us. We're standing fairly straight and tall and even the bum leg, 'tis doin' good, eh John? I'll say a prayer of thanks fer us."

"Ay," John sarcastically retorted, "And say one for those blokes we left behind in that stink hole while yer at it. They were all prayin' as well—if ye recall."

"'Tis nary a way ta forget that, John—we all remember, but yer always the first one ta say we have ta keep a stiff upper lip and move on. So, put yer pence where yer hole 'tis, ye grumpy arse, if ye ken find it—that is—yer mouth, I mean."

"Oh, shut yer own hole, Alexander Maxwell. It muddles me when yer right." His stomach rumbled, he belched, shrugged, and strove to look contrite.

The tirade had relaxed them all somewhat and they went back to the business of staying alive. One foot was again placed in front of the other in a bizarre sort of rhythm that kept them in step and let them move forward less tediously.

Nightfall found them collapsed and huddled together—passed out in yet another wet grassland. At dawn, they, and others who could, instinctively crawled up and started out once again—increasingly hungry and down cast.

Alexander was dragging along, but about noon he instinctively lifted his head as he began to recognize familiar scenery, "Bide a wee—gaze about, lads. Surely it must be—ay—'tis Morpeth," he croaked out. "I know this area well. I was born in Caerlaverock; 'tis near here—but thankfully blessed ta be over the border inta Scotland. We're gettin' deeper inta England, needless ta say—been headin' nearly straight south all the way. Anyway, in case ye dinna know it, Caerlaverock, 'tis at the mouth of the Nith River, nary so far ta the west from here. My family once owned a manor and great lands there. Everythin' was plundered by the English, and our home razed ta the ground."

Those memories still cut deep, but he pushed them aside, took a deep breath, and went on, "'Tis more than grand, eh? If ye look to the east we could suppose that we were amongst Scotland's misty moors. Dinna we all wish it? Instead, 'tis here in Northumberland we be."

John had picked up that the guards seemed edgier than usual. "They kenna be hoverin' about fer nay, Dan. What do ye ken they be up ta now?"

"Surely ye know much better than the rest of us, John, that they'll let us in on it when and if they care ta. It seems they get paid eight pence a day, at least the infantry does, more fer the Cavalry—two shillings, they say."

"Zounds, 'tis a hell of a lot more than we be gettin'. Once we're out of this muddle, 'tis sure I'll be ta beg that our pay be jacked up."

The guards' odd actions became very clear when shots rang out and the column was steered off the trail. "Look there, lads," Alex spouted, still fighting memories of his home. "It seems we're in the midst of a garden, or at least the remains of one. Those *hoar* frosts sure slammed this place hard. My God—come on—wake up—look! Grub! Cabbages, loads of them! Get a move on—get at 'em fast— pull up as many as ye ken."

Indeed, the column had been steered into a large, walled in garden. Due to the ravages of war, the crop had not been harvested. The four fell to their knees, yanked rotting cabbages from the ground, held them fiercely and gnawed at them. The rest of the starved prisoners did the same. They wrenched and pulled until they tore the garden apart in record time. Starved and desperate, they gobbled the plants, roots and all, plus anything else they could lay their hands on in the field, including mice, bugs, worms, and snakes. The ground was soon scraped and dug clean while frantic raw hands searched in vain for one more bite.

All the while the English guards, with their bellies full and comfortable, looked on and made fun of them. "Go to it, you Scottish pigs—rut around—why not have a race? Show us who can be the wildest and snort up the garbage the fastest!"

Chapter 12

CABBAGE DEBACLE

THE DECAYING cabbage was the only thing that even resembled real food that the prisoners had eaten since Dunbar other than the two stony biscuits, and it soon had worse effects. Their abused and shriveled stomachs recoiled at the insult.

The garden's rotting cabbage crop was no more—in its place was a blanket of men who seemed to be vomiting in unison. Daniel spewed only once, Robert several times, but John and Alex had been hit the hardest of the four, and John was so sick that he neither moved nor noticed when Alex heaved in his hair.

Sleep did not come kindly, and those who managed a few winks woke up in distress. Waves of nausea came back with a vengeance, and moans of agony joined the strange cacophony. The cabbages refused to stay down and the runs soon followed to boot.

Morning brought more trials and found John in trouble. In his bossy way, he had been a strong beacon of hope to all around him, cracking jokes and even singing softly from time to time when he was sure the guards couldn't hear. Now he was just plain sick; the stomach cramps and dysentery had made him pay dearly for chomping such shabby cabbage much too quickly. His great body shook, and he couldn't seem to haul himself out of this utter misery.

Bullies among the guards berated, taunted, and threatened the prisoners as they attempted to rise. Unmoved by the sight of the obviously ill men, the frustrated and resentful guards yelled and pushed at them to get up and get going.

John rolled around and tried to pull himself up, but the effort just made him look like a wounded bear. Daniel, not feeling quite as queasy, forced himself to his feet, reached down, placed his arm under his friend's limp shoulder, and gagged—the smell of his vomit-stiffened locks stunk worse than the rancid smells that surrounded them.

Taking on most of John's weight, he urged, "Come on, get up and move, yc kenna quit now. If we could only get a sip of good soup, 'tis cured we'd be in a wink."

"Ay—indeed. But fat chance of that. Now, dinna ye worry yer head lad, I've a tough skin and 'tis nary a cabbage I'll die from, nor from exposure like so many of these poor buggers. The bastards may bend me, but I'll be danged if I'll break."

Daniel felt bad, "I know yer tough old bird, but ye shouldna need ta be."

"Hey, dinna ye *should* on me, lad."

In spite of himself, Daniel felt a chuckle slip out, "I know better than that, ye ornery, pigheaded old goat."

To get John moving he joshed, "Ye, know, my *máthair* was a great cook and very creative with cabbages—but I'll tell ye, hers nary tasted as good as these little honeys. Must have helped that they were just a bit over ripe!"

"'Tis nary a bit of humor I see in that. Yer killin' me, Danny—Zounds, I dinna ever wanna see another cabbage."

Alexander was as white as a sheet, and Robert was doing his best to hang on. None of them knew how they did it, but they made it up, and between them managed to keep John on his feet. Bilious and dizzy, he continued to lean heavily on Daniel, while Alex picked up some of the slack from his side.

They looked around the rummaged garden that had turned into another torture chamber. Nevin MacGreggor had vomited blood all night and was obviously dead. Many others did not move, and any man who could not get up was simply shot.

As usual, Leighton urged his horse on while he sported about. He leaned down over men still on the ground and ran them through with his claymore, wielding his very heavy two-handed, double-edged sword with an ease that came from intense dedication and zealous practice.

He haughtily goaded the prisoners and boasted that his beloved weapon was a battle trophy that he had taken from what was left of a high-ranking Highlander. As he brandished it about his aides continued to help him finish off others with their carbines.

Daniel got a prickly feeling on the back of his neck—he looked up and felt heavy eyes on him. A guard was checking them out—especially eyeballing John.

Aware of the seriousness of their situation, Daniel took charge and asserted, "Come on, me friends, fancy ye ken hear bagpipes squawkin' in those thick heads—let's do a wee dance fer the buggas."

He tugged as hard as he could on John, and with Alex's help he kept him up while Robert put pressure on the tether and kept them all balanced. They somehow gathered the strength to stagger off to join those who had started to move.

"In the name of all 'tis holy," Robert gasped as he looked back into the garden and pointed to the high stone wall on the north side.

The gasp caught the guard's attention, he forgot John and took off toward the back wall where suddenly all eyes were glued.

"Zounds, 'tis Walter Gragon tryin' ta climb the wall, with George Mackay right behind him. They dinna stand the chance of a snowball in hell. Someone get them down."

Walter had actually made it almost half way to the top. He yanked wildly at loose cracks and brittle vines for support. Poor George barely got his feet off the ground.

"Too late, Rob," Alex exclaimed as musket shots ended the frantic hopes of escape and the two fell back into the remnants of the garden.

Their bodies were added to the pile of others who had died or been killed that morning. As of this dire day, more prisoners had been murdered on this trek than had perished from all their other sufferings.

At the sound of the shots Leighton turned and was at the north end in a flash. He assessed the event, nodded his approval, and slapped the guards on the back.

Somehow, stubborn pride and defiance mixed with a subconscious urge to survive took over, and in response to the Major's orders, the column advanced.

Even though most of the survivors continued to have dysentery in various degrees, no one was allowed to stop even as excrement rolled and dripped down their legs. The stench was so strong they could taste it; the ground slippery with feces and vomit. Hopelessly they glanced at the River Wansbeck that ran adjacent to the far wall of the garden and longed to dive in, but they could only yearn as they passed by.

"Ye sweeties are by far the ugliest dancin' partners I've ever had the pleasure of holdin'," John croaked out with a lame chuckle.

Daniel tried to smile and teased, "Just dinna step on my feet, ye clodhopper."

Robert kidded, "Me thinks that means he's feelin' better, eh?"

The humor helped, but each thought to himself, *I dinna know how much longer any of us can survive this brutal bitch of a death march.*

They continued to help each other along, and John, still supported by his friend's shoulder, strained to speak, "I fear 'tis ye I'm beginnin' ta sound like, Dan. Me throat hurts, me arse hurts, me feet hurt. I ache, I itch—me stomach—well—best ta ferget that. I dinna believe any of us have ever been so tired and hungry. The way they push us, ye ken bet they just would love fer us all ta fall down dead. But ta hell with them, me friends, whatever it takes, dinna flinch—we nary ken give them the pleasure of thinkin' we be whipped."

Robert piped up, "It perturbs me ta think that we've been abandoned by our own. The farther south we traveled, the faster any hope of rescue fizzled."

Alex agreed, "Ay, Rob. That dream died long ago—but John—ye knew that it would all along. I'm just too tired fer any wild adventures anyway—but dinna fret friends, I will keep goin' while I still have breath. Watchin' ye keep movin' on with that mess of a leg, John, 'tis nary a way that I will give them the pleasure of seein' how fed-up I am."

John gave a puzzled look down toward Robert, "*Perturbs*? What does that mean anyway?"

"I dinna have a clue," Robert smugly answered. "My Da used ta utter it ta my Ma, and she would get really riled. Might mean—who knows? *Pissed off?* Mayhap."

"Then, why in hell dinna ye just say that?"

"Well now, John, what bit o' fun would there be in that?"

"Fun, eh? Oh, ya—fun—aaah—now there 'tis somethin' that seems ta have slipped me mind—what the hell 'tis that anyway? Ring a bell with any of ye?"

Daniel grinned and shook his head in feigned disgust, then winced as his muscles complained. He frowned and doggedly knotted his eyebrows together while he tried to blot out the hurt. His weary legs shook from exhaustion, but he was determined to show more spunk, "Let's move our arses, we're missing the sunrise. And—just look at us woeful souls. What say ye? Reckon ye that the Kirks would regard this army *Godly enough* fer 'em at last?"

Chapter 13

SCOTLAND
THE TURMOIL LINGERS

BACK IN Scotland the horrendously devastating *Wars of the Three Kingdoms;* (the *English Civil War; Irish Confederate Wars* and many related conflicts) were still very much alive after almost ten years.

Clashing politics, treachery, disrupted families, mayhem, and hostilities continued as more men and youths were earmarked for warfare, while women and children were left to fend for themselves. Life was hard.

The bitterly trounced Leslie had abandoned the core of his *Covenanter* army and hightailed it from Dunbar with its remnants, and as John had learned via the grapevine, he had bypassed Edinburgh, left it defenseless and at Cromwell's mercy while he proceeded to Stirling where he immediately set out to recover from his defeat and regroup.

• • •

The word was out that Leslie had been offered help from MacLean of Duart's Highland regiment and that he had accepted volunteers from the Burntisland garrison under Barclay's command as well. With these newly conscripted recruits, Leslie reorganized and built up the strength of his army in Stirling to the point where he felt confident that he could prevent Cromwell from advancing further into Scotland.

After celebrating his great victory at the battle of Dunbar,

Cromwell had swiftly descended on Scotland's weakened capital of Edinburgh. Resistance was fierce and the defenders did their best, but without reinforcements and help, the outcome was preordained. Cromwell took command and made it his base.

And indeed, although Cromwell now controlled the southern part of Scotland, he was unable to dislodge or seriously threaten Leslie, who felt confident in his stronghold at Stirling, where he commanded the lowest crossing point of the River Forth as well as the inland ways into Fife and north-eastern Scotland. The *Covenanters* dug in and continued to steadily build up forces.

This prolonged crash and burn of egos now continued in the form of the *Third English Civil War.*

Cromwell was not exactly sitting pretty in Edinburgh, to add to his adversities, he was constantly harassed by the Moss Troopers, or *Mossers*—knots of raiders that had been formed by absconders from Dunbar who had not rejoined Leslie's army. At first, small groups of the Moss Troopers, led by a Captain Augustine, started out by involving themselves in highway robbery and the murder of English laggards or unaccompanied couriers, but they soon formed into greater, more serious groups.

Always cogitating, Cromwell recognized that Fife was crucial to his plans to out maneuver Leslie. Since the English fleet had undisputed command of the sea, he made preparations to outflank the *Covenanters* by designing an assault onto the Fife coast at Queensferry. This strategy was interrupted and delayed when he was taken ill and his army became seriously bogged down.

In the meantime, many Scots, who—rather than allow themselves to have their lines of communication cut—followed the young King Charles II and his *Royalists,* who were making a final desperate bid to invade England and capture London, while Cromwell remained in Scotland.

During this time Cromwell's régime approved a policy to destroy the power of Irish Catholics in Ireland who would not become Protestants; they labeled these stubborn Catholics as dangerous savages and probable followers of Prince Charles.

With the exception of Connacht, which was deemed to be an extremely *stark* western part of Ireland, the bulk of Irish properties were seized and many of these people were forced into the wastelands of Connacht where they died of starvation and disease.

As planned, Irish land owned by Catholics dwindled rapidly. The aim of the Cromwell régime was to relocate more acceptable Godly Protestants to the island and offer them the best lands, along with power over any Catholics that remained. Needless to say, there was no love lost between Irish Catholics and the English.

Unfortunately for Daniel and his comrades, they had been caught up in the middle of the muddle. Their days of hell continued while death and destruction were reprehensible back home in Scotland. Small wonder that not much, if any, thought was given to Leslie's unfortunate *Covenanter* pawns-of-war. Surely their loved ones missed them and Parliament and Cromwell had taken steps to be rid of them—but for the most part they were expendable—forsaken and forgotten.

So, the hapless death march continued and the ill-fated prisoners struggled on as their numbers ebbed—after all—who had the time or inclination to be concerned about the fate of a bunch of forsaken men and boys who had suffered the misfortune of being captured and discarded after a battle?

Chapter 14

HANGING ON

ACROSS TO the east, clouds glowed as if aflame while the sun made a promise of warmth it could not keep. Too soon it yielded and the grey of the day took over.

Starvation in addition to the rotten cabbage incident had been just what the flux needed to batter the prisoners once again. Some were dreadfully ill, all were worn out, and many simply hung on to life by a thread. John still felt wretched, but he looked healthy when compared to many others. Robert, on the other hand, seemed to have improved.

"Good grief, John, yer soakin' wet and 'tis freezin' here."

"Ay," John groaned, "and —'tis pretty shitey I feel at that."

Daniel knew he'd better not appear overly concerned, so he came at him with, "And . . . oooo, ya, I be gettin' a good sniff of that all right. 'Tis nary a sweetness award ye'll be winnin'. Nary a lass in the hills would come within fifty miles of ye, even up wind."

John got it and tried to laugh, "'Yer nary a rose yerself, lassie."

Alex joined in with, "This trail beats me up more and more every day. It pounds on me from my heels ta my head."

"Ay, indeed 'tis a bitch," Dan grunted.

Robert saw his chance and pounced, "Ye *bairns* have been plankin' yer arses all comfy on a horse fer so long yer soft as wee ones."

"Oh, blow it out yer arse, old man, and watch that ye dinna trip over yer own feet."

"Now leave him be, John, ye know he's just comin' back from that fierce bout with the flux. More'n likely 'tis left him soft in the head."

The three managed a weak laugh. Robert made a face, but eventually joined in. As the march and the day wore on, a short, cold downpour fell from an over ripe cloud, as if in sympathy with the prisoners' plight. It temporarily helped shower off some of the filth and almost felt good on feverish heads that were turned up to catch welcome drops of rainwater.

Further along, a rainbow broke forth that brought a faint smile from even the toughest Scotsman. Seemingly from out of nowhere, a huge flock of birds landed out of reach on both sides of the human train, ignored it, and busied themselves seeking out lunch.

"What do ye reckon they be up ta?"

"After worms, I'd say—fat juicy worms," Alex ventured. "The mud 'tis sure ta bring 'em out."

"Most likely headed fer a warmer place," Rob suggested. "Wonder if they'd like ta take some lads along for the ride, eh? Be they robins, Dan? 'Tis fond of robins I be, always so perky and cheerful."

"I kenna say, I dinna see any flashes of red, but ye ken be damn sure that, if I could get my hands on one, he'd nary be makin' the trip."

"Ay, they look like meaty little critters."

The birds were oblivious to the plight of the downhearted humans until some faint sound startled them and they took off, fast and free—gone as quickly as they had come.

Lucky bastards. The thought was echoed by all.

Alex reached down and almost pulled John off balance in his haste, "We could keep a closer eye out fer worms. I know they're out there, if those little buggers could find so many of them, there must be a lot more fer the pickin'." He tried to prod about in the earth near his feet, but couldn't slow up or stop long enough to work it. He tried to manifest worms and held on to that thought for later; but none showed themselves, nor did anything else that even vaguely resembled food.

"Pluck up, ye dogged scalawag, dinna ye know that eatin' worms ken ruin that grand build of yers."

"I say, John, I do believe ye be jealous!" They all chuckled at that, but the thought of a wormy lunch wasn't the least bit offensive to any of them.

John had been right about Daniel's hipflask. The four men felt that the precious shared water had made them feel stronger and less hungry on the way to Alnwick—and while they were incarcerated there Daniel had been able to refill it. Once back on the trek they had managed to sneak and share a few sips every now and then, without being caught by Leighton, who now was called, the *monster* by all. They were well aware that he was always on the lookout for even the slightest sign of weakness.

The scanty water was almost gone, but it had saved them from drinking from the filthiest puddles, and most likely had saved John's life by keeping the wound on his leg as clean as possible.

It seemed to the four that the road was never ending, and they had mostly lost count of the endless torturous days. Their sense of humor and ability to banter had played a huge part in spurring them on, but the fun had begun to fade. Most of the time they just trudged stubbornly along, but when they could, one or the other would make some attempt to lighten the load.

"'Tis a wonderful day I be havin', myself. How be ye doin' lassie?" Daniel baited.

John grunted, "I am so danged cold me jewels are shriveled inta acorns."

"Well now, what will ye do when we go ta the pub this week then, and ye havin' ta hang behind 'cause yer nary up fer it?" teased Alex, whose vision of worms had cheered him up.

"Always with the smart remarks. Shut yer face and get off me back," John shot back with a weak inane laugh.

"Ah, ha . . . Well clearly, John, I now know why 'tis yer croaky voice has gotten so much higher!" Robert was reserved, but he was full of surprises and had proven that he could hold his own in every way, including the pun department.

Staying alive got tougher and the days blurred into each other, but they all did their best to keep their spirits up while they dragged themselves over the windswept countryside. Each night the flicker of torches and the smoke from the guards' campfires made the merciless cold seem worse while the smell of roasting venison drifted their way, swirled up their noses, made their mouths water and stomachs ache.

∴

Daniel was constantly on the lookout for comrades he knew and was beginning to recognize some. A few of them returned his nod and that gave him some comfort. He felt numb as he thought of them now and tried to seek some out. *What in God's name ken we be doin' here? Possibly 'tis a dream? Or, nightmare—moreover.*

Daniel shook his head in bewilderment as he filched glimpses to search the mass of naked, icy cold bodies, *Zounds, what a wretched bunch. We've been brow beaten, robbed of our dignity, and ken hardly move, and yet we trudge on.*

He searched conquered eyes and thought he could still see a faint glint of pride, but defeat and abuse had done a good job of crushing spirits. It was hard to believe that many of them were the same men and youths he had lived and laughed with such a short time ago. They had all been so full of life then, cheerful and happy.

What in heaven's name do they think about? What are their greatest fears? He pondered. *Nary of death, ta be sure, every soldier must face up ta that. Same as me, I reckon—saddened that they may nary see home again, or troubled that they might lay dead, forsaken and unclaimed in a ditch—their remains nary ta be placed lovin'ly in familiar soil.*

How long will their families mourn them, or hold onta the futile hope that they might still live? When would that hope die? Unknowns like that would frighten anyone.

Daniel knew in his heart that they treasured thoughts of home and family, as he did—remembered the warmth of fires, parents, wives, sweethearts—children they longed to see grow up—even a favorite horse, or dog. Maybe they dreamed of a spot where they once hunted or fished—even a great tree to sit under and just be.

Fer me, 'tis always my Mora." A painful moan passed Daniel's lips, *Oh God, Mora. 'Tis yer warm body I'd give all fer ta hold next ta mine.*

So, what's ta be done then? What's left, my dearest love? He doubled over and thought, *I see a mirror of myself in all those worn, sad faces— that says it all.*

Both John and Robert felt Daniel slump at the same time and each instinctively placed tension on the tether, "Dan, Danny lad, what goes with ye anyway? Wake up! 'Tis nary a place ta take a nap. Snap back, *bráthair,* be ye with us?"

Vaguely, Daniel heard voices and brushed them aside—he reached out to Mora and tried, but couldn't grasp her hand—he watched as her image slowly slipped away.

Abruptly reality splayed back—he glanced into his friends frightened faces, remembered where he was and roughly shook off the vision. "Uh, fer sure, old man, just missed a step, 'tis all. 'Twas a blunder. Just a wretched blunder."

"Zounds, Dan, ye scared the shite out of us."

Chapter 15

SNAGS & SURPRISES

IT HAD taken the column three days to crawl barely from Alnwick to Morpeth, and the lengthy days since then had simply grown sorrier and worse. Any shred of hope that had managed to endure had dwindled; every captive wondered how soon he would die and didn't care much if he did.

As they lumbered further south the coast disappeared and the glorious shades of heather that had hugged the hills most of the way had given over to much rougher flora that closed in on both sides of the trail.

Robert's right hand was scarred from grabbing heather up whenever he could manage to reach some. Any scraps he could conjure up were precious and valued for their healing potential.

"Me Ma always made tea from flowerin' heather stems and fed it ta us fer most any ailment we came up with," Daniel offered, "Nary a chance of any tea here, though! But we'll keep stuffin' down any of it ye can catch, Rob—that means ye as well, John."

Robert agreed, "My own dear *máthair* used ta make it inta a liniment fer her rheumatism, and she was always cookin' up a hot poultice fer my Da's chilblains."

Alex recalled how it had worked for him to kill a cough or cold.

"Okay, let up, lads—I hear ye—I hear ye—I hear ye." John barked. "Whatever ye give me of the nasty rough stuff goes down my throat ta shut ye up—but I believe those scratchy flowers would be put ta much better use ta make beer, ta hell with the tea—'tis what my Da always did with 'em."

Various types of moss obscured any rock that dared show its head among the juniper and brambles that now replaced the heather. Not to be outdone, some stubborn thistles popped up here and there. Meadows that had been burned by the army emerged, and many of these open spaces had taken on new life—some even boasted short bushes that bore delicious berries. The captives in the front of the column shoved these into hungry mouths, but the bushes were bare and the berries long gone by the time the end of the column arrived.

An unexpected surprise was in store, however. Word had spread of the large column and some sympathetic, supportive citizens were among spectators that seemed to appear from out of nowhere to line the trail and gape at the flood of pitiful captives as they passed through tiny parishes, villages, and hamlets.

"Will ye look now?" Alexander's jaw dropped. In open defiance of the ever-vigilant guards, plucky women and children along the trail tossed table scraps, bits of bread and an occasional potato to the prisoners.

The Scotsmen had lost so much bulk from being starved that their ropes were a bit lax, although not loose enough to wriggle out of. They carefully held them close about their wrists and made it appear that they were still taut, but now they could move more freely and the possibility of food gave them a surge of excitement and energy.

"Cozy up ta the edge," John cried out eagerly, "The nearer we be ta the folks, the better chance of catchin' anythin' that flies our way, just be sure ta keep out of the *monster's* sight."

They moved as one, and a limping John seemed transformed as he urged the four quickly to the side of the mass. Almost managing a jump, he made a catch, took a second to smile a thanks to the gaunt matronly woman who had thrown it, and hugged it to his chest. "Could ye stand a lovely potato fer supper, ye ornery old scavengers?"

Daniel didn't hear, he was too busy trying to catch something on his own. A skinny lass tossed him an apple, an unbelievable treat. He held it up and tried to thank his benefactor, but just as he made eye contact, a scrawny kid dashed out of the crowd, pushed him from behind and snatched the apple out of his grasp. It happened so fast and the lad had moved so quickly, Dan hardly knew he ever had it.

No use trying to get the fruit back, the young whippersnapper had faded back to where he came from and had quickly blended in. Daniel could not see him, but he was sure he heard his apple crunch.

He didn't give up the quest, and when a small lad with a club foot caught his eye and gave a slight nod, he caught the dried piece of meat that flew his way. The youngster smiled; Dan smiled back and felt his mouth water.

Once the young lassies spotted Alexander, they made sure he caught the best of what they had. He held his handsome head up and tried to smile while he waved back at them as best as he could while at the same time he struggled to cover his nakedness and catch some food. He didn't manage to do any of it very well—how dearly he wished that he had on his sharp uniform instead of the mud and dirt he was wearing. He finally gave up and just went for anything that flew his way.

"Do ye believe it? Morsels of bread, meat, and potatoes, and Robert even caught an apple, how about that?"

"Good fer ye, Rob Jonkings, at least ye managed ta hold on ta yers," Daniel gloomily griped as the four of them shared their booty and gulped it down quickly.

"John, 'tis nary all, I caught two coins from the same lad that flew the meat," Daniel whispered as he showed him, "Could ye hide them fer me?"

"I ken, since yer trustin' them ta me—I got just the place." The precious coins were handed over straight away with no questions asked.

Signs of life appeared more often as the column tramped deeper into England. This prompted the guards to refresh the captives' ropes and tethers so they could keep a closer reign on them while they dispersed any sympathetic bystanders.

As expected, this area's inhabitants' politics leaned much more heavily toward the English cause, and the few that had no use for Cromwell had very little that they could share. Moreover, they were threatened and knocked about by the guards when they tried, but those who persisted found spaces to wiggle through and managed to toss bits of victuals to the grateful prisoners. Their efforts lifted hearts and spirits as much as the scanty food did. Grateful words of thanks resonated from the ranks in response.

Robert opined, "It touches my heart ta see that there are still some folks out there ta cheer us on—'tis good ta know that nary everyone in this area 'tis a Cromwell fan! It makes me grateful that we ken still make a difference and we ken make sure that the English have ta spend resources on us."

John came back with, "Dinna kid yerself, lad—they be spendin' nary a shilling on food fer us, 'tis fer sure—but they be killin' as many Scots here as anywhere."

Robert wasn't about to be shut up, "I am sick ta my soul of this shite, same as ye, but, I believe that every step I take 'tis another spit in their faces. Yer the one ta always say that the best thing we ken do 'tis stay alive in spite of the bastards. Well, I aim ta do just that." He managed to stamp a weary foot then added, "Even if it kills me."

"That so, lad? Ye dinna need ta get pious on us—ye know we be with ye."

Even John couldn't help but smother a laugh as Robert went on, cussing and muttering to himself, "So there—know it all—pain in the arse . . . ornery bully . . . ."

Alex threw in, "Well, 'tis nary a need ta chide him like that—ye know better."

Constantly battered by the wind, damp, and cold, the bare weary bodies continued to waste away as the barren roadside unrelentingly became graves for too many of the starved, ailing, and demoralized men.

Some of the most depressed and dispirited gave up all hope and chose not to take another step. Andrew Ross, John's friend, was one of these; he had somehow managed to free himself, but rather than try to make a run for it, he looked his captors straight in the eye and limped toward them. John caught sight of him as he yelled and made wild gestures to the guards.

"Andy, Andrew Ross," he shouted frantically to his friend and begged him to return to the line. "What the hell be ye doin'? Get back over here."

"Ah, 'tis Johnny MacKinney? It does me heart good ta see ye, old friend. I wondered if ye'd made it this far."

"I be here, Andrew. Get yer arse over here and join us."

"Oh, nay . . . nay-siree, I kenna do it. Dinna ye worry yer head none about me, Johnny. I be goin' ta a better place—I be pissin' blood fer Christ's sake. Just done fer—kenna run if me life depended on it—heh, heh—'tis a good one, eh?" He shook his weak head, ground his feet into the dirt, and stood firmer, "Ay, I be cashin' in on me own terms—this croakin' by bits and pieces dinna work fer me. 'Tis as far as I go."

John pleaded, "Andy, nay—dinna do this. Dinna give 'em the satisfaction."

There was no dissuading him, "I be claimin' me own satisfaction, Johnny.

The *monster* rode up at that moment, flashed Wilbur a dirty look, and cockily waved his sword in the air to order the kill.

Andrew received a painful fatal shot to the stomach and went down in obvious agony. Death did not come easy, but he never cried out or uttered a word.

"Oh, nay—fer God's sake, Andrew," John moaned. He was so shattered that his shoulders shook as he lowered his head and tried to hold in sobs. When he could speak again, he told Daniel that Andrew had been with him when he and another friend had escaped from the church after being imprisoned by the English at Preston.

They scuffled on in silence with heavy hearts and heads down.

Chapter 16

A FATEFUL SLIP

THE CAPTIVES watched sullenly as a hazy sun tried to rise on another unusually cold fall day. The heavy freezing rain from the night before had made the cold even more unbearable while the thinly iced-over mud it had created made walking nearly impossible. The prisoners' pace was slowed to less than that of sluggish snails.

Here and there a dog howled or a bird had the nerve to welcome the day with a cheery song. Hawks soared intently as they searched for a careless mouse or squirrel.

As the shrinking chain of prisoners attempted to inch on—as had become the norm—the dead and dying were left behind to stiffen in the early fall frost that clung so beautifully to the hills and foliage. That same frost also stuck and clung viciously to the men's hair and beards and assaulted already aching muscles.

A smidgen of unwelcome news that had managed to filter down through the grapevine added to the captives' anguish. Word was that William Key had overheard it from a couple of braggart guards and passed it along. John downheartedly broke it to his friends, "Lads, the grapevine says Cromwell took possession of Edinburgh. 'Tis still a lot of resistance there, but it seems he basically seized it, four days after Dunbar—we were barely at Alnwick then."

"Ye foresaw it, John, our General Leslie left Edinburgh undefended and moved on ta Stirlin'."

"God help 'em," a frantic voice was heard from the row behind;

"My people are there. I need ta be home, nary tied up like a pig here."

"Stand firm now," Robert nearly tripped as he turned his head and tried to comfort the man, "We all know 'tis a nightmare in every way, but we ken only do what we ken. 'Tis nary a way we ken control fate."

"Fate, me arse, I need ta be with me family."

Alexander sadly mumbled, "Forget it, friend. Pray fer them, 'tis about all we ken do fer now."

Captain Hugh Leighton, the monster, was in an especially foul mood. His brow was furrowed, his eyes flashed, and his jaw was tight. He had not been at all pleased when the onlookers had thrown the paltry scraps to the Scots. He was even more upset with the slower progress they were making. He rode like a mad man up and down the east side of the bogged-down prisoners, roughly pressing his loyal horse—his double-edged sword flaying about. He leaned into his stirrup and beheaded the prisoner nearest him with one swipe, and then slashed at three more without even slowing down.

His valiant steed struggled to keep the wild pace Leighton had demanded of him, but suddenly a hoof caught in a rabbit hole and he lost his stride. The action was so abrupt and strong that the heavy *monster* was caught off guard and thrown into the air. He crashed down hard and landed forcefully on his head in the mud. The horse flipped and fell on top of him, started to struggle, but couldn't get up. Leighton's bulky body twitched several times, then lay still.

Lieutenant Wilbur Barlow and other guards rushed to the *monster's* aid. It took four of them to turn and move the frightened horse. When they finally managed to get the great beast up they recoiled at the spectacle of Leighton, stretched out face down in the mud, his throat cut to the bone by his beloved sword.

Wilbur inspected the body and reveled secretly, then he very coldly informed his subordinates, "He either smothered in the mud, bled out or both. Too much mud was packed into his face to tell what got him first, but either way, he is quite dead.

"Move the corpse onto that knoll over there and clean it up as best and fast as you can. Our replacements from Newcastle should arrive tomorrow. Sargent Evans, form an escort and get it ready to accompany Major Leighton's body when we leave."

With that ordered, Wilbur smirked, set his jaw, matter-of-factly took command, and shouted out, "This doesn't change anything for you Scots, so just stay put."

The prisoners did not move; no Scot made a sound. Not one yelled, cheered, cursed, or danced at Leighton's demise, although they had all wished it from the first cruel act he had directed at them. This was a good choice, although they did not make it consciously. The guards were nervous and ready to shoot full-out into the column.

As full realization hit, John made eye contact with Daniel and tugged at his arm. "A fit end fer him, Danny Boy. I only wish it had been yer sword, or my dirk that got him.

"I ken tell ye, now that he's done fer—that 'twas Leighton—ay, the *monster* was the one I saw strike down William, and I thought then that he had killed ye as well."

As he looked into cold blue eyes that had opened wide in disbelief and rage he begged, "Dinna hold it agin me, Dan, I feared only too well that it would rile ye ta distraction if I told ye before. I had nary a doubt but that ye would have gone fer him regardless of anythin' else, and that would have been the end of ye."

"Thanks fer finally comin' clean," Daniel spat on the ground and choked out, "'twas wrong, John, just wrong—ye know damn well—he should have been mine."

John waited quietly while Dan wrapped his head around the painful revelation, all the while hoping that his friend could find it in his heart to forgive him.

After a long pause, Daniel conceded, "Ay, the bastard's damn well where he should be alright. And—well—'tis sure that ye reckoned what I would have done—and 'tis naught a doubt—I surely would have killed him with my bare hands—even if I had ended up dead along with him—and mayhap that would have been a better thing mullin' over where we be now. But at least I would have had the sweet taste of tellin' him ta his face ta rot in hell—although even hell—'tis too good a place fer that son of a bitch."

"Hang in there, Dan—we may get out of this yet." Daniel did not reply, but shook his grief-stricken head disgustedly, unconvinced.

The sound of troops appearing from the south startled the captives, but a big roar arose from the guards as they welcomed their replacements. Wilbur had his hands full trying to keep order and set up the transfer. His uncle had told him a while ago that troops would be relieving them as they neared Newcastle, but they had shown up sooner than expected. Sooner proved better; after the formal greetings and acknowledgments were accomplished, the exchange with the Newcastle guards was arranged in an efficient, speedy manner.

Lieutenant Wilbur Barlow, with a new-found confidence, had unfeelingly ordered his uncle's remains wrapped in a blanket and thrown on the back of his loyal horse. The gallant animal seemed confused, but fully recovered from the spill. The hurriedly formed escort fell in behind the line of trail weary initial guards and headed toward Newcastle.

Daniel's eyes followed the muddy corpse. It looked like a bag of garbage—only partially covered by the blanket, it flopped around and bobbled oddly in time with the horse's hooves as the beautiful stallion moseyed along with the group. He didn't say another word, but looked back at John, gently punched his arm, and gave his friend a nod along with a resigned half smile.

The replacement guards were fresh and all business; they established their authority and ordered the dazed Scots to move out; the column slowly and silently trudged on through the mud.

Nothing had changed, but everything had changed. A bit of the dark burden seemed to have lifted and the dispirited mood of the defeated Scotsmen seemed lighter.

Not far down the trail, a handful of bystanders tossed scant morsels of bread their way. Some prisoners, Daniel among them, made catches.

"Anythin' new with ye, John?" as they wolfed down the moldy crusts.

"Still freezin' me arse off, Dan." They smiled, shrugged, and struggled on.

"Come on, chaps—as the jolly English say—hit the road. 'Tis nary like we have somethin' better ta do." Robert's turn to be cheerleader.

Alex got in the last word with, "Yer a wee pain in the arse, Rob."

They carried on, painfully and quietly until dusk as they had been doing every day. No one missed the wild sword furies; however, men who could not go on for one reason or another were still killed by the replacement guards and left behind.

Mist nestled among the crevices on the soft rolling hills before it lifted into the sky; the effect was striking, but the splendor of it was wasted on bitter, sick men whose distraught mentalities focused solely on survival; they had two choices—move or die.

Twilight welcomed the night as the shrinking column stumbled through gates that stood upon what looked like part of an old Roman wall. This crumbling piece of history soon led to an old stone church, Saint Nicholas of Newcastle.

The guards stuffed the remaining captives into the church. It had no heat, but at least they were under cover. Men who could took refuge on sparse pews; most collapsed on the bare stone floor. Again, no food, water, or hygiene was provided. By sunrise, more than five hundred tormented souls lay dead or too ill to move. Not one of them was ever heard from again. Still, the wretched survivors got moving.

Alex queried, "John—Newcastle, 'tis the king's country—the biggest base the English military force has. What do ye think's goin' on? Will they stash us here?"

"I dinna know, but if they do, we'll be so well guarded there will nary be a chance of escape. 'Tis Cromwell's own man, Hasselrigge's, quarter."

"I fear that soon there will nary be a Scotsman left fer Cromwell ta bother with."

"Dinna give him that pleasure."

Chapter 17

DURHAM CATHEDRAL

THE WEATHER had brightened slightly and patches of blue had broken through the clouds here and there. The Newcastle guards had quickly realized the futility of pressing their haggard charges, so they just kept them in line and let them progress at their own pace. It became obvious why, when around noon an exhausted Daniel nudged John lightly and mumbled in a barely audible tone, "What think ye 'tis on that hill ahead? Fer sure 'tis Durham Cathedral, and I know 'tis a castle up there somewhere as well. I reckon the Wear River formed that gorge boundin' it."

Wandering rays of sun bounced off the Cathedral towers and were reflected back from the river as the enormous structure emerged before them. In spite of the faint warmth, Daniel shivered and felt as though he had been swallowed up by a foreboding black cloud. He decided to shrug it off and made a feeble joke, "Dinna that water just look temptin'? Mayhap we ken drink up and perhaps even catch a couple of fish ta fry."

John shot him a dirty look, "Nary a bit funny and a lofty dream, me shabby lad—it sounds tasty—but as ye well know, 'tis a beef man I be." He paused, glanced up, and muttered, "Ay, 'tis the Cathedral ta be sure. 'Tis said the place was founded by monks. I seem ta recall somethin' about a milkmaid searchin' fer her lost dun-cow. Hmmmm, I reckon some milk might be tolerable about now."

Robert was not in a gabby mood, "Cut the puns. Have ye gone

daft? 'Tis nary a josh that a good feed of about anything would be really tasty after this starvation hell. Ye heard that, Alex, *h e l l*. Ah, Zounds—ferget that—I take it back—my head—'tis weird—I dinna know anythin'—'Tis crazy with hunger I be and the mere thought of food gets me perturbed."

Alexander, was a bit edgy himself, "Yer always perturbed about somethin', ye droll lad. Anyway, put that out of yer mind and get grateful. 'Tis hungry we should be—we've moseyed about one hundred and twenty miles from Dunbar, half dead and with barely a bite ta eat.

"I know that we started out with over five thousand souls on this death march; now nary even half of us are still breathin'— and barely doin' that—if ye ken call us alive, 'tis stretchin' it. Those miles have taken a heavy toll. What day do ye reckon 'tis, Robert?"

Robert wasn't about to be cajoled. He turned his head aside and curtly came back with, "I kenna give a rat's arse what day 'tis, Alex. I dinna see what difference it makes anyway; 'tis all pretty fuzzy ta me, and dinna tell me that *fuzzy*, 'tis a cuss word."

"Be ye well, Rob?"

"Indeed? Now, just what do ye reckon I be?"

"Cheer up, Robert—if it gets any worse ye'll only be dead." Dan grumbled.

"Hey there, Dan," John rebuked him, "What a wee bundle of joy ye are! 'Tis great support—Zounds—like hell 'tis. And, by the bye, I know it feels like a hundred years or more, but if my count 'tis good, 'tis only been fifteen days since we left Dunbar—and that makes today September nineteenth."

"How ken so many strong men be dead in such a short time? Added ta the slaughter, I mean."

"Well, if ye plucked a half-starved, half-dead bird of his feathers and made him fly north all bare arsed in this weather, I doubt that he'd end up very bright eyed and feisty any more than we have."

• • •

The Durham Cathedral stood ostentatiously on its scenic knoll in northeastern England—its spires arrogantly joining the sky. The magnificent structure had been built in 997 by monks as John had heard.

During its history it had been ravaged by religious conflicts beginning with the Anglicans, under King Henry VIII; then the Puritans and Presbyterians from both sides of the border. The territory was regularly raided by squabbling clans, even before the civil war.

Once the Bishop had been deposed, the Cathedral was closed by Cromwell, and so it remained until he ordered Hasselrigge to convert it into a holding prison for his *Scottish Rebel Prisoners*.

The fabulous piece of real estate had, as Daniel had observed, been built on a loop in the meandering Wear River. The west end of the towers hung over the gorge, and very steep embankments dropped down to the river. They were scattered with rich haughs that were blanketed with grass and overgrown with hazel and alder.

• • •

The prisoners trekked on as the trail widened briefly, then narrowed again as they stepped onto a bridge that crossed the Wear River.

"That water's movin' right along. All that rain seems ta have brought it high."

Dan seemed mesmerized by the rushing water and slurred, "I swear, John, maybe Andy Ross had the right idea. How about we just jump in and be done with it—just float away, and who the hell but the four of us would care anyway?"

John heard, but barely. He couldn't believe his ears. His temper flared and his eyes went wild—he was hoppin' mad, "Oh, the dear English would care, Dan," he growled. "And happy they'd be as well—make their day we would—and in front of all their admirers.

"Now ye hear me good, Daniel MacDhughill, there will be nary more talk of Andy escapades, be ye listenin'? After all we've been through how ken ye even think of such a thing? Mark me words, ye'd best nary do it again or—I'll—I'll kill ye meself."

Daniel was certainly sorry that he had opened his mouth.

Alex had heard the exchange and jumped at the chance to rub it in, "Ye sure got the old bat's dander up on that one. Nary a good subject, that!"

"Jings, Dan," Robert added, "Ye cut ta the bone there—and I dinna mean the funny bone!"

Dan tried to shrug it off, "Come on—'twas nary earnest—only a josh—ye both know that I ken swim like a fish. Besides, it would be damn cold anyway."

Less than a minute later, Alex was hit in the face with a nasty rotten tomato—welcome to the village of Durham. Sullen onlookers lined the street on both sides just waiting to harass. They pelted the pathetic looking Scots with filth, kicked at them, and shouted obscenities; it was worse than Berwick upon Tweed.

The residents' ugly greetings still rang in their ears as they left them behind and started the tedious climb up the hill. They had crossed the river alright, but the only fish they got were the rotten guts that had been thrown at them.

When they finally made it to the top they found themselves facing the colossal Cathedral and were brought to a halt in front of its massive double door. The heavily carved entry looked out onto the beautiful Palace Green. It boasted an ugly bronze sanctuary doorknob that dated back to its monastery days. Those seeking safe haven had only to knock and they would be welcomed in. The prisoners were forced in through this entrance; what type of sanctuary would be offered remained to be seen.

"May God help us—did ye see that craggy carved skull on the wall over there? I kenna say 'tis a very welcomin' sight."

Chapter 18

COLD WELCOME

SIR ARTHUR Hasselrigge was the member of the English Parliament for Leicester and was Cromwell's Commander-in-Chief at Newcastle.

He had followed Cromwell's orders and hastily converted the desolate Durham Cathedral into a makeshift prison—but, his order to ensure that the prisoners had adequate food, water, and other basics had been completely ignored by his subordinates.

The supplies Hasselrigge had instructed them to have ready and waiting for the *Scottish Rebel Prisoners*, had been absconded with before the captives were ever near the Cathedral. The goods had been sold for profit and misdirected to ministers and guards, or bartered cheaply to local merchants in the surrounding burgs.

Déjà vu! Nothing welcomed them. Not a trace of water, food, bedding, clothing; not even a stick of wood or basket of coal to warm the huge hollow place.

• • •

The Scots were naked as jaybirds. Daniel's treasured leggings had long since been ripped and shredded to bits although his precious water skin that held his brother's brooch still hung precariously beneath the remains of the ragged waist band.

A couple of grass-like pieces of John's knitted whatevers looked completely bizarre as they hung by a thread just below his empty gut.

Robert was no better off; his scarf had disappeared into the brambles way back, and of course, Alex had been traveling bare and free from the start. Foot gear had practically disintegrated, and feet were raw and throbbing.

The prisoners were numb from the cold—gaunt and starved, their filthy bodies were as torn and ravaged as Daniel's leggings. Goose bumps stood out and continued to cover them like a second skin, their teeth chattered loudly, and they shook constantly as uncontrollable spasms racked them.

These stumbling sad remnants of General David Leslie's *Army of the Covenant* were herded, pushed, and shoved into the much-revered house of God that would prove to be a death trap for many. Shudders ran through them as a dank smell irritated their nostrils. Mildew soon confirmed that the building had been left closed up and empty for some time.

"'Tis a tad bare, dinna ye think? It seems the welcome committee may have been delayed." Robert coughed out as he peered into the massive structure. "How long do ye reckon they plan ta hold us in this stink hole? Saint Nicholas church was nary a treat. Mahap the food's better here. At least they've freed us from the damn ropes."

"The grub kenna be any worse, since we dinna get any. Ahhhh—I so would be grateful fer it ta be fittin' fer a change, I reckon I still had hopes—ye'd think I'd know better by now. Fer sure, 'tis a pipe dream—and fer what? Well, every now and then dreams do come true, dinna they? —and, any food would be better than nary a bit of food, eh, Rob?"

Discouraged by Daniel's rambling, Alexander felt he'd better offer up some kind of encouragement, so he uttered, half-heartedly, "Most likely they will want ta get us settled in before they bring it on, along with the water, beddin', and coal fer heat."

John didn't think so, "In a pig's arse," he bitterly spit out, "Nary a way these Newcastle guards be any different than the first bunch we had—they kenna change their stripes that much. But—waitin' fer us they seem ta be. The place feels more like a fortress than a church, 'tis all battered down and tucked in.

"We be trapped and crammed in here like rats in a cage—nary a bit better than Alnwick. I dinna reckon they intend ta treat us as we should expect and ought to be held—as proper prisoners-of-war. They dinna honor that creed so fer, why on earth do ye reckon the tide would turn now?"

"It dinna look quite as bad as Alnwick, John. At least 'tis a lot more spacious and 'tis some light reachin' in. Let us give them a chance and see what happens. In the meantime, keep yer eyes open—we be freezin'—dog-tired and raw—we gravely need a corner ta sprawl in. But—feast yer eyes on this place, will ye?"

The Cathedral was breathtakingly beautiful in spite of being neglected, and even these wretched men were in awe of it.

As his eyes slowly adjusted to the dim light, Dan ventured, "'Tis the nave fer sure. Zounds, 'tis huge—it must be over seventy feet high. Seems 'tis about forty feet wide here and it must be at least two hundred feet long."

Alexander made a feeble attempt to whistle through his dried-up lips, "Those carved pillars are bigger around and taller than most men—If nary else, 'tis God's house—surely He will find a way ta help us."

Daniel couldn't help but think, *Ay, like He helped our wretched comrades in Alnwick Castle and Saint Nicholas Church.* However, the last thing he would ever want would be to crush Alex's spirit or question his faith, so he ignored the comment and said, "My Da helped build lots of churches and even worked on a Cathedral. I dinna reckon he ever saw one like this though. The stone ceiling has rib vaulting with pointed transverse arches. *Magnificent* understates it.

"I nary had the love of workin' with stones as Da did, but I do know how Cathedrals are laid out. 'Tis lucky we are ta be among the first in. How's about we move around a bit ta fight these goose bumps?"

The only response he got to that invitation was guffaws, but he went on anyway, "Let us keep our eyes open, our wits about us, and check the place out." He managed to flash a little wink to John, who reluctantly forced himself to budge. They were being pushed from behind anyway, so they put a bit more energy into it. Their feet ached, and they were a sad looking mess, but the disheveled friends shuffled deeper into the widely revered Durham Cathedral.

Dan looked a bit smug and took on the role of tour guide, "Ay, 'tis the nave alright. Just look at that those wood carvin's over the arches and doors. Zounds, the walls are covered with 'em—will ye look at that."

They all gawked in wonder at the spires of superbly detailed delicate carvings that artistically adorned the walls and stretched up toward the amazing arched ceiling that went on for what seemed like miles on end.

The nave offered no place to sit or rest comfortably. If there ever had been pews there were none now, so they continued down the lengthy aisle and tried to take in everything on both sides. They passed the Bishop's throne and a slab of rough stone that had been built into the floor—this marker was to give women notice that they were not allowed to go any further into the Cathedral. More splendid stunningly beautiful wood carvings decorated the choir loft and organ.

They were taken aback when they spotted a vault with its doors slightly ajar. Robert was puzzled and asked, "Did any of ye know that they buried people inside a church?"

"Mostly only saints or very rich lords," Alexander answered. They all jammed together and struggled to peer into the abyss. Tired eyes followed a faint ray of light that filtered down from a shaft and highlighted at least four coffins. Resting on top of each heavily engraved casket was a masterfully sculpted lifelike image. As far as Alex knew, he was the only one of the group who could read so he enlightened them. "It seems that 'tis the vault of some of the Neville family. Hmm—a bit of the history comes ta mind—nary friends of the Scots fer sure—they defeated King David and his Highlanders at the Battle of Neville's Cross. One of them was a bishop, Ralph, I think—or Robert. I kenna be sure because, as I recall, there were a lot of them. The Neville's were the Lords of Raby."

He pointed eagerly, "Will ye look at that—Ralph, Alice; John and Matilda—the names are right there, ken ye see them?"

Daniel peered over his shoulder, straining to see and hear more. John hung back and waited while Robert leaned on the heavy vault door.

Alex, enthralled by the find, went on, "Imagine that—old tombs always fascinate me—these bones have been restin' here fer the past three hundred years, and we know who they were and the effigies give us a good idea of their appearance. These must have been about the first lay burials allowed in the Cathedral. The Raby legacy—'tis carried on by their descendant ta this day."

"A lot of good that will do us," a completely overwhelmed Robert groaned as he, Daniel, and John pushed back into the oncoming wall of men, "Ken we keep movin'? I need a place ta rest my own bones."

"Ay, I'm lookin' forward ta that myself." Alexander attempted a pretentious bow before he turned his attention back to the present and joined them, "Such an honor ta make yer acquaintance, Sir Ralph—Alice—John—Matilda. Oh, please, dinna get up—we'll see ourselves out."

"Zookers, Alexander," Robert shook his head and mumbled, "Ye've finally gone dippy fer sure—ye danged scatter-brain."

Chapter 19

THE CLOCK

MOMENTS LATER they saw it, in the south transept, a tall masterfully and elaborately decorated clock stood regally beneath the stained glass Te Deum window. It was by far the most stunning thing any of them had ever seen. There was no way that anything around it could compare.

Not even Alexander was aware that this was the famous Prior Castell's clock. It had been furnished by Thomas Castell, a monk who had been Prior from 1494 to 1512, when the Cathedral had been a monastery.

It was immense, rested on two legs, and loomed up toward the magnificent window. The face of the clock had only one hand and was divided into forty-eight rather than sixty segments. These segments represented quarter-hour intervals rather than minutes.

Above the face, three astronomical dials showed the change of the moon, the month of the year, and the day of the month. The four comrades glanced up and were caught short. They swallowed hard and eyeballed each other in disbelief as they ogled the single upright thistle that was the crowning glory of the clock. It was perched on the very top; its stem firmly planted as it stood tall and straight in its handsome round frame. The embossed thistle was exquisitely detailed and a brilliant royal purple as it should be. It appeared as fresh and untouched as the day it had been set in its place of honor.

Seemingly oblivious to the shuffling hoard behind him Alexander scratched his head, stopped short, fell to his knees, and gazed up in awe. "What a stunnin', outstandin' work of art. Ye see it, dinna ye, dear friends?"

Daniel quickly grabbed his arm and dragged him off to the side where he sputtered out, "Zounds, what in heaven's name? What could that lonely thistle be doin' in the midst of this English stronghold—restin' comely atop that clock?"

"Clearly, 'tis a message fer us from God," Alex exclaimed. "Our thistle—ours! 'Tis a symbol of Scotland's best—our fortitude, honor, and good. Ay, our thistle—'tis us! 'Tis resilient, nary matter how many times 'tis crushed it bounces back, stronger and better than ever."

As John and Robert moved to the side as well, Robert piped up, "'Tis good that somethin's stronger and better than ever—I feel like I'd been beaten with a cat-o-nine tails fer weeks on end. 'Tis truly whipped I be." He looked about for a comment on his play on words.

Actually, Dan was the only one who noticed—Alex was entirely enthralled by the clock, and John was uncharacteristically quiet. "A bit of a jibe there, eh, Rob?" Dan quipped and gave him a weak thump on the shoulder—then, after he observed the massive timepiece for a moment, he said softly to Alex, "Ye may be right, *bráthair*. It strikes me heart ta the core ta see that handsome Scottish thistle, and in here mind ye."

"Ay, Dan, 'tis our thistle. Speakin' ta us 'tis, biddin' us ta keep our heads, stay strong, and cling ta the faith. Hold up—let's claim our spot right here before 'tis taken."

Daniel rubbed his head and said, "I thought perhaps a wee place in the chapel might be best, but now, I reckon this would be a great site—it sets off from the nave and out of the mainstream. What do ye say, John? Rob?" The two were encouraged by Alex's and Dan's enthusiasm, but in truth all their bodies yearned for was to just flop down and get some sleep—still somehow, they conjured up a weak grin and nodded their approval.

Alexander seemed to be frozen on his knees. Robert laboriously reached down and offered his hand, "Buck up, Alex—move it—before ye end up stuck ta the stones."

He dragged Alex up as best he could and admitted, "I must say that it touched me—what ye said about our thistle. Treasure those thoughts, Alex—hold tight ta them fer all of us starvin' wretches."

Once on his feet, Alex pulled himself erect. His face was drawn and pale, but he grasped his friend's hand firmly in his, "I thank ye, Robert Jonkings, more than ye know, and rest easy, ye ken be sure that I will persevere."

Half dead as they were, they rummaged about just enough to find the ideal position that would give them a great view of the clock and also enable them to peer out into the nave on one side and into the cloisters on the other, which would allow them to catch any faint slivers of light that might sneak in through the barricaded windows.

John let out an involuntary gasp of pain as he eased himself down onto the stone floor. The others looked at him—greatly concerned—that was not like him, they knew he must be in trouble if his leg hurt that badly. Daniel felt his friend's head and exclaimed, "John, yer burnin' hot. Give us a look at that leg." He took a step back at the sight of it and stifled a gag, "Holy shite, why dinna ye speak up?"

There were no complaints; he simply grimaced, clenched his teeth and stayed put while they took a good look at the leg. It was obvious that the swelling was worse and the red area around the wound had widened; it felt hot to the touch and was very inflamed. They all felt shaken and powerless. Daniel reached for his water skin—a little water might cool it and help some—he poured the few remaining drops into the gash.

John glowered and moved about a bit, then shifted his body as he tried to settle into as comfortable a position as possible. "Ay—aaay," he groaned. "I reckoned it could be a lot fitter. Hey, I see those long faces. Now quit yer worryin' about me." With that he closed his eyes and fell into a sound sleep, almost before he got out the last word.

Relieved, Daniel remarked, "'Tis the best possible medicine right now. Hopefully, his fever will go down by mornin'." That said they all collapsed onto the cold stones beside him and sunk into a similar deathlike sleep that lasted until the middle of the next morning. They made no effort to get up but merely tried to stretch the hurt and stiffness out of their bodies—grateful that no guards were prodding them and there was no reason to haul their weary bodies up to get back on the trail.

John kept snoring away until he finally roused just before noon.

He glanced about, then straight away nodded at his friends that the leg felt better.

A bit too quick with that response, Daniel thought. He laid his hand on the burly forehead and found it cooler, but the leg was still a sorry sight and no one had to convince the big man to stay put—his friends were more than inclined to do the same.

Chapter 20

THE NEW DIGS

HUDDLED LIKE four starved dogs in their bare newly claimed digs, the four fell in and out of sleep for the second night. When they finally awoke well into the next day, they tried to shake off their twinges and stomachaches and convince themselves that they hated breakfast.

Daniel ventured, "How's about we explore our new digs? We should know our surroundin's on the chance that an opportunity ta escape opens up." They had a good laugh about that, but no one could discard the thought, so John stayed behind to rest his leg and guard their spot while the other three shuffled listlessly off.

The trio first confirmed that the cloisters were barricaded from the outside. Even in the dim light the lawn could be seen through the cracks, and it was green in spite of the fall frosts. They found that the former Prior's lodging had also been strongly barricaded along with any other doors or windows.

Distressed Scotsmen were sprawled throughout the Cathedral— they sat propped up against walls and in corners or simply lay on the floor. "Zounds, I dinna reckon on so many young lads. They be all over the place."

As the friends weaved between and around them they couldn't help but notice many bare and bloody feet—some showed green, or worse still, the black signs of gangrene, while others were swollen to three or four times their normal size. They stepped carefully to avoid vomit, feces, and urine that had already accumulated around obviously infirm captives. Healthier comrades attempted to clean, and they did manage to scrape some of the waste off into corners, but they didn't have much to work with.

The beautiful chapel was inviting—much smaller and cozier than the other areas. Daniel had first thought that it would be a more comfortable and warmer location for them, but it was badly overcrowded, smelled worse than the rest of the place—if that was possible—and it brought back too many memories of the crammed conditions in the dungeon at Alnwick. That confirmed that the site Alex had chosen was better for them.

The exploration continued quietly until Alexander cried out, "Look at that block of fancy green marble in the floor, I've heard of it—'tis said ta hold healin' powers from Saint Cuthbert! Gilded with gold they say, but I dinna see any sign of that now, only some kind of letters. Ah ha, I ken just make them out, 'tis Saint Cuthbert's name. That must mean that his body was laid ta rest here.

"I knew that Cromwell had destroyed the shrine—'tis pretty amazin' that the stone survived. Mayhap 'tis another message fer us—mayhap a healin' fer John's leg."

Even that short a jaunt had exhausted them, so once they calmed Alex down they headed back to their spot by the clock. Dan brought John up to date on the Cathedral's general layout, and Alex told him excitedly about the block of green marble that supposedly held healing powers from Saint Cuthbert. "We must get ye over there, it ken help—anyway—it kenna hurt."

John gave no reply, just grunted, not at all impressed until he saw Alex's face drop in disappointment, then he made it a big point to thank Alex for thinking of him and agreed that he might wander by later. "From what ye've told me, that Cuthbert fella has his work cut out fer him. This whole place seems infested."

"Yer so right, John, I've already started prayin' fer help."

"Pray fer supplies, Alexander, everyone needs those. We willna last long in here without food or water."

Nearly every soul in the Cathedral prayed, and waited and listened for some sound or smell that would announce food's arrival. Not a peep. They heard only the heavy, labored breathing of dying men along with quiet sobbing, and groans that escaped from bodies in agony.

The afternoon dragged until, out of the blue, the guards escorted a doctor in through a door near the south transept where the four friends were camped and John's infected leg was one of the first things he cleaned and tended. His forehead wrinkled into a deep frown as he observed the serious state of the wound.

John thanked him and, at Daniel's insistence, gave him one of the two prized coins. The doctor smiled his appreciation, placed a small jar of salve in John's hand and instructed him, "Rub it on twice a day for as long as it lasts, my boy. Be sure you do it regularly, that leg needs all the help it can get if you want to keep it."

Before he moved on, he tugged at Daniel's arm and spoke softly, "A friend of mine is a guard—Ellery is his name. He is sympathetic to your plight and might be able to get some supplies to you, for a fee. Tell him I sent you—and—make sure your comrade applies the salve properly. I plan to come by again next week."

Once the doctor moved out into the main part of the Cathedral the prisoners yelled and clawed at him, begging for help. When he saw the extent of disease, filth, and despair, and most especially more signs of typhoid fever and the bloody flux; he left as speedily as he could, obviously in fear of his life.

They never saw the doctor again, but thanks to his visit and the salve he had left with John, perhaps combined with healing vibes from Saint Cuthbert—according to Alex—the leg started to heal nicely in spite of the disgusting, unsanitary conditions.

• • •

A short time after the doctor's hasty visit, armed guards entered the Cathedral and methodically pushed and shoved to clear spaces and make room for some wooden buckets full of cloudy water. They placed them just inside the Cathedral doors, no doubt in answer to the physician's orders. A communal sigh was the combined reaction.

When the word *water* was heard, adrenalin clicked in and prisoners shoved each other about in a mad rush to get to it first. Everyone was surprised when the doors opened again and more buckets were brought inside.

Dan, Alex, and Rob, along with some other kind souls, carried some of the buckets closer to less fortunate captives, including John who couldn't get around yet.

The guards had delivered no fuel, food, or other supplies, but they assured the prisoners that things were *in the works*. And sure enough, not too much later, a few buckets of something called *food* were brought in. Daniel and Robert tried to put a name to the stuff, but all they could figure was that it was a strange sort of watery mush. They took a guess and thought it might contain potato roots and maybe some oats, but there was not a big enough chunk of anything in the mess that could be recognized.

The starved men went after anything they could reach, shoved what they could into their mouths, and spilled most of the potato water on the stone floor. Oblivious to the stench of excrement and death, many of the men lapped up any sip they could get to, like animals. Most did not get a taste of any of the so-called food. Those who managed to slurp a sample lapped their lips and were heard to say that they had never tasted anything so good, and then they cried out for more. No matter, at least it was something, although it was not nearly enough to sustain the ailing men or to quash the firm grip of disease that beset indefensible bodies.

Two days later more armed guards burst in, very official looking, complete with loaded muskets and carbines. The mayor of Durham had requested twelve Scottish weavers, and to the amazement of the guards themselves, they found them—half of them feisty men from Paisley. They were all hastily rounded up and whisked away.

The day after that, about twice the number of guards rushed in. Ordered by Hasselrigge, this time they searched through the prison and hauled off about one hundred Scotsmen, mostly very tall pike men. No one knew what tale these men had been told, but they all had gone quietly without a word. It soon became evident that they had been misled. According to whispers between prisoners and guards, these captives had been sold as slaves to English salt mines.

• • •

The guard, Ellery, who had been recommended by the doctor, was happy to bring some basic supplies in exchange for one of the well-hidden dirks that John *found* and offered up. The famished friends wolfed down the bread and cheese it had made possible and spread the small patch of straw on the floor. "God bless Ellery," Alex gratefully commented.

"And farewell ta one of the best dirks ever," John added. "Ellery told me that Hasselrigge had written the mayor of Durham and instructed him ta make sure that we had food, water, and coal and whatever else was fit fer prisoners. The mayor told him that a daily supply of bread had been ordered from Newcastle along with pottage made from oatmeal, beef, and cabbage—enough ta ensure that each one of us would have a quart of the stuff twice a day, every day."

"Well, doggonit—small wonder that we be so fat! It would be grand if we really got some of that," Robert scoffed.

John went on, "Ellery reckoned that Hasselrigge's officials had set up a hospital fer the officers over in the Bishop's castle and he heard that the ailin' were ta be stuffed with mutton and veal broth. Ay, and lest we ferget—coal. Hasselrigge told his men in charge ta be sure that we got enough coal ta keep fires burnin' day and night."

Dan groaned, "Someone must be warm somewhere, but 'tis sure as hell naught us. What a stomach-turnin' tale. Still, I suppose we should be grateful they are bringin' us some of that slop every other day."

The four friends settled in, grateful for the meager things John had been able to hustle from Ellery. They even affirmed Alexander's prayers of thanks. It felt so good to have something in their stomachs and a bit of straw between them and the stone floor.

Chapter 21

WINDFALL

THE WEATHER took a very cold snap and frost penetrated the stone prison with a vengeance. Yanked awake by a ruckus of bangs and loud yells, Daniel's group carefully peered out into the nave and spotted the source. Several of the stronger prisoners were pounding on walls and doors and bellowing at the top of their lungs for some real food and fuel. The potato slop had not done much to appease the captives, but it had strengthened them a bit. The full realization of their predicament had panicked them—desperate—some of them had decided to take things into their own hands.

Their demands fell on deaf ears of guards who could have cared less. Many of these guards had been in on the sell-out of provisions meant for the Scots, had money in their pockets, food in their bellies, and were not in the least interested in the prisoners' welfare. To quiet the unruly some promised once more that provisions were on the way.

"Bullshite," harried voices cried out. "More empty promises." Memories of Alnwick resounded in every captive's mind. There was nothing they could have done to help themselves there, but now they felt they had nothing to lose. Cries of a few incited others—they threw all caution to the winds and joined the horde.

The ear-shattering racket mixed with the rowdy outcries reverberated throughout the Cathedral as handsome wood carvings were savagely ripped from the walls. They splintered and clattered to the cold floor where they were yanked up and heaped into hearths throughout the Cathedral. Stone clinked on stone and sparks flared to ignite the dry wood. It wasn't long before warmth filtered about and took the edge off.

The uproar had been instigated by a few prisoners—but now every captive who could join in did. They helped pull down anything made of wood, including more of the priceless detailed carvings from the choir area and the organ. These priceless artifacts were heaped in piles ready to add to the flames, in an effort to make themselves and their sickly comrades more comfortable.

Dan was stunned, "'Twas fittin' that we took a good look at the place a while back—such grand stuff 'twas." All four friends grimaced at the destruction, but they also agreed that the first heat that they had felt since before Dunbar was welcome. It felt so good that they soon joined in and stacked more of the ruined artifacts for the fires.

Sadly, the warmth was short-lived—the fuel was gone all too soon. The delicate wood had been dry as bones and burned with a wild fury. The height of the beautiful arched ceiling enticed most of the fleeting heat to rise away from bodies that craved it so. The thick stone walls absorbed some of it and offered a little comfort and a brief respite from the penetrating dampness that constantly chilled every man to the bone.

Only the symbolic Prior Castell's Clock was left standing as they had found it in the south transept of the Cathedral, its wood was every bit as dear and precious as any piece they had burned, but even the most frustrated prisoners had agreed not to touch the clock. The significance of the dearly loved Scottish thistle that posed on the top touched their hearts and they reveled in its glory.

Alex constantly sang its praises. He reminded his fellow Scotsmen of the thistle's importance and every captive was inspired by his enthusiasm. All eyes looked to the venerated time piece to help them keep track of the hours and days. Many just sat and stared at it, dazed and enthralled. They seemed to take solace from it and gleaned a tiny thread of hope where there appeared to be none.

The search for firewood was not abandoned, at least not by the rowdy group who had begun the uncouth search for anything that would burn. Some of these disgruntled prisoners were part of a shoddier element and they robbed in desperate attempts to stay alive. As the battle had neared and the Kirks kept shrinking his army, General Leslie had ordered the release of a lot of ruffians from jail with the understanding that they fight for the *Army of the Covenant*. Many of them had been the first to turn tail at Dunbar. Some of these captured criminals had survived the death march and now ran rampart in the Cathedral. They robbed anything they could from the dead and as much as they could from the living. The dry wood had given them an idea—bones, *dry as bones*. They opted to rob Neville's vault. Like wild animals they rushed through the now widely opened vault doors, assailed the coffers and demolished anything they could with makeshift tools that they had snatched up. Pieces of stone struck at the likenesses of John, Alice, Ralph and Matilda. The heads and limbs were broken off, the ornate coffers damaged—pried open and violated—but little was found that could be thrown into the flames.

Daniel and his friends refused to join in the desecration. Maybe they still had some scruples, or perhaps Ellery's help had kept them from being that desperate.

Tired of sitting around, a hungry John decided to test his leg to see just how much it could take. "I'll be takin' a wee jaunt—off ta look fer Ellery. Mayhap I ken get him ta feel sorry enough fer us ta slip us a bite or two out of the kindness of his heart."

Alex joshed, "That'll be the day—it dinna do much good ta go beggin' a hawker; but go fer it if ye must! At the least, the walk will do ye good."

Ellery was not on shift at the time. The hunt had left John disappointed and tired, plus pain grabbed at his leg, so he headed straight back to his straw mat. The vandals were still ravaging the Neville's vault as he limped by, so he kept as far to the opposite side of the aisle as possible. He scowled in dismay at the unruly spectacle, then his head snapped and he stumbled as he felt something hit his foot. Without thinking, he stooped down, snatched it up and kept going.

Once he got back to his mat, he edged himself painfully down onto the floor, took a moment to catch his breath and thought carefully about what to do with his windfall. His principles were torn, very briefly.

He motioned to his friends to come close, then professed, "Ye know that I would have nary a part in any tomb raidin'. I could nary lower meself ta it. I saw what they did ta Alice and Matilda though—they smashed their crypts and defaced their likenesses.

"The culprits were still in there when I passed by on me way back from Ellery's post. I was way on the far side of the aisle and this just happened ta roll me way. I lowered me hand and it just slipped right inta it. It most likely belonged ta one of the Neville women, but they certainly have nary a need of it now, and we surely do."

He opened his hand and a most lovely gold ring that held a sapphire stone gleamed in his palm. "Dinna blather a word, any of ye. I've already decided ta keep it, and nothin' ye ken say will sway me because—I reckon they want us ta have it."

Speechless moments were rare between these friends and this one was huge. They stared blankly at the stunning gem until finally Daniel got out, "*Zookers,* out of the blue, eh? An amazin' stroke of luck! *Zounds!* What ken we say? Just—that 'tis a godsend and we be with ye all the way with it—whatever ye decide. Ye dinna do wrong, John, and 'tis nary a way we would ever judge ye."

Robert confirmed, "Ye know what I always say about destiny—well, 'tis a piece of destiny that has made its way here today. 'Tis nary a way ta place it back on the ancient bones. So, I agree, put it ta good use, John."

Alexander made it unanimous, "Fer sure, it ken get us supplies that will keep us goin' fer some time, and when Ellery sells it, I have nary a doubt but that it will make its way back ta the Raby family—eventually."

That settled they waited for the change of shift—then while Rob and Alex guarded their camp, John and Dan went to find Ellery and see what bartering they could do. He was more receptive than ever and promised to get back to them the next day.

Ellery was a kind man with a soft heart. He was also shrewd and very open to doing business, and he was cleaning up with his prisoner trades. True to his word, the wheeler-dealer guard slipped a package to John the very next morning. The ring had been a windfall for him too—he had made a great trade and promised to bring his *clients* three more bundles to complete their share from the sale.

John discreetly brought the first package back to camp. There he quietly and gratefully opened it and carefully showed the contents.

There were two loaves of bread, some cheese, and four whole apples. Ellery had even included some scant clothing. The four friends now sported loose brownish under shirts and baggy short pants. The clothing was obviously worn, but whole, and offered some very welcome protection from the ever-present damp, cold surroundings.

As they tried not to wolf down the wholesome food, John cautioned, "Take care now. Dinna go moseyin' about in these hand-me-downs. Ye know that there be ruffians in here who would steal yer back teeth given the chance. I've seen them in action, and 'tis nary a pretty sight."

Alex gratefully added, "God bless Ellery and God bless this piece of destiny."

Dan agreed, "And thanks ta ye, John, fer bein' generous enough ta share it with us. I do believe ye have saved our lives."

Robert and Alex murmured, "Amen."

Ellery was not the only guard that was open to bribes—or to doing business as they called it—others were cutting deals with prisoners who had something to barter for favors. The problem was, many of the men had nothing to trade.

Scant pails of cloudy water were delivered daily, and every other day a few buckets of the grey, thin potato root mush were thrown in for the emaciated prisoners to fight over. In addition, some bread and a few table scraps were sent in—not by the authorities—but by sympathetic and kindly parishioners. In spite of this, ailing Scots died at a rate that soared more alarmingly each day.

Chapter 22

RIGHTEOUS INDIGNATION

DANIEL NUDGED John, "Get off yer arse, and—if the leg will take ye—put it ta use, old man." Alex and Rob were moping and couldn't be convinced to budge. Alex, who was almost always optimistic, didn't even glance up at the thistle he so revered. John considered their sad state, forced himself up, and declared, "Well, let's be about it then, Dan, and leave the lassies ta mull things over and hold our place."

"I know how they feel, when those heavy black feelin's fall over ye, they sink down ta yer toenails and 'tis hard ta crawl out." Dan grunted.

A short stint into the nave was all Dan and John could take. Dreadfully sick men and youths burned with fever, were soaked with sweat and in pain. They complained of terrible headaches, distended and cramped stomachs. *Cast and scours*, as Robert preferred to call the miserable states of vomit and diarrhea, were their constant companions. The strange reddish spots that signaled typhoid adorned many chests. It was never quiet, sounds of moaning, sobbing, and worse, were echoed and amplified throughout the Cathedral. Although various small groups clumped up and sat about gazing into the air, other captives were comatose and lay curled up in fetal positions, while more were sprawled out as though glued to the nave floor. The ever-present stench of humans jammed together for too long hung in the air and clung to everything.

Daniel was heartsick, "Ken ye look at this? So many of our fine lads just dyin' by inches. The more I see of it, the more disgusted I be. 'Tis nary a need fer it. All of these lads deserve ta be treated worthily. 'Tis way too much hell they've been through ta have ta die here in this house of God like dogs."

There was not much John could add; he felt the same way, "I dinna reckon it, naught in a thousand years—war 'tis bad enough—but this—'tis worse."

The heavy black condition was not reserved for the friends—it had shrouded the entire Cathedral. The incredible structure was never envisioned as a prison nor designed to put souls down, but rather to lift them up and fill them with joy.

The fact that so many were so much worse off than they were had shaken John more than he'd care to admit, but somehow it settled him and made him grateful for what he had. Downheartedly, the two survivors slowly made their way back to their shabby straw mats. The little alcove looked like a palace to them, and Daniel thanked his lucky stars that Ellery had kept his bargain and had come through with the additional goods they had agreed on from the sale of the Neville ring. Those provisions had kept them as well and sane as their incarceration would allow.

• • •

Signs of winter had begun to sneak in and made the constant struggle to keep warm an even bigger challenge. Without fires, body heat was all that warmed the frigid air. Ellery had become a good friend since the ring business, and Daniel had finally convinced John to barter the last coin for blankets. He had tried for four, but Ellery had stood firm at two. Dan and John shared one, and Alex and Rob the other.

In the middle of an especially cold night, John felt a breeze that shook him from a sound sleep. He felt his half of the precious, thin blanket being slowly pulled away. His first thought was that it must be Dan, seeking more warmth for his side. A muffled thud alerted him—he shot one glance at a soundly sleeping Daniel, turned, and in a flash slipped his remaining dirk from its hiding place in his matted bushy hair, held it sharply at the invader's throat, twisted him around, and stared him straight in the eyes.

The astonished thief stopped in his tracks, stiff and immobile as a statue. Much to John's surprise, he recognized him as a Cavalry man from his own brigade—a usually model soldier, Niven Morray. John calmed himself from his initial shock and fury, and snarled, "Zounds, Niven, 'Tis sure I be that yer as cold and hungry as we be, but touch that, or anythin'' of ours again, and ye'll have nary a need fer more. Got it?"

"Ay sir—truly, 'tis sorry I be—I dinna recognize ye, sir," he stuttered, "Forgive me, John MacKinney—ye ken be sure that it willna happen again."

Out of respect for his brigade and everything they all had gone through, John lowered the dirk and gestured to Niven, who quickly crept away. He felt bad for the lad and knew that it was sheer desperation that had driven him over the brink.

Shaken awake by the ruckus and unsettled about Niven, Robert decided to placate John with their old joke. He hoped to change the subject and get him back in good spirits, "Now, just how tasty was that side of beef ye gobbled at first light?"

But John was still much too agitated from having to turn Niven away and nearly bit his friend's head off, "'Tis nary even a wee bit funny, ye wreck of a man. Utter it again and I'll cut yer stones off, or at least what's left of 'em."

Not a peep from the rest—they were shaken up, but not surprised by the desperate act, although they would have supposed it to have been one of the bunch of hooligans, rather than one of their own. The friends wrapped their flimsy blankets tightly about their legs and went back to sleep. Daniel took sentry duty that night.

They didn't have much, but their blankets increased their chances of survival. The slight shield took some of the bite from the constant piercing chill and gave them a faint, but no doubt false, sense of security. As things grew worse, they eventually agreed to barter the precious things they had left—John's last dirk, Dan's flask, and his dear brother Willy's brooch—which his friends adamantly refused to let Dan part with.

"I be grateful ta ye fer that, me *bráthairs*—but, 'tis certain I be that Willy would be the first one ta offer it and ten times more—if he could—and I reckon we all know that we would do the same fer each other. So—let's thank the dear lad, send him a smile, and get on with it."

And—get on with it they did. As Ellery sold each cherished treasure in turn, the welcome booty enabled them to get through more dreary days.

Once the spoils from the final sales were gone, Ellery had continued to slip them a few morsels from time to time out of the kindness of his heart. Overall, the four friends had been able to somehow hold their own since the day they had staggered in through the Cathedral's sanctuary door.

Robert had given up attempts to cheer his comrades since the last rebuff from John. He was still indignant, felt put down, and made it known, "Well, it looks as though beef 'tis the least of our problems. Nary that it matters much—'tis dead we'll all be soon enough. I kenna be sure we ken get out of this one."

John tried to bring him around, "Ferget it, Rob. Hey look, we be here now. Quit the whinin'—our comrades left dead along the trail be the victims. I reckon we have a duty ta live—if only ta be sure that they be nary fergotten."

"The old fart's right, of course," Daniel glumly validated.

Alex wasn't exactly a bundle of joy either, "Between typhoid fever, the bloody flux, cast and scours—and God only knows what else, how ken things improve?"

Daniel shook his head, "What the hell's with ye? Be ye turnin' inta another Robert the Grump? Yer the one who always looks on the bright side, Alex."

Robert's eyes threw Daniel one serious *if looks could kill, ye'd be long gone.* But, he hadn't realized he'd become so edgy, *'Tis nary like me,* he thought, and made up his mind that he would put a stop to it right away. *Nary more Robert the Grump. If 'tis ta die I must—I may as well do it cheerfully,* he affirmed to himself, none too sincerely.

"Well, agreed—I usually am an optimist, ye know," Alex commended himself. "'Tis the same price, my friends, doom and gloom or a bit of hope, but right now I just kenna see many flashes of hope. 'Tis nary a secret that over two hundred and fifty children of the mist have died in this house of God in just the past week alone, and there dinna seems ta be any sign of a let up. Nary a doubt, with so many ailin', the death toll will go straight up."

"Alright then. What ken we do fer it?" John looked stumped.

"Keep at it, John, 'tis all." Dan encouraged, "Alex, ye get on with yer prayin', and the rest of us will try ta help out where we ken—keep askin' and look around more closely fer possible escape means. We must stay alert and as fit as we ken, so we will be able ta move fast should we get the chance."

"Move fast ye say, eh? I dinna even recall how ta do that," Robert sighed.

Fed up as they were, they constantly tried not to get dragged down. They strove to keep warm—scratched graffiti on the walls—dreamed of escape and anything but their predicament. When one fell ill, the others tended him. They spoke less and less, and even the jokes had worn thin. There was never enough food, but since the death toll had risen so radically, the potato mush was thicker and almost had some taste.

Daniel said the first thing that came into his mind, "Remember how we loved ta ride amongst the glens, while we teased Cromwell's *New Model Army*, and kept them frustrated and at bay fer our General Leslie? We were so proud of him then."

Alex nodded, "Ay, those were good times, Dan. Often we were so close ta the Roundheads that we could almost feel their breath—and them without a clue! But as luck would have it, we ended up here. Nary more cat-and-mouse games fer us, we be the mouse now, and a cornered one at that."

Chapter 23

FALLOW HOPE

MORALE HAD never been lower. Daniel had struggled to retell an old tale but could get no one to listen. The Cathedral reeked of death, and sanitation was non-existent. With virtually nothing to slow or stop them, the diseases of filth spread quickly. Previously at least thirty Scots perished daily—now more than one hundred succumbed each day.

"I say there—Daniel—John." It was their friend, Ellery. He had entered the Cathedral with a group of ten armed guards. "We're looking for men strong enough, and willing to help bury the dead. I'm sure you've noticed how many have passed, especially since the typhoid fever went crazy. If you and your comrades would volunteer, it could earn you some doles—and maybe even a few bobs."

Daniel glanced at John, took a huge swallow as he tried to overcome the revulsion that the thought of such a conscription conjured up, and ventured, "Thank ye, Ellery, but might ye let us have a minute ta speak with Rob and Alex about it?"

Ellery was more than a little shocked at the hesitation, but he needed good men, and after a quick look out into the nave he agreed, "Sure, but make it short, once we have enough volunteers, that's it." He raised a finger for the guards to go on.

Daniel presented the conundrum while the comrades huddled about. "Well, 'tis nary a doubt about it, 'tis frightful work—but I feel that they be our dead, and we should honor them. Somebody needs ta.

That aside—twill get us outside where we ken peer about, evaluate and plan our escape. So—what do ye reckon?"

On Ellery's return he caught Daniel's eye and waited for an answer. He was taken aback by their audacity—they knew that they really had no choice in the matter—he could just force them to do his bidding. *They sure have balls,* he mused. The four agreed to volunteer for the burial patrol, and Ellery nodded his head to seal the deal, *this should work for all of us,* he thought, *they need food and I need the help.*

It was worse than they thought. They were used to the putrid smells inside the Cathedral, but their stomachs turned at sight of bodies disrespectfully stacked like fire logs all over the scenic lawns—noticeably with no decent burial plans for them.

Volunteers or draftees, the Scots were slave labor, and they were forced to dig massive trenches along the north side of the Cathedral. The guards ordered that the pathetic, skeleton-like corpses be dumped unceremoniously into the ditches on top of each other as they had been doing. The Scots determinedly refused to toss their comrades' remains in the hole like garbage, and they would not budge, even when threatened.

The English were fed up with the horrible job themselves, so rather than execute the Scots for refusing orders, they conceded the point and allowed the sad bodies to be placed in the forlorn common grave in a gentler manner. The need for more space soon forced them to dig trenches on the Palace Green.

Alex's lips never stopped. Tears ran down his face constantly as he prayed his heart out over the valiant men they laid to rest. It broke his heart that there would be no Trinity trees or markers of any kind.

As tough and disturbing as this task was, the friends' decision to join the burial patrol had proven useful. In spite of the hard work, they thought themselves blessed to be able to offer some semblance of respect to their fallen comrades. And, on the mercenary side, their plan was working. Ellery saw to it that they had extra rations, plus working outside gave the four chances to nail down a viable way to freedom.

Daniel affirmed, "'Tis time—John, even yer leg 'tis less worrisome and we be stronger than most of the poor souls in here. Buryin' our comrades has been sheer torture, but I dinna regret it. I would much rather be placed in the ground gently by me own than be chucked carelessly in a ditch by my enemy—so, there ye have my pennyworth. Now then—what's been learned from our pokin' about outside?"

Each of them had come up with hopes and plans. They went over each one and began to settle in on a composite that they thought had the best chance for survival.

John was quick to offer his opinion. "Fer me, our best bet 'tis the river—it will offer us the most cover. Once out of the water we'll roll around in fallen leaves ta dry off, then scrounge about fer supplies and—head fer home!"

It was agreed—they would go northeast—the direction they reasoned the English would consider their least likely route. They chose to head for Caerlaverock, where Alex's family had once lived, and from there west towards Galloway. They knew friendly Scots in that area would be glad to hide them until they could find a way to rejoin their army. They all felt they owed their comrades that.

The friends realized that they needed time to get their heads on straight so they decided to fake an attack of cast and scours. It was not difficult to convince Ellery—they already looked half-dead. They rested for a couple of days, then felt ready.

"Once we go back on burial patrol, I reckon we ken slip down ta the river without bein' missed right away, especially if we ken convince Ellery ta turn a blind eye. He has been a good friend, whatever his motives, and 'tis nary a way we ken ever repay him. Rob has picked a good spot and 'tis that we'll go with."

Robert hesitated, "But—the water 'tis freezin' this late in the year. Yer right, John, we kenna stay in it long—we have enough trouble tryin' ta keep warm in here. And then there are the strong currents. We'll have ta catch some driftwood ta hang onto and hide us, and . . . ," he stopped, brandished his arms about, then threw caution to the winds, "Aw, hell—'tis dead we'll be if we linger here, so—wilt away inside—or grab at a wee chance that we might survive out there? Some choice. I say, let's go fer it."

That sealed it; it was now or never. Daniel reported to Ellery that his group could return to the detail the next morning. To avoid any suspicious eyes so soon after their recovery, they'd work the whole day of the ninth—but they would slip out of the patrol as early as possible on the tenth. "Ay, 'tis time," they asserted, "After nearly two months in this place—added ta the merciless cruel horrors before—we ken do this!"

• • •

The best laid plans of men—as they say. On the morning of November tenth, before any light peeked through the barricaded windows or the burial patrol was even awake, heavily armed guards burst into the Cathedral in force. Daniel woke up abruptly and gave John a sharp nudge. They jumped to their feet followed by Alex and Rob—all shocked, appalled, and disappointed beyond words.

They were relieved briefly when they recognized several of the guards. Maybe this wasn't as bad as it looked. Ellery's burly superior, who rarely set foot in the Cathedral, yelled out, "All Highlanders, stand up and be counted."

Scores of the Highlanders could not stand at all, but as many of them as could hauled themselves proudly to their feet. During the ruckus, Dan caught Ellery's eye and moved cautiously near him.

"What the hell 'tis goin' on, Ellery?"

"Out of my hands, Dan. It's an order from the *Council of War.* Highlanders, one hundred and fifty of you, are to be sent to London today. I'm not sure of the plan, but the order is for us to take the strongest, healthiest-looking Highlanders that we can find."

"'Tis a tall order from this outlandish place." Ellery didn't hear; his attention was called to his superior, who gave him orders and left. At the same time, Dan was yanked and shoved into the line of selected Highlanders that was being formed in the nave.

The guards had strict orders not to take any captives who couldn't stand, looked feverish, had distended stomachs, or rashes on their chests. They dragged Highlanders out to make up the quota while John, Alex, and Robert stood together, nervous and worried, while they watched them pick and choose. As the selected group increased, it looked as though they would be left behind. John seized the moment and motioned to Daniel to make room, which he carefully managed. John slipped in beside Daniel first, followed by Robert, then Alex—who stole a glance up at the thistle, nodded, and joined his friends. That extra moment almost cost them as a guard turned their way, but a sympathetic Ellery caught his eye by feigning a question. Once in place, John whispered to Daniel, "Think yer goin' ta have all the fun? Where ye go, we go!"

"Thanks be ta all of ye. I hope ye know what yer doin'!"

"Dinna sweat it, Danny Boy. 'Tis another plan we be needin'—but at least we'll get out of here." A sharp look from Ellery, and they sank into silence and waited.

Once they had gathered the quota, the guards prepared to march them out the Cathedral door. Just as they were about to give the order to leave, Alexander—to the absolute astonishment of his friends, and everyone else within earshot—yelled out at the top of his lungs, "A nod fer our thistle lads, 'tis our inspiration and our strength. Remember what it stands fer, and hold it fast in yer hearts."

Then he boldly chanted, "Scotland, Scotland"—and the chant was echoed by every captive who could find breath throughout the Cathedral. Then dead silence. All were stunned, especially his friends who had taken a stand protectively by his side.

Just as amazing—rather than reprimand Alex, the guards, at Ellery's directive, did an equally strange thing. They stood at attention and saluted the Highlanders.

Claps and cheers were heard all around as the Scotsmen were marched out the Cathedral door—not a dry eye among them.

Chapter 24

NOVEMBER 10, 1650—68 DAYS SINCE THE DUNBAR BATTLE ABOARD THE GOOD? SHIP *UNITY*

EERIE FEELINGS ran through the selected Highlanders as the huge sanctuary door slammed shut behind them with a resounding thud. Scots who had not been outside the Cathedral since they had slogged in through this same door, shrunk back in horror at the sight of the twisted remains of their comrades that waited—piled higher than ever—on the edges of the burial trenches. They felt deep sorrow and guilt about leaving them behind.

Alex choked, "Zounds, 'Tis so wretched—feels like we be abandonin' them."

"Yer prayers helped, Alex. We must trust that others will follow yer lead."

"Amen ta that," John and Robert affirmed, almost in unison.

As they moved on past the remains with heavy hearts and heads down, a gust of fresh air blew up from the river, smacked them in the face, and roused them to the reality of what had just happened—then an inkling came to them as one, *Whoa—perchance we ken still work our plan—all we need 'tis an openin' and we ken slip away NOW.*

Not to be, those thoughts died, dead as the corpses that had surrounded them as soon as they raised their heads. There, across the Palace Green just past the latest open trench stood one of their original guards, the monster's nephew, Lieutenant Wilbur Barlow, now *Captain* Barlow. He had a new-found confidence and couldn't hide his haughtiness as he announced that he was in charge of the prisoners. He paid the captives no mind and immediately ordered the sharp unit of armed guards that accompanied him to bind the wrists of the Highlanders—a routine with which the captives were quite familiar.

Moments before the changing of the guard, Daniel got a chance to hurriedly inquire of Ellery, "What's the story? What be happenin'? Any gist?"

Ellery whispered, "It seems that you've been sold to some business men . . . ." Before Ellery could get out more, he and his men were left behind on the Green as Captain Barlow abruptly ordered the captives to march. Daniel faintly heard Ellery call after them, "Good luck, safe journey."

Robert noticed that Alexander was not listening, but was staring back at the corpses, dazed and lost in thought. He had not heard a word that Ellery had uttered.

Rob took advantage of the moment to exclaim to the others, "Holy shite, dinna let Alex hear that sellin' bit. He'll call down the wrath of God on all of them, and we'll most likely be the ones ta get it."

"I wish he could call down somethin', Rob. What do ye think? Could Cromwell truly sell us?"

John had heard the last of that exchange and answered for him, "Methinks he has the blessin' of the War Council, and that takes the pressure off Cromwell, so indeed—I think he ken do just about as he damn pleases with us."

"What a hypocrite." Dan said shaking his head in disgust, "But then, Leslie's nary an angel either. I kenna ferget how he saved Cromwell's arse at Marston Moore then changed sides."

Robert was *perturbed!* "Well, 'tis just a dandy mess. We'd better hope that a chance ta escape presents itself, and soon."

Nothing presented itself but disappointment. Barlow had given no indication that he recognized any of his charges, but he was well aware of the gallantry and prowess of the Highlanders and was determined that not one would escape on his watch.

The prisoners were marched north, away from Durham Cathedral and back towards Newcastle, where they finally stopped at a quay on the river's bank. Barlow, without so much as *Godspeed*, turned them over to a group of sea dogs who ordered them onto their boat, tied them in place, and held them under close scrutiny all night.

At break of day, their well-thought-out escape plans completely dashed, Daniel's heartbroken group and the other Highlanders were sculled to Gravesend, where a small ocean going sailing ship, the *Unity*, awaited them.

All this had been arranged after the War Council passed the order back on September nineteenth that had encumbered the *Scot Rebel Prisoners* to be sold as slaves. Unknown to the Highlanders, their passage had been purchased by Joshua Foote, John Becx and Company of London.

The *Unity*'s captain was Augustine Walker. Born near Berwick on Tweed in England, he knew full well the plight of the *Scot Rebel Prisoners* and was not at all empathetic. This wealthy flesh-trading sea captain now resided in Charlestown, Massachusetts, where he was respected, had a wife, three children, and belonged to the church. The tough little ship that he commanded from Boston Harbor was readied to return from London to its home port once its bowels were stuffed with human cargo.

The Highlanders stood on deck and waited. The looks they shared exposed how completely miserable they were. John was very down in the mouth, but he made an attempt to at least appear in good spirits, "It seems we might be dinin' in this evenin'," he observed as a wiry, weather-beaten deckhand who waited near the hold motioned to them and handed each man a piece of dry moldy biscuit as they were pushed forward.

Daniel raised his eyebrows and gave John one of his *what-now* looks as he accepted the familiar rock-hard thing. He managed to gnaw a bite, but couldn't stomach it all. Most of it fell to the deck, but the crust lingered tightly in his fist.

The one hundred and fifty *Scot Rebel Prisoners* taken from Durham Cathedral were unceremoniously shoved into the small, damp, and dark hold of the *Unity*. With some still chewing their biscuits, the captives were haphazardly pushed down a flimsy temporary ramp that led below deck. Hearts sank as the comrades shared another look of dismay. "Look ta the bulkhead, John." His gaze followed Daniel's direction, traveled up, and came to rest on a cannon that was firmly mounted, loaded, and trained on the hold.

The formidable weapon made the impression that was intended, and the two acknowledged it as they took another glance into the glaring hole, then back at each other. John cleared his throat, "What the hell 'tis with the English and biscuits?

"Anyway, they dinna seem ta take very kindly ta us, 'tis probably best if we dinna offer them any guff."

"Dang it," Robert cussed, "What do ye think 'tis waitin' fer us here?"

Uneasily they shuffled down the ramp, stared warily into the black abyss, and clearly heard the sound of rats scurrying about. The first thing that came to some battered minds was the possibility of meat. Most of the captives grumbled, while others tried unsuccessfully to crawl back up the ramp to stop the grate before it fell into place over their heads. That didn't work—the seamen easily jostled the men out of the way, hauled up the ramp, and let the grate slam, neatly trapping the Scots below with the rats.

"Shut your faces, you scum. You're getting a free trip to the *New World*—whatever more could you want?" The surly voice snarled down at them, "You'd better settle in and get used to it, luvs, you'll be our guests for at least five weeks, and that's if it's smooth sailing." To add insult to injury he added, "Oh, I should tell you that none of us are planning to do any house cleaning down there. You can take care of that business yourselves. Of course, just ring and the butler will bring up and dump the crap pails." His laughter made a sick echoing sound as he walked away on the deck.

A heavy hush fell over the Scots as their unsavory quandary began to sink in. Packed in so tightly that there was barely room to move, they warily squashed down onto dirty floor planks that were sparsely covered with straw. No surprise—no matter how much they fidgeted and rearranged themselves, they could not get comfortable or stretch out. So, as they had done before, the friends arranged their straw and settled into their *camp* as best they could. Then, as they had on their first night in the Cathedral, they slept like the dead they were convinced they would soon become.

Daniel opened his eyes to feel John poking his leg and smothering a laugh. "Yer quite a generous bloke. Yer friend the rat just treated himself ta some of yer leftovers."

Startled, Daniel shook himself awake and reacted instinctively, the rat ran, and the crust flew, but only to the nearest hand. "Ye well know 'tis nary a friend of mine. The dirty things only spread filth. 'Tis good he cheered ye up a bit, though."

Already queasy from the rocking of the ship that was still at anchor, he moaned, "That piece of biscuit I managed ta get down landed like a rock in me gut, and right now I dinna care if I ever eat again, if ye ken believe it."

Once the ship was underway, the crew threw down a bunch of scraps and lowered some buckets of water. Everyone tried to eat something, but John was the only one of the friends who had sea legs. Others gagged at the very smell of food.

The hold was abhorrent. The Scotsmen could not see the light of day, but now and then they glimpsed a flicker of lightning through the grate. Mostly they could barely make out the face of the nearest man. They called out to each searching for answers. "Anybody know anythin' about this *New World?*" "Anyone know what happened ta my friend—*Andrew? Henry? George? Philip?*" Responses were few, far between, and rarely what they had hoped for.

At first most complained and refused to eat the slop and moldy biscuits that were flung down, but before long they were hungry enough to devour every bite and fight to keep it down.

Old friends, cast and scours, now had a new companion, *scurvy*, and it soon caught up with more than half of the Scots stuck in the filthy hold that creaked and rolled relentlessly.

Chapter 25

**ABOARD THE *UNITY*
JOHN MACKINNEY**

THE PRISONERS sat shocked and devastated. They struggled to make some sense of their new quandary—they felt drained and swept away by overwhelming feelings of frustration and helplessness. The complete inability to do anything to change their situation weighed them down the most. Their world, life as they knew it, and the war with the Roundheads was no more. They had no idea how to face this new threat—how could they fight the unknown?

They clung to memories of what used to be with a preciousness brought sharply into focus by absence. They grasped onto any bit of happiness and love they had ever known, no matter how small. In the ways of old men, they reminisced about days that had been lost in yesterdays. They smiled resignedly to themselves as they recalled their special moments, said goodbye to their past, and gave up any hope of a future.

Then, when it was calm enough to hear, they started sharing their stories. Names were called out from time to time in a weird sort of roll call so the living could be assured that others were still with them. Niven Agnew yelled his name out from the back and told his tale of life before the war; then James Berry, Alexander Cooper, and Daniel Ferguson. Someone razzed, "What a blowhard, yer full of it Ferguson—'tis nary a one who would believe all the shite ye piled on there."

"What ken I say," Ferguson retorted, not bothered in the least by the crude remark, "I be an unusually interestin' person."

Cheers went up and cries rang out for more stories, and others followed—John Neal, William Furbush, William Gowen; John Ross got up his courage and told a great tale. They all loved Peter Grant, and they eagerly listened to his wonderful stories about his clan and wild adventures. The forsaken lot even tried to laugh and fit in some jokes.

Then the malaise would set in again. "Oh, God, help us. 'Tis nary a way ta joke this off. 'Tis a lost cause." No one offered words of encouragement—there were none.

A thoughtful John MacKinney commented, "That poor lad—'tis right he be. What a pathetic bunch of baggage we be. Nary a one would ever guess that we were once soldiers and actually had lives. I kenna recall when I have felt so completely useless. Me hunger—'tis more than fer food."

The stories had moved John, and he conceded, "It dinna seem we'll be goin' very far from here. We've been on a slippery slope fer a long time now, and I dinna know any one who could fault us fer how we've handled ourselves and persevered along the way." He suddenly felt an urgency to rise above this morbidity and share a special part of him, so he decided to broaden the picture they had of his life.

"Me *bráthairs*, fer 'tis what ye be ta me. Ye may reckon I be gone wholly over the edge, but me heart 'tis full sittin' here listenin' in the dark while ye share yer pain and the things ye hold dear—I must confess, 'tis a good feelin'—so ye may be surprised ta hear that I've some ta share meself.

"And 'tis how it was—I be John, I be from Tobermorey, just across the hills," he started out with his famous introduction. "Just sits there perched by the sea—ay ya. 'Tis the jewel of Scotland, ta be sure, and I long fer it. But as ye may suspect 'tis far more ta the tale. Fer a bit, and the best of all times—this grizzly, rowdy, poor excuse of a bloke had a most dear and beautiful wife, Jean, a more bonnie lass there nary wus—and even more flabbergastin'—she loved this wretch that I be."

This was news to all but Dan, who had heard him mention his late wife briefly on rare occasions. He realized though, that he knew much too little about John, and he welcomed the opportunity to hear more. The idea excited him as it did the others and they leaned closer, all ears.

John had made up his mind and wanted to do this, but now he a hard time getting to it. Suddenly it came blurting out, "Died she did—givin' birth ta our son, Gavin. He lived fer two days, but he had come early and was weak—just couldna make it."

"Zounds, John, 'tis awful." After a sad silent pause, Daniel asked, "And what was yer Jean like—reserved, I suppose. Dutiful?"

That brought a smile to John's drawn face and the memories rushed back. "Reserved? Dutiful? Me darlin' Jean?" He laughed aloud.

"Hell nay, 'twas a spitfire she be! Nary anythin' but feisty, bossy, and a lively handful. She loved ta torment me—she'd shake her head and send her flamin' red hair flyin'—and me knees would go weak whenever she did it.

"Me dear Jean was the tomboy of all tomboys. The lads and I would wrestle and play our war games, and she'd just ache ta join in. She was especially good with the wooden swords—she'd laugh and tease the whole time.

"Then, she'd get fired up and real mad when we wouldna let her get in on the rock kickin' or wrestlin'. Her cute little nose was sprinkled with freckles; they seemed ta dance about when she would wrinkle it all up, and whoa—could she pout.

"Ye ken just imagine the uproar if we'd have let her wrestle—every *máthair* on the island would have been after us! Thing 'tis, she probably coulda whipped us all. I must say, I taught her a few great moves later, though." John chuckled at that and his eyes twinkled at the memory he enjoyed for a moment before he went on.

"She was a wee one, but feisty as a Bantam rooster. She'd as soon tell me off as look at me, yet she'd fall apart if some foolish thing I said hit her the wrong way. We laughed and fought and then did it all over again. Such fun and joy as was ever known.

"Do ye recall, Dan? I told ye that she sewed up the kilt fer me. I dinna tell ye what a time we had makin' it!

"She'd place the plaid out on the grass or on the floor in our place—had me help her spread it all out—ta measure, she would say, and we'd end up makin' love every time. Nary a cloth ever got measured so often or so much. 'Tis a wonder the old kilt ever got finished—but finish it she did—and ye saw the wonder of it."

The friends smiled, they could feel the love and couldn't help but be amazed at the gentle side of this fierce giant of a man.

John took a few moments to enjoy the memory, but when he went on his mood changed, "We both thought birthin' would be easy as rollin' off a log fer her. We were so happy about it. Most likely her bein' so tiny did her in. Gavin was breach and too big ta turn. 'Twas nary a doubt that he was goin' ta be a hulk, same as me.

"Choosin' the name was sort of one-sided. I reckoned Wallace would be great, but I swallowed it, and we agreed ta call him Gavin Francis. Nary me favorite name, but she was strong on it. When she gave me one of her looks, 'tis about anythin' I'd agree ta."

Grief overcame him—in his mind he was back with them. "She nary knew that wee Gavin dinna make it, he lived the two days as I said. She was so proud ta have given me a son. She got ta hold and hug him before the bleedin' finally wore her out—and—me darlin' Jean—she nary woke up."

Obviously deeply shaken, Daniel tried to remain calm, "'Tis more than sorry, I be, John. Grief—'tis a terrible nightmare—one that nary leaves ye."

"Ay, Dan, but the dear ones nary leave yer heart either. I dinna realize that at first. The loss came so out of nowhere, neither of us ever dreamed such a thing would happen. There was nary consolin' me. I was wild with fury and struck out at anyone who tried ta help me. I would have gladly died fer either of 'em, but there was nothin' I could do ta save them. So I jolted off and welcomed the chance ta join up with Leslie outside of Preston. I was happy ta fight and kill fer him, and I did plenty of it. It seemed I turned inta a monster of sorts meself, although I must say I nary touched an unarmed lad as he did. None of it brought me any peace. I was just a bitter, twisted, pathetic nothin'.

"Then after I escaped from the church, somehow me old self started ta come back. Once the Battle of Preston was behind me, I caught up with the Dragoons, rejoined them and met ye, Dan—then Will, and ye, Alex.

"Bein' back with the Dragoons seemed different this time; it lightened me up, and I started ta feel more human again. I owe ye fer that and will always be grateful."

All were enthralled by his story, sad as it was, and yearned for more, but they could tell that John was finished, and they were lucky to get as much as they did from the burly Scotsman who had never before spoken of his private life.

Surprised and encouraged by John's heart-rending tale, John Taylor and George Grey spilled out yarns of their lives—then David Hamilton and John Key—and on and on—William Thomson, James Warren, John Reed, David Livingston, and Thomas Holmes. Micum MacIntyre told the chronicle of his close call as a tenth man at least a dozen times and everyone roared whenever he recounted it. All were taken in as they reveled in each story—and the distraction help ease the pain of their reality.

Chapter 26

**ABOARD THE *UNITY*
DANIEL MACDHUGHILL**

THE NIGHTS in the wretched hole let too many dark thoughts run through Daniel's mind. He struggled to clear his head. It helped to think of the stories—especially John's amazing revelation. He knew only too well the horror and helplessness of loss.

Memories of times gone by weighed heavily on him—he tried to think of different things. *I kenna recall much about where I was born,* he thought, *Fer sure 'twas in Alness, way up north in the Highlands— and then we moved down south ta the Galloway Hills. I have many fond memories of that place. I hated it when Da moved us up the west coast ta Oban fer better work—but I soon came ta love that wee parish. Oban, the Charing Cross of the Highlands. It somehow pleasured me that it bordered on Argyll ta the south, Lochaber ta the north and Breadalbane ta the east, ay ya—where the Firth of Lorne so beautifully separates Mull Isle from the coastline.*

The thoughts kept coming as he drifted on—*I had nary a bit of trouble pickin' up the new dialect and just seemed ta naturally slide inta the lifestyle there. It dinna seem as light and carefree as Galaway, but I made up my mind ta fit in and fit in I did.*

As recollections of his yesteryears washed over him. He knew that he wanted to share as the others had—about Mora and more. *Ay, I ken do it—and I will, as soon as I get the chance.*

The next day the time felt right and he tested the waters, "Ken ye

The Resilient Thistle

recall when I mentioned how the plague first got ta Scotland? I told ye when we were visitors in the glorious Durham Cathedral." The friends were a bit foggy on that, but they implied that they thought so—they sensed that a story was coming on and tucked in.

"Hearin' about yer family touched me in the heart, John. I grasped the wonder and the heartache—I felt it hard because I know it so well."

Not sure where to begin, he stared into the darkness and felt the putrid stench of filth run around his nostrils and up his nose. That set him off, "The foul black death filched the ones I held most dear. It came from out of the blue like it always does, spread out its dreadful claws—snatched the innocent—nary a way ta know where it came from or why. The minister who said the prayers at their graves was the one who apprised me that our own soldiers brought it home with them from England years ago.

"Our Da, William and I were the only ones spared. The others were gone in less than two weeks. My Ma was first ta go, then me precious wife, Mora, and our dear little daughter, Ellen. She was only two, runnin' about full of it—just started talkin'—it was great fun listenin' ta her rattle away—she'd go on and on!

"Ay, I know only too well where that pain worse than death comes from—that wholly empty feelin' that overcomes ye while ye have ta stand helplessly by and watch their agony—and all the time wishin' with all yer heart that ye could take it from them." Dreadful images splayed back and it was too much—he couldn't go on.

After a few moments John nudged him and coached, "Cough it up, dear lad, ye know we want ta hear it."

Daniel closed his eyes, cringed and more poured out, "After Ellie, it took me brother, Duncan. We always teased him about being a bit stout, same as our Ma—he'd just laugh and tease us back—then he'd call William and me skinny string beans.

"He was the youngest—was often sick and nary did seem ta get very strong, just a mellow, happy lad. Duncan was the only one of us that had dark hair like Da—and he always messed with it till we razzed him that he'd wear it out and end up bald if he kept it up!

"Fer a while it looked as though he would beat the beast, but the dreadful thing was too strong—he dinna make it ta fifteen."

After another pause Daniel smiled as more musings came to mind, "Me Ma, Mary, was all heart—she always enjoyed cookin', sewin', and fussin' over us.

"As far back as I ken remember her hair was pure white. Me Da once told me that she had been tiny and a towhead like me when they met. Her carin' face was always quick ta break inta a smile and she was pretty as could be.

"Da recalled ta me that he had been taken with the plague once himself, when he was fairly young. He remembered bein' really sick—fer what seemed like forever, but once his fever broke he had recovered quickly. Anyway, it dinna touch him this time.

"He always wanted me ta grow mutton chop whiskers like his—and yers, Rob, but Mora loved me with a clean-shaven face and that settled it fer me."

There was no stopping him now, even if they had wanted to—which they did not—he was back home just as John and the others had been.

"Mora, oh, dear God—me sweet Mora. She was everythin'—kind, beautiful, sweet, warm, lovely—and she was mine. I felt so blessed when I held her close and whispered our secret words. What ken I say? She was perfect!

"Her soft raven hair danced about her waist when she moved—and her eyes, they were a clear violet on most days, with curly thick lashes that touched her soft ivory skin when she was asleep.

"On the rare days, when the sky and the ocean were the clearest blue, Mora and I would wrap up and just sit at the top of the hill where we could gaze out and watch the sun skip across the Firth of Lorne. 'Tis where we did most of our courtin'. It seems like a million years ago, and it might as well be.

"She called me her golden warrior. 'Tis glad I be that she dinna know I went off ta war and ended up in this mess.

"Quite different from yer Jean, I reckon, John, but as fiery in her own way. We both loved the bagpipes and dancin'. She was reserved and quiet on the surface, almost bashful—but beneath the blushes—and the covers—she had an intense passion that always caught me off guard and made me love her more and more!

"Birthin' dinna take a bad turn fer Mora. Me Ma said she was built fer it, even though she was slight. We were expectin' our second when the fever struck. Gone . . . Gone . . ."

Daniel's voice faded as he reminisced so his friends pressed in closer to better hear. "Ellie was a miniature of Mora, except fer her hair—'twas light same as mine—and she had my eyes as well. She was our adorable little towhead, and already a tease like Duncan. Zounds, how we loved that happy wee imp.

"Then—suddenly—the scourge was gone—just like that—leavin' almost everyone in the village dead and the rest ta grieve.

"A few weeks after we lost them, me Da took up his tools and went back ta the trade he loved. He could create anythin' with stone or wood, and I had worked with him a lot. I enjoyed his company, but nary a bit his craft. Da knew that—he loved William and me too much ta force it on us and urged us ta choose our own way."

"With everyone gone, the place was too sad and empty. Willy and I decided that there was nothin' there fer us either so, with the minister's strong encouragement, we took off and joined the army—nary the best decision—now Willy's gone as well.

"He was two years younger than me, and the most handsome, of course. Ye recall how the lassies were always gigglin' after him, John. He'd blink those blue eyes, flash his dimples at them and play hard ta get. That nary slowed them down, they'd only giggle more—and he dinna seem ta mind a bit, did he?"

The two friends shared a silent private moment as they recalled Willy's happy nature, then Daniel added, "Ours was a great life—William, Duncan, and me, we rode horses or just gallivanted in the hills—played, danced, ate good food—with Mora and Ellie—always there fer me ta come home ta—ay, 'twas a great life indeed—until that damn Black Death destroyed it all." Daniel lost it, utterly and completely forlorn—he broke down and sobbed like a baby.

John didn't say a word but fought back his own tears. He heard stifled sobs from Rob and Alex and more of the same from all sides. It seemed as though Dan's tears had burst a giant dam and released a great flood.

John finally managed to get his voice back, "Ye know—'tis blessed we be, Danny, lad—in spite of all the tough times—we've been dearly loved. 'Tis nary everyone who gets that lucky."

"Amen—'tis fer sure," others mumbled.

They all sat quietly for a long time; it was Daniel who finally broke the silence, "Thanks ta ye all, me *bráthairs*." He was overcome and felt a need to change the subject, "Zounds—I kenna wait ta settle in on these comfy planks fer the night."

John managed a faint chuckle and thought of a feather bed before he tried to get comfortable on the filthy bare boards. He wondered how many dead lay among them this night, and had serious doubts about the chances any of them had for survival.

The *Unity* shook and rocked as lightning flashes flickered down through the grate, but if any of the Scots cared, they gave no sign of it, and those who fretted gradually fell into their usual troubled sleep. They had lost count—but, this night marked the end of four nightmarish weeks that they had been held cramped, disheartened, and depressed in the ghastly hold.

Chapter 27

**ABOARD THE *UNITY*
ROBERT JONKINGS**

ONE STORM hounded another over the next week—any thought of comfort was a delusion. The captives continued to envision each day as their last—but eventually the sea blustered itself out and was as silent as a cat stalking a mouse.

Robert had listened intently to tales that had filled the murkiness. He had been moved deeply by how the telling had helped his comrades and felt that he could use some of the peace they seemed to have found.

Even now his round baby face belied his age and condition. Dirty brown hair had grown down over his wide forehead and covered tension lines that gave away the agony he felt when his home came to mind. He recalled the Esk River and salmon fishing. *Those were fair and fun days. Olden times,* he told himself, *'Tis best ta bid farewell ta them and ta everythin' about our beloved Scotland fer I know in my heart that 'tis all vanished fer me.*

It took him some time to get up the courage to bare some of the hurt he had kept so deeply buried in his heart. His friends seemed in a relatively good mood after they finished their delicious lunch of kitchen scraps, so he thought, *Well, 'tis now or nary.*

"I reckon ye've all been itchin' ta learn more about me." His kind face looked sad, but he managed a grin, "Well, 'tis ready I be ta spill my beans—be ye up fer it?"

"Let it loose, Rob, 'tis overdue," Alex quickly agreed.

"Ay, yer right, we be a nosy lot, so spout off," John spurred him on.

Daniel followed, "Ye've been a mystery fella long enough. We kenna wait ta hear what brought ye ta this wild adventure."

Zounds, 'tis kind of like a confessional, he thought, *Ah, so what—that kenna hurt,* and his voice shyly ventured into the darkness. "Well, I reckon 'tis nary that much ta say—really—but 'tis important ta me.

"'Tis nary a secret that I hale from Careston. Netherside and Balbinney are part of it. Tiny hamlets in Angus, part of our beloved Scotland, I dinna believe there were ever more than four hundred souls livin' there. Too small fer ye ta ever have heard of, I suspect.

"'Tis a beautiful, hilly place where the soil could be better, but the grass 'tis the greenest green and makes great fodder fer the cattle, which by the way, I dinna think I ken ever even stand ta look at again—fodder—ugh!" They all laughed and knew that he meant the horse feed the guards had spilled and they had grabbed and gobbled.

"William and Elspet Maul Jonkings—the best Da and Ma—and my sister and I were their world. My Da worked hard ta become a land owner and bartered fer Balglassie in 1600. It did really well and he was very proud of it, but times got hard once the political situation became so entangled.

"I recall me Ma recountin' that it cost Da twelve shillings ta enter their names in the Session Book ta arrange fer their marriage in the church. She told me 'twas a big deal then—and when they took me ta Brechin ta be baptized as well. 'Tis sure that Agnes made that same trip. We both grew up on Balglassie and 'twas a great life fer us, but nary fer the area—it seemed as though 'twas always in turmoil.

"I dinna care ta spread it about, but I had some learnin' in Brechin. All the lads were required ta attend grammar school and go ta church every Sunday. I hated it. Agnes got off the hook on that—nobody gave a hoot about a lassie's schoolin'.

"Brechin was the closest touch ta civilization, and the parish church was the center of it all. Alex, yer nary the only one brought up with an excess of religion. Surely mine dinna stick as much as yers did, though! Nary a fault of theirs, of course, they were constantly at me, tryin' ta pound the fear of God inta me along with readin', writin', and good manners.

"My family couldna afford the tuition, so 'twas paid by the Sessions out of their penalty monies. That plainly marked me as poor—and humbled me pretty good."

The friends all listened with their jaws hung open. Already this was the most they had ever heard come out of Robert's mouth at once, and they loved it. Robert felt their surprise, gave a little shrug, swallowed, and kept going.

"That wild Montrose, he came and went with his army—he occupied the area five times and our Scotts' army led by the Marquis of Argyll was always on his heels chasin' him in and out. Everyone was forced ta run fer the hills—then come back after things quieted down and try ta start over.

"The place was plundered and ravaged time and again, each time the attacks were meaner and more vicious. Montrose kept the people in constant fear so my family and others stayed in the hills a lot."

Rob's bottom lip quivered, but he got a grip on himself. "'Twas 1645, on a clear beautiful Sunday afternoon, the twenty-third of March. I recall the date well, 'twas her twentieth birthday and we had planned a party ta help her celebrate. Montrose came roarin' out of nowhere, made a merciless attack on Brechin and started burnin' the town.

"Annie MacNab had things that were precious ta her that she wanted ta put in safekeepin' before she ran ta the woods—things ta surprise me with fer our weddin'. She was among the villagers who were caught as they tried ta hide some goods in the church steeple."

It was Robert's turn to have the past catch him in the throat. Indeed, this was way tougher than he thought, but as John and Dan had done before him, he stuck out his chin and carried on. He thought he could hear his own voice echo back, and it seemed to sound like a klaxon blaring from some far-off foggy moor.

"The soldiers plundered the town and murdered many folks, but they saved the fair and dear Annie MacNab fer last. They raped her and her two friends over and over. When they were done, they carelessly shot each of them point blank in the face.

The slave pit audience waited in breathless silence for Robert to go on, "I ken nary fergive meself fer nary bein' there when she needed me—but she had shooed me off with a wink after church and promised that she and her friends would hurry on up into the hills as soon as they tucked away a few things. She stuck out her cheek fer a kiss, but I was too shy ta give her one in public." Robert stopped abruptly. "Sweet Jesus," he muttered.

His friends could feel his anguish and shivers ran through them as they waited quiet and motionless, hoping he would go on, and then he did—ever so faintly.

"'Twas where Annie and I met—at that church. Her parents were tenant farmers fer the Careston estate that was owned by the Carnegies of Balnamoon, and she was obliged ta attend church on Sundays, same as me. She was the only thing that made goin' there worthwhile, and I looked forward ta it every week. I was so nervous—it took me forever ta finally get up enough gumption ta ask her ta be my wife.

"Annie wrapped her arms about my neck and said that she loved me and no other and had been plannin' on it all along. She said she nary thought I'd get around ta askin'—that she reckoned she would have ta tie me down and beat it out of me—and that she had been strugglin' fer ages ta find a way ta get the deed done!"

"We both had a good laugh at that because she was so gentle that she could nary even hurt a fly. 'Twas the happiest man on earth she made me that day.

"Our weddin' plans moved slowly because I wanted ta save up enough ta start out properly. I had finally gathered the monies required fer the ceremony and the witnesses—me Da had given us a lovely spot of land on a knoll with a small cottage that sat pretty as could be on top of it, and we were ta be married that next Sunday.

"We buried her instead, under a beautiful tree she loved, just up the hill from the cottage that we were ta share. I nary got ta hold her as me wife and I ken always regret that." Robert paused and was lost to them all again. Finally, he gathered his broken heart—closed his eyes and took a deep breath—he was determined to finish.

"Shortly after that, in 1647, the bloody plague broke out in our region as it did in yours, Dan. It raised hell and over half of the folks in our hamlet were dead by the time it was gone the next year. 'Twas another great tragedy fer such a small community.

"I stayed on after all of it ta be near Annie's grave. I fixed up the cottage, helped with the farmin', and aided as many of the stricken families as I could and before I reckoned it—I was twenty-nine years of age—I still kenna be sure how that came about! 'Twas then that the ministers of Brechin were ordered ta fill the quota of recruits. In such a small place I was high on their list.

"Ye ken imagine, 'twas very hard fer me ta leave, most especially because I realized how badly my help was needed. But, there was nary a way out of it.

"Agnes was very upset, but she felt better after I signed over the cottage ta her and made arrangements fer her ta maintain it. It had nary been the same without Annie there ta share it with anyway. Then—off I went, and that was the last time I saw my home or the Brechin Cathedral. Nary a word have I heard from Careston or my family since, and I now feel strongly that I nary will."

Sadly resigned he drew his tale to a close, "So, I soon counted myself among the Highlanders who marched down from Doon's Hill—and ye know the rest of it."

Daniel spoke quietly for them all, "Ay, and ye know how we all ache fer ye, Rob."

Alex was stunned, "I nary realized, me dear *bráthairs*, the deep pain ye have suffered—strangely—I understand, even though I've nary had the privilege of loves like yers. Dearest God—'tis all so horrible and yet so—special."

Chapter 28

**ABOARD THE *UNITY*
ALEXANDER MAXWELL**

DAYS CONTINUED to be dark and foul, fetid smells wafted up from half filled slop pails, sick bodies, and the filthy straw that masqueraded as bedding. Groans echoed throughout the hold like rolling thunder.

The four friends sat in the dimness bored beyond belief and tried to forget about the queasy feeling that gnawed at their stomachs. Robert, Dan, and John poked each other and decided to zero in on Alexander—they wanted his story.

"Go ahead, Alex—'tis time ta come clean! After havin' yer way with all those eager lassies there must be some bonny tales ta tell!"

"Ay, ye ken, Alexander," Robert goaded, "Ye must have a steamy tale ta tell. Take it slow now—and try nary ta get us over excited all at once!"

Alex took the chiding in stride, but he had hoped to join in at some point, so he felt them out, "Now, do ye really reckon my dull escapades would be of any interest?"

All three stammered over each other and started to speak at once, until Rob finally got it out for all of them, "Ye ken bet yer jewels we do. Fer sure we wanna hear all about it, Alex—details—particulars. Ye kenna leave us hangin' here."

Alexander stood up and tried not to wobble, "My story kenna compare ta yers, and ye know most everythin' about me anyway. Needless ta say—I'm nary one ta kiss and tell . . ." he paused, scratched

The Resilient Thistle

his head and added, with a twinkle in his eye, "Then again I be pretty much an open book, especially when it comes ta the lovely lassies."

He couldn't resist the opportunity to frustrate his eager audience. He rubbed his chin slowly, pulled his whiskers, and tried to sound thoughtful. "I reckon I might be able ta fill in a few blanks fer ye," he teased, "'Twill suit ta make it short and sweet."

The ship lurched and threw Alex down sending his friends into a laughing jag, but he was not about to let that slow him up, quite the contrary, it egged him on. He was feeling a part of things, and he liked it—a lot. He wiggled into a more comfortable position and kept going—but surprisingly, along a more serious vein.

"Ye guessed that I was born ta the free abundant life. Growin' up near the castle at Caerlaverock was great fun fer me. I dinna know that the border area was under constant threat from both sides, but I got the full picture when both my Ma and Da were murdered by the English—our home, everythin'—wiped out.

"I was ten and had been visitin'—playin' war games with my friend George Warren who lived over ta the west. We were havin' a grand old time until the dreadful news arrived. I dinna believe it at first and had a hard time takin' it all in. It dinna make sense ta me then—I still kenna fathom it. My folks were wonderful ta me and we were close—I nary even got a chance ta say goodbye or ta really thank them fer all the great things they had done fer me, things that I had taken so carelessly fer granted.

"I'd be the first ta admit that I had been spoiled. As the only son I had ta merely ask fer anythin' I wanted, and there it was, and usually more came along with it. So, it was quite an adjustment indeed when my aunt took me off ta live with her in Inverness. I dinna exactly go quietly—I put on a real show and acted as mean and hateful as I could.

"I'll give my aunt credit—the old bat kept me out of the orphanage, but she dinna want me anymore than I wanted her. I raised holy old hell and kept her in a state of furious disgust, so much so that she was nary in any way a delight either and took advantage of every opportunity ta get back at me whenever she could. Mostly my fault—I was such a cocky pain in the arse—but I must confess that those years with her dimmed my opinion of the fair sex. More than likely 'tis why I've nary chosen ta settle down. The minute I felt myself gettin' too serious, I'd split. I took ta the foot-loose and fancy free ways with married life the farthest thing from my mind. I must say that after hearin' about yer dear ones, I ken see that I've missed out on a lot and the fact that ye lost them kenna dim the joy that will always be yers." His friends nodded as he went on.

"My wonderful stallion, Star, was the closest companion I had. I raised him from a colt and we practically grew up together. He was about the only thing that came with me from Caerlaverock. We both loved the openness of the ride and went fer it any time and any place we could. It was on his back that I rode ta join Leslie's forces. Why did I join up with Leslie? Simple—I did it because the opportunity presented itself and because I wanted more than anythin' ta get away from my aunt—and several lassies, fer sure—who were just achin' ta pin me down."

"Ay, that must have been really rough, eh lads?" John couldn't help but rib him, and they all laughed.

Alex laughed as well—then he couldn't resist, tilted his head and tauntingly threw in, "Well, what ken I say? What lass could ever resist such a lordly, dignified, and remarkably handsome devil, eh?" His comrades just shook their heads.

"As ye know, before the battle, most of the officers were confident that there was nary a threat from the Roundheads on such an awful night. They left their posts in the wet cornfield and jumped at the chance ta sleep over in nearby farm houses, nary far from where ye were all tryin' ta get some rest and keep dry. It gives me a pang of guilt ta admit it, but I followed their lead and hightailed it ta the farm nearest Broxburn Brook where a fair bonnie lass invited me ta share her warm upstairs chamber." They moaned; Alex grinned. "I had planned ta leave after a hearty farm breakfast at first light. I dinna care fer the fastin' bit, either!

"When I heard the sounds of attack, I refused ta believe that such a bazaar thing could be happenin' and tossed it off ta thunder. Within a minute I was certain that we were in big trouble. I hastily left her—inconsolable and disappointed. . . ." He paused again, dramatically, to give his friends the opening he knew they wouldn't be able to resist. They jumped on it and the comments flew.

"Zounds, dinna ye know she was glad ta be rid of ye?"

"Of course her heart was broken, 'tis probably still bawlin' she be."

"Good try, but we kenna swallow that bull. Just who do ye think yer joshin'?"

Alex raised his eyebrows, rolled his eyes, and wriggled with pleasure before he carried on, "I tossed on my uniform and jumped on Star who, thanks ta all that ever was, I had left on the farmer's front porch out of the rain. I nary got the farm breakfast, sad ta say, and I know ye'll be pleased ta hear that I felt like a real arse."

"Hold it right there, Alexander Maxwell," Rob sensed a payback. "I let a *hell* and one arse slip by, but this makes it one arse too many—ye got carried away a bit with the cussin' there, dinna ye, smart arse?"

"Zounds, ye got me, Rob—I guess ye dingy blokes must be rubbin' off on me."

"NOW, Rob?!? Ye had to butt in NOW?!? We wuz just gettin" ta the good stuff."

They had their laugh and Alex went on, "Nary ta mind, that part was over anyway, I left the sweet lass and raced back ta the cornfield, keen ta get inta the fray—and ye all know how that went—just about as badly as it could. Star and I jumped inta the fracas and were holdin' our own until my beloved mount dropped like a stone and me with him. It was most likely a stray shot, but it hit Star just right, and he was dead as he fell.

"The Roundheads stole Star's saddle and took me. That clearly dinna go too well, either. I suppose 'tis grateful I should be that they dinna kill me on the spot, most would have done the deed and enjoyed it. Anyway, here we are, and I dinna see how we could be in a much worse fix, but I have decided ta belly up ta the bar and survive."

His friends gave up—they couldn't envision any bar to belly up to at the moment and were in no way assured.

"Ye heard me, I mean it. We dinna come this far fer nothin'—nary a way, I refuse ta believe it. God has a plan fer us—the thistle affirmed it, and it demands that we survive so we ken give testimony ta the courage and sufferin' of our lost comrades.

"I ken just feel that one day we will sit by a warm fire and rehash our miseries. 'Tis a vision I have. The thistle speaks! Believe, me *bráthairs*—'tis true. Pray fer it."

"Indeed, Alex. 'Tis a goal ta be sure. Let's hope we ken—meet as ye say."

After Alex fell silent they all sat placidly and mulled over each other's memoirs. They recognized the value of the intimacies they had shared and felt that their kinship had been strengthened to a deeper level, and secretly in their hearts they held onto a slim hope that Alex might be right.

John felt emotions he had forgotten he had, "Who would ever think that in this stinkin' hell hole, most likely on our way out, that a bloke like me could feel decent and whole again, but strange as it seems, 'tis so."

"'Tis true, John." Dan felt it as well, "We nary had a chance ta speak seriously about anythin' on the trail—the guards hated it when we tried to talk, and as ye know, many a good man was cut down fer doin' just that. Moreover, we were much too harried just tryin' ta stay alive. Same thing in Alnwick and the Cathedral. We were always focused on survival and chances ta bolt. Strange that it came up now, but somethin' made it important fer us ta validate our loved ones—and I reckon—ourselves."

The others listened intently and knew exactly what he was talking about.

"At least," Rob teased, "it took our minds off the scuffle of rats and worse, eh?"

"Ah, Robert, knock it off."

Robert had no more than got that out when the vessel went into a wild dance from a nasty storm that caused the small ship to roll more than usual, but the comrades were in another place in their heads and had blocked out all but cherished memories.

Chapter 29

BOSTON, MASSACHUSETTS
THE *NEW WORLD* WELCOME

THE *UNITY* slipped into Boston Harbor just before Christmas of 1650. The sailor's guess that it would take five weeks to cross the ocean had turned to six and even for the crew it had been a rough long voyage. As for the prisoners, they regarded their stint in the dark, filthy, vermin-ridden hold as another taste of cruel hell.

Unexpectedly there were voices and action above the grate. A conversation was in process that obviously concerned the Scots. "We'll get as much as we can for what's left, Jerry. They told us that Highlanders were tough—but maybe not so much I guess after so many of them croaked on us—but I'm sure the live ones will bring in enough to make it a profitable voyage anyway.

"Destroy the manifest, Charlie, it wouldn't look good with so many of the damn scum dead and all. Orders were to select only the strongest from Durham so we could make the best profit—somebody slipped up somewhere. But like I said, that will still happen, even with the losses. I bet they'll go for about twenty or thirty pounds each—eh?"

"Oh aye, Captain Walker will still do alright and that means we will too. Let's get ready to get 'em out and rope 'em up. Hey, Jer, if any can't make it up the ramp, we'll just tie them up, put them aside and throw them over when all is quiet. They'd just make us look bad if they died at the auction."

"You got it. Hey, it looks as though we've made it home just in time to spend Christmas with our folks! Can't you just hear the smell of that good cookin'? That's what my Ma used to say, 'I can hear the smell'. It would always make us laugh."

His companion came back with, "If I don't stand too near that damn pit I might just be able to *hear* it!" They both laughed loudly as they walked away.

Apprehensive Scots waited below, "What the hell was that all about, Dan?"

"Beats me, I dinna know, but fer sure, John—my nose smells land! We may have just reached the *new world*. What that means fer us I kenna say."

Robert had been listening, "Well, 'tis a beginnin' or an end, eh *bráithers*? One thing 'tis sure though—we'd damn well better get ourselves up that ramp. Get ready fer whatever, Alex."

Disoriented and confused, Alex finally managed to blurt out, "Ay, lead on." *Dear God, help us, 'tis fer sure we're in fer somethin'—nonetheless—the thistle calls.*

The orders finally came to haul the cargo out, the flimsy ramp was lowered and one by one those of the dazed prisoners, who could, managed to drag their smelly, bony bodies toward the light. The men were then pulled and pushed out onto the deck.

The cold winter air stung their lungs as squinted eyes tried to adjust to the light of day. No sooner had feet found the deck than each man was smacked in the face with a dipper full of water—gasps and shivers ran rampart as wrists were roughly grabbed and bound, then feet were tethered. Almost immediately, frost formed on scraggly beards.

The overcast grey sky made it a bit easier to focus. Fuzzy outlines of their comrades came into sight, and the emaciated men looked so grisly that they actually scared each other. Shoulders pulled back, they blinked and stood up as straight as they could. Pathetic as they all looked—they refused to see themselves as so.

"At least 'tis off this damn ship we'll be," one Scot mumbled.

Another said, "I sure as hell willna miss that mess."

"Ye got that right."

"Amen ta that."

The first scene that met their smarting eyes was the port of Boston, in the *New World*. "*New World*, me arse," Ferguson was heard to garble.

Daniel and John said nothing at first. They looked about and tried to orient themselves to the strange surroundings. Dan ventured, "'Tis a bit like Edinburgh or maybe more like Stirlin' from here. I kenna say fer sure, but dinna those appear ta be hills over there? 'Tis a welcome sight."

"Glance at all those ships, and folks gathered on the dock and shore."

"Zookers, ye reckon we will ever find our way home from here?"

"We'll have ta see how it goes, Danny. We still be alive—or at least sort of—ye reckon? Anythin' could happen. Keep yer eyes and ears open."

Although Captain Walker had no feelings for the Scots, he was a shrewd business man and had given orders to fatten the cargo up a bit, so they'd bring a better price. So, for the last week more food—mostly bread and cheese, in addition to the usual leftovers from the crew's meals and any rubbish that was handy—had been thrown into the hold. It had been very welcome and every scrap was eagerly devoured, but the sickness that had taken some of the captives' lives had taken its toll on the survivors as well. Similar to Morpeth, run-down bodies hadn't been able to process the food fast enough to make much of an improvement in their appearance.

The prisoners were a wreck. Their eyes looked sick and every bone in their ailing bodies was on display. John's hair and beard were matted and bushier than ever, God only knew what had been growing in there along with all the dust, dirt, and whatever else had stuck to his face and head—he looked quite mad.

As they were shoved down the gangplank Daniel noticed that John was staring at him as if he were a stranger. "What be ye gawkin' at, ye mangy old critter?"

"Ye recall when ye told us that yer Ma's hair was pure white?"

"Ay, John, I remember well and yer right—white as snow and beautiful."

"Well, me friend, yer goin' ta be in fer a hell of a shock when ye see yers in the light of day! 'Tis as white as snow, Dan—but 'tis sure as hell 'tis nary beautiful."

Dan was surprised, but he shrugged and did not reply; his looks were not high on his list any more. His handsome face was haggard—the bright blue eyes that were once his best asset were sunken in with black circles beneath. They belied evidence of scurvy, and that made him look even more ghastly. The sunshine wavy hair that Mora had so loved and had kept cut short for him about the face with longer strands neatly tied in the back was now a very dirty sticky white, as John had mentioned, with a disgusting scrawny and unsightly beard to match. His straight nose was red and peeling. He was a sorry-looking site to behold.

He wasn't alone—the surviving men had sores all over their bodies. Many had bloody mouths and blotchy, spotted skin, sure signs of the scurvy that had attacked nearly all of them. They were itchy, had cracked lips, scars, scratches, bites, and were bruised, unrecognizable relics of their old selves; many could not walk without help.

Robert's once innocent-looking, clean-shaven baby face with well-trimmed pork-chop whiskers, now held a scruffy disheveled beard, and above it, his eyes were hard and flashed bitter glances in all directions. His gaunt body didn't even have the slightest remnant of a muscle and spoke its own tale of woe.

As aristocratic and meticulous as Alex had always appeared—he was now unrecognizable—a scrawny scarecrow would appear better looking than he did in his present undernourished state. He was trying his best to think positive, but his stomach was woozy and he felt very weak in the knees. *'Tis best I put my coppers where my mouth 'tis,* he thought. *Dear God, if we ever needed Ye and the thistle ta show the way—'tis a good time.*

The crew confirmed that all wrists were securely tied as they continued to push the *valuable beasts of burden* down the gangplank. The *Scot Rebel Prisoners* stepped skeptically into the *New World*—classified as traitors and banished from Scotland forever—each one's dreams of home knotted in hapless hearts and faded further away.

"Keep coming, you stinking pigs. You'll get what you deserve now, you reeking animals," the sailors taunted, as though the prisoners were at fault for everything wrong with the world.

Dispirited, hobbled men were marched from the dock over to

Brattle Street Square where the Scots entered a decrepit-looking structure with what looked like an altar at the far end. The run-down building had been pathetically decorated with evergreen branches scattered about, obviously to give a flavor of Christmas.

Robert was taken aback, "Whoa, the Kirks would nary like this, eh? How long has Christmas been banned in Scotland now? We made of it anyhow, on the sly—me Ma loved it. Did ye know I was born on the day before Christmas?" Robert groaned, to no one in particular.

A nasty seaman overheard, gave him a sharp poke and grunted, "And, you well may well find yourself dead on Christmas if you don't get your arse moving."

Once out of hearing Alex nudged Robert, "Dinna pay him a bit of mind, Rob . . . and a bonny Happy Birthday ta ye, dear *bráthair*."

"Very funny Alex. I may cramp up from laughin'. Nay—I thank ye—'tis indeed a happy day just ta be out of that vile shakin' tub."

The barn like building had been cordoned off and converted into a slave pen. The Scots that came off the *Unity* were confined there and held to be sold as slaves in *Brattle Square, Boston, Massachusetts Bay Colony* in the *New World*.

Chapter 30

BOSTON, MASSACHUSETTS
FLESH PEDDLING—BIG BUSINESS

BUCKETS OF water were brought into the slave holding pen. The closely guarded captives were taken aside in small groups—their wrists and ankles were temporarily freed, and they were ordered to clean themselves, which they did as best they could. Once the guards were satisfied, ten of the Scotsmen at a time were led off into a rough cold basement where they were firmly grabbed and held while their heads and faces were shaved—and none too gently. Daniel held his breath expecting John to explode—but the big man just bit his lip and seethed sourly inside. Further violations continued when their muscles, eyes, ears, teeth, genitals, etc., were inspected.

Daniel's group was still furious and feared the worst when they were pushed to the rear of the room. The very skeptical and wary Scots gawked into the dark area where they glimpsed piles of clothing. New guards approached them, and in an effort to calm them down, the tallest one ventured, "You've nothing to fear here; you're safe. We heard that Richard Leader is planning to buy a bunch of you Highlanders once we've done our going-over. He wants his slaves to be clothed and he's paying, so each of you gets a set of duds." He removed a rumpled list from his pocket and related, "That means you'll get a pair of long johns, pants, a shirt, and one of those nice warm sweaters. I'm sure you'll be glad to hear that you'll also get some socks and boots plus a jacket, hat, scarf, and mitts. Just don't try any monkey business or, believe me, you'll be sorry,"

Warily, the Scots accepted the clothing—it fit poorly—was obviously worn and patched—but fairly clean and warm. Then wrists and ankles were bound again and the shorn bewildered group was returned to the pen as ten more Scots were led down.

A small group of prisoners in the next pen were also clad, and they seemed more at ease. One of them noticed the puzzled looks on the Scots' faces and said, "Quite a shock, eh? You'll get used to it. We did. Our bunch has been sold before. Our first owners have no use for us anymore, so here we go—up for grabs again."

He looked over at the men caged up in the various sections and first pointed out some restless youths with very black skin and said they were called *Negros*—then to a small group he called *Orientals*—they were clearly in deep distress.

The man, Barney, kept rattling on. He seemed bent on educating the newly bald group and told them that many of the Negros were kept bound especially tight to quell their tempers and force them to accept their fate. "Not going to be a good one," he commented. "They most likely will be sold off to the Barbados. Just hope you don't get sold to that place," he snorted, "No slave lasts long there."

A still dazed Dan found himself staring at the young Negros, "'Tis a bit unusual, eh? I dinna recall ever seein' anyone with skin that dark before, have ye? So soft and smooth—like a moonless sky."

"Ay, I ken. I saw some lads same as them in Inverness," an equally disoriented Alex confirmed, "Drivin' coaches fer rich folks—and they had on fancy outfits."

Robert still hadn't recouped his senses, but he looked ponderingly at his fellow captives, "Soft, eh? I dinna reckon it—'tis proud I'd be ta lay claim ta those muscles."

"Well, small wonder," Barney went on, "I've heard that most of those buggers had ta row those heavy cargo ships when the wind was down. I would say that would be enough ta build muscles on a mouse and put hair on your chest, eh? Oh, by the way, look over there." He pointed off to the far side of the pens and seemed especially smug to report that there were also some women awaiting their fate. "They're Irish—I think from the looks of them."

Barney pointed his finger toward the frightened women who

clung together in the west end of the pens, "I've heard it first hand, from a most reliable source mind you, that those poor womenfolk are from Cromwell's devastation of Ireland. Word is that Richard Leader snapped them up right away. He has many ventures, you know." Barney cringed as he caught a nudge and a dirty look from one of the guards. He glanced about and without another word, slithered off toward the back of his pen.

The early morning auction was declared open, and the first piece of humanity was dragged and placed on what the Scots had first thought was an altar but was more like the auction blocks used for cattle or horses back in Scotland. The turnout of buyers was huge. Lost souls seemed to make good Christmas gifts in this *New World*.

The incorrigible Barney returned just as the Orientals had been lined up for the block. "They will sell fast," he smugly apprised, "It's said that they make jolly good servants and cooks." They all went quietly with their heads bowed.

Next the Negros, as Barney called them, were forced onto the block for display and inspection. He smirked that most of them were *returned goods* (he seemed to have forgotten that he had been *returned* also). "Those slaves are incorrigibles who ran away from their owners who want to get rid of them and regain their investment. Like I told you, they will likely be sold to flesh traders who will carry them off to the Barbados."

According to Barney, some of the milder Negros might be slightly luckier. They would be hustled off to Virginia, where, he believed, they would work on plantations under conditions that should at least be better than the Barbados. Some resisted and struggled, but that only got them knocked on the head and dragged off by their feet.

There was no shutting up the seemingly know-it-all Barney. He went on to brag that he had seen ships deliver cargos of what he called, pure *wild* Negros, from time to time. He said that those were auctioned off quickly, and many of them sold for a lot more than thirty pounds each because of the high demand for such strength and durability.

The area was suddenly filled with a loud uproar as the first of the Scots were hustled and crammed onto the auction block. Within minutes the gavel had crashed heavily down with a thunderous bang

The Resilient Thistle

that declared a large group *sold* to Richard Leader, a name that was suddenly becoming familiar.

Peter Grant was among this batch of about sixty-five bedraggled Highlanders. Under guard, he proudly marched them out to face whatever fate held in store for them. Their wrists were still bound, but their ankles had been freed. Their shorn heads were held high under their warm caps but their eyes were cold and furious at the indignities that had been forced on them.

Leader had paid for them, but his man, John Giffard, would take them away. Their official *owners*, Joshua Foote, John Becx and Company, were based in London. The newly purchased slaves were now bound to *The Undertakers of the Iron Works of Lynn* that had locations at Saugus and Braintree, Massachusetts.

"Foot and Bek? Dinna we hear that name afore?" John MacKinney, as well as most of the Scots within earshot, recognized the names Foote and Becx as the company that had paid their passage on the *Unity*. Richard Leader's involvement had them puzzled, but it seemed certain that he was important at the iron works.

A voice was heard from among the remaining Highlanders, John thought he recognized it as Andrew Rankin's, "God keep them—may we all be as brave as Peter Grant. 'Tis said they are off ta Saugus and 'tis a two-day march from here. So here's ta Peter and the more than one hundred forty lads of the Grant Clan who fought at Dunbar."

While the remaining Highlanders watched their comrades head out for Saugus, the auction had picked up its pace. Abruptly Daniel, Alex, and John were startled and shocked as Robert Jonkings, much to the dismay and helplessness of his friends, was hauled out along with six others for a man called Valentine Hill to inspect.

Valentine Hill lived in Rollingswood where he owned the most land in the area. He had a house on the north side of the Oyster River and a sawmill nearby. His trip to Boston had been for the sole purpose of purchasing seven Scottish prisoners-of-war to work in his mill and on his five-hundred-acre farm. He had interests at Sturgeon Creek and Quamphegan as well as at Salmon Falls.

Robert had been picked right away. Daniel recognized the wiry Micum MacIntyre and Andrew Rankin among the six others purchased by Hill for the seemingly going rate of thirty pounds each.

Alexander went berserk—beside himself, and obviously not in a prayerful mood—he screamed and bellowed like a wild man. "Rob, Robby, lad—get back here. Dinna let them take ye. Unhand him, ye bastards. Release him—let him loose, I say!"

Hill had made all arrangements before taking possession of his slaves, and he whisked them away quickly. They had no time to orient themselves or ponder their fate. Robert's new cap fell off as he managed to look forlornly back at his friends, bewildered and understandably distraught. He heard Alexander yell after him while he and the six others were tied up like hogs and thrown in a wagon, but there was nothing he could do. A guard picked up his wool cap and stuck it roughly back on his cropped head—then the back board was shut with a bang and tied closed.

Robert was beyond fear for himself, but his sweet face scrunched up in agony at the thought of not knowing what would happen to his friends. He relaxed some when he felt a nudge from the bundle on his left and turned to face Andy Rankin. A nudge from the other side revealed a wide-eyed Micum MacIntyre. "More are here as well," Andy hoarsely whispered. They gave each other a silent nod and hoped for the best.

His friends tried frantically to at least find out where he was being taken, but they were cut off as guards shoved them forward into the viewing spot off to the side of the auction block where they stood, shocked and worried about Rob. They were grateful that at least the three of them were still together, but their qualms soon took on a new concern—it was their turn to be sold.

Chapter 31

BOSTON, MASSACHUSETTS
LOGISTICS

"DID YE hear that, lads? The filthy cruds." Alex, furious, with his mouth agape, spit out, "Zounds, Robert is *sold* . . . for thirty pounds . . . in this ghastly place . . . nay . . . nay . . . NAY . . . I kenna stand it. *SOLD* . . . ye hear? The same's a worthless bauble. Where are Ye, Dear Lord? We need Ye."

Daniel tried to calm him, "Get a hold on yerself, Alex. What's come over ye? John and I be troubled same as ye. We yearned ta stop it . . . but look at us . . . we be in a hell of a fix here . . . helpless as a teat on a bull. Ay, sure an' Rob sold fer thirty pounds. But ye saw what some of the other poor wretches went fer, and if ye want ta regard it in that way, think of that wee Negro who sold fer only ten pounds, yanked right out of his *máthair's* arms he was, and God help the poor *bairn*—thirty pounds is a top price. 'Tis almost a promise that Robert will be safe. Who would want ta harm a good investment? Now, take charge of yerself. Wake up, dear lad! Where be that cockeyed optimist attitude we all love?"

Alex vigorously recoiled, "What are ye jabberin'? Have ye gone daft? Dinna ye watch the *Unity*'s Captain Walker saunter by us like a cock o' the walk? Come ta collect his fee fer deliverin' us, nary a doubt. I heard he got paid five pound fer each of us, which if anyone in a sane mind should be interested, amounts ta at least a fifteen hundred pound profit on the trip, even after so many of our brave comrades died in that hell hole.

"Holy shite, damn it." He ranted on, "Thirty pounds fer Robert? And only God kens what will happen ta those poor souls that Richard Leader's man, John Giffard, took away with Peter Grant . . . what do ye reckon could be in store fer us?"

No sense asking him where his positive side had gone; Alex had not been rational since they had staggered off the *Unity*. Among the nicks and cuts where his abundant hair had been chopped off, small remnants of black bristle stuck out every which way on his white scalp, and his sunken eyes searched wildly about. He looked outrageous although strangely still handsome. Even worse, he had stopped praying or preaching to them and had taken up cussing. His friends' attempts to liven him up had been met with sullen responses, or no reply at all. They were worried about him.

He dove into another tirade, "And ay, yer right. 'Tis *sold* we'll be as well. Dinna ye hear me? Those sons o' bitches sold Rob—like so much manure, and we be next. Ken ye believe it? *Zounds*. Damn it. Damn them—Damn them all ta hell."

John grabbed him by his shoulder as roughly as he could with his bound wrists, looked him in the eyes, and barked, "Alex—yer gonna get yerself ended, calm down."

Daniel yelled, "Stop it *bráthair*," at the same time.

With eyes glazed and tormented Alex yanked John's arms away and screamed, "Calm down? Stop it? Ye both must be daft. How ken this be? Robert is sold ta a hooligan named Valentine? 'Tis some kinda josh? He owns him fer thirty pounds? Who the hell be these creeps anyway? Bastards. All bastards."

Dan firmly slipped his bound hands over Alex's head and butted foreheads with him. "*Bráthair*, ye know that John and I feel every bit as helpless and dire as do ye about Rob but hear me—'tis possible 'tis a solace. While we were waitin' we got some news—and yer right— the man who took Robert was Valentine Hill. Micum MacIntyre and Andrew Rankin were sold ta him as well. Hill dinna seem ta be tied in with Foote and Becx or Leader. 'Tis said that he hails from Salmon Falls and Durham. Ay, same name as the shameful Durham Cathedral that nearly done us in. Fer now we must stay on our mettle so we ken

The Resilient Thistle

track Rob down and get him back when we be able."

Alex ducked his head and pulled himself loose of Dan's hold, then went on ranting even louder, "Like hell ye will—bullshite—yer joshin' yerself if ye reckon that. Nay, Naaaaaay—NOW—we must get him back NOW."

No amount of coaxing could quiet Alex. He continued to draw attention to himself, striking out at anything or anyone in sight demanding that Robert be released. Neither Dan nor John could subdue him, and his raging got so frantic that a guard finally yanked him aside and knocked him on the head. He dropped like a log, out cold.

No bystander paid the least bit of attention except Richard Leader who walked over, calmly caught the auctioneer's eye, waved his hand, and *procured* Alexander Maxwell from where he had fallen unconscious. He ordered him tied tightly and thrown into the extra-long wagon that had pulled into the yard. After he brushed off his gloves, he and his brother, George, looked the remaining Scots over and *purchased* twenty-three more men. Among them were Daniel MacDhughill and John MacKinney.

The crowd thinned and started to wander off past the accounting stands, where straight laced pious Puritans recorded the *sales*. The bedraggled men looked like freaks to the clerks who could not understand the Scots' thick Gaelic accent, and as a result many of the proud names of Scotland were turned into peculiar and sometimes illegible scratches that were unrecognizable. Earlier, Robert Jonkings had been recorded first as Roberd Junkes, then Junkings, and finally ended up as Robert Junkins—and at that, his name was a lot nearer to its Scottish origin than many of his comrades would get.

No one came even close to understanding the name *MacDhughill*. They made out the *Daniel* alright, but they were rushed and quickly got tired of attempting to understand him. "Dooll? Wheel? M'Deel? Dill? Da? I can't fathom such garbled talk. How about *Dill* then, heh? A-aah, I believe that *Daniel Dill* will do just fine." So it was written in the record as Daniel was pushed to move on. His MacDhughill heritage now obscured, he would be legally known thence force in the *New World* as *Daniel Dill*.

John MacKinney muttered his name which they spelled wrong also, but if John knew or cared, he gave no indication.

Fortunately for Alexander he was literate so he had dutifully written his name clearly for the clerks earlier—before he had realized what it was for and before Robert's sale had driven him over the wall.

The remaining Highlanders were sold off one by one to various establishments or persons from towns and cities in the Boston area and the auction closed.

Richard Leader's second lot of Scots, their feet freed, were lined up and escorted to the long wagon where they found Alexander propped up on one of the benches that were built into the dray's high sides. He was still unconscious, but all ropes that had bound him had been removed except those on his wrists. It was a crowded fit even for the twenty-four Scots, but they were told to squeeze up while two armed guards tied them to each other and jammed them in. The wagon was hitched to six rugged mules, and with one big *hey-ya* from the driver, the captives found themselves off on a journey toward another unknown.

Alexander finally revived, glanced dazedly about, and tried to orient himself without much luck. His confused look made his friends realize that he would need some time to sort himself from his mind-numbing stupor. Dan had slickly maneuvered to sit next to him, and John had done the same to be near Dan who manipulated his tied wrists to pat Alex on the leg and smiled to encourage him.

The guards were occupied and seemingly oblivious so John spoke, but softly, "Dan, it seems that Richard Leader 'tis a Boston business man, he be."

Daniel interrupted, "I heard, 'tis said he hailed from Ireland around 1645, and Barney thought that he was some sort of merchant in Boston."

"Another lad said that Leader owns four hundred acres of land on the Little Asbem—or whatever—River, includin' some buildin's and abandoned mills," John went on.

"Ay, that rumor reached me as well," Daniel agreed. "They think he's settin' up a twenty-saw mill ta be water powered by the falls on that river, ken ye fathom that? I dinna know what our place would be there; shite work at his sawmill most likely. But if 'tis so, it might nary be very far from where Rob's been taken—it seems that Hill owns a sawmill same as Leader." He glanced at Alex and muttered, "At least we three are together fer now."

Alex, whose wild outbursts had been so unlike him, seemed to hear some of that. He perked up a bit, sorted out some sense of where he was, rubbed his sore head, and said, "Ay, Rob is partial ta that crazy wee shite, Micum and Andrew as well—they may indeed be of comfort ta each other. Yer right, *bráthairs*, we will find a way ta learn more about where 'tis they've been taken and how we ken free them."

Dan quietly and firmly addressed Alex, "Ye know that 'tis nary a choice we have but ta fend fer ourselves first. 'Tis then that we will see what's ta be done about Rob." Alexander reluctantly nodded his head.

Daniel and John exchanged glances and had to cover a smile. They were thankful to see that their friend had rallied, but they couldn't help but wonder how Alex, even in his current mental state, had the nerve to call anyone a *crazy wee shite.*

There was no sign of Richard Leader as they headed north. The man who looked back at them with contempt was Richard's brother, George Leader. He was almost the complete opposite of Richard. George resented how people were drawn to his brother—how his presence sent out a sense of calm and conveyed his firm take-charge attitude.

George on the other hand turned most people off. Unlike the attractive, tall, and well-built Richard, George was short, heavy, and his pepper-salt hair and thick eyebrows overpowered the small eyes that were deeply set in his chubby clean-shaven face. His portliness combined with his deportment made him come across as pompous and haughty. In reality he was an anal-retentive man who had no sense of adventure and no use for Scots. He did want to impress his brother by doing a good job of managing the mill Richard had placed in his care. He looked back occasionally at his *slaves* and seemed very pleased with himself as he rode up front with his gloomy driver, Ellsworth Drew. Two more armed guards followed the bouncing wagon on horseback.

The Scots looked skeptically at everything around them. The gray sky leaked snow onto the bare trees and seemed to send an ominous message. There was nothing familiar—even the fuzzy sun appeared to be coming from the wrong direction.

"I reckon 'tis even colder here than 'twas in Scotland." Daniel shuddered as he recalled the many cold goose-bump days and was grateful for the warm clothing.

John shook his head in dismay, "Folks have put up with a lot worse than we have and survived." He mumbled, mainly to himself. Louder he said, "I dinna reckon what more we ken handle. Me mind's as boggled as a crosswind in a thunder storm."

"And 'tis somethin' new—that? Ye mean that the rattlin' around in yer head . . . 'tis somethin' different?" Dan joshed.

"Yer akin ta a rowdy fox scuttlin' about in a hen house, Daniel MacDhughill."

"Soooo then . . . it takes one ta spot one, eh, old man?"

John decided to quit while he was ahead, "Ye got me there, laddy."

Daniel got more serious, "They say 'tis a boundless land this *New World*; it goes on and on. Appears 'tis called the *Massachusetts Bay Colony* and 'tis wide open. Folks are fightin' ta get here. Yet here we be—free passage, so ta speak, eh!? Dinna snigger. Mull it over, John. Mayhap 'tis the best chance yet ta escape."

"Ay, some chance that be—*sold as slaves* and tainted as *traitors*—ta be shot like beasts should we be caught . . . right . . . oh, ay . . . that should get us off ta a grand start. Let's just hope we dinna go from the pot inta the fire."

"Stop yer whinin', John MacKinney. We kenna give up. Nay—nay, I nary will."

Alexander hadn't heard a word of that exchange. He dozed, still worried about Robert.

Chapter 32

**THE LAST DAYS OF 1650
ON THE MARCH AGAIN?**

SEVENTY MILES to go, the *slaves* were told. Their eyes wandered and took in the surroundings as the wagon led them on a trek up the grey rock covered coast. Most trees were bare and sparse but a few evergreens mixed in to add a touch of green.

There was no breeze and in spite of the cold, the slaves felt almost hot in their newly acquired clothing—no complaints. Daniel relaxed and watched the light snow flutter down. One of the guards nudged him and introduced himself. "I'm Tom, Tom Eagan. That's Ralph Taylor on the other side; we both work at the falls. Richard charged us to help fetch you. It's extra duty—extra pay too. Aaa-ah, he's quite a man, that Richard. As good a boss as they come, he is. A-yup, that's right."

Tom was tall and lanky with straight stiff grayish hair that shot out all around his woolen cap. Longer strands coiled around his large ears and framed a long, clean-shaven face that boasted an especially generous nose. Strange as it seemed to Dan, the man went on, "Aaa-ah, we've got a lucky break with the weather; folks here call it a January thaw. Most likely much colder air's a comin' with a lot more snow cha-sin' it. Aaa-ah, yup, that's right."

Even colder? Dan thought, he didn't know what to make of the odd-looking man.

After what seemed like forever, the wagon made a turn up the edge of a river just above where it met the ocean. The banks were covered with crusty patches of ice and muck, but the water still flowed freely. That wasn't the case as they forged farther up—the river was frozen solid in most places, but some areas showed sizable cracks that spit out torrents of wild water that surged and splattered frantically before rushing over the ice to battle its way to the sea.

Out of the blue, the second guard, Ralph Taylor, started talking to any of the Scots who would listen and sensed that those within earshot looked interested. The fact that the two guards were being nice to them made the captives very suspicious—from their experience this seemed a bit too good to be true. Ralph went on, "The place where you'll be livin' is called "Newichawannock." Yup—that's *Newy cha wann ock*—got its name from the Abenaki Indians, they called the river, "Asbenedick"—that means *river with many falls*. Two of those falls let loose the power for Leader's saws."

It was hard to hear above the sounds from the wagon, and Ralph was even harder to understand than Tom, but from what Dan could make out, his words seemed to mesh with what they had heard at the slave market. He and the others leaned forward to hear more but were almost sent flying from their seats when, with a sound jolt, the wagon stopped abruptly. It was soon obvious that they were bogged down and there was no way to get through the vast swampy area that had come into view ahead.

On George's orders, Tom and Ralph released the Scots and ordered them to lay hands on the back of the wagon in order to push it around the inlet and up onto more solid ground. Not an easy task. "Don't try to rush it, put your backs into it, but take it slow and careful—and watch your foot gear, believe me, not good to get them feet wet in this weather." This from Henry, one of the guards from the back.

Too late for that, the slushy snow had already seeped in over the tops of their boots. Even George had to abandon the wagon, wrappings and all, while the guards and slaves tried to free it. For nearly an hour the mules pulled, while all but George, pushed, tugged, and heaved, until finally the wagon came loose enough to get around the inlet and back on the trail. They were all left wheezing and panting from the effort.

It was Tom who insisted on a break, "A rest is in order, Mr. Leader. Now that I think about it; this is as good a place to camp over tonight as any. There's rough going ahead, and we need to be up for it." George reluctantly agreed. The driver, Ellsworth Drew, pulled and Tom pushed to get their boss into the back of the wagon where he quickly adjusted his warm furs and robes, immediately fell into a sound sleep, and sent loud snores off into the quiet woods. None of the others sat down for fear of getting wet, but they did lean against the wagon which gave them some relief.

"Who would ever reckon we could be so completely out of shape—eh? And us nary a mite more than lads . . . and whoa . . . dinna gawk me over so." John complained.

"I kenna say what the cause, but what makes ye think ye ever were in good shape?" Dan pestered. "Anyway, our muscles kenna be weak, we dinna have any left. We be paltry bags of bones. Musta been the rubbin' and rattlin' that got us so winded."

Alex, still irritable, but more himself now, shook his head and quieted them with, "Shut yer faces both of ye—added together ye wouldna make one puny old biddy."

John gave him a dirty look, "Still nasty, eh?"

Ralph, Harvey, and Ellsworth rounded up some firewood and soon had a roaring fire going. They chopped some fir limbs, and the Scots helped spread them out for makeshift beds, then they threw down felts that had been stored under the benches in the wagon. Tom heated up some grub and roused George who hastily gulped down his food, then promptly fell back asleep.

While they ate, Tom took advantage of the stop to continue the story he and Ralph had going. His eager audience nodded, all interested now. "About seventeen years ago three partners, James Wall, William Chadbourne, and John Goddard came from England under contract to Captain John Mason to buy land and build a sawmill and a stamping, or gristmill on the Asbenedick River, near the Assabumbadoc Falls. This is part of that river right here." He noticed the Scots' confused looks and gave them a few moments to think and wonder about their fate while he grinned. "A-ah, yup, I know, it will take a while to get used to those Injun names, but anyway—carpenters and millwrights were sent over from England to build the mills.

"After they caught on, Chadbourne stayed on in the area; Goddard moved out, and after a few years Wall left too. The mills passed through quite a few different hands after that, all of them ripping off more of the profits, but not putting much into repairs, so eventually the mills fell into shabbiness and the debts fell back on Captain Mason—then his heirs. None of them wanted the mills, so they were closed and abandoned. That's when Richard Leader seized an opportunity and bought the *water corne mill* along with its buildings and lands. Yup, that's what he did, a-yah, that's right."

George was roused by his own snoring. He threw dirty looks at Ralph who hastily interrupted Tom and motioned for him to stand guard. Tom snapped himself alert and moved nearer the wagon, but still managed to wind down the history, "Early last year Leader recruited a master carpenter, Peter Weare, and moved him and his wife, Mary, into a house near the river. Then he and Peter got right down to organizing all that was needed to get the new sawmill underway. It was a mess, but twenty beautiful saws were completed and put in place this year; and that, in a nutshell, is why all of you sorry lookin' slaves were brought here. George Leader, up with the driver, is mostly in charge since Richard is still tied up with duties at the iron works in Saugus and other places."

"God help us." At last, a familiar sound from Alex.

At first light Ellsworth, Tom, and Ralph got George refreshed and resituated him on his side of the wagon's front seat. Back on the trail the terrain had changed and the going was rougher—the trail twisted around huge rocks and giant hardwood trees that peered down at them from great heights. Mixed in everywhere were straight tall pines. There had been a lot more than light snow flurries here and as the hills grew steeper the snow got deeper, the trail slicker, and the gait slowed. The mules could no longer pull the heavy load as they had down river, so the *slaves* where tied on a leash behind the wagon and only the driver, Ellsworth Drew, and George Leader rode.

"Just look at those trees," Alex gawked, "We dinna have the likes of them in Scotland that I ever saw or heard of. They must be at least four or five feet round. They are so tall and straight they'd make perfect masts, fit fer the ships of kings."

John smiled to himself and thought of Tobermorey and its beautiful harbor—no kings' ships—but trim fishing boats. He said only, "'Tis most likely the idea, eh?"

The wagon kept to the right as the trail split into a fork, and the group settled in for another night. Sitting around the fire, Ralph motioned back to the left and said, "Look over yonder—that's the way to Quamphegan and Salmon Falls."

Alex hadn't been paying much attention to the guards' ramblings, but that got his attention. "Dinna ye say Salmon Falls?" He was alert now and wanted to hear more.

"That's right. There are sawmills over there too. Can't compare to ours though."

Alex's eyes lit up and he checked to make sure Daniel and John had heard the same thing he had. Dan winked, they both smiled and nodded. "How far ta Salmon Falls?" Alex asked, but Ralph did not hear, he'd followed Tom off to gather more wood.

White freshness brightened the woods the next morning as the terrain rose even sharper. The heavy snow made it hard to deal with deep icy ruts that were hidden beneath the heavy snow. Footing was treacherous. The mules grunted as they dragged frozen wagon wheels along.

Once the snow that had chased them from Boston petered out the temperature continued to plunge and they could feel the change down to their toes. George felt it too and ordered Ellsworth to pick up the pace, but he firmly refused and insisted that the mules couldn't take it—he declared that if he pressed them any harder, they could all end up pushing the wagon. The memory of how long it took to get the wagon around the inlet was still fresh in George's mind, so he grumbled, wrapped his robes and blankets more tightly around his ample body, and gave in to his driver's judgment.

Chapter 33

NEWICHAWANNOCK

LARGE CLEARINGS emerged as they traveled out of the thick woods, and soon what appeared to be a hamlet came into view. Ralph pointed and said, "Yup, that's right, we're here, Newichawannock, ain't it a sight for sore eyes?

"Hanker over to your left, that first house belongs to Chadbourne; next to it is the home of our George Leader. Those houses over to the west belong to foremen and other townsmen." He motioned to a small house that sat back a way from George's and told them, "That's where Richard Leader stays when he is on site. He and his family now live in Portsmouth, where I hear he has a grand house. I've been told that he has a wife and two daughters, but as far as I know the daughters have never been up here."

Dusk waned into nightfall as the wagon moved on past the hamlet and further into the complex. The Scots recognized the smell of fresh-cut wood and knew that they must be getting near the saw mill. Although they couldn't see much, there was no way to mistake the loud roar of the falls. The wagon stopped abruptly in front of a cabin and the airy smell was soon replaced by smoke that curled down from its chimney.

Ralph and Tom helped get George, with his blanket and fur robes still wrapped tightly around him, into the cabin. "Henry, Harvey— you can go as soon as we are all inside," he yelled over his shoulder. The two wasted no time and scurried away while Ellsworth Drew quieted the restless mules and waited.

"Okay, now let's get you fellas inside." Ralph motioned to Tom who lowered the back of the wagon. The Scots didn't need to be coaxed to follow him into the building, where a warm, clean aroma enveloped them. They found themselves in a modest sized room with eight large beds secured along the walls. Small windows sat high above them and heat radiated from a pot belly stove that squatted in the center of the room.

"Well," George Leader said flatly, "This is where you will bunk. The layout is simple, but adequate. There is one bed for every three of you. The wash center is over there, and you sure smell like you could use it." He motioned impatiently, "Ralph, Tom, take over and get them settled in. I'll come by to explain more in the morning. I've arranged for four fresh men to help you here if need be."

The Scots stood motionless and shivered in their frozen boots while their uneasy eyes tried to take in as much as they could. A sigh of relief went up from all inside when George, with the help of two of the men from the back, disappeared out the door.

Ralph took the lead and addressed them in a calm firm voice, "I know this is hard, but listen up, this is important. You're in a fine place here, whether you know it or not, and a lot of it has to do with Richard Leader and John Cotton. They both have strong opinions concerning this slavery business, and you'll hear more about that down the line. Now this here is the plan: Tom and I want each of you to take off your jacket, hang it, along with your scarf, mittens, and hat, on those hooks near the wash area. Then, by threes, go sit on the edge of a bed."

The Scots noticed that two of the armed men were standing in the shadows with their feet firmly planted. They did not know what to expect any more than the Scots did.

Daniel, John, and Alexander moved first. They hung their things, rubbed their wrists and stamped their feet in an attempt to get the circulation back, then moved as one toward the nearest bed, where they perched on the edge and, with a nod of permission from Ralph, removed their damp foot gear.

They couldn't help it—they slid their hands down to feel the mattress and confirmed that it was filled with straw covered with some sort of sail cloth. Laying on top were two generously sized felt blankets and three pillows that hinted of feather stuffing, scant but ample. "Been a lot worse, eh?" John grunted, "The straw smells fresh."

The routine was continued until all twenty-four Scots were sitting on the edges of the eight beds and awaited the next move. A loud bang announced that the two other guards had returned from sending George on his way in the wagon. Ralph acknowledged them with a curt nod and pointed to his workmate, "Tom, here, will explain the layout."

Tom looked over the sorry lot and scratched his head, "Leader bought you, and I'm sure he knew what he was doing when he chose you to help with this business; although I must say, your sorry state makes me wonder.

"George—ah, Mr. Leader, will explain all the business details tomorrow. I'll tell you how the day to day routine works, and I'd advise you to make the best of it. You'll be expected to keep this cabin and yourselves neat and clean. That sums it up for now. More chairs will be brought in and placed around the stove. In back there is the outhouse—only in this case you're in luck: it's an *inhouse*!"

Tom stopped and laughed at his own joke. "There are plenty of holes in there for your use. Later you will be expected to take turns cleaning that out also. It cleans from the back, by the way, outdoors. The door over on the left leads down to the mess hall, where you will be fed, most always, twice a day. Breakfast at daybreak—where you can pack up a lunch as well—and supper is at twilight. Work hours are dawn to dusk and often later. You're wearing your first ration of clothing and will get one more set, all paid for by Richard Leader by the way.

"All of this is *if* all goes well and you obey the rules. Anyone who does not will be sent back to Boston and shipped to the Barbados—no exceptions. Any runaways will be shot if they don't surrender immediately. Life is give-and-take, and the Leaders have a big investment in the mill and in you. Any questions?"

The Scots had none. "What the hell ken we say," John muttered.

Tom ignored the grumble and went on, "Okay then, starting with the three men sitting on the first bed . . . yup, that's right . . . you three." He gestured toward Dan, Alex, and John, "Walk over to the wash area, clean your hands—head over to the mess hall door and get on into the mess hall."

The friends were first again and did exactly as they were told. The minute they entered the mess hall their mouths watered as they recognized the unmistakable aroma of baked bread. Their eyes closed and their heads rolled as they let it fill their nostrils. A strange guard beckoned to them, and they walked over to a counter. He motioned for them to each take a metal bowl, which they did. Then they followed their noses down the line where their bowls were filled with a piece of meat, baked beans, and two pieces of the homemade bread slathered with butter.

"Grab a seat at one of those tables up back," Tom said and motioned to rough hand-hewn tables with benches along each side. The hungry men made a bee line for one and had dipped their bread into the beans and stuffed meat into their mouths almost before their butts hit the bench. They gobbled their meal and were finished well before many of the other Scots even had theirs in hand.

Amazingly it all stayed put in the abused stomachs. No one could hold back, all groaned with sheer pleasure, but at the same time they were filled with apprehension. What on earth waited for them this time? What did all this mean?

After all the Scots had finished their meal they were directed back to the pot belly stove room, where they sat and listened while Tom went at it again.

"Okay, things change from time to time, meals may be better or worse, but that's more or less the general routine. Get a good night's sleep. See you all at daybreak.

"Oh, by the way, I'm sure you noticed those nice gentlemen." He motioned to the four guards who were still vigilant in the back of the room. "They are leaving with Ralph and me. You will be locked in for the night, but the cabin will be guarded in case any of you should get crazy ideas about wandering off. A good night to stay in—if you don't want to freeze to death." The room shook as the door slammed behind the six men.

Alex was sitting in the middle on the edge of their to-be-shared bed. He looked first to one side, then the other, and took a minute before he stuttered, "What ken ye make of this? I reckon 'tis mayhap a bit overmuch ta be real, eh?"

It didn't take Dan long to answer, "Well, 'tis warm I be and me belly 'tis full—all good. But the idea of sleepin' with ye two stinkers scares the shite out of me."

That broke the ice, and they couldn't help but laugh. They all headed for the *inhouse*. It could have smelled better, but they had been subjected to more horrible stenches. A long bench, with its top about four hands wide, stood about knee high and was attached to the back wall. Several holes of various sizes were cut out of the top of it. The holes appeared bottomless—they had no covers and some of them looked big enough to swallow up a small Scot. Old rags and leaves sat by each opening. The inhouse was not heated, so no one dallied any longer than he had to.

Once they got in their bed, Dan said, "Let's try ta get some sleep. Then we'll see what another day brings. As yer always sayin' Alex—*the world 'tis full of surprises*."

"How be ye Alexander?" John probed warily.

"I dinna be certain yet, my mind still nags at me, but ye heard Ralph—Salmon Falls may nary be far from here. I know in my heart that the thistle will watch over us, and I pray that Robert stays as warm and full as we are."

"Well," John went on, "at least yer prayin' again, 'tis good enough fer me!

Hum . . . Hill only took seven men, eh? Mayhap Rob has a whole bed ta himself!"

Without another word, the three friends rolled into the first bed of any kind that they had slept on since . . . they couldn't recall when. Alex had ended up in the middle and mumbled, "I thank God that we are nary as squeezed in as I reckoned we would be."

Chapter 34

FOUR PENCE A DAY

THE SCOTS had been rousted out early next morning by Tom—who had given them a flash course on bed making, not that it was a difficult task. All they had to do was straighten out the straw mattress, tuck the felt blankets around it, and place the three pillows back on the bed. Tom then directed them to wash up and get over to the mess hall where breakfast was more beans and oatmeal. "Thanks be ta ye, dear Lord," the satisfied sigh from Alexander had been echoed by all.

Once they had returned to the pot-belly stove room each slave made an effort to sit tall and confident on the side of the bed and waited edgily for George Leader to arrive . . . and waited . . . and waited.

George eventually appeared at mid-morning. The cabin door swung open and he blew in along with a blast of frigid air. He walked over to the pot belly stove, held his chubby hands over it, and rubbed them together. Then he looked over the sad looking human mess that his brother expected great things from and said, to no one in particular, "Last night was as cold as it's ever been since I came here."

He turned toward the Scots and found every eye focused on him—he liked that and addressed them, "Seems you have settled in. You're all looking pretty dastardly. I hope we can improve on that. You sure are a sundry raunchy mess."

The captives sighed and grumbled quietly at the last remark and tried not to take offense. They had no misconceptions as to their appearance or condition.

More to the guards than the Scots, George commented, "It's good in a way that the weather is so dastardly frigid and will most likely stay that way for at least a week. That makes it much too cold for even the dumbest of fools to give any thought to running away, and it will give us and them a chance to get oriented, and hopefully more able to get down to production."

All twenty-four sets of eyes stayed glued to George and waited impatiently for news of their future.

"First of all," George seemed to finally be getting to the business of the day, "Sam Lawrence, the company doctor, will be here this afternoon to check you all out. You're ugly and no doubt lousy as hell even with your heads shaved. He'll get rid of any bugs and see if there is any way he can fix up what ails you and try to help shape you up."

His manner came across as condescending, and to make matters worse, he took what seemed like a threatening step forward, looked down his bulbous nose, planted his body in a rigid position to put firm emphasis on his authority, and bawled out, "NOW LISTEN UP—BECAUSE HERE IS WHAT IS EXPECTED OF YOU."

As soon as those words exploded from George's tongue, Dan vomited up an eruption of beans that ended up on the pine planks at his feet and splashed onto his new foot gear. "Oh shite, seems Alex was utterly right—he reckoned worse was comin'." He moaned as nightmarish memories filled his head.

He wasn't the only one who felt shudders run through his body. George wasn't on a horse, but the stance and tone of the almost verbatim words Hugh Leighton, the monster, had bellowed when he laid down the law at Dunbar flashed back into still tortured minds. They remembered the hell as they watched his sword flash—his hateful eyes and sneering mouth—murders, brutalities, hunger, pain, exhaustion, death, and worse. They were back in a place they had never wanted to think about again.

Jaws and fists tightened in the stifled silence, eyes narrowed—but no Scot opened his mouth. Tom broke the chill when he walked over and gave Dan a pat on his leg, reached down and quickly cleaned the mess from the floor. He then shot George a perplexed look, but the callous man neither realized or cared about the ache that sank to the soul of every Scot.

George did take notice of the mood change that had descended onto his slaves and thought, *Good, it's sinking in. I'm the boss, and these poor excuses for men are collateral in my charge, and they had just better respect me and my authority.*

He stuck out his chin and blurted, "Your duties will be varied, some demanding and grueling, many dangerous—some boring. They will all be explained as they come up." He'd loved how his own voice had sounded, and he just had to belt out another, "YOU WILL PERFORM ALL TASKS ASSIGNED YOU."

He glanced quickly around, and when he got no resistance, he let up a bit, convinced that his firm directive must have sunken in, "You may think that because Richard bought and paid for you and that makes you his property, that this is the end of the line for you. I've no doubt that's what you darn well deserve, but—my brother, Richard Leader, is an exceptional man. Against my better judgment, he has a plan for you that I believe super generous—you will have to judge that for yourselves, of course.

"As I said, the work is no picnic. Working conditions are the best we can make them, but you'll need to be tougher than you look to work the ten to twelve hours and sometimes more each day that will be required, besides being able to stand up to the harsh weather that you only have gotten a small taste of. However, and again against my better judgment, you will be paid."

The sound of breaths being sucked in filled the room.

"You will work every day, and your pay for the first three days of the week will go for board and room along with a measured amount toward paying off Richard's investment in you. He put out a lot of money—top price of thirty pounds each, I believe."

Most of the Scots' backs stiffened again as they heard their worth defined in such a way, but they had developed tough skins and the blow was softened by the word *pay*.

"You will work the remaining four days of each week for Richard's sawmill same as the other three, but your pay for these days will be your own. It's no windfall, going rate is four pence a day tops, some positions pay less, and don't worry, you will earn it—and I might add that some expenses will be taken out of that as well. Let's be clear, it doesn't look to me as though you're worth even that, not at the present anyway."

It was a good thing that the Scots were sitting down because pay was the last thing in the world that they had expected to hear, especially after the monster flashback. All twenty-four mouths gapped open. They wanted to believe what they heard and let their guard down slightly. They didn't trust him, but as nasty as George was, they felt that he couldn't hold a candle to Hugh Leighton when it came to being a monster.

It seemed that they were indeed slaves, and this certainly wasn't freedom—far from it—but it wasn't the hard-core slavery they suspected would be their lot either.

George added, "I'm sure that Ralph explained to you that Richard has insisted that you receive another set of clothing, including boots and gloves, that will enable you to have a change so that you can keep clean and dry out, if need be—the cost of this set will be taken from your pay. You'll be no good to us if you catch your death or freeze. As mangy a bunch as you are, you are a still a big investment that requires upkeep.

"That about sums it up for now." He put his mega loud voice back on and yelled, "REMEMBER, YOU WILL BE UNDER SURVEILLANCE AT ALL TIMES, AND ANY INSUBORDINATION WILL BE DEALT WITH HARSHLY—I'LL MAKE SURE OF IT."

After that last hurrah there was no doubt that George had said his piece, and without another word he nodded to the guards before he stiffly dashed out the door and disappeared into the cold that had been waiting for the chance to deliver another freezing blast into the cabin.

The Scots were flabbergasted and had a world of questions, but they would get no answers from him. Ralph, on the other hand, filled them in a little more.

"I expect yer first question is, *When do we start getting paid?* Eh?" Ralph smiled and explained that they would have to start producing first. Then he affirmed that it was true, they would be getting some pay and by the means George had explained. He went into a few more details, "No matter what George Leader says, his brother, Richard, dubs you *indentured servants*—not *slaves*. After you work off your expenses—if you dig in and do well—you may be free in seven to ten years."

That was it—the meeting was over and the stunned Scots were left to mull things over. Dan was the first to speak, "Seven ta ten years . . . Zounds . . . that feels long."

"Ye got that right, 'tis long . . . but it dinna be forever . . . and after what we've been through . . . well, 'tis at least a thread of hope." It seemed that Alexander's sunshine was back. "We're bein' offered an opportunity ta build somethin' fer ourselves and ta show them just what kind of stock we are made of."

Daniel agreed and added, "Ay, and mayhap we ken save up enough ta get back ta Scotland."

"'Tis nary a chance of goin' home fer us, Dan. Dinna ye ken that? We're considered traitors by the English. Besides I dinna be sure that I want ta go back, I dinna have a thing left there. Our country, 'tis in ruins. And dinna ye fancy 'tis over yet—nary fer a long shot—and I reckon 'tis bound ta keep on that way fer years."

This coming from Alex surprised them all, and whether they agreed or not, there was nothing they could do about Scotland at this time. Survival had to take priority.

Cooperation it would be then. They all agreed and vowed to take it one day at a time until they could determine what would work out the best for them. Since it was the only real option, they couldn't see what they had to lose. They were aware of their state of affairs and realized that they needed time to heal and better evaluate their situation.

Chapter 35

THE GREAT WORKS

TRUE TO George's prediction, the weather remained in the deep freeze for two weeks. The small windows that rimmed the walls were covered with dazzling white frost that clung to them like ermine capes.

Although the Scots made endless trips to the generously stocked wood bin and kept the pot belly stove roaring so hot that the stove pipes rattled and glowed red, there was no way to stay ahead of the sub-zero temperatures that slinked outside. The men were grateful for the felt blankets they could wrap around their shoulders and for the stove they could huddle around and soak up the heat.

In spite of the severe weather, Dr. Lawrence had managed to come every day to continue treatment and evaluate the progress of his newly acquired patients. He had taken a personal interest in them and was rewarded when they began to thrive.

Most of the Scots received treatments of physic for scurvy, remnants of typhoid, dysentery, pneumonia, and just about everything else. They were all ordered to take a horrible tasting tonic daily.

John's leg had gotten the doctor's full attention, but it continued to be inflamed and seeped puss. The good news was that it was less painful than it had been in months.

After they followed the doctor's ritual for a full week, the inhouse began to get a lot less business. They all rested, ate, rested again, and although they had a long way to go before their health could even begin to be restored, most had started down the road to recovery and felt almost human again, even restless.

The wood bin was filled daily by Ralph and Tom, who usually stayed to visit and share the lunches they had all packed at breakfast. Each day they explained more about how the mill worked, where the wood was harvested, how the water from the falls powered the saws, plus many of the other things that they would need to know.

The Scots were attentive and eager to learn. They enjoyed hearing about anything that might affect their future, and they liked what they heard about the sawmill business—it had been too long since any of them had performed any physical labor, and they wanted to get back in shape.

"Well, Dan, 'tis in a lot worse places we've been held—at least they dinna seem hell bent on slicin' us up, kickin' us about, or shootin' us. They dinna yet anyway!" Alex appeared in good spirits and relieved.

The Scots thought it was some sort of jest when Ralph and Tom came through the cabin door at the crack of dawn on the second Monday. The two were so completely encased in snow that even their eyelashes were covered. The snowmen shook their hats and jackets then smacked their feet to kick the cold stuff from their foot gear.

The two guards usually surprised the Scots with some silly antic, made witty or sarcastic comments and had a little fun to keep them in good spirits, but this day Ralph wasted no time and got right down to it, "As you probably guessed from all this snow, the weather has finally broken; it's a lot warmer, and this storm is just about finished. Sooo . . . the three men from the first bed and first man from the second bed fall in by the wash basins. Hop to it, grab your jackets and hats—you're off to see the real world! Yup, that's right."

They did just as Ralph said while Tom lined up the second team behind them and Nyven MacLeod moved in to make it four on Dan's team.

For the first time in over two weeks they went out the front door and found it to be a clear day. The brisk fresh air they inhaled shocked their lungs and dared them to feel alive. Over two feet of thick heavy snow lay on the ground along with a fresh batch that had fallen during the night. It clung to both bare and evergreen branches and the weight of it bowed the trees gracefully to the ground. Rays from the morning sun flooded through them and spread a glow over the entire hamlet making it sparkle like a fairy land. The Scots had to admit it was a gorgeous sight. The cabin door slammed shut behind them, and Ralph guided them onto a narrowly shoveled path.

The path led directly to the site where the larger of the two falls harnessed the full force of the river and drove it into the water wheels that would power the giant saws. It was an eye-opener, although the noise was deafening and the spray just missed soaking them all. A row of open huts that bustled with activity came into view along the river. Canvas covers had been removed and the huge saws with their large benches, ropes, and pulleys were exposed. The Scots couldn't help but be impressed as they watched one saw strip a huge log of its bark in what seemed like no time at all. The other saws were shut down, however, while the operators and other workers shoveled the heavy snow.

"That's a big job in the winter, a-ya." Tom said. "There is a lot of it and it keeps on coming—not much work can be done until the snow is cleaned up. So, every man is expected to do his share until all areas, trails, and homes are opened up."

They moved toward some giant wood piles. "It's hard to tell right now with all the snow cover, but this bunch of logs is all pine. We try to work with one type of wood at a time because of the special features of each group. Softwood is easier to work with and we sell a lot of it, but the real reward is in the hardwood. Oak, maple, and birch head up that list, and you will be harvesting and working with those trees most of the time.

"A-ya, let's head over there toward that wooded area. We get a lot of logs from these woods because it's close and that makes it easy to skid them to the saws, plus it's a good way to open up more land for the complex.

"Buck saws, hatchets, axes, and all the tools you will need are kept in that barn over there behind the skidders. You will be expected to keep the ones you use sharp at all times to ensure cleaner, trouble-free cuts. In addition to precise cuts being good for business, a sharp tool could also save your life. Yup, you better believe it."

All the Scots could see was another huge hump of snow, but they were excited and eager for more. They were ready to get on with the work and be out in the open air.

"What reckon ye, Nyven?" Daniel asked.

"Same as all of ye, I be sure—I dinna wanna stay—I wanna go home so bad I ken taste it, but at least twill be good ta be doin' somethin' with my hands again."

"Me as well." Dan agreed. "From the looks 'tis a big task, eh?"

Alex joined in with, "Ya, and 'tis a bloody cold one as well. Just cast yer gaze on that froth risin' off those falls. *Brrrrrrrrr.*"

Tom guided them right out into the mist onto a rugged iron bridge that was attached to the huge barn that rested just above the falls. As they looked down, the water pommeled and thrashed onto rocks below before it slinked quietly on.

"The river is twenty-seven miles long," Ralph cupped his ears and yelled above the din, then he pointed to the east where there were rows of racks covered with vines. "Now, what do you think of that, eh?"

He quickly answered his own question. "Ayah, that's right, it's a vineyard right here in the complex. It takes a lot of care, but the grapes grow well here—and look further down behind the vineyard—apple trees—different kinds, and trust me, the apples are the best you will find anywhere. They just snap when you bite into them, all juicy and tart." He smacked his lips at the thought of it. "A-ya, the best, that's right."

It was hard to tell the vines from the trees at the moment, like everything else they were so completely covered with snow, but it was clear that Ralph loved grapes and apples. He was also proud and relished showing off what he considered to be the best of the compound.

He went on, "See those empty acres over to the west?" Again, he pointed to more snow. "You can grow your own food there if you want, on your own time of course. We have a central garden that we all tend. It provides supplies for the mess hall and locals."

On the way back to the cabin Ralph pointed out a busy trading post that he said Peter Weare had acquired some years back to trade furs with the Indians. "Peter used to do a lot of business with them, but they haven't been seen around here in years—must be getting a better price for their furs someplace else. I've heard that there has been some Indian trouble down below Plymouth Plantation, but we've had nothing but good relations here in Newichawannock. It's been years, but while the Indians were here they were easy to do business with—we were good to them and they were good to us. By the way, this store will be a good place to come when you get some pay coming in. You can buy a lot of things here, including booze and tobaccy. A-ya."

They plowed their way up a bit further and passed a small church that sat on the river bank. "You're welcome to attend church," he told them, "under escort of course, but no one is obliged to go." Alex and Nyven showed interest—they were Presbyterians, and this was a Puritan church, but they knew that they would like to attend.

Ralph wound down with, "Once the logs are ready, most are slid into the water over there." He pointed to quieter water below the falls. "They go down to the mouth of the river to get loaded onto ships. Some end up in shipyards and a lot more will go to England. A few loads will go by wagon, but you saw how rough that going was. That's it for now—a-ya—this will give you the gist of it. Yup, by golly, that's right."

That night at supper the mess hall was filled with excitement and anticipation. They were grateful that they would be able to get out and do something. The future was a mystery—but then—it had been for some time now.

Chapter 36

EMPLOYED

BY APRIL, with the peak of the winter behind them, the Scots were heartier and most of them were working full time. The stronger Scots started out as choppers, scalers, or teamsters—they were sent out to cut and haul logs or work on the river—while those still in poor health did a lot of cleaning, repair jobs, or yard duties.

And so it began, a sort of routine was established as these survivors of the Battle of Dunbar, the Death March, the diseases of Durham Cathedral and the eerie ocean voyage, learned all phases of the sawmill business that included the hard and dangerous tasks of keeping the falls harnessed and the great undershot water wheels working smoothly.

The completed products that consisted mostly of masts for ships, beams, rough planed boards, planking, etc., came from trees that they selected, toppled, stripped, and finished. One section of the mill even made dowels, wooden nails, knobs, and kindling—not much went to waste. Businesses and private citizens were crying out for these services, and it didn't seem as though the mill could put them out fast enough, so much was needed to build a new world.

"George Leader be right about this sawmill business, 'tis nary a picnic!" Dan panted while he sat on a rock beside a giant oak that he and John had felled.

"But take a hanker at that, will ye? We landed that mighty piece of forest all by ourselves with only buck saws and wedges! Part of me hates ta see it layin' on the ground like that, but just know how happy 'tis gonna ta make some folks."

"And well-off—ta be sure," John added, then adjusted his hat and asked Daniel to give him a leg up so he could sit on the rock. They both sat a few moments and looked at the beautiful oak tree that lay prone at their feet.

"Now then, lad—tell me straight—just how did they say we be goin' ta get the damn thing out of here?" They feigned a good poke at each other and had a good laugh while they listened for the horses that meant Bill Gowen would appear with the skidder.

Dan had noticed how slowly John had pulled himself onto the huge boulder and he ventured to inquire, "The leg—'tis healin', eh, John?"

"Ay, the Doc's been makin' a big fuss 'bout it . . . surely 'tis the best 'tis been in months. But I must own up, 'tis nary same as new and nary ever will be. But as ye ken see, I get along with it quite well, eh?"

"Indeed, John—yer one tough shite. 'Tis the truth, old man."

"If ye say so, me lad! And, what do ye make of this sawmill business?"

Dan took a moment to think and smell the freshness of the day—gazed about him—at the sky, the downed tree, the thick woods and at John, who looked healthier than he had seen him in months—even had a short ginger beard and some hair again.

"Ye well know my intentions, John MacKinney—I yearn always fer Scotland. But Richard Leader has surprised us all, and I dinna have any complaints that would make much sense fer any of us right now. The past few months have softened me heart a bit and wrung out some of the bitterness since Dunbar. I kenna make much sense of it all—and as far as the sawmill business goes—I ken take it or leave it. I dinna feel settled by it in any way, yet somehow it heartens the hope fer freedom—hazy 'tis ta be sure—but I feel 'tis still there. What say ye, me *bráthair*?"

John scratched at his hair, hot and damp beneath his wool hat, and smoothed his regrown whiskers, "'Tis as though we've been wacked off the land by a giant hand—tossed so high and fast that 'tis nary a way ta feel the solid ground ever again. In one wink I feel trapped same's a rat, and the next I be grateful ta be alive . . . then . . . alive fer what?

I kenna figure that out yet—but the same as ye—I have some itch fer new starts, although I dinna have hope as ye do ta return ta Scotland, but, mayhap, me friend."

He was glad to see the skidder appear, "Look ye there, here be grumpy Gowen."

• • •

The Scots sweated and worked their butts off. Their muscles complained, their hands were full of calluses, and their feet sore and blistered. They ached all over and every back cried out in agony at even the slightest tug.

Their days were so full they didn't have time to do or think of much but work. Once up at dawn they ate, dragged themselves to work, ate again, collapsed and fell asleep as soon as they hit the sack, only to get up and start all over the next morning. Slowly, as the days passed, they found themselves with a bit more strength and vigor.

Eventually, the Scots even found a bit of time to visit the Trading Post and during supper the monotony was broken once in a while when Walter MacKee would play a tune or two on the mean fiddle he had traded for at the post and repaired. William Gowen had bartered for a harmonica, and he would join in, usually along with David Hamilton on his juice harp—then George Grey's feet would start stomping and Alex would sing while the others danced or skipped about the mess hall.

As the mill began to prosper their bodies continued to rebuild and shape up. Before they knew it, they had learned how to run the various machines, even the gigantic water powered saws. They dug, sawed, chopped, carried, and ate humble pie from foremen and locals, and they did it all with no complaints.

Time passed, business was good, and by summer Richard Leader had finished his business in Saugus and was spending more and more time in Newichawannock which had already earned a reputation and had become well known as *The Great Works* and the Asbenedick River as *The Great Works River*.

Richard Leader, whose roots were in Ireland, abhorred slavery. Where his brother, George, always called the *Scottish Rebel Prisoners, slaves,* he insisted that they be called *indentured servants,* and always treated them well. Although many of the locals and most certainly his brother, George, complained vehemently, he took advantage of John Cotton's qualms of conscience concerning this camouflaged slavery. He applauded Cotton when he took steps against it and made sure it was known that he would back him all the way. Cotton sent a letter to Cromwell on July 28, 1651, and Richard insisted that a copy be posted outside his offices and in the mess hall:

> *"The Scots, whom God delivered into our hands at Dunbarre, and were of sundry were sent hither, we have been desirous (as far as we could) to make their yoke easy. Such as were sick of the scurvy and other diseases have not wanted for physick and chyrurgery. They have not been sold for slaves to perpetual servitude, but for six, seven or eight years, as we do our owne, and that he brought most of them (I heare) buildeth houses for them, for every four an house, layeth some acres of ground thereto, which he giveth them as their own, requireing three days in the weeke to worke for him (by turns) and four dayes for themselves, and promiseth, as soone as they can repay him the money he layeth out for them, he will set them at liberty."*

The posting was read aloud by Alexander Maxwell. It gave every Scot a sense of pride, gratitude, and hope. It bestowed a greater sense of appreciation every one of them had for Richard Leader and boosted the moral of *The Great Works!*

Alex and a few of the others attended church every Sunday along with the locals, some of whom worked at the sawmill with them. They had to sit in the back where they were closely watched and looked down on by most, but Alex didn't care—he felt he had regained some of his dignity, and he just knew that the congregation admired his full rich baritone voice as it filled the room when he belted out the hymns he loved.

Richard Leader had taken to Alex from the start when he had first seen and heard him spouting off at any and everyone at the auction in defense of his friend.

He had laughed at the outburst and admired the spunk of the

captive Scot who had been knocked on the head and had landed unconscious at his feet.

He had a good feeling about him and whisked out the thirty pounds on the spot, not realizing that he had saved Alexander Maxwell from being shipped out with other incorrigibles to a less palatable place.

He sought him out to see how he was doing at *The Works* and as they talked it came out that Alex could not only read and write, but had a gift for mathematics. Richard realized the value of this and had taken him under his wing, approved of his work right away and promptly promoted him.

Alex had excitedly reported back to his friends, "Wait till ye hear—Richard and I had a great talk about a million things, and he ended up askin' me ta do some financial and other book work fer him."

"Well done, Alex, mayhap 'tis somethin' right up yer alley, but—be aware there. Yer gettin' inta George Leader's place, and we all reckon that he dinna care ta share," John stated flatly.

"But 'tis easin' his load I'll be. I reckon he will welcome the help."

"Let's hope yer right," Daniel said echoing John's feelings, "but be ye mighty careful and watch yer back.

"Zounds, yer always thinkin' the worse. Lighten up a bit, eh? 'Tis the best thing ta happen ta me since—since—I kenna recollect when!"

Dan felt some support was called for, "'Tis lucky ta have ye, he be. Richard Leader made a first-rate choice." John gave a weak nod.

Alex was a bit disappointed with his friends' reactions, but he smiled and shook his head in agreement as they patted him on the back.

In fact, George was not at all happy about Alex's new position. He kept his thoughts to himself, but in the back of his mind he was furious and already trying to come up with a plan that would enable him to get rid of the lowly Scot in a way that would not offend his brother. He watched and waited.

Chapter 37

SAD NEWS

THE NEWLY assigned duties came easily and effortlessly to Alexander. He enjoyed working with Richard and they became good friends. Before long Alex spent much more time working with Richard Leader than his brother, George Leader, did.

Usually over supper in the mess hall Daniel, John, and Alex enjoyed going over the day's events. Through his new position and friendship with Richard, Alexander had access to information that opened a window for the Scots into the world they had been shut away from. Alex loved to share the news and to sing his new friend's praises.

"All that we heard when we landed here showed us that Richard Leader's an outstandin' fella, eh? Ay, 'tis true indeed. He's been decent and kind ta me—the more I learn about and from him, the more impressed I am." Alex was in his glory, and knew he had stirred his friends' interest.

"We all figured when we first heard of his feats, 'twas more ta him than met the eye. Well, he was hired by Joshua Foote, John Becx and Company up at the *Saugus Iron Works* back in 1645. Owing ta the standin' he had earned from his minin' and metal skills, he soon replaced a fella named John Winthrop and was made the head of the *Company of Undertakers of the Iron Works in New England*—and they had all the rights ta iron manufacturin' in the settlement.

"Richard dinna waste any time. He started ta improve things right away. First off he chose a new location fer the iron makin' on the

Saugus tidal river where fresh water meets the ocean. This placed him nearer ta the raw materials and water power he needed, and was the perfect set up fer loadin' the shallow flat-bottom boats with the heavy iron products at low tide ta be sent down the river at high tide."

"Same as we send our logs a floatin' down the river, eh?"

"Indeed, Daniel MacDhughill. A lot of the things we do here came from Richard's doin's at Saugus." Alex went on singing Richard's praises, and they all agreed with him that Richard was a fine man and that they all admired him. That finally settled, they turned their attention to their supper.

But one such evening it was obvious that Alex did not carry such friendly news. He started out slowly, "As ye may have heard, Richard Leader just got back from a rushed trip ta the *Iron Works* in Saugus. Ay, the very *Iron Works* he strove ta build up. Richard helped it take off in the early days when he sent Peter Grant and our other comrades there.

"The bad news be that Saugus grew too hastily—and shortly after Richard left there ta focus more on his sawmill here at *The Works*—things changed—in a big way.

"First off, the work load was boosted ta keep up with the vast demand fer the iron goods. The owners wanted ta fill their orders faster ta get more return—so they grumbled ta the new manager that he was wastin' too much profit on room and board fer the *indentured servants*. Against Peter Grant's protests, they crammed our comrades in and fed them smaller helpin's of poorer foods.

"Out of the blue our Scots started dyin'. They looked as healthy as horses, but somethin' was vastly wrong. Before long, they started droppin' like flies. Out of the more than sixty Scots that marched off with Peter Grant, it grieves me ta tell ye that less than half still live this day."

All jaws dropped and there was dead silence in the mess hall as the stunned comrades tried to grasp this latest tragedy. They twisted, groaned, sighed, and hurt—then a flood of questions came, "Why? Zounds, how could this happen?" "How could our comrades just fall down dead?" "What ken ye be sayin'?" "Zounds, this kenna be."

Alex was at a loss, but he carried on his report, "Richard told me that the doctor blamed the typhoid fever and other diseases they suffered in England. Thought it had weakened and damaged the lads' hearts ta the point where they couldna handle the relentless fatigue and gruelin' work. Seems that when the pace at the *Iron Works* was increased, and our comrades were forced ta carry out the intense hard labor needed fer iron makin' with nary enough food nor rest—sad ta say, the mishmash did 'em in."

No one wanted to hear that, but at the same time, they all needed to know what happened, "Fer one thing, they had ta push heavy carts full of ore ta the top of a steep ramp and across a bridge where heat blasted them straight in the face. Then they had ta dump the load inta the deep stone chargin' hole of the blast furnace ta make sure it stayed red hot—then back they'd go—outside fer more loads.

"On top of that they had ta deal with the molten iron and slag that came out of the bottom of the furnace and the massive bellows that had ta blow all the time on the charcoal fire ta keep it so hot—water powered by the way—most likely where Richard Leader got his idea fer our water powered saws.

"The work went on in all kinds of weather and all areas of the iron makin' mill. In addition ta feedin' the blast furnace they worked the forge, water wheels, the rollin' and slittin' mill and more—much more. And, as ye know—same as us—they wouldna' complain, they just carried on. Kenna ye just see them—their jaws set rigid in their smudged faces and their weary soot stained bodies set on doin' their job?"

Grunts were heard throughout the mess hall as the Scots took Alex's meaning to heart. "Well, it seems that the quick change from hot ta cold proved ta be deadly. Sweat would drop off from 'em one minute, and the next that same sweat would be frozen all over 'em—and without a break—nary a chance ta wipe up and throw on covers fer the cold outside nor ta fling them off in the heat.

"The stampin' machines and other tools they worked with were danged heavy as well. Richard said that the forge hammer alone weighed over five hundred pounds, nary ta mention the iron goods themselves."

Dan injected, "Zounds, the very things we handle all the time were forged at the *Iron Works*—the saws, shovels, pots, pans, anvils, iron nails, even the pot belly stove and stove pipes and—we nary mulled over much about where they came from."

Alex shrugged and nodded in agreement before he went on, "The owners wouldna' let the pace slow—they demanded that the outfit run all day and all night every day. Nary enough hands fer that broad a task, they were stretched too thin. The Puritan locals—Cromwell loyals—resented and mistreated them and helped push them beyond their limits whenever they got the chance. Again, ye know how proud and stubborn we Scots be—'tis nary a way they would give in or back down."

Alex stopped and shook his head, "Peter Grant, John MacAllen, Alex Innes, and several others made it through. I've posted the complete list of survivors outside Richard's office door."

Dan, John, and their mess hall comrades had no appetites—the tasty venison stew they loved sat before them cold and cast off. "'Tis sad news indeed, Alex. What's ta become of our comrades that are left? Has anythin' been done fer them?"

"Richard told me that the hours have been lowered ta take some strain off the lads, and it seems that they are now gettin' more hearty food as well—also the owners plan ta purchase more *indentured servants* ta help with the heavy tasks."

"We been doin' the long days—luggin' and liftin' hefty logs and loads—'bout the same as those lads—how come we dinna be dead as well?" John's question echoed the troubled the minds of all.

Alex had no real answer, and it bothered him as much as it did them, "Well, fer one thing—iron 'tis a lot heftier than wood—'tis fer certain. But I dinna ken—it boggles my mind, same as ye—it seems they were simply worn out and their scarred hearts just couldna take it—may they rest in peace."

The tragedy had them all trying to make some sense of the puzzle. Daniel felt he had to put out his thought, "'Tis odd, eh? Most of us had the typhoid, as John said, and went through all the damn nightmare stuff along with them—and again, we work really hard as well. How ken we reckon it? Seems 'tis blessed we be indeed. We toil only ta dusk and we have good clothin' fer the frigid open-air—'tis ready fer the worst of it we are—and back in the cabin we manage ta keep warm. Mayhap, thanks should go ta Richard Leader, eh? We get enough shut-eye, we're fed good—and, as heavy a load as we carry—nary a thing we do ken hold ta the strain 'twas forced on our comrades, Alex. Poor lads—and afta they made it all this way."

John joined in, "Another bloody nightmare, just add it ta the rest."

"Indeed, 'tis just horrible, fer everyone," Alex agreed then went on, "The deaths shook Richard up real bad, even though it all happened after he left. He felt partially ta blame because he had *purchased* the men fer Foote and Becx and had them delivered ta the *Iron Works*—Richard was riled and 'tis why he made a special strip ta Saugus and made it known that he was dead against *slavery* and deeply resented the way our comrades that he had placed there were used.

"He offered ta transfer the debt owed the *Iron Works* ta *The Great Works* fer any survivor who wanted ta change over and come work off their time with us at the sawmill—and James Warren, Dan Ferguson, John Neal, and John Taylor took him up on it. As ye might have guessed, Peter Grant refused ta leave the *Iron Works*—felt he should stay and watch out fer the remnants of his crew—must have broken his heart ta have watched such ruin. If anyone ken look after the survivors and see that changes be made, 'tis he who ken get it done, or die tryin'."

The Scots fell silent, mourned their comrades. Later, all comfortably tucked into their big bed, secretly thanked their lucky stars that they had ended up at *The Great Works* rather than the *Iron Works*.

Chapter 38

OPTIMISM? POSSIBILITIES?

AFTER THE distressing news Alex had passed on about Saugus he was thankful a few nights later to be able to bring information of a better nature to the mess hall.

"Relax friends," he opened, "I have somethin' ye'll want ta hear this night."

The look in his eye convinced Dan and John to listen closely. "As we've mostly suspected, all the sawmill folks in the area know each other, more or less—eh?"

"Ay," Dan agreed, "So, Alex?"

"Well, Richard knows most of them well and visits with them from time ta time. When he told me 'twas Salmon Falls he would be travelin' ta—ye ken well guess who flew inta my mind!"

Impatient, John pushed, "Aw, come on, Alex—dinna drag it out—have ye news or be ye lollygaggin'?"

"Dinna be so tetchy, ya grump-arse." The impish Alex stopped to scratch his head before going on. "Well, some 'tis good and some I dinna reckon if it be good or nay. Anyway, I pressed Richard ta find out about Robert, and he agreed straightaway."

The wiry fox had their full attention now, "He said he would be glad ta inquire if they had a Robert Jonkings workin' there! And, what do ye ken? Richard traveled ta Salmon Falls this last week. As soon as he got back he told me that he had news that our lad, Robert was naught there . . . ." Big groans all around, "Hold yer horses—but he ran inta Andrew Rankin . . . ye recall Andy, who was sold and hauled off with Robert? Well, he informed Richard that he and Rob are friends and that he's alive and thrivin'!"

A cheer went up at the table that drew curious looks throughout the mess hall.

"It seems though, that Rob hasna been at Salmon falls fer a spell but has been over ta Oyster River workin' fer Thomas Broughton's ventures fer some time now.

"As a favor ta me, Richard tried ta find out as much as he could about Rob. Andy said that the last time he saw him he looked very fit. He said that Rob was held in high regard . . . that he fits in good and 'tis trusted ta do a lot of special tasks.

"Andy told Richard that he would remember all of us ta our friend when he heard from him. He was relieved ta hear that we are alive and well . . . he was also very upset as were we, when Richard told him about our *Saugus Iron Works* comrades."

"Oh, thanks be ta God—our Rob 'tis found and 'tis fit he be. What a blessin'. Oyster River, eh? We reckoned that he was sold ta Valentine—then nary another word. Did Andy say anythin' about young Micum MacIntyre and the others, Alex?" Dan asked hopefully.

Looking a little wistful, Alex went on, "Nay, sorry ta say. That was about as much news as I could get fer this time—and lucky ta get that, ye know. I hinted ta Richard that I would love ta travel with him on his next trip there. He felt bad but said that he dinna reckon that would be possible. He has too much other business ta care fer personally, and he kenna take me—at least nary fer now."

Dan and John lowered their heads and looked downhearted. "Nary a surprise there. But we are grateful indeed ta hear about Rob."

"Thanks be ta ye, Alex. Ye know how much this means ta us. We were as worried about our Rob as ye. 'Tis such good news and 'tis an extra bonus that he dinna be as far away—or worse—as we feared he might be.

• • •

When they had first arrived from Boston, George Leader had mentioned that the pot belly stove room would be temporary, but he had not explained anything further. Richard had proven good on his promise of better housing that had been mentioned in John Cotton's letter to Cromwell. Six cabins had been built for his *apprentices,* as he now chose to call the Scots, and the new housing was a big improvement over the original thin-walled cabin that had bunked all twenty-four men.

The new cabins were actually quite roomy. Each had a *Great Room* with a fireplace, a cooking area with cupboards, a wash area, table, chairs, and more, and in addition there was a bedroom that easily held a separate single bed for each of the comrades. The Scots were required to buy only pots, pans, bedding, and other sundries, the cost of which was taken out of their pay and they all readily agreed to this.

"Once you can repay me the debt I have invested in you, you will have your freedom." Richard reaffirmed to them and added that he hoped that most of them would stay on after and work for him as free men. Many of the Scots thanked Richard, shook hands, and agreed on the spot to stay on. He assured them that he would go even further for them if they did. He would see to it that anyone who wanted to build a house would be granted a piece of land from the colony.

Most of the Scots were very impressed and underwent a serious change of heart. They had been working day to day, not really venturing to think much about their future. None of them had dared to even consider a permanent arrangement, let alone the possibility of a new life in the area.

This promise changed their perspective. They became more dedicated and took a personal interest in their work. They wanted to show Richard their appreciation for his faith in them and became more productive workers. They set out to prove to him, and anyone who cared, what honorable men of Scotland were made of.

John shared their resolve and admired his comrades for their mettle, but he had other irons in the fire. He had become very fond of a lovely Irish lass, Eliza O'Hara, and he was not sure how she would feel about this plan.

Eliza and John had met when he found her crying while she was doing the washing one day. When she looked up at him he was lost at once in her beautiful tear-filled green eyes. He wiped her little red nose, consoled her, and used the excuse to help with the laundry. Then, she in turn helped him put away supplies he had delivered. They hit it off from the start, enjoyed each other's company, and snatched a few moments whenever they could to be together. The visits happened more and more often, and somewhere along the line they found themselves in great need of each other, and the need soon turned to deeper feelings.

John, especially, was in for a surprise when Alexander told another Richard story at the mess hall, "I have another bit of interest that I bet ye dinna know about Richard. He was in another deal when he bought us in Boston, one with a David Selleck. Ye recall the Irish lassies that we were told were on hold fer him?

"Well, Richard Leader and David Selleck rescue lassies and *bairns*—wanderers who were forced ta flee from Cromwell's invasion of Ireland. That's how Eliza O'Hara got ta Boston last winter. How about that, John? Small world, eh?"

John exclaimed, "Quit yer joshin'—that means that me Eliza was in that wretched place with us and I dinna grasp it."

"She's nary at all the same as my Jeannie," John thoughtfully told his friends, "but the tiny dear thing has grabbed my heart, and I kenna shake her from it, nor do I want ta. We have nary more than touched each other's hands, but we just know what the other 'tis thinkin' and that we are meant ta be together."

As soon as he could, John met with Eliza and asked more about her story. She confirmed that Richard had personally placed all the women and children she knew of in various homes or businesses that required cooks or household help, and that he kept an eye out for all of them to make sure they were treated properly.

No Scot was allowed to marry while in service, and they all were aware of this, so when John heard of the house and land plan he thought seriously about taking Richard up on his offer to stay on at *The Works*.

"We dinna be *bairns*—we know the rules and grasp that we have a while ta wait fer our freedom, but Lord willin' 'twill happen and when it comes, we'll be ready!"

"Zounds!" That summed it all up for Daniel and Alex. "What ken we say, John? 'Tis grand news, *bráthair*. We wish ye only the best, eh, Alex?"

Alex was looking a bit down in the mouth, but his happiness for his friend overrode it, "Indeed, John. Eliza 'tis a lovely lass, and yer lucky ta have her. Ye really got us this time, ye old dog—we nary saw that comin'! Now, let us know what we ken do ta help with anythin' ye might need."

"Thanks, 'tis great of ye ta offer—just be sure ta keep our secret under yer hats, lads, ye know that Eliza still has ta work off the debt time she owes George and Joan Leader, eh? They'd nary take ta it if they found out, and she would land in big trouble."

Alex grimaced, "'Tis nary a doubt about that. She could be workin' fer kinder folks—ye ken be sure that our lips are sealed, John. 'Tis grand ta see ye in such good spirits."

Daniel confirmed, "Amen ta that, ye wild ginger bear." All puffed up and happy, off they all went back to work—smiling all the way.

Chapter 39

A BITTER PILL

THE END of October 1651 closed on an exceptionally beautiful autumn. *The Works* continued to prosper with no complaints from the Scots.

Not so good was that Alex once more had distressing news for those in the mess hall. He felt sick himself from the dark report that had come from Scotland. He flinched but decided that he'd better get right to it.

"Leslie and Cromwell did it again," he yelled out.

Those two names mentioned together in one breath drew the immediate attention of the entire mess hall. They all felt a cold chill, held their breath, and waited for what they knew couldn't be good. Alex quickly confirmed their inkling, "We reckoned that when Cromwell left the Battle of Dunbar and moved on ta Edinburgh that he planned ta take control of Scotland ta prevent Prince Charles from reclaimin' the throne and bringin' back the rule of the Crown of England.

"A twist of fate, on September third of this year, one year ta the day from his victory at Dunbar, Cromwell attacked General David Leslie's army—led by King Charles the Second—at Worcester— and would ye believe it? General Leslie and our lads were beaten again."

Disbelief filled the hall as they cried out, "Zounds, what happened this time?"

Alex explained, "Leslie wanted ta make a stand in Scotland where support fer the king was the strongest. Well, Charles had other ideas

The Resilient Thistle

and took the refurbished army south ta Worcester where they were overcome by Oliver Cromwell and his restored army of thirty thousand Roundheads. Our lads were outnumbered two ta one.

"As before, the fightin' was bitter, with the hand ta hand combat inflictin' severe losses. They put up a good fight, but eventually our Scottish troops broke. The rumor was that when city was surrounded our men were captured by Cromwell's soldiers as they tried ta flee.

"And if they did, 'tis nary a wonder, Cromwell lost about seven hundred men and between two thousand and four thousand of Leslie's army under King Charles were slaughtered.

"The reason ye dinna see Nyven MacLeod among us tonight 'tis because he was deeply distressed when I was the one ta tell him earlier that over eight hundred MacLeods alone were cut down at Worcester in support of the Stuart cause."

"Sweet Jesus," Daniel muttered, " 'tis most of his clan."

"And 'tis nary all, Dan—as many as ten thousand Scots were taken prisoner.

"Of course, the English reported that the Scots were defeated by the better General with his larger army, which 'tis what the English always say.

"The most humiliatin' news was that Charles left his bodyguard behind ta cover his back while he fled the field. 'Twas said that he hid from Cromwell's men in the lofty sunshade of heavy foliage in an oak tree, where he stayed until he was retrieved by a royal guard who took him ta the coast from where he later sailed ta safety in France. Leslie survived, fled again, and eventually returned ta his castle in Fife.

"Seems they executed the Earl of Derby though, about mid-October I'd say, buried in Ormskirk Church. Ah—*Yn Stanlagh Mooar*—the Great Stanley, indeed.

"And there ye have it. 'Tis sorry I am ta bring ye such ghastly news."

The Scots thanked Alex and assured him that no matter how the news might have been delivered, the effect would have been the same. They were grateful that he had been the one to tell them.

There were a lot of bowed and shaking heads as the Scots left the mess hall that night as they tried in vain to fathom this second demoralizing defeat and pondered the fate of its countless victims.

• • •

A few months later, in late January of 1652, they got direct news of these captives when Richard arrived with another *purchase of indentured servants* he had completed—this time from Charlestown.

This batch of Scottish prisoners of war—from the Battle of Worcester—was placed in the thin-walled cabin with the pot belly stove, where the *Unity* group had first stayed. It didn't take long for the word to spread and as many of *The Great Works* Scots as could jammed into the mess hall that evening to find out what happened.

They shuddered at their first good look at their comrades. The more they tried not to stare, the worse they were at it—no one could help it, they all stared.

The new comers reminded them of how far they had come in a year. These men were as pathetic a looking mess as they all had been after being auctioned off in Boston.

After the new *purchases* had dug in and enjoyed their meal, Ralph decided to let everyone linger and reconnect with comrades from yesterday.

Daniel broke the ice with, *"Ciamar a tha sibh?"*

Being asked how they were in the old language encouraged one of the weary Scots to step forward. His face broke into as much of a smile as he could manage, and in a croaky, faltering voice said, "Dear comrades. I am James Grant, I speak fer us all. I kenna say that any of us are fit, but as bad as things have been and as much as we want ta be in Scotland, we are comforted ta be here with fellow Scots who had been given up fer dead long ago—and I must say—yer all lookin' pretty lively ta me!"

Once the laughter died down, he perked up some as he informed them, "The best news I've had since I got here was ta learn that my *bráthair*, Peter, lives. We should have known that rascal was a survivor, but I must admit, hope had worn thin. Richard informed me that 'tis in servitude in Saugus he be—at the *Iron Works* and that he's had a rough time there—but survived that as well."

James got a well-deserved round of applause at the mention of Peter. Then he pointed and said, "Over there towards the back 'tis my cousin, another James Grant and beside him, if ye ken believe it,

The Resilient Thistle

a third James Grant. That young soldier 'tis a drummer he be, and a brave one at that."

Everyone cheered the lad and urged James to go on, which he did. "I recalled ta Alexander earlier about our ordeal, and he said that one would have thought that the English would have been kinder a second time considerin' the harsh criticism they got after the first death march. Well I ken assure ye, that dinna happen. They seemed even more dogged ta shove it ta us and used the same old nasty tactics. Well, I reckon, 'twas an easy way ta be rid of a bunch of us, eh?

"We were stripped and marched as cold-bloodedly as ye were, only this time ta hovels all over London rather than ta where they took ye.

"Nary a pardon was granted this time, naught even fer the dyin'. They and countless numbers of our wounded comrades were forced ta either keep up or be slain—and ye ken be sure that any that fell behind were murdered or departed this life on their own.

"They stuck us in any place they could find that could hold us. We were spread all over London and other areas. We waited in those filthy places while many more of our comrades died, until finally, the Council of State decided what they wanted ta do with us. It took weeks and weeks—felt like forever—sounds familiar, eh?

"'Tis sorry I am. I know how sorely this must remind ye of yer own horrors—so much hopelessness, exhaustion, hunger, and death."

John spoke up, "We needed ta hear this James Grant, but 'tis a mean blow indeed. We all feel deeply fer ye and fer all the brave souls who gave their all."

James had more, "Richard Leader received word that they sent a thousand of us Worcester prisoners ta East Anglia, wherever 'tis—yet another thousand or more ta another strange place called Guinea ta work gold mines there. And more were sent ta the Barbados or ta Virginia.

"They started shippin' us out in November, and the Scots ye see here with me were among the two hundred seventy who made it ta Charlestown aboard Captain John Greene's *The John and Sarah*. We were herded below deck where most of the cargo space was taken up with iron, household goods, and other provisions. They crammed us in behind all that. I willna go inta it. Ye know that tale well enough.

"They dinna *auction* us in Boston though—where Alex told me ye were *bartered*. We were lined up ta be *sold* in Charlestown by a merchant named Thomas Kemble. He was given full reign ta get the best price he could fer us so that any profits he made could be invested in goods that would be hawked in the Barbados fer higher prices. 'Tis due ta Richard Leader's project that we ended up here as *indentured servants*. And after findin' ye here, we are very grateful that we did."

Applause filled the room. He waved it aside and went on to add one more bit, "Some say that Worcester's battle ended the Civil Wars, I hope ta God it did. Oliver Cromwell called our defeat the *crownin' mercy* and said that it secured the government. Could be true. I seriously doubt that any Scot's army will try ta confront him again."

"The bastard," Daniel growled. He stamped his foot so hard that he felt the force of it in his hip. "'Tis a miserable tale indeed, James Grant. Sad fer us all."

The Works' Scots embraced their comrades with open arms. Although the locals still held resentments and blamed the Scots for usurping some of their jobs, they eventually came around, and it wasn't long before the newest indentured servants proved themselves, fit in, and regained their health and some self-respect as well.

Chapter 40

A WOMAN SCORNED

BY 1653, urged on by long days of hard work and exhaustion, time in its usual sneaky way had moved along seemingly unnoticed. Business was good, and Richard Leader was proud that his apprentices had worked out well for the mill. He felt sure that they had coped well personally. He hadn't missed the fact that their bodies and minds had healed more than they would have thought possible. It pleased him that most of them had settled in Unity and Berwick and dared to look forward to a new life.

The Great Works mill and *Great Works River* had become household words in the *Massachusetts Bay Colony,* and Leader's management was mostly responsible. Since finishing his contract with the *Saugus Iron Works,* he had been on-site more often, although he still had other enterprises in process, one of which required that he travel to the Barbados. He was restless and looking forward to his next adventure, and since *The Great Works* was doing so well, he felt very comfortable leaving it from time to time.

It was while he was away on one of these business trips that his financial assistant found himself in deep trouble.

Alexander Maxwell enjoyed working with Richard and didn't even mind his additional other duties which included delivering firewood to three houses. One of these houses belonged to George Leader and his wife, Joan Searle Leader.

Joan's father, Andrew Searle, had a shop nearby that was frequented by most of the Scots. Alexander had seen Mrs. Leader there several times, and she had smiled sweetly at him as she looked him over in a hungry way, looks he was very careful not to return.

Whenever he came to fill her wood bin he would see her curtains move, and she would just happen to appear on the porch as he approached it. She always over thanked him for bringing her wood and invited him to sit with her on the porch and share sweets or a drink, which he repeatedly refused, docilely but firmly, and reminded her that such a dalliance would be against her husband's rules for his *slaves*.

She'd just giggle and say, "Oh, Georgie wouldn't mind," and made it obvious to him that she liked his looks and more. She wanted him in her bed and wasn't going to take no for an answer. She was confident that she'd wear him down one of these days.

Alex's only thoughts of her were that she was George's wife, and he didn't consider either of them pleasant to be around. He always tried to stay downwind of her and as far away as possible. She reeked of some kind of fragrance that he couldn't place but reminded him of smells that he would rather forget.

One of these times he was ahead of schedule and brought the wood early. He was just approaching with a wheelbarrow full when he heard a sharp cry. The cries got louder as the Leader house came into view. There on the porch was Joan Leader, looking very frumpy and disheveled in her nightcap and gown, beating on Eliza O'Hara with a cane.

Alex would go to the aid of any damsel in distress, but he had a more personal interest in the lovely Eliza, she was John MacKinney's future wife. The sight of her in such misery made his blood boil. Joan repeatedly struck the helpless lass as hard as she could while incessantly chastising her the whole time.

Alex let go of the wheelbarrow, which tipped over spilling the wood, and rushed to Eliza's aid. Eliza was sobbing, and Joan Leader didn't seem to have any intention of stopping the abuse.

Alexander yelled at Joan to leave Eliza alone. "Drop that stick, ye stinkin' bitch." She looked up in shock, furious to see him so early, and dropped the cane. One of the reason's she was so angry with Eliza was because she wanted her to hurry her chores and leave. Once that was finished, she wanted to get George out of the way, freshen up, and be ready for the wood delivery she expected within the next hour.

A very shaken up Eliza gave Alex a grateful look, shuddered with fright, and ran off still sniveling, hoping that John would not hear of the encounter.

Joan was livid. She had so looked forward to dallying with the handsome Scot, she had even made arrangements for a private place where they could meet. Now he had taken up for that slut and had the audacity to call his boss's wife abhorrent names. He chose to take the side of a *slave* when he could have had a lady! Who did he think he was? She'd show the insolent brute.

Screams filled the air as she went into a frenzy to cover her embarrassment, "Get away from me you . . . ignorant, ungodly . . . Scottish scum."

Alex, his ego offended and his dignity crushed, lashed back with, "Ye gross old cow. Yer nary worthy ta wipe the dirt from Eliza's feet. And ye have nary a right ta call me ungodly. Ye dinna know a bit of me. My father was an Earl and my clan—high, honorable and very Godly. Ye insult me, ye insult my heritage."

Then he remembered where he was and how Richard depended on him. *Zounds,* he thought, *how could I let myself sink ta her level?*

He changed tactics and tried to calm her down, but his ego couldn't resist berating her for beating Eliza at the same time—not a good combination.

Joan Leader was not good at rejection—she would have none of it and started shrieking, "Georgie, Georgie, come quick . . . hurry . . . help, help."

George, annoyed to have been rousted from his nap, ran out of the house, more agitated than concerned. The porch floor planks groaned and his increasingly hysterical wife nearly tripped on her dressing gown as she threw her arms around him, conjured up tears, and cried into his shoulder, "Georgie darlin', my sweet darlin', can you believe it? This animal threw wood all over the yard and then he insulted and attacked me just because I disciplined that poor excuse for a *slave*, as was my duty. Why just look at him—he is still defiant. I was so frightened," she whined. "He threatened me with harm and got me so upset that I feel faint."

George couldn't believe this bit of good fortune. He placed his arms about his distraught wife, and the wheels turned in his brain as to how he could take advantage of the situation and get even with the Scot who irritated him in every way.

"Now, now, Joan, sweetie, you just go inside and refresh yourself. You'll need rest, my dear. I'll have Dr. Lawrence brought over to give you some relief."

Joan Leader dabbed at her dry eyes for her husband's benefit, gave Alexander a vicious scornful look, and disappeared into the house. Once inside she ran immediately to the living room window, pulled back the curtains, clutched her breast in an outraged gesture, and peered out to make sure that the uncooperative *slave* got his due.

George turned on Alex with a satisfied smirk on his face, "So, Alexander Maxwell," he sneered, "I can't believe that you would sink to something this depraved. How dare you attack my wife? You filthy pig. You're not even fit to speak her name.

"What made you think that you could forget your place? No matter what my pious brother says, you're a stinking *slave*, nothing more. I own you—you lousy piece of crud—and you'll soon see how that works."

Not wishing to dishonor Richard in any way, Alex bowed his head to humble himself. "I be sorry Mr. Leader, Yer utterly right. I fergot myself. It willna happen again." He knew that he was in deep trouble, and he made an unsuccessful attempt to placate the irate George by acting as contrite as he could manage.

"I've always thought that Richard was giving you more authority than you deserved. You of all the *slaves* should know better than pull something like this after the affection my brother has shown you.

"I believe you're about to learn who's in charge here—and learn it the hard way." Leader roughly grabbed Alex, who instinctively struggled to escape his grasp. Harvey, who had heard the yelling from where he had been clearing a ditch just down the road, ran up and with his help the Scot was subdued and hauled off.

"I will see to it that you get your just desserts. Joan was right—you are nothing but an animal." Then he and Harvey threw the irate Scot into a cell and left him to ponder his fate while they gathered up enough of George's colleagues and friends to help throw together a speedy trial.

No time was wasted. The cunning George impressed upon his peers that this was a very serious offense, and one that should not be put up with in any way lest it lead to worse offenses on their own loved ones. He made a big point of saying, "My brother prefers to give his *slaves* special treatment and jobs, but this is a good example of what a waste of time that is and of how gross and low they really are."

Anyone within sight or earshot had been gathered up to witness the makeshift hearing. Alexander had no chance to speak up and the exceptionally prompt and unanimous verdict was $GUILTY$, with a good public lashing ordered as punishment. Not all of the jury shared George's interpretation of *slave vs. indentured servant*, or even Richard's choice of *apprentice*, so it was also ordered that any time the defendant spent recovering was to be made up in addition to his current *bondage*, and if he ever caused any more trouble, he would be sent off immediately to the Barbados. Only his known relationship with Richard Leader saved him from being on the next ship.

George spoke boisterously and insisted that they make an example of this gross offence. He pressed on and insisted that the *villain's* punishment be dealt out immediately. The judge complied— *"Alexander Maxwell is to be flogged for grosse offence and exobinant and abusive carages towards his master and his missus."*

Alexander Maxwell, with his hands tied firmly behind his back, was dragged off toward the square.

Chapter 41

THE GREEN MONSTER

THE NUMBER of lashes had been set at thirty on the bare skin, and Alex was booed as he was hauled off to a small straight sapling next to the horses' watering troth. His shirt was ripped off, and he was roughly yanked into position facing the scruffy but strong tree and was bound tautly around back of the trunk.

As the injured party, George was entitled to select the punisher, so he offered Ralph Taylor the whip, but he feigned that his hands were too sore. Tom Eagan refused with an equally lame excuse. Able and willing to do the deed, Harvey Urban stepped up.

Pleased that he had drawn blood on the first snap of the whip, Harvey prolonged the delivery of the thirty lashes to Alexander's bare back, purposely halting after each blow to ensure that as much pain as possible had its full effect. Some spectators cheered him on, but a surprising number of locals as well as indentured servants, whose attendance was mandatory, just stared in silence.

Alex stood as straight as he could, gritted his teeth, and made up his mind that he would not scream or grovel. As pain worsened, he bit his lips and tongue until they bled, but he did not cry out. After twenty-five lashes had shredded his bloody back, he passed out and his body slumped down.

The crowd called out, "Enough, enough," but George gave the order for Harvey to continue. Happy to oblige, Harvey nodded and struck Alex's unconscious body with five more hard strokes. The crowd booed and began to disperse shaking their heads in revulsion. George smirked, raised his head in defiance, and savored his private victory over his lowly slave.

John had just returned from a repair job down at the dam when loud voices caught his curiosity and caused him to leave the path and come up to see what the ruckus was all about. He couldn't believe his eyes when he barely recognized Alex all bloodied and sagging down the trunk of a tree. Ralph and Tom grabbed him as he tried to go to his friend's defense. He struggled fiercely—bellowed, screamed, and lashed out at them—but the two strong men held him firmly.

"There's nothin' you can do for him, George made sure that the whole business was all tidy and legal. Alexander was found guilty and the judge ordered him to be flogged for gross offence and exorbitant and abusive carages towards his master."

"Yup, that's right, George testified that Alex had badly offended his wife and him."

"Nay, that kenna be. 'Tis he breathin'? Will he live? Loose me up, both o'ye."

"Yup, he is alive—barely. Don't go near him yet and we will release you. Eh-ya, I think Dan is workin' in the vineyard. Go fetch him. George should be gone by the time you get back. Then Tom and I will be here to help you get Alex down and care for him. He'll need plenty of mendin'. Yup, that's right, by gorra, he surely will."

John could hardly control himself but ran as fast as his bad leg would take him to the vineyard. Daniel was nowhere to be found, but a worker told him that he had seen him leave about an hour before. He said Daniel had waved and yelled that he was headed over by the chopper to gather some kindling.

It took him longer than he would have liked, but John finally caught up with Dan, gave him the bad news, and continued to fill him in as they rushed back toward the whipping post. George had lingered a bit to gloat, then had strutted away, much to Ralph's relief. He knew how the stout man would fare if Dan and John got a hold of him.

The friends worked their way through what was left of the thinning crowd that had wandered away from Alex, who was left to hang by his wrists, unconscious with the full weight of his ravaged body pulling heavily on his shoulders.

True to their word, Ralph and Tom were standing by, and with Dan and John's help, they carefully cut Alex down. While others carried him to his cabin and gently placed him face down on his bed, Tom made a rush for the doctor and found him a short way from George Leader's house where he had calmed Mrs. Leader, given her a sedative, and was headed home for the day.

"Ye'll need yer God and the thistle now, Alex—yer back 'tis a bloody mess and ye've broken ribs." John muttered as he ogled exposed bones and gaping wounds.

Alex groaned and tried to move, but could not, and flopped back down. He turned his head to Daniel and made an attempt to speak.

"Whoa, my *bráthair*, ye need some doctorin' before ye ken get up. Yer back looks like chopped liver. Dinna fight it, ye need yer strength—shut yer face now and lay still so ye ken get treated and start ta mend."

"I shouldna let him bait me. The bastard, I couldna help myself," he moaned.

Dan and John each rubbed a bruised arm and agreed. "'Tis nary a doubt about that." Dan spoke for both. "We know how long and hard George has been lookin' fer somethin' ta wield over ye. Ferget it fer now, *bráthair*—just get this back healin'."

Dr. Lawrence rushed in with a very out-of-breath, exhausted Tom at his heels, took one look at the sorry looking back, and shook his head. "I don't have much that will ease that raw pain. He's been severely wounded. Those lashes are from a whip with a metal tip, and they are very deep and serious. He'll face the fight of his life to recover from this thrashing, and that is if there is no infection.

"The best thing we can do is to get him liquored up before he regains consciousness so you can help me trim up this mess and cover it with salve. Tom, Ralph—can you get us some strong spirits? . . . No wait . . . Tom, would you run and fetch my wife?"

The worried men looked at each other, Ralph took one look at the wasted Tom and said, "Umm . . . eh . . . Yup—you get the booze, Tom, and I'll go fer Mrs. Lawrence. You know where we keep the boss's extra stash—get some of that special Scottish whiskey—that seems very fittin' and he'll never miss it."

A relieved Tom returned shortly with the medication. It wasn't an easy task to get anything into Alex, but John and Tom helped hold him on his side while Dan held his mouth open and the doctor poured small doses of the spirits down his throat. The fact that he wasn't used to hard liquor made things even more difficult. He coughed and choked at every attempt, but finally, with patience and impatience, they got him to swallow enough to deaden the pain. He didn't flinch when the doctor and the newly designated medical team carefully applied the smelly salve.

The doctor emphasized that the patient would need constant care, and they were all relieved when Ralph returned with Mrs. Lawrence. She took a look at Alex, then a dismayed glance at her husband, and said that she would be happy to stay and watch over the patient for as long as she was needed.

"Thanks, Catherine, you're a gem," the doctor tilted his head and gave his wife a peck on the cheek, "We've got a rough case here. I knew I could count on you."

"I'll do the best I can, Sam," she answered with an uncertain smile.

The recovery was arduous and painful. The wounds appeared to get uglier and festered as pus started oozing from the deeper cuts. Days passed. They were all frightened when Alex spiked a fever and became delirious.

"If he can fend off pneumonia, he'll have a chance. Continue the treatments and keep him very warm, my dear. No sense bleeding him; he's lost enough blood already." Catherine nodded and pressed the doctor's hand before he left to attend other patients.

From time to time Alex rallied, muttered through his teeth that he'd like to kill both George Leader and his wife. Catherine assured the worried Scots that it was just the fever talking. They weren't so sure when he rattled on, "She's a bitch, John. She abused Eliza, and she insulted me and my family."

It was four more days and long nights before the fever broke and the doctor felt that Alex was out of danger. It took an additional two weeks before he could sit up for any length of time or even think of lying on his back. He constantly insisted that he was ready to resume his duties, but the doctor firmly told him that he wouldn't allow it until he was certain of a full recovery. By this time, a less appealing Scot had been assigned the job of wood delivery to George Leader's residence.

When Richard Leader returned from his voyage to the Barbados, he heard about Alex's whipping and his brother's part in it—he was mad as hell. He had come to depend on his financial assistant. He had not been aware of his brother's deep-seated resentment of the Scots, although he was familiar with his jealous nature and well acquainted with the whims of his quirky sister-in-law. It finally dawned on him that George had taken his friendship with Alex as a personal rejection and affront.

Richard caught up with Alex as he sat by the river where Mrs. Lawrence had him helped to a bench every good day to get some fresh air. He apologized for his brother's harsh actions, asked Alex if he would carry on as his assistant, and he assured him that he would be honored and pleased to stay on. "I need you more than ever now, my friend. Let's put this nastiness behind us. I vow that I will make it up to you.

"If you will set aside a space in your great room, I will furnish a desk and cupboard that will make it into a small office for you to work from. That would keep you and George out of each other's hair, and be a big help to me."

"I kenna think of a thing that would please me more. As always, I am happy ta help ye in any way I ken. And, Richard Leader . . . 'Tis grand ta have ye home safe!"

Chapter 42

**THE CHANGING WORKS
NOVEMBER 1655**

MOST OF the *indentured servants* from the Worcester battle accepted Richard Leader's offer to stay on at *The Works* once they had completed their service. True to his word, Richard provided cabins for them. *The Works* continued to run smoothly, and the Scots worked diligently and constantly looked forward to the day they would be free men.

Alexander's body had healed, and he had seemed to be his old self again—then his sparkle began to fade. Unusually quiet at supper on a cold, snowy evening, he picked at his favorite mess hall beans until he could stand it no longer—he pushed his bowl aside and blurted out, "I dinna have anythin' but bad news this night."

"Zounds—from the way ye sound, 'tis best we hear it straight away. I dinna reckon 'twill get any better fer the waitin'."

"When ye hear it ye willna josh. Ye'll wish ye nary had heard it as do I." He drew a deep breath and let loose, "Richard Leader has made plans ta leave *The Great Works* totally by the end of this year. He has already sold all his dealin's ta John Becx, Richard Hutchinson, Colonel William Beale, and Captain Thomas Alderne."

This would take a while to sink in, "Be ye sure, Alex?" A stunned Daniel stammered, "Mahap 'tis some mistake."

"Nay, Dan, 'tis fer certain. 'Tis definite he's goin'. Whatever 'tis that he's inta 'tis a mystery ta me, but 'tis sure that he has scheduled a trip ta the Barbados. Seems he and Thomas Broughton have a partnership goin' that involves some crops on those islands. 'Twas the real reason fer all the visits ta Salmon Falls.

"Damn, 'tis shitey indeed," John grunted. "I ponder where that leaves us."

"He told me nary ta worry on that account. He assured me that his *apprentices* as he has always called us, would be taken care of before he left."

The word spread quickly and the Scots were deeply disappointed. They had come to rely on Richard. Nevertheless, when the day came they wished him well as he went off to carry out his latest project. His constant search for new and more challenging adventures was no secret.

George would have more authority, although by now they all knew to keep a low profile around him. The London people had selected their own financial assistant, much to Alex's relief. He didn't want more conflict. He had plans of his own.

Ever a man of his word, Richard made sure before he left *The Great Works* that his Scottish *indentured servants* would have the grants of land he had promised them from the colony. When the first land grant came through in early 1656, it was made out to Alexander Maxwell. Along with the help of his friends, he had a house put up on it as soon as the mud season ended. His land was in a picturesque spot along the *Works River* in Berwick. James Warren and John Taylor were offered grants in this area as well. These three grants had been handpicked by Richard Leader as his way of saying thanks for special services he had appreciated.

Down the river in Unity, grants went to John Neal, Daniel Ferguson, and others. Most of the Scots who had arrived on the *Unity* had been granted land on the river near *The Great Works*, which is where Alexander would have chosen on his own; however, he couldn't find fault with the land Richard had chosen for him and had to admit it was better in every way than the place he'd picked. Many of the Battle of Worcester survivors would be his neighbors in Berwick.

Daniel was too stubborn to accept a grant. He felt it would tie him down, and he was still adamant about returning to Scotland.

John refused one also because he and Eliza had made plans to marry, and she did not want to live anywhere near *The Great Works*

The Resilient Thistle

once they were free and wed. "The further away we can get from this place, the better 'twill be for the both of us."

This was a change for John. He had been thinking about staying on at *The Works*, but Eliza's aversion to it sealed the deal for him. He had some thoughts, but he was not sure where they should go. Then the unexpected happened.

Ansel Jackson, a former fisherman from Gloucester had taken a job at *The Great Works*. While Alexander was processing Ansel's paperwork, they started discussing boats and fishing. He mentioned some fishermen that he admired, and an Abraham O'Hara, who fished with his son, Frank, was among them.

A light went off in Alex's head, "O'Hara? Now why does that ring a bell? Of course, 'tis Eliza, John's soon ta be wife."

As soon as he could—he *just happened* to walk by the laundry where he knew Eliza would be, and he slowly worked up the nerve to ask her about her family.

She sadly told him that her mother had died while they were in captivity and that she had a father and brother but had no idea what had become of them.

He would hate to get her hopes up for nil, but then he thought, *If 'tis them—this could be life changin' fer her,* so he bluntly asked, "What 'tis their trade?"

She didn't hesitate, "Oh, they are dyed-in-the-wool fishermen." Her face lit up as she thought of them, "Abraham and Frank O'Hara are the best there is."

Treading carefully, Alex went on, "Well . . . hum . . . ah . . . more 'n likely 'tis a coincidence, ye know . . . but Ansel Jackson just moved here from Gloucester. We were shootin' the breeze while I filled out his paperwork, and he started tellin' me about some of his fellow fishermen and the names Abraham and Frank O'Hara came up."

Eliza jumped up and nearly knocked Alex over, while the dress she had just carefully scrubbed fell back into the wash tub and splashed them both.

She started laughing, shaking, and crying all at once, "Do you know what you're sayin', Alexander Maxwell? 'Tis them!" Eliza was so elated that she could hardly go on, "It has to be them. 'Tis my Da and my brother, Frank. For certain that's who he spoke of.

"Oh! Thanks be ta God—I'm forever grateful to you, Alexander. They're alive! How many O'Hara's do you think could be a fisherman named Abraham? Tell me more! Tell me more!"

The laundry was forgotten, and all she could think of was finding John to tell him of her good fortune—that Alex had stumbled onto her father and brother, and they were not only alive, but had ended up in Gloucester, which was not nearly as far away as Ireland.

"Bless you, Alex, what do I do now? I know, John, yes, of course—John will know what to do."

John didn't know, but Ansel Jackson did. He had a brother, Samuel, who was still in the fishing business in Gloucester, and he was more than happy to help.

It took some time because the O'Hara's were out fishing down around Cape Cod, but once they returned, Sam made contact with Abraham and confirmed that he and Frank were indeed Eliza's family. Disappointed as they were on hearing the news of the death of Abraham's wife, the two of them were thrilled to learn that Eliza had survived.

Communication was set up, and the parties shared their stories and convinced themselves of their good luck. Yet another surprise—it didn't take the O'Hara's long to send their future son-in-law an invitation to join them in the fishing business. Abraham even offered to get a boat lined up and ready for John by the time the couple received their freedom and were wed.

Except for the best forgotten voyage in the bowels of the *Unity*, John had always loved the sea and the idea of having his own boat roused his heart. Fishing had always been a part of his life in Tobermorey, and he had missed and yearned for it, but never believed he could get back to it. The thought of how much Eliza would love to be close to her family confirmed it for him.

Once the deal was sealed, Alexander convinced John and Eliza to be married in the little church by the river before they left to start their new life in Gloucester. He also suggested, in the meantime while they all awaited their freedom, that Dan and John move in with him. Liza was required to stay on at the *indentured* women's house.

"'Tis just the thing," he encouraged. "Though we all wish we'd be leavin' tomorrow. 'Tis still time that we must serve, and I dinna have ta tell ye that George has increased the rent on the company houses a lot. If we all share the house ye helped me build on my land grant in Berwick, we ken keep workin', share expenses, and save up more money until our freedom 'tis a reality—'twill make the perfect bridge fer all of us."

"Dang it, Alex, ye drive a hard bargain. What say ye, John?" Without a moment's hesitation, John and Dan both agreed. They brought their belongings over to the new house on their next free day. Alexander kept his downstairs bedroom, while Daniel and John set up their goods at opposite ends of the roomy upstairs loft.

They all respected Alex's plan. He made sense. It was indeed a great way to tide them over comfortably while they awaited the freedom that was still a few years off.

"Freedom. Dare we even ponder on it? Ken it be? And, what will it mean?"

"Life, John, our dear *bráthair*—LIFE—a free new life fer all of us." A big smile opened on John's face as he thought of a life with Eliza. He grabbed Daniel, then Alex, and flabbergasted them both with a giant bear hug.

"*Zounds,* John—bugga off! Fer sure 'tis yer wits that be gone at last."

The idea of freedom becoming actuality within reach at last made their heads spin, and they hardly dared breathe. They tried to appear calm and confident, but their stomachs were secretly filled with butterflies, doubts, and impatience.

Chapter 43

THE THISTLE CALLS

JOHN'S PLANS for himself and Eliza had put a slight hitch in Alexander's, and he certainly couldn't fault him for that. So, as freedom drew near, he revised his vision and hoped that Daniel would be a part of it. The opportunity to speak with him alone came up on a clear fall night after John went out to meet Eliza.

"Daniel, me *bráth* . . . ," Alexander started out.

Daniel's eyes rolled from side to side, he smiled ruefully and said, "Hold it right there—*bráthair*, eh? What's rattlin' about in that head of yers now? By gosh and by gorra, I ken smell it—yer plannin' somethin' fishy and ye want me tangled in it."

Alexander returned the laugh and asked, "Ye know me that well, eh?"

Dan's grin and nod gave Alex his answer, but that didn't stop him from going on, "'Tis well aware I am that ye have a lot on yer mind and that John's plan has ye shaken up." He paused a moment, smiled, and quipped, "Ye know what Rob would say, *'tis perturbed I am as well*—and indeed, 'tis bitter sweet—as painful as losin' that dear friend all over again, but 'tis nary a doubt that we both agree with John's decision ta take advantage of the chance Eliza's Da has offered —eh?"

"Agreed, nary an argument so far, *bráthair*." Daniel raised his eyebrows, cocked his head, and smiled suspiciously.

"*Zounds,* we both know his leavin' willna be easy. But, in spite of our deep friendship, neither of us jumped at the chance ta take him and Eliza up on the kind offer they made when they invited us ta share their home in Gloucester. The simple truth 'tis—the fishin' business—'tis *naught* fer us. Ye know we'd make miserable fishermen and John knows it as well. So . . . tell me, truth be told, what are yer plans, Danny lad?"

Daniel didn't hesitate, "Scotland, Alex, ye know it well, 'tis Scotland on my lips and in my heart every moment of the day and night," he repeated. "I dinna reckon I could return there once my Mora and my family were gone—but now I kenna abide anythin' else. 'Tis where I was the happiest, and 'tis where I will feel closest ta them."

"Aw, Dan, I know that, but ye also must know in yer heart that the English will nary let ye go back. How would ye even begin ta start over back there anyway?"

"I was hopin' I might find my Da and work with him again. Now that the war 'tis over, things might be quieter, and I feel I ken be of some comfort and help ta him."

"Dream on then, and inquire about it as ye should—but once ye are sure ye kenna go, would ye consider goin' in with me?"

Daniel really wasn't listening, "I've already asked around ta find out how we Scots could return home if we had resources and could pay our own way. Nary one gave me much hope, and I was reminded that Cromwell and his hate fer Highlanders are both alive and well. Anyway, 'tis a step further I've taken it and contacted the *Scots Heritage Society*. They've set up a group in Boston ta aid Scots brought here against their will like us. I dinna know if any help 'tis, but I have ta try."

"Dan, Billy Stuart has a wife and four wee ones back in Scotland—Peter Grant has three *bairns*—as do others. They willna let them go back, why would ye think ye would be different?"

A glum Daniel looked up at Alex, then down at his feet. No answer.

"Daniel MacDhughill, listen up ta me, will ye? Ye know how we reveled in our scoutin' trips about this area while we looked fer the straightest tallest trees ta blaze fer ship masts? Ye recall how it reminded us of Scotland as we traveled down toward the sea?"

Dan scratched his head, "I reckon I know where ye mean—mayhap."

"Well, I've spoken ta ye before about my searchin' around those parts. I've found that most of the region 'tis level, but there are three hills that rise a hundred feet or more above the sea. I took a fancy ta the one in Brixham—'tis called Cider Hill. I checked with the surveyors, and they told me that the York tidal river runs right by it, up seven miles from the ocean—beautiful that—with craggy cliffs and sandy beaches.

"The land around 'tis as much like Scotland as ken be—mayhap, even better. 'Tis grand, Dan, with good soil fer plantin' corn, wheat, fruit, vegetables—whatever a bloke could want, and 'tis a lot of prime wood—oak, maple, and pine about."

Daniel interrupted, "And, I am sure ye know 'tis a short growin' season it has as well, eh? Wolves, bears, freezin' arse winters—and ay, eh—best ye nary forget the rattlesnakes—one jumped out at me just last week." He looked thoughtfully at Alex and asked, "I dinna grasp it—'tis a snag fer ye stayin' on in Berwick?"

He was caught off guard when Alex answered, "Ay, fer me 'tis, *bráthair*. In any case, I've laid down the first payment—'tis done."

"Holy shite, Alex, ye dinna. Nay, it kenna be. Have ye gone completely daft?"

The chuckle in Alex's throat grew into a thunderous roar as he watched Daniel's mouth fall open and his eyes bug out. Once his laughter petered out, he asserted, "Nay, I dinna be daft and ay, indeed, I contracted fer it. My life 'tis tied ta my dream. Ye know how I've salted away every penny I could, and ye know as well that Richard was sorry fer me because he figured out that I was flogged fer naught—and 'tis why he made sure I got that fine land grant we're livin' on here in Berwick.

"All well and good, and 'tis grateful I am, but 'tis nary the place fer me. So, I made plans ta sell the grant along with the cabin and put the earnin's, with the most of my savin's, inta my land on Cider Hill—ta improve and build on it!

"Our comrades deserve great respect and admiration fer makin' Unity and Berwick into such laudable hamlets, but I dinna aim ta spend the rest of my life in either of those places. Their namesakes alone would always hark back the misery we went through and the dead we left behind. So, fer me . . . nay. I kenna—I willna—do it.

He shook off the musings and got back on track, "Dan, I have a great need fer ye ta walk on my land, get the feel of it and look it over with me. 'Tis sure that workin' it willna be easy, but I dinna be a wee one. I know that winter lingers inta the heart of spring, that the river usually stays frozen over till at least then, and ay, it could snow inta May and hang around in the woods fer even longer. But . . . 'tis nary frozen now . . . and we could fit in a walk and a take a look at it. In fact . . . 'tis a scoutin' trip logged in fer next mornin's sun up. What say ye?"

This was by far the happiest he'd seen Alex since before Dunbar. The jaunty aura and the lively eyes were back. There was no way that he could even think of hurting that dream. "Now that ye've described it so well, I reckon I recall that stretch—and indeed, 'tis truly fine. Ay, ye old goat, ta be sure, I'll mosey over there with ye."

The next morning opened onto a stunning September day. Its breathtaking wide open blue sky, clear as crystal, brightened the countryside and enhanced its vibrancy. The route that Daniel had taken more or less for granted when he was simply scouting for logs looked quite different as he made an effort to take in the whole picture in the way his friend had portrayed it. By the time they arrived at the Maxwell parcel of land Daniel could understand why Alex considered it a special place.

He couldn't resist. He kept Alex in suspense while he turned, twisted, and over-inspected the land from all views. When he finally called a halt to his charade, he grinned and admitted, "I must say yer right, Alex, 'tis incredible. Standin' on this hill and gazin' out over the marsh ta the river . . . well . . . 'tis a remarkable site indeed."

Alexander breathed a sigh of relief then put on his most serious look, "'Tis friends we've been fer a long time now, and we've gone through more than most men ever do in a lifetime. I felt sure ye'd take ta my land, Dan. But ye know how much I value and trust yer opinion, so I had ta hear it from the horse's mouth—standin' right here next ta where I intend ta build, settle myself in, and create a refuge, ye might say. 'Tis what I've been tryin' ta get through ta ye—our own hamlet—Scotland Parish. Danny, the thistle cries out fer us ta build a fresh new Scotland where the strength and fortitude of our heritage will shine and brighten this new world."

Daniel plopped himself down on the soft grass and thought, *that was quite a mouthful ta be sure, the old fart's nary at a loss fer words, eh?* But he couldn't deny that Alex's enthusiasm had made an impression.

Interpreting the silence as a sign that his friend had softened Alex followed up with, "I mentioned part of my plan ta Richard before he left. He dinna say much—I am sure he hoped that I would stay on in Berwick—but he did mention that more grants will be available ta the likes of us, in Unity and Berwick—and in this area as well. We ken do this, Dan. Birth my dream right here. And soon, Scotland Parish will be a reality."

Daniel took in the wide sweeping view that sparkled beneath the pristine sky. As he looked down at the river intermingled and defined by the clean-cut lines of the marsh, it tugged at his heart, and he had to admit that it reminded him of home. The trees radiant in their autumn colors, the welcoming hills and gentle stillness encircled and tempted him.

He shook it off and heaved a big sigh, "Ay, Alex, 'tis truly glad I be that I've come ta see yer land. 'Tis certain that I love it, and I admire yer idea, but 'tis Scotland that I wanna get myself back ta—Scotland—the home I carry in my heart."

"Ay, and I kenna be the only one who has told ye, Daniel, that the English will naught let ye go back. 'Tis banished by Cromwell and his cronies we've been. When are ye goin' ta get that through yer head?"

His resolve wavered, but his stubborn side won out, "I kenna give up my dream any more than ye ken quit yers. Moreover, even if I wanted ta throw in with ye, I nary could afford it."

"Dinna whimper, Dan, ye kenna bullshite a bullshiter—ye could do it, and easily—'tis part of my plan. I need help. Look, I could pay ye instead of strangers, and ye could save up fer your own place. That would help us both and get the vision underway."

A gentle breeze came up from the river, glided through trees that bowed and answered by rustling their leaves, but Alex didn't notice, he simply pressed on hoping to convince his friend. "We've learned so much from our *slave* days or *indentured* time, or whatever they want ta call it ta try ta disguise the truth. Fer sure—a chunk's been ripped out of our lives, but we ken make it all pay off fer us.

"We get along and work well together. We trust each other and ken do just about anythin' we put our heads ta. 'Tis wiser we've grown since we were *shipped* here—we know how ta harvest huge trees, prepare heavy lumber, and shape it inta beams, logs, boards—and so much more. We ken deal with all types of wood and most metals, we ken do the work, and all we need 'tis close by. After so much hurt and brutality—'tis so welcome, Daniel. We have a chance ta make somethin' fer ourselves and others."

There was no stopping him. It was obvious that he had put a lot of time and research into his plan. He pointed, "Gaze over there—do ye see that cabin? 'Tis mine—comes with the land. Thomas Moulton owned it before me. He lived in it along with his wife and two wee ones. We could fix it up and live there while we're gettin' started. I've already walked off my house's cellar hole. We could start ta dig whenever we could fit in the time. Dinna pass this up, Dan. We ken have it all. What say ye?"

"I love the madness of yer soul, Alexander Maxwell. I promise ye that ponder it I will. And I thank ye fer yer kind thoughts ta include me in yer plan."

Chapter 44

THE EMERGING VISION

AFTER THE visit to Cider Hill, Daniel intensified his efforts to find a way back to Scotland. He ran into more dead ends and got nowhere with James Grant or the *Scots Charitable Society*. They made him the offer of a small loan to help him get started once he had collected his release papers, but that was all they could do. It was the same story everywhere—Cromwell would not let the Highlanders return to their homeland. They had been deemed traitors, were not wanted, and that was that.

"And . . . ," James impressed upon him, "hear me well, Daniel, 'tis sorry I be, but yer wastin' yer time and mine, lad. 'Tis nary only Cromwell that willna let ye back, 'tis the *Council of War* and their cronies as well. We are deemed thorns in their sides—as well as traitors. They see us as bitter good-fer-nothins'—menaces and scallywags that could stir up old conflicts—they willna take the risk that any one of us could get loose back home ta threaten their peace."

Obviously distraught and discouraged, Daniel acknowledged, "I hear ye, James—AGAIN—but I reckon, 'tis yet another battle lost fer me." As he walked away, his thoughts echoed his thwarted hopes. *That surely blew away any chance fer me ta be gone from here—mayhap 'tis meant ta—aw, nay, that kenna be.* He sat down under the nearest tree and bent over with his head in his hands, then, like the sun bursting out from a cloud it hit him, *Zounds—more than naught—'tis the danged thistle that calls—Alex swears ta heaven 'tis. I dinna know* *why, but 'tis fated I seem ta be—it appears I be meant ta join that befuddlin'—bamboozlin'—flabbergastin'—**bráthair**—ta help create the new Scotland. That schemin' foxy geezer—he finally wormed me inta it.*

That evening John was out as usual with Eliza, and it didn't take much coaxing to get Alex to walk over to the mess hall and enjoy a good meal of beans and hot bread topped off with apple pie. Alex said nothing, but watched him with a puzzled look, curious as to why his friend was so quiet and serious-minded. A perplexed Dan had painstakingly mulled over the day's events. He ate slowly and rethought them once more. When he was finally ready, he pushed his plate aside, eyeballed Alex, and flat out informed him, "'Tis home I still hope ta return ta one day—but in the meantime 'tis honored I'd be ta help ye get the new Scotland underway."

Caught off guard, Alex breathed deeply and murmured a quiet prayer that ended in a long sigh. For a moment he sat in silence, as though frozen in place, and just stared at Daniel. Once he shook himself loose, an irrepressibly wild smile exploded over his handsome face. The bench toppled over as he jumped up, grabbed his friend by the shoulders, clapped him on the back, and exclaimed, "And, 'tis honored indeed I am ta have ye, Daniel MacDhughill. Thanks be ta God, 'tis a good choice, ye willna regret it. Feels good—dinna it?"

"A bit better than I reckoned it would," he grudgingly admitted, "Fer the most part, Alexander Maxwell, I'm lookin' forward ta givin' it a go." Alex was too emotional to say more. A rare occasion.

• • •

Since Richard Leader's departure, the inside information Alexander was once privy to was no longer available to him; however, he still managed to keep abreast of most of the news through *The Works* grapevine. A rare plum fell into his hands one afternoon in late October when word reached *The Works* that Oliver Cromwell was dead.

After work that night, Alex sought out Daniel and John and found them at their old table in the crowded mess hall. There was no way he could wait. He burst out with the information straightaway. He let the news sink in before he blurted out, "Ay, 'tis true comrades, 'tis a great day—*Old Warts and All*—dead—died of complications from malaria and typhoid fever, so 'tis said—and get this—it happened on September third—INDEED! Ay, ye heard that right, SEPTEMBER THIRD—on the very same month and day as the battles of Dunbar and Worcester! And—from the typhoid that took so many of our own as well. Dinna ye reckon 'tis a wee speck of justice there?"

"A wee speck, 'tis indeed—our lads deserve more than that—but it surely sits well that his nasty hate 'tis finally ended," Daniel asserted amid shouts and cheers that filled the mess hall. He rubbed his head to try to blot out bitter thoughts that ran through his mind, but an especially raw one gripped his heart. *It would have pleased me more had it come sooner and that he had taken all of his cronies with him. But, ahh—'tis fittin' indeed ta have another closin' on the hell that was.*

He wasn't alone—memories of atrocities flooded back from the depths every Scot there constantly strove to rise above. Alexander called for a toast to their lost home and comrades. Then he roused them all with a familiar song and soon they all joined in, including his musical friends on the juice harp, harmonica, and violin. The music comforted them, settled them down, and brought them back to the present. Finally, Alex raised his coffee mug and offered a sort of benediction, "We will nary forget the horror of the loss of our comrades. Now and forever 'tis embedded in our hearts and 'tis nary a way ta shake it." His fellow Scots banged their tin mugs loudly on the tables.

George Grey took up the torch, "So, let us hold those memories dear. Hark back ta the lads with pride and hail them by makin' our future worthy of their sacrifice."

They did just that—tucked their past close in their hearts, dug into their work, made the best of their plight, and before they knew it, the day that had seemed as far away as eternity became a reality. The first batch of Scots who had been auctioned off in Boston and had been trudged through the snow to Newichawannock just after Christmas in the last days of 1650—were finally free men. They had all dreamed and hoped, but none had dared believe that it would actually happen, especially once Richard Leader had left *The Great Works.*

The *indentured servants* from the battle of Worcester had another year to serve, and Alexander had heard via the grapevine that Salmon River's *indentured servants* were still in bondage. Sadly, he had been unable to contact anyone there since Richard Leader left, and in spite of repeated attempts, could obtain no information about Robert Junkins—there was just no news as where he was, his well-being or when he would be released.

Alexander blamed George Leader, he knew that George had access to information at Salmon Falls as well as the other saw mills, but there was no doubt that he would be the last one to get any news from that man or his office.

Uplifted Scots had their papers in hand—evidence of their freedom—the reality gradually began to sink in, although suspicions and fears lingered at the back of their heads. Could this be true or a trick? Could their freedom be taken back? Slowly they accepted their good fortune and began to unwind.

True to form, George Leader made sure that Alex stayed on to serve the six weeks he had lost because of his flogging and recovery.

Many Scots, like John had made plans to marry women they had built relationships with during their servitude. Some married daughters of foremen or locals they had worked for, and they settled down to raise families and etch out new lives.

Christmas, freedom, and John and Eliza's wedding were ingredients for a wonderful celebration. Because Alex had an in with the pastor he was able to arrange for them to be married in the little church by the river.

A radiant Eliza O'Hara was led down the aisle by her father, Abraham. Her eyes focused on an outrageously anxious John MacKinney. The gentle giant's wild ginger hair had been shaped up, parted neatly in the middle, and smacked with a bit of gunk to hold it securely down. His gold eyes gleamed as he shakily placed the ring on his bride's finger.

A proud Daniel did well as best man. He choked up when memories shook him, and he stumbled about a bit—but no one seemed to notice. The touching service was made even more so when Alex's rich voice filled the air with Eliza's favorite hymn, and all joined in to freely sing Christmas carols that were still outlawed in Scotland.

The bride's brother, Frank O'Hara, sent his love and a keg of rum, but had stayed in Gloucester to oversee the fishing business the family's welfare depended on.

Catherine Lawrence, the doctor's wife, had become close to all of them since she nursed Alex back to health after the flogging that had nearly killed him. She and Daniel organized a wedding reception at Alex's home in Berwick. They decorated the place, sampled all the food, and Daniel cracked open the keg of rum with perhaps a bit too much gusto—a facade to cover the fact that he couldn't tolerate spirits.

Dr. Lawrence helped Catherine dish up a beautiful cake she had baked and decorated for the occasion. It served to top off a delicious meal of roasted wild turkey, mashed potatoes, carrots, turnips, and gravy that Alex and Daniel had paid the mess hall cooks a hefty fee to prepare. It was a whale of a party, and a huge success.

The bride and groom slipped out early to take advantage of a break in the frosty weather and headed off for their new life in Gloucester. Eliza sat straight in the wagon and laid her head on her husband's shoulder. As he held his wife close, John couldn't resist a glance back at his two best friends. He smiled at them, gave a nod of his head and a final wave before they disappeared in a swirl of light snow.

Daniel and Alexander stood like a couple of statues and watched them go. They hated to see John leave and were horribly upset, although they tried not to show it; however, the joy that radiated from the happy couple made it all worthwhile. John's promise to stay in touch wasn't enough to console them, but they had all made their choices and life moved on.

Chapter 45

GENESIS

AT ALEX'S urging, Daniel had repaired the cabin and moved to Cider Hill in the early days of January shortly after John's wedding. It didn't take him long to settle in. Soon, wood from the pile he and Alex had stockpiled crackled in the fireplace and the welcome heat spread throughout. Before long, the cupboards had been stocked and Daniel had ordered some of the building supplies they had agreed upon. When the weather permitted, he got down to the outside work at hand. When the snow and cold kept him inside, he put his considerable carpentry skills to work and made furniture.

In the meantime, Alex took extra care to avoid George Leader while he worked off his extra weeks. It was a torturous time that seemed to drag on forever, but with the sale of his land grant and house in Berwick finalized, he had everything ready for the big day and as soon as he stuffed his freedom papers in his pocket he took advantage of the unusually mild February day and left straightaway for his cabin on Cider Hill. Once on the trail, he straightened his back, lifted his head, and welcomed the sun that warmly caressed his face; he took a big gulp of the fresh free air and prayed that God would enable him to release the miseries of the past and bless the new Scotland.

A bright fire, the smell of venison stew, and Daniel's smile greeted him as he entered the cabin door. They shook hands and Dan stunned Alex when he enwrapped him in a giant hug, "Welcome home, *bráthair*. 'Tis good ta see another free Scot, even such a poor excuse fer one as yerself!"

Alex gave Dan a quizzical look, along with a feeble punch on the shoulder, took a step back, and jibed, "I think ye've been alone here fer much too long." He shook his head, feigned a disgusted cough, and flashily wiped his mouth on his sleeve, "Ugh, one of those will last me fer a life time. Zounds, I reckon that was a bear hug, 'cause ye sure smell like one of those critters." Then he turned, laughed in the old carefree Alex way, faked a growl, grabbed a startled Dan, and gave him a hug back. "At least 'tis a friendly bear, *bráthair*. Truth be told, 'tis good ta be home and the smell of yer lousy cookin'—'tis the best greetin' of all."

"Lousy indeed, 'tis a paltry gratitude fer me bustin' my arse. Evidently bein' free dinna improve yer manners nor ye brain too much—yer still daft as a cuckoo bird."

Alex freed himself from his heavy clothing, and between helpings of the tasty stew, they delved into ideas for their new endeavor.

By early March they felt that they had forged a beginning, and although they were working harder than ever, they were enjoying it a lot more.

"A mild winter mayhap, but more 'n enough snow ta shovel, eh?"

"All the better ta keep us in shape and warm, ye snowy haired old buzzard."

"'Tis a lot of extra pay I'll be needin' fer this duty, ye know."

"Umm—'tis fair of ye ta ask, and ye'll get it as well . . . after I dock ye fer all the extra food ye shovel inta that endless hole ye call a mouth."

When it snowed they shoveled, laughed, and threw snow at each other—then laughed some more. "Just look at us! Frolickin' about like two *bairns* without a care in the world. 'Tis grand, eh, Dan?

"Surely 'tis. Ah, wouldna Mora and the wee ones just love this? I ken see us all hootin', hollerin', and rollin' about in the snow." The wishful dream dimmed abruptly, he dropped his shovel and lowered his head, "Ahh, shite, what do I reckon? Naught good ta go there. Forgive me, Alex, I dinna mean ta fall back, but 'tis when I be the happiest they come ta mind the most."

"Dinna regret it. 'Twas a wonderful life that ye shared, and they are a part of ye forever. It warms my heart that ye ken remember them in that way. Dinna ye see though, Dan, 'tis what I've been tryin' ta tell ye. Mora dinna linger back in the old Scotland, 'tis here with ye she rests—here in yer heart—where she belongs."

"Yer pressin' yer luck, *bráthair*."

Alex bit his tongue—for once he knew when to quit. Still, he felt uplifted as he grabbed his shovel, moved to a new spot, and whistled softly through his teeth.

Once signs of spring began to show they dug right in—fenced off the garden, cleared away more trees and rocks, pruned apple trees that had been left by the former owners, and finished other odd jobs while they waited for the last frost of the season to leave so they could get on with some of the heftier jobs.

"Since the *Old Mill Creek* sawmill 'tis just down the road a piece, we'd best purchase the heavy foundation beams from them. They tell me 'tis run by an overshot wheel 'cause the mill 'tis above tide water. Just contrary ta *The Great Works'* wheels—seems fittin', eh?"

It was a happy day when the huge beams were delivered. No time was wasted. They carefully sawed and carved the dovetails into the strong, rough wood until they fit precisely into each other to set the level for the entire house.

"Eh, Dan, 'twill pay off now that I marked off the cellar hole earlier. I kenna wait ta get movin' on the house."

"Yer right, Alex, time saved, and 'twill be good ta have yer home built before we get to the barn, since we dinna have much of anythin' ta keep in a barn yet anyway. And by the time we ken work a good deal fer enough stock, we'll be settled in yer grand place. The animals ken then be kept in this old cabin and crops stored in the loft. Good fer us all, eh?"

"As Ralph and Tom would say, *Yup, by gorra, ye be right,* eh, Dan?" That brought on a good chuckle and fond memories of their old friends.

Travel to *The Great Works* was much too long and hard a haul to tackle in the depths of winter, but as soon as the mud season dried up, more logs, boards, and other materials were on their way from the greater distance, and their friends and former co-workers made sure to send only the choicest lumber in every order.

They were pleased to find that there was a brickyard just a short way down the trail that led to the village of *York*. Handmade bricks delivered straight to the site were carefully fashioned into a large hearth. The garrison design Alex had chosen for his home included a shelf built into the fireplace that would serve as a base for a beehive oven that would be added later. The chimney went up fast, and within a month the house was framed and the roof was on. Crops had started to show green in the fields. Alexander and Daniel were over the moon with excitement; the dream was in motion.

By fall they had realized a good profit from crops and logs, plus a special bonus from the sale of saw grass from the marsh. Their hired hand, Albert Dexter, had informed them of its value and had helped them harvest it. Albert had a small piece of land and a cabin up the trail. He was slightly disabled and wasn't up to working a farm of his own, so their mutual arrangement was just what they all needed.

The coolness of October found them seated on the back porch of Alex's sturdy home looking straight out over the marsh and river. The last soft shades of the setting sun played with the water and marsh grasses as Daniel, Alexander, and Albert rocked quietly and enjoyed the full beauty of it until the sun disappeared and a big old yellow harvest moon took over the sky. A handsome buck ambled by, not a hundred feet in front of them. They watched as the white tail caught a lingering flash of light as the buck headed for the woods and deeper cover for the night. Once the stunning majestic animal was out of sight, Albert headed up the hill to rest his bones.

"Alright now—what's buggin' ye? Let's hear it, Alexander, out with it. I ken see that ye have somethin' cookin' in that poor excuse fer a head. 'Tis a bit stumped I am, 'cause we be doin' so dern well—yer home 'tis fine and a thing ta be proud of, the crops are in, ye have some stock, and the root cellar 'tis packed full of food fer the winter."

"These apples are snappin' good, eh?" Alex took a bite of the delicious fruit while he gathered his thoughts. "Remember how Ralph bragged about them when he first took us out to explore the *The Great Works*?"

Dan waited impatiently until Alex went on, "Okay, yer gettin' so ye ken see right through me—my mind's been dwellin' a lot on *The Great Works* of late. By now I had hoped that more Scots would be here. I know that many like John Warren and John Neal grew ta love

Berwick. They chose with their hearts when they agreed ta settle there. They knew the risks. 'Tis nary a secret that we are considered defeated Scottish dogs by most of the locals there . . . and most likely here as well fer that matter."

"Ay, Alex, I know that. 'Tis even legal ta shoot any of us dead with a bow and arrow—Scotsmen, Negroes, Irish, any sort of bondsmen—we all be considered chattel, free or naught. So? Zounds, 'tis old news that, somethin' else 'tis itchin' ye."

"I often reckon that the biggest thing we had in our favor at *The Works* was the strong Irish heritage of Richard Leader. We've come a long way, and we Scotsmen demonstrate our worth every chance we get. I respect that, Daniel, but I hope fer more here in Scotland Parish, and I had dreams that more would join us."

"So, there 'tis. Ye've placed yer dreams on them, Alex. Let go. We've made our move. They must have the choice and time ta do the same. 'Tis nary a doubt I hold that more will come here in their own good time. Call on some of that faith yer always totin'—relax. Let the thistle do its work."

"Ay, *bráthair*, 'tis wise ye be. 'Tis the thing ta do indeed. I truly know that the thistle guides us and will bring our new Scotland what it needs. 'Tis my own impatience that I let get the best of me, ye know me well. Wait and trust—'tis the order of the day."

"A worthy resolve, ye old fart, since 'tis nary a say ye have in the matter at all. Just hold yer horses, *bráthair*—dinna be in such haste."

Alex grumbled to himself and reaffirmed that he would be grateful and count his blessings.

Chapter 46

GOOD TIMES

I SAY, Alex, mayhap 'tis time we meet more of our neighbors. We dinna visit many of 'em since ye got here. Some of 'em have lived in the area fer years."

"Um," a distracted Alex mumbled, "'Tis a thought, Daniel."

"Indeed 'tis, Alex, and 'tis some serious thinkin' of my own I've done as well. I reckon 'tis time ta have that talk with Rowland Young, and make a deal fer that twenty-acre parcel of land just down the trail from here at Bass Cove—that set back piece ye told me about. If he will take the down payment I ken offer, I reckon I ken pay it off in a year or so. It kenna hold a torch ta yer seventy acres, but I want it saved fer me before ye sway more Scots ta leave their nests, get ahold of all the land, and settle here."

Alex snapped out of his trance and was instantly alert—he had been hoping for this, he tried to play it cool, but he was too elated "Well, 'tis staggered I am—but nary more pleased. 'Tis a great plan, *bráthair* and 'tis about time." Cautiously he ventured, "Ken this mean yer set on puttin' down roots here, Daniel?"

"Hmm, I nary reckoned I'd own up ta it—but 'tis true. I've grown ta like it here . . . and the land—'tis fine . . . suits me indeed. 'Tis good it feels ta me just as this place did ta ye when ye first sat on it. It comforts me and feels like home, fer now anyway. Besides, I have need of my own homestead. I could nary stand livin' with the likes of ye ferever."

"Ye should be so lucky!" Alex chided, "Anyway, ye know how I feel about it, Dan, I love ownin' my own land and it will cheer my heart ta watch ye enjoy yers. I believe 'tis a wise venture, and if ye need help with the down, 'tis pleased I'd be ta offer it ta ye."

"'Tis sure I be that I ken work it out on my own, but 'tis kindly of ye ta offer, Alex."

Nothing more was said until a week later when Daniel breathlessly burst through the front door upon his return from a trip to York. "The Bass Cove land—'tis a settled deal, Alex. Rowland Young and I hit it off from the start, and he offered ta let me begin building whenever I am ready." He rattled on, "Did ye know that Rowland was one of the first people ta buy land in this area? He said that five lads bought in at about the same time. It seemed that he wanted me ta know that I was in good company." Daniel cricked his neck and raised an eyebrow, "Funny, he dinna mention ye a bit!"

"The old scallywag, I'll get him fer that! Anyway, cheers ta ye, Daniel. First, let's celebrate, then, as soon as yer set on it, I say—*let's get buildin'!* But, where ye plan ta build the house, though—so fer down, near the river—'tis quite fer back from the trail, Dan. Ye might want ta start afresh on that. Ye'll have a ton of shovelin' ta do all winter."

"I dinna give a shite. I reckon yer right, *bráthair*, but 'tis the spot that called ta me. And I reckon ye and Al will be more'n eager ta help me handle the white stuff, eh?"

"Gettin' pretty cocky there, ye snow topped old buzzard."

Build they did, and it wasn't long before Daniel Dill was living in his own home, soundly built in the garrison tradition, on his scenic land at Bass Cove. He continued to work with Alexander and still managed to clear out more space for himself. He even added a cow, some chickens, and two pigs. He then made an agreement to winter them in Alex's new barn while he saved up to build his own.

Albert Dexter hired on to help Daniel and kept on with Alex as well. Once again the friends enjoyed a good and profitable harvest with apples and saw grass high on the profit list that they called *easy money*.

Sooner than they wished, the weather turned grey and dictated that the two former prisoners-of-war face up to the coming winter's responsibilities. They knuckled down, tightened up their walls, winterized the chicken coop and Alex's new barn to protect the farm animals, then organized indoor work for the cold spells. They took pleasure in their accomplishments, and on rare sunny days they sat on whoever's porch happened to be the nearest, enjoyed the beloved view, and counted their blessings.

After a soft January snowfall, Alex's snowshoes made the only marks in a perfect blanket of white as he broke a trail through the new fluff down Cider Hill to Bass Cove. "Danny, my *bráthair*, rotten news," he blurted out as he burst through the door and slumped into the nearest chair, "Ye recall Richard Leader's adventures ta the Barbados in cahoots with Tom Broughton?"

Dan nodded curiously while Alex took a moment to catch his breath, "Well, the bad news . . . 'tis that a nasty fever took him and he died there on his latest trip—in early December. He be dead, Daniel."

"Zounds, I be sorry, Alex, I know how close the two of ye were. It hardly seems possible, he seemed so healthy." Searching for words, he added, "'Tis a nightmare indeed ta hear of it. Such a loss."

"'Tis grateful ta him I be. He turned my life around, encouraged the deep wish in me fer a new Scotland and paid me well fer the financial work as well. That and the yield I gained from the land grant he gave me in Berwick got me started here. His son-in-law, Robert Jordan, was appointed executor of his estate. The end of an era, Dan."

"Amen ta that. He'll be sorely missed, *bráthair*."

Not much more was said, but by the spring of 1661 Alexander had built a meeting house in memory of Richard Leader on land he purchased at Gallows Point.

A complete change of pace was welcomed in June when Dan and Alex quietly celebrated the burning of Daniel's note to Rowland Young. Daniel reveled in the free and clear ownership of his homestead on Bass Cove.

By early November Daniel had news to share, "Alex, I just came from town. Yer tobacco and goods are out on the porch. The whole place was talkin'. Ken ye believe it? The York folks be havin' a big fuss about Maine's planned sale ta Massachusetts. We gotta hustle right down there ta get our two cents in." The two attended the meeting, but the fuss was for nothing—the sale went through in spite of protests.

"Amazin', dinna ye reckon? Some of those York folks at the meetin' dinna even know that Cromwell's been dead, and fer a while now"!

"Oh, I heard them Dan. They called him *the wonderful Oliver*. They've nary a notion of his atrocious dealin's. I had ta leave before I started another war."

Dan's head snapped and he began to rant, but Alex raised his hand to hush him and went on, "I know how ye feel, my friend. Yer right of course, but remember, the people of York heard only what England wanted them ta hear about the war. I guess it all hinges on which side yer bread 'tis buttered. Yer harborin' a lot of bitterness, Danny. How long are ye goin' ta try ta undo the past? Zounds, let it be, if ye dinna, 'twill just keep eatin' at ye. All this gettin' agitated, 'tis just nary good fer ye."

"Ye may be right, but I kenna do it. The hate catches me right in the throat every time I recall our lost comrades or anythin' ta do with them. I still see their bodies all bloody and crumpled along the way, and those in the ditches at Durham. Only lads Alex, mostly all young lads who deserved a life. The thought of it makes my head whirl and my stomach boil up. How ken ye ever even begin ta ferget or fergive all that?"

Alex tried to respond, but Daniel didn't give him a chance. "Well, I reckon what yer goin' ta say, and I am glad that prayer works fer ye, but nary fer me. Dinna worry, I'll keep strugglin' with my demons and try ta keep my thoughts ta myself."

Fat chance of that, Alexander thought as he gave up and retreated up the hill to his garrison home. He felt empty and helpless to relieve his friend's anguish.

Daniel resolved that he would suffer in silence on the matter, but held a dogged satisfaction that Cromwell was history, and he felt sure that Alex shared that feeling more than he had let on.

A few days later Alex brought up a subject he thought his friend might find more encouraging, "Imagine, Dan, King Charles the Second 'tis finally restored ta the throne. 'Tis somethin' ta reckon, eh? A lot of water over that dam."

Daniel chose to see that glass half empty. "Indeed, and a lot of bloodshed, as well—and fer what I dinna know, my friend. I reckon 'tis best we put aside all that blatherin' fer a while, ye grasp how cantankerous those things make me."

Nary a doubt about that, Alex raised his eyebrows and silently affirmed.

Daniel made an attempt to clear the air, "Anyway, ye'll be glad ta hear, I have news fer ye of a much happier nature, *bráthair*—John Carmichael and James Grant have come ta make Scotland Parish their home. Ye remember that James Grant be the one called the *Drummer,* or the *Welsh James,* eh?"

The change of topic pleased Alex in more ways than one, "Indeed? The two of them, eh? Indeed, I know them well. At least three James Grants came ta *The Works* from the Worcester battle, eh? Same clan as Peter and the other James Grant. They surely gave their all, dinna they? And the little Drummer Grant 'tis settlin' here—and John Carmichael as well—truly great news 'tis!"

"'Tis quite a year, eh, Alex?" Dan watched as his friend nodded, smiled in grateful agreement, and then frowned, glanced down and tightened his lips.

"Ay, but yer still down in the mouth a bit, eh? I reckon I know what ye be thinkin', Alexander Maxwell, the loss of Richard Leader pains ye still—and on top of that, neither John Carmichael nor the Drummer James Grant had a thing ta offer about our Rob. But dinna ye give up hope on that one, *bráthair*—hear me—come he will."

Chapter 47

FRUITION

PEEVED AT a hard persistent knock on his front door, a startled Daniel looked up irritably from his late lunch of venison stew and all but dropped the cornbread he had just dunked mouth-wateringly in gravy.

He figured it was Alex, wolfed down the cornbread, and yelled out, "Be done with yer joshin' now and get yourself in here. The door 'tis open, as always, ye pesky pain in the arse—yer in luck, grab some grub, 'tis more sittin' there by the hearth."

"Pesky pain in the arse, eh? Am I ta suppose 'tis the best ye ken offer an old friend, ye cranky ole fart?"

Daniel's head snapped as the door swung ajar, his body shook in disbelief and his mouth fell open. Gravy drooled down his chin as he stared aghast at a man of distinguished appearance who stood straight and tall in his doorway, hat in hand with a wide grin on his face.

Words finally came, "As I live and breathe, Robert Jonkings. Zounds, ken it be?" Daniel sucked in his breath so hard that it caught in his throat "'Tis really ye then, Rob?"

"Indeed—in the flesh, Dan!" Rob faltered, so choked up that it took a while before he added, "Nary another thing has been on my mind fer some time now, but it wasna easy ta loosen up from Thomas Broughton. I did a lot of business fer him in and about Oyster River—or Dover, as some call it now—but once I heard ye were alive and got news of Scotland Parish, I knew 'twas this place and nary another where I must be."

The familiar gentle face broke into a lively smile, "Ye look pretty much yer old self, dear friend, feisty and fine, except fer an even bigger pile of snow on yer head." He walked closer, ruffled Dan's silvery hair and said, "'Tis so good ta put eyes on ye, Daniel MacDhughill."

Dan ducked, jumped to his feet, grabbed the rag he had carried the hot bowl of stew to the table with, hastily wiped at his chin and hands simultaneously, seized Robert by the arms, and exclaimed, "Well, I must say ye nary ken hold a candle ta the bloke I last gazed at when he was *sold*, snatched and tossed inta a long wagon like a lump of fodder."

Dan held his comrade off at arm's length and took a good look at him, "Zounds, ye old weasel, ye look better than ever, pork chop whiskers and all. Ye even smell good!"

They shook hands and hugged, then did it all over again until Dan finally said, "I reckon that ye are tired and starvin'—nary a doubt—but 'tis sure I be that yer achin' ta set yer eyes on Alex even more, eh?"

Before Rob could finish his nod of agreement, Dan had grabbed his cloak and they were out the door. "The ornery codger has a grand homestead just up the trail a bit. What a godsend! I kenna wait ta see his face when he lays eyes on ya. 'Tis over the wall 'twill drive him!"

After Alex's heart nearly stopped from the sheer joy of it, he stood like stone until Rob reached out and clutched him to his chest. He went limp, slumped, and was about to slip to the floor when Dan quickly grabbed on to both men. They held tightly to each other for a timeless moment. When they slowly broke apart, Alex weakly managed to sputter, "How long we've waited and prayed fer this day, our very own Robert Jonkings."

"Indeed," Dan beamed as he released them. "And 'tis starvin' he be, Alex. In my rush I left some good stew behind, but I'll grab what ye have handy and join ye out back where we ken sit and begin ta catch up, eh?"

It didn't take long for the years to melt and mesh together—their close bond lived on stronger than ever and time ceased to exist.

"'Tis befuddled I be, Rob, how did ye get here—what took ye so long?"

"Ahh . . . long it seemed indeed, *bráthair*. Well, Andy Rankin got the first news from Richard Leader ta me that ye were alive! 'Twas a grand day, though I dinna hear of it till later. I rarely traveled back ta Salmon Falls 'cause I was steady in Oyster River by then, but I did hear some things via the good old grapevine. I knew that Andy received deliveries from time ta time from *The Works*, but those drivers answered directly ta George Leader and there was nary a hint of news ta be gained from them. One fine day though, he got lucky when a wagon arrived from *The Works* with a driver he dinna know. He introduced himself as Tom Eagan, told him the regular driver had been injured."

"Zounds, our friend, old Tom Eagan," Alex and Dan interrupted, almost in unison.

"I gathered that, because once he heard yer name, Alex, he told Andy that he knew ye well and was aware of yer friendship with Richard Leader and that ye had gone on yer way ta start Scotland Parish up near York. He told Andy of yer plan and that ye wanted more Scots ta settle there. Tom dinna know how ta get word ta ye though.

"On a rare run I made back ta Salmon Falls, Andy told me all about Tom's visit, and he and I pledged on the spot that we would get ta Scotland Parish as soon as we could. I stopped by *The Works* once I was on my way, asked around, and finally tracked down Henry Laird. 'Twas he who told me how ta get here. Turn right at the fork by the river, eh?" They all could laugh at it now, but it had been hell at the time. Visions returned of the cold wet trek along the icy river—the struggle to get the wagon around the inlet—with no idea of what might wait ahead for them in Newichawannock.

"And, John MacKinney," Robert's voice brought them back to the present, "Where does the hoary ginger bear hide out these days? I look forward ta seein' his ugly face as well!"

It took a while, but Daniel brought Robert up to date on John's romance with Eliza O'Hara and their marriage. It gave him pleasure to report that their friend was in high spirits working his fishing business in Gloucester. They all shared the empty space his absence left, but Dan assured Rob that the news they received from him was good. He smiled as he heard about John's son, Danny, who was five and allowed to take short fishing trips with his father, or occasionally with his grandfather, Abraham O'Hara, much to the dismay of his concerned mother, Eliza.

Alex jumped in to tell Robert of the arrival of John Carmichael and James (the drummer) Grant. Although Robert did not know them, he said, "I look forward ta meetin' up with them. It seems that Henry Brown and Patrick Jameson are staying on in the Salmon Falls area, they signed on with Broughton ta work at the Quamphegan mill.

"As ye might suspect, Alan Rankin and I became good friends while we were at Salmon River, and he assured me that he had high interest in the new Scotland, as did Micum MacIntyre. I feel certain that both of them will turn up once their duties allow.

"Alex? This Scotland Parish—I reckon 'tis even more than ye hoped fer, eh? Fer me as well. I feel really free, whole again. It seems that I'm Robert Junkins now, my friends. Did ye manage ta keep yer own monikers?"

"Alex did," Dan explained, "but 'tis *Daniel Dill* they call me in these parts." That caused them some pause, but they managed to brush over it without too much ado. They had too much to catch up on to dwell on that sore subject.

Once they had told and retold every good and gory detail of their slavery days, Alexander could stand it no longer, "We must hear more of yer doin's in Oyster River, Rob—but ye mentioned that ye were interested in land, and right now I am burstin' at the seams ta take ye out and show ye some nearby that will grab yer heart."

They trudged up Cider Hill and checked out several parcels before Robert was keen on one he liked. "I reckon 'tis the place ta start—right here. 'Tis a dandy site. I'll build on top of this knoll where I ken be far enough away from the river and still look out over it. It very much brings ta my mind Careston—Netherside and Balbinney. Seems 'tis just as 'twas meant ta be. Dinna wake me—tell me again 'tis real! The three of us relics, neighbors in Scotland Parish. These six acres will be only a start, mind ye. Plans are comin' ta my mind already. I'll spread out—farmland and orchards. I ken see it all now . . . my new Scotland homestead."

Robert was completely immersed in visions and hopes for his new home, so Alexander and Daniel took the hint, smiled at each other, and agreed, "Let's leave him be ta dream fer a bit. How grand 'tis. Mark and honor this day, we must, Danny! We stuffed Rob pretty well earlier, but let's cook up somethin' special fer supper!"

Robert easily found his way back down the Cider Hill trail and relaxed on Alex's back porch. He savored every bite, then loosened his pants so he could breathe and laid back in one of the comfortable chairs Dan had crafted. Twilight gradually slipped over the marsh as they set aside the remnants of the huge steak dinner with roasted potatoes, carrots, greens, and all the fixings. The beauty of it was not lost on Robert, "I dinna mind tellin' ye, that was the best feed I've had since many a day past in Angus. Makes me hope I could someday forget that those hungry, grim, and dire years ever befell us." He stopped, closed his eyes and shivered, "Dinna we yearn for it, eh, my *bráthairs*?"

They nodded and hung their heads in silence, and Alex held his breath as he watched Daniel struggle with himself and was grateful when he firmly changed the subject, "Lads, such fine a day 'tis been, eh? Surely there 'tis more ta tell, eh, Robby."

That did it, on he went and soon the others joined in. Slowly the full moon emerged and swaddled the marsh in its warm glow—hours later, heavy clouds drifted over, softly veiled the light and let out a soft drizzle. Oblivious, the *bráthairs*' tales kept pouring out.

Chapter 48

SECOND CHANCES?

SCOTLAND PARISH suddenly seemed to have taken on more zest, meaning, and purpose. Alex was noticeably relaxed; he laughed with renewed gusto and life took a lighter turn. Robert had been impressed by how rugged and strong his friends' homes were from top to bottom—practical, safe, and comfortable—so, in a surprisingly short time, another solid home built in the garrison style was standing on Cider Hill, and Robert was sitting pretty in it. He was very proud of the two-story design and loved the front overhang. He had acted on Alex's advice to expand the original size, raise his roof higher, and extend the east side to include two more rooms downstairs and two more bedrooms upstairs. The result was handsome and impressed them all.

Cultivating the land came naturally to Rob. His garden put both of his friends' weed patches to shame. He filled the rest of his six acres with apple trees that he carefully pruned and tended. "I dinna have the saw grass ye two have, and I have a need ta make up fer it, so more apples!"

Daniel and Alexander continued to upgrade their homes and stock as well, but they also kept their hands in the major points of the area's political affairs and signed petitions they favored. Robert showed little interest in politics. He was too busy working on his beloved homestead.

"'Tis sick I am of signin' all these articles. They always list me as yer servant and that irks me ta my very core . . . that dinna be me. Ye grasp it, Alex, 'tis bad enough they took my good name and call me Daniel Dill. I kenna stand all that bullshite."

"Now, Dan, there was nary ever a doubt about yer workin' with me. Seems their record keepin' hasna improved. I dinna care what they call ye; ye will always be Daniel MacDhughill ta me. But, we are what we are, and as long as we ken keep doin' what we're doin' and bein' there fer each other, 'tis pleasin' ta me."

"'Tis pleasin' ta me as well, Alexander Maxwell."

• • •

By the end of 1663, Robert had already made arrangements to purchase more land and obtain some of the land grants his friends encouraged him to apply for.

The residents of Scotland Parish loved to keep up on the news of the area and of the mill at *The Great Works* and were sorry to hear that Eliakim Hutchinson of Boston had taken over the mill in 1665 and that Richard Tucker had been placed in charge. Tucker didn't last long, nor did the several managers who followed him, including Roger Plaisted, William Spencer and Walter Allen. Allen stayed until Hutchinson rented the mill to Thomas Doughty. Thomas then convinced James and Peter Grant along with John Taylor to be his bondsmen. It gave Robert Junkins pleasure to hear this—Doughty was one of the seven Scots sold along with him to Valentine at the Boston auction.

Scotland Parish continued to flourish. Alexander Maxwell, Robert Junkins, and Daniel Dill were all doing well as were most of the newcomers. Robert had fired up their enthusiasm and continued to inspire them.

Shortly after dawn on a quiet Tuesday morning in early May, Daniel was out feeding the chickens when John Parson, a shoemaker who plied his trade in York, called to him from the Cider Hill Trail. He was on his way to deliver some boots to the Hooke farm and had volunteered to ask a favor of Daniel Dill.

They exchanged their *Good Mornings* until John skipped the small talk and got right to it, "The ferry's in trouble, Dan. I think you know my friend William Moore. He is a fisherman, and he also runs the ferry at Stage Neck. He's married to Dorothy Dixon; they're raising their family nearby in the lower towne on Varrell Lane. Going at it pretty good, I'd say; they have quite a bunch of kids.

"Ah, well, back to the subject, Will owns the ferry and has been running it for years, through all weather and conditions, you name them. The ferry has always been dependable and has provided a great service for us, but this being the worst mud season anyone can remember about these parts, it only took that wild thunderstorm that just went through to get the thing bogged down bad, and I'm telling you, Daniel, it's in grave danger; if Will doesn't get help fast, we could lose it.

"That's why, when the town council sat wringing their hands and not knowing what to do, I spoke up and told them that Daniel Dill would be just man for the job. So they told me to get myself up here and ask you if you would help out—you being so really good with the wood and all. Do you think you could find someone to keep an eye out for you here, while you take a ride with me down to the lower towne to check it out?"

Dan didn't hesitate, "Ay, John, I've met William Moore, 'tis a fine man he be, and 'tis pleased I'd be ta help."

The Stage Neck ferry was a muddy mess alright. William pointed out the most damaged parts; the planking and aprons were ripped and the rope trolleys and windless needed work as well. The ferry could be completely wrecked if the windless did not work properly, so they tackled that first and finally got it to go up and down properly. Daniel, Will, and four of his fisherman friends worked sixteen hours straight before they got the top planks replaced and the cracks filled with oakum and hot pitch. By then they were completely exhausted and William insisted that Daniel stay with him to rest up and get the job finished. Dan did not object and was happy to crash in the Moore's barn for what was left of the night.

Up early and anxious to get back to work, Daniel had just washed up and was about to tie the rawhide thong to hold back his silvery mane when his eye caught a glimpse of something familiar darting around the corner of the house just past the kitchen door. He couldn't place what it was, but he could not ignore the loud jolt to his brain. He dropped the cord, took off after the mystery, and barely caught sight of shiny, long black hair bouncing saucily as it flipped around the west side of the building.

He felt his breath catch in his throat as he overtook the vision. "Zounds, it kenna be," he gasped as the owner of the lavish head of hair spun about to face him. "Mora," he sputtered. "Mora, my God, This kenna be. Surely I must be dreamin' again," and he dropped down like a log onto the damp grass.

The flabbergasted girl gazed down on Daniel who looked like some sort of old sack with white wool sprawled on top, "Who in the world are you? I couldn't hear you. What did you say? What's with you anyway? Are you ill? Can I get something for you?"

Daniel put his hands up, shook his head, and tried to speak. Unfortunately, nothing came out but projectile vomit that landed on the vision's shoes. The girl swallowed, tried not to gag, and ran for her father, who rushed out of the house.

"Dan, for goodness sake, what's wrong? Did the breakfast upset your stomach?"

"Nay, nay, Will . . . I dinna eat yet, must have over done it a bit yesterday, eh? 'Tis bound ta be that. 'Tis fit I'll be shortly." He tried to contain himself but was overwhelmed by the dream still standing before him and heaved again.

"Let's get you into the house and fix you up. We've got a long day's work ahead of us if you're up for it. We still have the aprons to deal with. This is my daughter, Dorrie, you just scared the wits out of. Dorrie, help me get him inside."

They each took an arm and as Daniel accidentally touched her hand he missed a step and almost passed out. As he looked down onto her head he would have sworn it was Mora—the height, size, all were the same.

Once inside, Will sat him down and Dorrie brought him a drink of some concoction he did not recognize, but that he had no desire to ever taste again. It did the job though, and in a short time he pulled himself together, quickly excused himself, and went back outside to clean up. Will came out to check on him and brought a bewildered Daniel back inside where a few smothered giggles snuck out. Will silenced those with a glance, welcomed Dan to the bountiful breakfast table, motioned to an empty seat, and began the introductions starting with Elizabeth, around eighteen—John, maybe thirteen—Robert who seemed a couple of years younger, probably eleven—and Thomas—who piped up and declared, "I'm, Tommy, I'm nine." They all laughed, and William Sr. said, "Over here is the baby—for now—Annie. She'll be two next month." Then he pointed to his obviously pregnant wife, and said, "And this is my wife, Dorothy."

The very attractive Dorothy Dixon Moore smiled and nodded, "It's very nice to meet you, Daniel Dill. Thank you for helping Will with the ferry. Everyone about here depends on it." Then she turned and admonished a still disheveled Dorrie sharply with, "Tuck that messy hair into a cap, young lady, and sit down."

Dan was struck by the varied shades of hazel eyes that stared at him. The resemblance stopped there; for not one of them bore a likeness to the other. Had he met them elsewhere, he would not have guessed that they were related. It was easy to tell though, that this was a close and loving family. He searched out the unbelievable, his Mora, whom he never dreamed he would see the likeness of again. She had slipped quietly into her place, the stunning hair now confined beneath a simple white cap. Dorrie, named fer her ma, he reasoned as he sent the name to his heart.

Cautiously, he sneaked a better look—she was precious. As he tried to casually observe her face, she surprised him and looked directly back at him. He gulped and cleared his throat, tried to ignore his trembling, and gazed steadily back into the wide green-golden eyes that lured him from beneath heavy dark lashes. How well he remembered Mora's flashing, vivacious violet eyes that had constantly driven him to distraction. William and his wife, Dorothy, shared a not too happy what's-this look.

It was too much. Queasiness overtook Daniel once more and breakfast was forgotten. He acknowledged them all and begged to be excused.

Chapter 49

CHASING YESTERDAY

BEFORE ANYONE else had a chance to move, Dorrie darted from her chair and filled a bowl of chicken soup from the kettle that slowly simmered on its hook in the fireplace. She moved so quickly that liquid slopped onto the hot coals below, unfazed, she dashed out the door, off to the befuddled Scotsman.

A confused Dan accepted the offering and tried to act natural. He ate the soup as slowly as he could, took in her beauty with every breath until he finally fumbled the empty bowl to Dorrie, smiled out "thanks be ta ye lass," and trudged off to catch up with William, who had motioned for him to follow then rushed past them the toward the ferry.

Dan half turned about, only to find her watching him, and almost tripped over his own feet. He swore she gave him a wink and a flirty wave.

They were not even half way down to the water when a breathless, edgy Dan caught up with William and blurted out, "I need ta speak with ye. 'Tis yer permission I beg. Wait up, Will, I wanna . . . I must . . . marry her."

Uncomfortable couldn't even begin to describe the astounded father. William Moore stopped in his tracks, frowned, forced his hands to his hips, and looked around at everything but Dan until he finally focused on him as he would a wild crazed creature.

Daniel would not stand down, "What ken I say, Will . . . Mr. Moore . . . Sir? She be the one fer me, I ken it . . . 'tis simple . . . 'tis."

He knew he needed more, so he gulped, "'Tis only the best of everythin' she'd git from me, ye ken it fer sure."

"What? Who? What in heaven's name are you talking about, Daniel Dill?"

"Why, yer daughter, Dorrie Moore, of course—'tis Dorrie I yearn for . . . I need her, Will . . . ah, Mr. Moore . . . 'tis her hand I be askin' ye fer . . . I gotta make her me own."

"WHOA NOW, that's out of the blue. A bit sudden, to say the least; what the hell are you thinking? You only just met her!" He looked Dan over carefully and added, "And look at you—you must be near thirty, eh?"

"Indeed, I am thirty-seven, sir, and I be sure ye are aware that nicely set up on Cider Hill I be. I ken take good care of her. 'Tis nothin' she'd want fer."

William rubbed his head. His first thought was to kick him right in his insolent mouth; however, Dan's very serious manner prompted him to think twice, so he responded, "Well, she's nineteen Dan, that's a marrying age alright—but as far as you being my son-in-law, I have no say what-so-ever on that one. It's up to Dorrie to choose her own husband, and you can bet your boots that her mother will have her nose in it if she can. Neither of them ever hesitates to speak her mind, as you may well find out!

So then, Daniel Dill—as far as I'm concerned, you can go right ahead and ask her—once the aprons are fixed." He guffawed, "And—I hope you take rejection well."

As soon as the ferry was up and running Daniel managed to meet with her in a quiet spot, barely out of her mother's earshot. He blabbed away, told her all about himself, how well off, and why she should marry him . . . and *would she, please*?

Dorrie had not uttered a word, but she had been bowled over by the tall Scotsman at first glance. The white hair made her think a moment, and thirty-seven years of age to boot; but he was so handsome and fine, and he still looked like a young buck, so she brushed that aside along with the strange heat that had come over her, and it didn't take much courting to convince her to be his wife.

"'Tis sure I must be that ye want me, lass—me age an' all."

"Oh, I do." She couldn't keep herself from blushing nor from gushing out, "I love you, Daniel Dill. I've loved you from the moment you spewed out all over my feet. You were a most pathetic sight and the strangest shade of green I ever saw."

"Guilty, and sick still at the thought of it I be—but, love ye I do, Mor . . . ah, Dorrie Moore. Moore—Dorrie Moore." He quickly covered his slip and hugged her before he caught a sharp glance from Dorrie's amazed mother, who was never far away.

William was shocked, he never expected Dorrie to accept the tall Scotsman, but he knew from past experience that there was no point in arguing with his women once they had made up their minds. He backed off and resolved himself to his daughter's speedy decision. It took some doing, but Dorrie gently wrangled her mother's reluctant blessing and set June eighth as the date for their wedding. Dorothy cautioned her daughter about rushing into a marriage with someone she hardly knew, but Dorrie had made up her mind about her Scot and wanted to become his wife as soon as possible.

"What do you think, Daniel Dill? It's barely a month away, you know."

"I ken ye be just beautiful—inside and out, and as fer the date, 'tis grand, Dorrie, the sooner the better fer me."

Daniel's thoughts of using his savings to return to Scotland fled his mind. He used the time waiting for June eighth to get ready. He bought more land from Rowland Young, and he and Albert Dexter cut out the dead wood and thinned out the brush. Then they took a good look at the entrance to his home and decided that it now appeared much more attractive and also provided an easier access from the Cider Hill Trail.

He lovingly carved a handsome headboard, finished the sturdy bed, and had a fine feather mattress made for it. Then he added a platform with a balustrade onto his house at the highest point of the roof so he and his soon to be wife could sit together, look down on the marshland and river to enjoy the sunset at twilight or the star filled sky on a clear night. *Just the way me and Mora used ta huddle together and look out over the sea. Ay, life, mayhap 'tis worthwhile once more,* he thought, and remembered good times back in a Scotland, where his dreams had been stolen from him by the plague.

It seemed that the wedding day was upon them in no time. Dorrie had no desire for a large wedding. She insisted on a small ceremony that would be performed at her home by the Reverend Prebble, rather than the plan that Alexander Maxwell had come up with to hold the wedding and a whopping party at the meeting house he had built on his land at Gallows Point. It seemed such a great idea to him, but Dorrie was not the party animal Alex was, so she gently but firmly declined the kind offer.

Alex was hard to back down, but Dan preferred a small wedding himself, so he refereed and smoothed feathers until his friend saw the light.

David Livingston had expressed interest in forty acres next door to Rob Junkins on the northeast side of Country Road, so Alexander was partially grateful that he didn't have to make arrangements for a wedding and reception while he was so busy closing the land deal in addition to showing property to James Jackson and Alexander McNair, who also wanted to buy land in the area.

James Jackson was a fellow comrade and a cousin to Ansel Jackson, who had been so helpful in locating Eliza O'Hara's family. Ansel and his brother, Samuel, had settled in Gloucester. James had been *indentured* in Quamphegan, but had been granted early release after his hand slipped while he was operating a saw that caused him to end up with a maimed hand and a lost finger.

Alex was disappointed, but try as he could, he could not convince James Jackson to buy some of the fine acreage he offered. James was a fisherman at heart and chose a site nearer the ocean at Cape Neddick, where he had eyes for a certain lass in addition to the sea he loved.

John and Eliza MacKinney came up from Gloucester a week before the wedding so they could have time to visit with their friends, catch up on all the news, and show off their strappingly handsome son, Daniel, who was now nine years old and the spitting image of his father, with even wilder and brighter red hair. "Be assured, in spite of it, he has a much gentler nature!" Eliza quipped.

"'Tis me heart it fills ta hear how well things be down yer way, John. We've heard rumors of some Indian troubles though—any of those bothersome ta ye?"

"Nay, me friend, a few skirmishes, maybe, but nary a thing fer ye ta worry yer head about. So, what do ye reckon about yer namesake,

Daniel Dill?"

"'Tis a fine lad he be, in every way, John. 'Tis such a treat ta meet him and ta see ye. Eliza has blossomed. I guess 'tis the salt air that has been so good fer her!"

"'Tis more than that as ye well ken, smart arse. But then, ye be right, me lad. 'Tis happy ta be back with her kin she be. And I admit that she be mad fer me and Danny—and, I gladly fess up ta it, me *bráthair*—me fer them as well."

"Ye surely have earned it. 'Tis about time ye got somethin' right!"

John's gentle giant smile lit up his broad face. "Ay, Danny, I hope yer Dorrie makes ye as whole as me Eliza does me."

"Ye old mutt! 'Tis my wish as well, *bráthair*." Dan thought briefly to share how much Dorrie resembled his Mora, but decided against it.

They stayed at the Dill house and Eliza volunteered to put a few feminine touches on the lovely but stark garrison home. She improved on some of Dan's feeble attempts, but she had nothing but praise for the huge feather bed and the balustrade.

Alexander, Robert, and Daniel were shocked to see what a mess John's leg was and how much it still bothered him. Eliza confirmed that there was no discussing its condition. He was just as bull headed about it as ever and worked like a horse in spite of it. She assured them that he loved the fishing business, never called it work—just enjoyed every moment. She glowed when she spoke of her John and Danny.

Chapter 50

A FINE KETTLE OF FISH

THE HEAVY snows of winter were behind them, but June 1665 turned out to be cold, even for Maine. In spite of it, summer had managed to bloom and York and Scotland Parish were eye-catching with their fresh greenery and colorful early flowers. The morning started out nippy, but the breathtakingly flawless blue sky transformed and warmed it into a perfect day for the simply charming wedding.

Later, after the service and small reception at the Moore home, John MacKinney and his family reluctantly bid their farewells and headed back to Gloucester. Having John around again had been so natural and good that Robert, Dan, and Alex had ignored the fact that he must get back to his new life. They wished once more that he and Eliza had settled in Scotland Parish, but they could clearly see that their dear friend's heart had led him to make the best decision for him and his family.

More hugging and tearing up came about when Dorrie said her thanks and farewells to her family before she and Daniel rode up the trail to the home they would share on Cider Hill. She was still sniffling when they rounded the bend to the cove, "Hush now, Dorrie, yer nary leavin' them forever. We'll be only a few miles away and see them often we will."

"I know that and there's no need to fret, Daniel Dill . . . *my husband*," she wiped her nose, dried her eyes, and looked adoringly into his before she squeezed his hand and went on, "I'm so looking forward to our life together, and I want it more than I have ever wanted anything—still, we both know that my old home and family will always be a part of me."

He prayed she would never know how deeply that remark hit home for him as he looked into her beautiful face of his yesterday. He shook off his feelings and smiled at his bride, whose tears were forgotten once he swooped her up—starry eyed and lovely, in her soft white wedding dress—and carried her over the threshold into her new home.

He held her, sweet and fair. But try as he would, she was Mora in his mind and he prayed, *Lord, dinna let her cherished name pass my lips.*

She was quiet in his arms, although she shook like a frightened little bird that had fallen out of its nest into a strange unknown place. *Mora was not quiet,* he remembered, they had melted together naturally, as if they had always been one.

Dorrie, Dorrie—God, help me—'tis Dorrie, he reminded himself.

He held her closer, untied her fancy nightcap, pushed back her soft black hair, and kissed her on the forehead while he whispered, "My sweet *Dorrie.*"

But it was Mora's hair he smelled, Mora's round firm breasts he felt, and it was Mora he made love to with a wild urgency and desire. He was back with her in every sense of the word. Every fragment and caress of their love was fresh in his mind, and he was swept away. He felt her warm body bend into his until the moon exploded into a thousand stars. His heart was full and he was home.

Once he was spent he felt deeply ashamed. Reality found him sheepishly in Dorrie's arms, his shoulders shook with sobs and tears ran down his face.

Dorrie was obviously frightened, but she held onto him strongly. She had never had a man in her bed and could make no sense of this outburst.

The first thing that came to her mind was, *Is that what it's all about then? Is this the love marriage is supposed to build on to make it strong and lasting? —And here it's me that should be doing the crying. What a strange kettle of fish this is.* She stared at the ceiling for what seemed an eternity and finally fell asleep, but not before she resolved to figure this marriage thing out.

The smell of sizzling bacon and freshly cooked biscuits woke him. He whacked his head and silently admonished himself. *Zounds, how daft ken I be?* He jumped out of bed, jolted himself back to the present, and braced himself for Dorrie's reaction.

He expected the worst, most likely she would leave him and be on her way back to York—but thankfully that was not the case. There she was, fully dressed, lovely and fresh as a daisy—the table set, coffee in his mug. Daniel was well aware that the entire Moore clan ate like kings, and it seemed obvious that Dorrie was bent on keeping up the family tradition. She turned and greeted him with a warm welcoming smile. He breathed a sigh of relief and his heart sang again.

So fetching, a great cook and fun, she filled his house with joy. *Dorrie joy* he kept telling himself—but try as he would—Mora still smiled through.

After his bad slip into the Mora fantasy, Dan took himself to task. He made a special effort to control himself and see Dorrie as Dorrie. *I ken deal with this—I must,* he promised himself, *'Tis my wife she be—she deserves better.*

He put his heart into it and his efforts seemed to help, and if Dorrie suspected anything was amiss, she gave no sign of it. He made sure that their lovemaking was gentler, and she responded in surprising ways. They became more comfortable with each other and a warm relationship began to take shape. It hit new heights when Dorrie announced to Daniel that he was going to be a father. "Next March, my dearest husband, we'll welcome spring with our first child." She cuddled in his arms and with soft, tender touches initiated caresses that pleasured them both.

• • •

A couple of months later, Dorrie's mother informed her that her black sheep brother, James, had died and had left Dorrie five pounds in his will. "Why did he do that, Ma? I hardly ever met or saw him."

"It would take more than me to figure James out." Her mother frowned and shrugged her shoulders. "Most likely he did it because he heard of your marriage and because he loved you, dear. Just enjoy it as he would want you to."

Dorrie puzzled over the unexpected wedding gift and shared her feelings with her husband, "He didn't leave my brothers or sisters anything. Don't you think that strange?"

"I nary met James, so I kenna say what his reasonin' is, but 'twas surely kind of him ta think of ye, strange or naught."

"Well, Dan, I've inquired around and no one seems to know much of anything about him, after his wife's death he just seemed to disappear into the blue. There was a rumor I overheard, that James was my father, that his wife died in childbirth and that he blamed the child and wouldn't even look at her—what's more, it could be that I was that babe, and my Ma and Pa took me in out of pity."

"Well," Daniel thought for a minute, let out a huge breath then said, "William spouted out yer birth date real fast when first I asked fer yer hand, so that rumor 'tis most likely just that. It makes nary a difference ta me, though—I love ye nary matter who ye are." He had said that to be funny, but then it caught in his throat. *What am I thinkin'? Zounds, I should listen ta myself—there 'tis plain as day—'tis true—I love her Mora, but every time I see or touch her, I burn hot fer ye. 'Tis selfish I know, but I kenna let ye go.*

He shook out the cobwebs and said aloud, "I'll check about quietly and see what I ken turn up about yer Uncle James. We may nary find the answer ta that one, but if any truth ta it there is, I feel sure yer Ma would have told ye by now."

• • •

The pregnancy was hard on Dorrie; nothing tasted good and she felt nauseous most of the time. One day she was feeling especially antsy and picked a bone with Daniel about church going. "You steer clear of going to church with me for even the most trivial excuse, and you certainly have come up with some of the dizziest ones I've ever heard of. You could make more of an effort, Daniel Dill. I know you are not fond of my church, but I feel obliged to attend. My family has a history in these parts. My mother's father, William Dixon, was living here back when York was called Gorges and Gorgeana—and the Moores go way back too. I owe them my respect. You offend both Puritans and Royalists alike with your outspoken ways and insolent remarks.

"Sometimes it seems to me you do it on purpose just to show contempt for their authority." She pouted, kneaded her hands, and tearfully went on, "I realize you'd much rather attend your friend Alexander's meeting house services, but If I don't go to my own church regularly I could be flogged or placed in the stocks; even tied to a dunking stool and dumped into the freezing river. I don't think I could survive such a thing. Please Danny, dear, do not embarrass me so."

Dan couldn't help but be amused at his wife's lame attempts to get him to attend services in town. She was right though, he had no use for Cromwell's church, but he considered her condition and suggested that they go to York one week and to Alex's meeting house the next.

Feeling that she could eventually convince Dan to take her into York every Sunday, Dorrie agreed, but she soon found that attending the meeting house was very comforting, although the hard backless benches were not. She felt sick and dreadfully tired most of the time and had to admit that the shorter service was so much easier on her and the lesser distance they had to travel, just up the Cider Hill Trail was very welcome. And moreover, she enjoyed the congregation and loved it when Alexander sang his heart out *for the Lord*, so he said—and it was hard to fault him since no one ever tired of listening to his golden voice.

For once Dan never said a word. He was happy and enjoyed their attendance at the meeting house. Albeit, he couldn't help but sanctimoniously observe that no one came to try to drag his wife away to the stocks or threaten to dunk her in the river.

Chapter 51

ERSTWHILE FEARS REVISITED

IT TRIED hard to be spring, but March had no reputation in either the new or old Scotland for delivering it, and in 1666, it definitely was not in sight. Ice and snow were abundant in the woods and the white stuff still fell when and where it felt like it. The air was absolutely freezing and not a bud dared peek out.

"Breach," the midwife shrieked at Daniel. "It's a breach birth and it's not going well. I don't think I need to tell you that it's hell. She'll have to be very strong and the babe too, just to get through it. I can't do this alone. Get going and fetch the doctor."

"What? Breach? What are ye sayin'—are ye daft, woman?" All he could think of was John MacKinney's first wife, Jean. She gave birth to their son, Gavin, who was in a breach position, and Dan well remembered that they were both lost.

"Let me in! I must see my wife," he pleaded with the midwife, "there are things I need ta tell her."

"I'm afraid that will have to wait. She's already in too much pain for a fireside chat. Settle in with your people and be prepared for a long haul—and a whole lot of praying would be good."

Daniel was never much for praying, so he started drinking, and alcohol was not his friend. It didn't take much to get him reeling. His thoughts raced back to Mora, their little Ellen, and the second child they had looked forward to.

What's happenin'? How ken this be? I ken take just about anythin', but nary more of that—*I kenna stand another horror like that. Nay.* His thoughts scared him.

Oh my dear, Mora—Dorrie is nary as strong as ye were. She is so delicate and frail. I need her, I love her—ye ken the need, dinna ye? She must stay—she must.

Alexander heard the commotion, saw the midwife arrive, jumped into his snow shoes, and rushed down to the Dill home to offer his help.

"The *bairn*—'tis breach, Alex—and dinna they say—the past dinna repeat itself."

"Sorry, but ye've got it wrong, my *bráthair*, unfortunately—it almost always does."

As soon as Alexander heard that the midwife needed help he called Albert out of the barn and sent him on his way for the doctor. He had started praying a while back and decided it would be best to take Daniel away from Dorrie's screams.

Robert Junkins appeared as if out of nowhere, and he and Alex coaxed a bewildered Dan up the hill to the Maxwell home where they sat around the table in the front window to wait.

No doubt a mistake—they all knew that Dan could not hold his drink—but he already had a head start and they couldn't stop him— he just drank more and more—grog, whiskey and any other hard drink Alex's cupboards had to offer—which was a lot.

Suddenly he made up his mind that he must go home, "And ay, I ken damn well make it on my own, thank ye very much. I'm goin' ta sit in my own chair til I hear that Dorrie and the *bairn* are well." Nothing his friends said could convince him otherwise, and he headed off down the blustery Cider Hill Trail.

"Let's stay far enough behind so that he's naught aware that we are checkin' on him. We'll join him later and keep him company. Who knows how this will turn out? I kenna get our *bráthair* John MacKinney and his Jean out of my mind, and we both know 'tis what swirls in the forefront of Dan's, along with the loss of his Mora and all."

Robert agreed and poured the two of them another cup of grog while they let Daniel get a head start.

A tipsy Dan was barely on the trail back to his home when he started to vomit, loudly. This drew the attention of his stiff necked, anal retentive, neighbor from the lower side of Bass Cove, John Card. Bad timing for Daniel—the current jailer just happened to be out shoveling and caught a good view of Dan. There was no missing the fact that he was three sheets to the wind. Card held a particular resentment toward all Scotsmen, so he took pleasure in his chance to make an example out of this inebriated Scot. He dropped his shovel, arrested him, and hustled him down to the jail in York.

It so happened that Dorrie's young brother, Robert Moore, saw Card push Daniel through the jail door. He told his brother, John, who beat it up the Cider Hill Trail to tell Alexander Maxwell—who then rushed down to York and after some fast talking and finagling—finally convinced Card to let him take his very distraught and sloshed friend home under his care, for a fee.

• • •

It had been many hours, but the doctor was still closed in the bedroom with Dorrie. When the midwife finally came out, she handed a contrite, but at long-last sober, Daniel, his son. He was mesmerized and ogled him with wonder. The child was wrinkled and squealing, but he looked—and especially sounded—very healthy. Dan's eyes turned to the bedroom door, but it had firmly closed behind the retreating midwife.

He forced himself to focus on the bundle in his arms, "Hey there, Johnny," Dan heaved a sigh, weakly smiled and told his friends, "Dorrie and I decided that if 'twas a son we had, John he would be, after my Da and our *bráthair*, John MacKinney, fer sure." The new father took to the little guy straight away, although it didn't seem quite mutual! Young Johnny continued to be quite vocal. Alexander and Robert laughed, and Daniel couldn't help but join them, "Whoa, I ken see which John ye'll be takin' after."

Dan's head snapped as the bedroom door banged open and the doctor emerged followed by the midwife. He handed his son back to the woman and asked, "Ken I see my wife now?"

The doctor shook his head, "I'm sorry, I hate to tell you this, but Dorrie lapsed suddenly into a coma, and I must say the news is not good. She has lost a lot of blood and is extremely weak." He added firmly, "This is very serious; I don't believe she should have more children—if she can survive this, that is."

"Nay, what are ye sayin? Oh, Dorrie, nay." Dan crumpled into the nearest chair.

"Chin up, Dan. Ye have a fine *bairn,* and I am sure Dorrie ken weather the storm and get through this. She is young and stronger than ye give her credit fer."

Alex placed his hand on his friend's shoulder, "'Tis as Rob says, my *bráthair*—have some faith, Dan—ye kenna give up. 'Tis always hope. We must pray that she is healed and restored ta us straight away."

Dorrie's condition lingered on. It seemed improved one day and dismal the next, but after seven days at death's door, she surprised them all when she finally awoke from the coma and started to mend quickly.

Dorrie's mother, who had recently given birth herself, took her new grandson, Johnny, down to the Moore home on Verrel Street and wet-nursed both him and her new daughter, until Dorrie regained enough strength to take on her own child.

Before they knew it, Johnny was an adorable toddler. The proud parents enjoyed and played with him like youngsters themselves.

Daniel cleared out a lovely area around a giant old oak log on the bank of the Cove down where the river wandered in. Rob Junkins planted a fragrant white lilac bush on the north side of the log that added ambiance to the surroundings.

Dorrie loved it. They had fun with Johnny, laughed, relaxed, and treasured their time there. Alexander and Robert came down often to join them, take advantage of the great fishing, or to just sit on the old log and shoot the bull with friends.

Then, Dorrie was pregnant again. Nerves were on end until the birth proved uneventful and normal. A second son, William—named for Dan's beloved brother and Dorrie's father—was born on June 10, 1667—and belying all the doctor's worst predictions, both young Willy and Dorrie came through it healthy and well.

Sure that Johnny's difficult birth was a fluke, Daniel and Dorrie were thrilled in 1668 when the birth of their healthy third son, Joseph, seemed to prove them right.

The Resilient Thistle

That year brought more good news—it was the first year that Scotland Parish was mentioned in the town of York records as a separate suburb. It seemed that the town had finally recognized the Scots.

At the same time, Robert Junkins happily welcomed his good friend from his Salmon Falls days, Andrew Rankin, to Cider Hill and listened eagerly to all the stories he had brought with him. He knew Alex would be especially interested in one of them, so he moseyed down the Cider Hill Trail and recapped the news for him.

"Everyone be still reelin' from Richard Leader's death. As ye know, Robert Jordan was appointed administrator of his estate back in 1661. Well, Andy told me that Richard's sons-in-law were selected as beneficiaries. Ye'll probably recall that Richard's daughter, Elizabeth, married John Hole of lower Kittery, and her sister, Anne—Samuel Clarke—they live in Portsmouth." Robert cringed, "I dinna agree with that, I feel that Richard's *bairns* should inherit direct. But I knew that ye would want ta hear of it."

Alex nodded, "Ye be straight, on both counts. I am always interested in any news about Richard, and 'tis pleased indeed I am ta have Andy here, Rob."

Another land search was on the agenda with Alexander at the forefront and Andy Rankin chose a fine site not too far up the Cider Hill Trail from Robert's homestead.

Not long after that Massachusetts invaded York and took control of Maine. Wild goings on—and Peter Weare was right in the middle of the action, where he was promptly arrested and accused of being a traitor. His friends and cohorts were so offended that such false accusations had been made against their loyal ally that they broke Peter out of jail, hid him out, and made him lay low until he woke up to the fact that Maine would not get out from under the thumb of Massachusetts for a long time.

Chapter 52

CUPID'S SURPRISE!

THE FOUNDING fathers of Scotland Parish were pleased with how well the hamlet had progressed in the years since Alexander Maxwell had made his first purchase on Cider Hill. The Scotsmen had settled into their *second chance* lives and were grateful and proud of themselves.

Nowhere was it more obvious than at Bass Cove—where, on an amazingly warm day for April—Alexander Maxwell, Robert Junkins, and Daniel Dill along with his wife, Dorrie, and sons, John, Willy, and Joseph, enjoyed a visit to their favorite spot by the Cove, down where the white lilacs grew. They all had fun teasing and playing with the boys until Dorrie caught a chill and trudged them up the path for their afternoon nap.

Once she was out of sight, Alex asked, "How is Dorrie doin', Dan?"

"She's full of surprises, that one, and she nary fails ta amaze me. 'Tis nary a doubt that she's still frail, but she's always tellin' me she's fine—that she loves me—her life and our family. And I must say, that even though my sons are a handful. She manages them and the house with an ease that puts me ta shame.

"Ye ken see that Johnny's gettin' real tall. Willy's growin' like a weed. And ye heard Joey, he's startin' ta spurt out words like a wee trooper, eh?"

Alex knocked him on the shoulder and said, "'Tis a beautiful family ye have, Dan. It pleases me ta be considered a part of it."

The Resilient Thistle

A bit later, as the inseparable trio sat on the old log, rehashed stories, and shot the breeze, Alexander nudged Daniel, raised an eyebrow, and crooked his head while he eyeballed Robert in a quizzical way. There could be no doubt that he was especially quiet. He had been acting quite strangely lately and had taken a lot of mysterious trips to Cape Neddick. He had made up so many excuses for the excursions that the two decided that this was the time to pin him down and ring the secret out of him.

"Spit it out, Robert Jonkings—dinna try ta tell us that nary a thing 'tis goin' on. We ken ye better than that. What 'tis with ye, anyway?"

Robert groaned, looked a bit sheepish, took in a deep breath, and threw a random stick into the water—then two. He finally convinced himself that this was as good a time as any to come clean, "Ye two are always sayin' that 'tis *better late than nary at all, eh?* Well, this may come as a surprise ta ye, but 'tis 'bout the best better late than nary that could ever be fer me *bráthairs.*"

His two friends rolled their eyes, twitched their mouths, and winked at each other, "Ay, umm," Alex teasingly thumped Robert on the shoulder and ventured. "So, 'tis *bráthairs*, eh? 'Tis serious indeed, this must be."

Dan winked at Alexander, smirked, bit back a grin, and nodded in agreement, "Could this be about a four-legged furry critter? Eye on a new wagon, mayhap? More land? Nary more apple trees, eh? What say ye?" Robert gave them both his most disgusted look and lambasted them.

"Listen up ye scallywags, 'tis nary a time fer yer tom foolery. Ay, 'tis serious—'tis damn right deep serious—and I've nary been more so," he blurted out.

He called up his courage with firm thoughts, *How about that? Jolted 'em, did I? Well, I reckon 'tis best I sock it ta 'em now that they are in my clutches and completely off-guard. Rattle their timbers 'twill fer sure! Rattle my own 'twill—as well. Here goes.*

"'Tis Sarah Smyth—ye blockheads—'tis months 'tis taken me, but I got ta the end of my rope, got up my mettle, and went ahead and asked her straight out if she would marry me, and—ken ye believe it? She utterly flabbergasted me and accepted! Dinna ye hear that? She said yes! I dinna stop shakin' yet! I am gettin' married!"

Heads turned, jaws dropped open, and eyes bugged out, "What?" His two friends almost fell off the log. They glanced at each other and gawked blankly at Rob, then back at each other. Dumbfounded, Alex searched for words and finally found enough voice to utter, "Well—*nary say nary*—I'll be danged—ta say the least!"

Dan was flat out pleased, "Rob, 'tis the best news we've been hearin' fer a long spell. Best wishes are in order."

"Indeed," Alexander exhaled noisily as he regained his composure, clapped Rob on the back, and added, "Well done, I am truly delighted fer ye."

Robert relaxed, his face lit up, and he smiled—obviously relieved and tickled that his friends approved and shared his happiness.

No way could Alex let him off that easy, "Now, might that be John Smyth's daughter?"

"Ay, 'tis . . . so?"

"'Tis well known in and around the Cape Neddick area that he be . . . well . . . are ye sure he wants ta put up with an old codger like ye fer a son-in-law? "

"Ye kenna leave it be, ken ye? What ken I say, Alex? Well, 'tis beyond me, but Sarah loves me—thanks be ta God. What's more, 'tis a lovely, charmin' woman she be—the same age as Dorrie, by the by. I am hopin' 'tis good friends they'll be."

Dan elbowed Alex and said, "We kenna fault ye on this one, Rob. We are thrilled fer ye, *bráthair*. When ken ye bring her up ta meet Dorrie and our little hooligans? I am sure 'tis love her they will, since ye seem ta be so smitten!"

Shortly after that visit, Robert drove Sarah up Cider Hill to visit the Dills, accompanied by her neighbor, Nellie Damon. Alexander walked down to join them and was impressed with Robert's choice of such a fine lady. As Dan had predicted, Sarah and Dorrie hit it off from the start, and she fit in straight away with Alex and Dan as well.

For a while Sarah was reluctant to add her touch to Rob's home, but he encouraged her to make it her own. He emphasized that she'd be improving *their* home, and he would be grateful for her help. That was all the encouragement she needed. She went right to it and brought a few things up from Cape Neddick on each visit. When Nel or Sarah's sister, Elizabeth, couldn't chaperone, Dorrie gladly took over and welcomed the chance to pay a visit and help Sarah put her future home in order.

Once the inevitable spring mud finally dried out and the soil was ready, Sarah jumped at the chance to help Rob with his garden. Her green thumb fit in perfectly with his, and she was as fussy as he was about planting the rows straight and neat.

When it was Dorrie's turn to chaperone, she embraced the change of pace and thoroughly enjoyed it. On a clear day she sat under fresh smelling apple trees filled with pink buds while her sons, Johnny, Willy, and Joey played nearby. From her vantage point, she kept an unnecessary eye on Sarah and Robert as they putted in their garden.

Robert Junkins married his beloved Sarah Smyth in June of 1670. It ended up being a beautiful double wedding that was held at the Smyth home in Cape Neddick.

Rob trembled as he watched Sarah walk down the aisle toward him. *She looks like an angel*, he thought. His head swirled and his wobbly knees barely held him up, but as soon as he felt her hand in his, he came alive and made it through the ceremony all in one piece, although he could never remember a minute of it later.

The ceremony that made Robert and Sarah man and wife also joined Sarah's sister, Elizabeth Smyth, to James Jackson.

Seems that James had been courting Elizabeth for some time, and they had fallen in love and become quietly engaged earlier in the year. James had built a charming house and barn on his land in Cape Neddick even before she had accepted his proposal, and once she had, Elizabeth and Sarah started to perk that house up between visits to the Junkins' place.

The brides were beautiful, the grooms happy, and the reception abundant with good food and good cheer. Of course, Alex sang at the wedding and the reception—as always, not leaving a dry eye in sight.

As soon as they thought it safe, the newly wedded Jacksons slipped out the back and jumped into a buggy they had hidden behind a huge tree. But, not so fast! Their friends had beaten them to it, painted all over the buggy, and attached shoes, tin cups, and other hodgepodges to it. The Jacksons laughed it off and noisily rattled off, giggling all the way to the home that waited to welcome them.

Robert did not escape so easily—Alex and Dan had other plans. A cocky Robert thought he had outwitted them as he drove his dear Sarah proudly up to the Junkins home on Cider Hill in a strong new wagon he had put out a pretty penny for. He claimed to his friends that he had purchased it for his bride, but he had to admit that the attention it got him from family and friends hadn't hurt.

Alexander and Daniel jumped out and trailed the wagon—as close to it as they could manage—rattled chains and threw out wise cracks all the way up the hill. They laughed and teased while Sarah blushed, and Rob tried to urge the horse on, to shake them off—it didn't work.

Alex frowned, pursed his lips, and stated the obvious to Dan, "Seems James Jackson ken what he was doin' when he bought those thirty acres in Cape Neddick rather than on Cider Hill. I dinna believe fer a minute that 'twas only the sea that called ta him. I be willin' ta bet he had his eye on Elizabeth Smyth the whole time."

With a scoff, Dan nudged him, "Ya think, Alex?"

"Well, I offered him some exceptional sites, ye know. Much better than he got."

"Sometimes ye baffle me, Alexander Maxwell."

"Takes one ta ken one, as ye be always the first ta say."

They loudly pestered Robert and Sarah until they arrived at Dan's long walk way. Then they got out a few more jibes, laughed, banged the wagon, and dropped the chains—headed for their own homes and let the newlyweds be on their way in peace.

Chapter 53

TRAGEDY AND REBIRTH

THREE MONTHS later, with fishing poles in hand, but hearts not in it, Daniel Dill, Alexander Maxwell, and Robert Junkins sat sadly at their favorite spot on the bank of Bass Cove enveloped in a black mood that hung over them like a shroud. Dan attempted to break the silence, "It dinna seem right—'tis such a tragic blow—and afta things all seemed ta be fallin' inta place."

Like three heavy stones, they remained hunkered together on the old log until Robert finally made an attempt, "I still kenna reckon it, our *bráthair*, John MacKinney dead. Zounds, 'tis like a sword through the heart, and him on top of the world."

Alex agreed, "Ay, and we dinna even get the chance ta go ta Gloucester fer the funeral. 'Twas rough hearin' the whole story after 'twas all over. What a terrible blow ta them and ta all of us."

"The damn leg." Dan lamented bitterly as he relived the sad tale they'd already repeated many times, as if saying it over and over would change the outcome, "'Twas a nasty squall that came up out of nowhere, and when he tried ta help get the sails down the boat skewed and he slipped and fell hard onta the wet deck. The leg snapped right at the spot that was so weakened by that sick old wound. The broken bone split, ripped through the skin, and left him in terrible agony."

"They said that all he did was bite his lip and call fer the scotch whiskey—that nary a one knew he had. Just like him, eh? His son, Danny, found it, and he and the crew poured it down John's throat.

By the time the storm cleared so they could get him ashore, the leg was such a mess that all the doctor could do was cut it off. Eliza gave him the go ahead while John was still out of it. Kenna ye reckon it?"

Rob dropped his head, bemoaning the very thought of it. "'Tis a good thing he dinna hear that order. 'Tis nary a way he would have let them take it." They agreed and couldn't help but chuckle as they pictured what John's reaction would have been.

Alex spoke up, "In this case, naught a bit of his stubbornness would have helped. 'Twas nothin' else ta be done. I cringe ta think about it.

"'Tis nary what we'd want. 'Tis nary our Scottish way, but since his wish was ta be buried at sea—a fisherman thing it seems—well, ye know, *bráthairs*—respect it we must. 'Tis the least we ken do."

Dan broke in, "So out he went fer the last sail—Eliza, young Danny, her father, brother, and John's crew took him. She said it was a perfect day, very peaceful with a glass smooth sea, and he would have loved it."

John had no qualms about the safety of the fishing business and had given Eliza instructions as to what to do should anything happen to him and had charged her to write a farewell to his friends as well, to be kept in case the need should arise. Rob pulled the wrinkled note from his pocket and read it aloud, as they had done a dozen times since they had gotten the news.

"Dinna ye dare ta grieve fer me bráthairs. 'Tis the best of both worlds been mine, and 'tis only due ta ye that I got through the rest. I swear I love ye—ye ornery buzzards—so smile when ye think of me, or 'tis back 'twill I be ta get ye."

"Leave it ta him, dinna ye recall how he loved ta boss us around? Now I reckon 'tis done it, he has, even from the grave! And 'tis best we move on out of respect fer him, or he'll be on our backs!"

They couldn't help but smile at that, and Robert affirmed, "'Tis sure I am that he could do it, if anybody could."

Easy to say, but sorrow lay heavy and refused to be shaken off. John's death had cut the friends' hearts to the core. Everyone tried in vain to get them to move on, but nothing seemed to help. Finally, some good news managed to lift their spirits, and Robert Junkins was the one to deliver it.

The Resilient Thistle

"Micum MacIntyre has finally arrived here in our Scotland. A lot of years 'tis taken him, but he said 'twas part of his plan ta come from the first time he heard of it. Great friends we were at Salmon Falls, and we spoke of settlin' up here, but 'twas nary quite sure I was, as time went on, that he would actually come."

Dan and Alex were elated. "'Tis wonderful news, indeed. What a long way he's come from that fateful day at Dunbar when he was a *number ten* and about ta be shot, eh? Nary one of us will ere forget how he took off from the ranks and scampered in and about like a weasel till he was caught and saved by Lieutenant Wilbur Barlow."

They all laughed and Rob affirmed, "'Tis one of the rare good memories from those times. Micum mentioned ta me that 'tis lookin' fer a piece of land he be, and he has his eye on that beautiful spot of yers, Alex. Said he'd appreciate it if ye were ta cut out a piece fer him on yer south side."

"Hmm, 'tis some thought I'll be needin' ta give on that one. Ye know how I value my open land."

"Dinna ye know that Micum married Alexander Makaneer's widow?"

"Nay, 'tis a surprise, I dinna know that."

"Ay, she was Dorothy Pierce. They married soon after Makaneer died."

Dan recalled Makaneer only too well. "Ye and he dinna ever get along, eh? Ye were at odds, even back in the *Cathedral* and on the *Unity*. What was it with ye two?"

"I kenna place it, Daniel. We just rubbed each other the wrong way. Ye must admit that he was an aggravatin' little bastard. He knew just how ta get my goat, and he loved ta egg me on. He always called me *Maxey*, and ye know how fast that got my dander up. That 'tis why I conked him a couple of times."

"Ay, I surely remember, nary yer most shinin' hour, especially since he was so spindly and walked with that limp."

A chastised Alexander decided he'd said enough, but the next day he met with Micum MacIntyre. He was grateful that he knew it was Micum he was to meet, otherwise he never would have recognized him—he had changed considerably.

But, haven't we all? Look at me—even wearin' English garb and all, he reflected, rubbed his pants, and reached out his hand to greet him. The spunky little banty rooster he remembered had transformed into a tall stately man who still had the soulful brown eyes of a lost puppy. A droopy mustache melted into his short well-trimmed beard, and hair that was almost black stopped just below his ears where it curled and was full—the crown, however, was a bit thin, and Alex noticed that there was a hat tucked into his side pocket.

The meeting was a bit awkward until Alex opened the conversation with, "Good ta see ye again, Micum. We're pleased that ye've chosen ta settle in Scotland Parish. I dinna know where yer home was in the old country."

"My family came from Glencoe," he answered, his Gaelic accent nearly absent—as was Alex's for that matter. "Andy Rankin's from there, lots of McDonalds and Campbells as well. 'Tis off to the east from Lock Linnke, near Bellachulish."

Alex tried to picture it, but nothing came to him, "I dinna know that area, although I think I recall Daniel mentionin' Lock Linnke when he spoke of Oben."

"Ay, we're a bit north of that. If I remember rightly, John MacKinney came from Tobermorey, on the Isle of Mull—which is to the west of Oben and Glencoe and sits right on the ocean—really rough weather there—no wonder he was so tough!

"Rob Junkins brought me up to date on John, told me he had moved on to Gloucester, was married, fishin' and all. I could picture him there. 'Tis so very much like Tobermorey by the Sea. He was an amazin' warrior, eh? A bitter shame that Dunbar got him in the end."

Sensing the pain the mention of John's death brought back, Micum wisely chose to move on, "Glencoe is a dandy place, a lot more snow than here, but no more than they get in the White Mountains that are not too far north in what they're callin' New Hampshire. I did a run up there for Doughty once looking for timber. Knocked me for a loop when I saw those hills. They were snowcapped and looked so much like the ones that surround Glencoe that I thought I was in a dream and at home. I wouldn't settle up there though, word is that 'tis not a great place to live. The area is only good for wolves and bear!"

The survivors got along famously, and Alex soon was persuaded to sell Micum a nice piece of land on the south side of his home.

He wasn't quite sure if he had been convinced to sell it because he respected and liked Micum so much or because he still felt guilty for his abuse of Alexander Makaneer, whose widow, Dorothy, was now Micum's wife, either way he felt he had made a good decision.

Besides, he told himself, *Micum was a great friend ta Robert at Salmon Falls, and they helped each other get through that time. I am sure a good neighbor he'll be.*

By the end of 1670 Micum and Dorothy MacIntyre had moved into their home as Alex's neighbors. Their house was built in the traditional farmhouse style rather than the garrison type Alex, Rob, and Dan had preferred. The downside was that Dorothy was not at all well, and she passed away less than a year after they moved in.

Chapter 54

ANOTHER KING—ANOTHER WAR

ON AN exceptionally brilliant day in March of 1671, the Junkins and Daniel were seated comfortably around the great room table enjoying a piece of blueberry jam pie Sarah had baked to perfection in her bee-hive oven. Robert sat quietly and fidgeted with his piece for what seemed to Sarah like forever. Abruptly he pushed himself away from the table, stood up, and tested, "Dan, I know how much ye love ta create things from wood. How's about ye render me an opinion on my latest effort?"

"Ye know I would be pleased ta."

With that, Rob slipped into the bedroom and returned grinning like a Cheshire cat. Under his left arm he lugged an adorable cradle. "I felled the tree, planed the boards, made the pattern, sawed it out, sanded and rubbed it—took what seemed like years." He halted and took a deep breath before he expectantly asked, "So, what think ye?"

Immediately alert, Dan flew out of his chair to examine the lovingly created work of art and said, "'Tis nary a craftsman who could have done it better. It rocks in perfect balance and 'tis finished with care. 'Tis just a little honey. Ye sly rascal, Robert Junkins. I dinna know, but . . . seems 'tis . . . er . . . 'tis . . . ah . . . be ye two . . . expectin'?"

Sarah smiled and nodded her head from the chair she had moved to near the fireplace, and Rob walked over and placed his arm around her. Dan couldn't hold back, he jumped in with, "Zounds 'tis the cat's meow—'tis! When will the wee one arrive?"

"Oh, the usual time, in a few months—about the time the leaves turn." Sarah purred and smiled at her husband. "We're very pleased."

And five months later, Sarah Smyth Junkins gave Robert, now fifty years of age, a son, Joseph. His wife and child had weathered the birthing well and nothing could have gratified Robert more. He was overjoyed at his good fortune.

• • •

Scotland Parish had grown more rapidly once its fine reputation had spread about. Fresh settlers put up new homes while established citizens enlarged theirs or upgraded. John Card, who had just been appointed constable of York and the surrounding area, built a new house on the Cider Hill Trail across from the south end of Bass Cove, which made him an even closer neighbor to Daniel Dill than he had been. None of the Scotsmen were elated about it. They all knew that he had no affinity for them. "I know 'tis yer neighbor he be, Dan, but whenever possible keep yer distance from the old grouch. He nary misses a chance ta put us down."

"And, mayhap I reckon ta be well aware of that, eh?"

Sarah gave Robert Junkins a second son in the spring of 1675. They named him Alexander, and Alexander Maxwell's head was puffed beyond belief.

"Old Robert's makin' up fer lost time, Dan, I nary thought he had it in him, but 'tis just great, and I kenna be more tickled about my namesake."

"'Tis quite an honor alright, but nary rightly deserved after all the bad mouthin' ye sprang on his Da over time."

"Why, I nary, what do ye mean, ye old goat . . ." Alex hesitated, caught in his own trap. "Well, could be I may have teased him a bit . . . in a rare moment."

"Rare moment? Ye were on his back all day, every day."

"Fer Pete's sake, Daniel . . ."

"Got ya, Alex, but needless ta say, if ye dish it out, ye must be able ta take it."

With that, Dan whopped his friend on the shoulder, and they shared a roaring laugh that hurt their stomachs, but at the same time felt good. When their bellies stopped aching, Dan added, "All joshin' aside, more'n any of us, Robert knows only too well that yer heart—well—'tis in the right place, Alexander Maxwell."

"And, thank God fer givin' me a sense of humor so that I ken stand yer lame attempts at one, ye snowy stinker."

"I love ye too, Alexander Maxwell, ye pious pain in the arse."

• • •

Happiness and contentment continued to abound, and there was no reason for any person in Scotland Parish to suspect that the happy life and tranquility they had worked so hard to create was about to take a nasty turn.

Called the *Red Indians* or *Algonquians*—they roamed the snowbound forests of Canada—down the rocky coast of Maine, west to the canyons of Colorado and south to the Everglades of Florida. In Maine they were called *Abenaki* or *Tarrantines*. They had been friendly until settlers had threatened and attacked them. In addition, many of their enemies had been killed off—mostly the *Mohawk* and *Iroquois*—by a great plague, small pox, and tribal wars.

No Indians had ever shown any interest in the town of York. They had no claim there and had not been mistreated in any way in the area. In addition, none of them had camped anywhere near the town from at least as far back as 1616. However, everything changed when the Indian chief *Metacomet*, King Philip, initiated a war with an attack on the Plymouth Colony on the twenty-fourth of June, 1675. The people in York, including Scotland Parish, were aware of it and empathized, but none believed that its consequences would seriously affect them—*wrong*.

Although this situation seemed to appear suddenly, problems and resentment had been simmering for some time. From the Indian's point of view, the war was justified, and it was no surprise that King Philip easily gathered many recruits. Within two months the war had worked its way up into Maine.

When the first raids shocked Wells and South Berwick, York responded by dispatching troops and ammunition. In addition, eight *big* guns were acquired from Massachusetts. Captain Ben Swett was placed in charge, and he quickly organized the men of York to patrol the district as his aides.

York soldiers that had previously been sent to Massachusetts were returned as extra protection for its estimated four hundred and eighty residents. Grateful to have their defense force back the citizens of the York area relaxed, felt much safer, and seemed to be so.

This calm continued into the summer to the great relief of Robert Junkins. His Sarah had just given birth to their third son—a little fellow they called Daniel. Their joy was shared by all—especially Alexander Maxwell and Daniel Dill—who now unreservedly shared in the puffed heads department.

The peaceful summer sailed by, but as the sun sank lower and the winds of fall cheekily filched color from the trees, all things changed. The bright harvest moon that lit up the serene September night was completely out of sorts with the gruesome message Daniel had to deliver.

"'Tis the most fowl thing I be obliged ta tell ye, Rob. Cape Neddick has been hit by savages—many were killed and most of the houses burned ta the ground."

Robert held his breath. The dismal look on Daniel's face sent chills down his spine, "My dear Sarah's folks?"

"Ay, my friend—Sarah's sister, Elizabeth—well, 'tis the worst. Her neighbor, Nel Damon came ta my house with yer niece, wee Lizzie. I dinna know how ta say this, so 'tis best I just out with it."

Robert flinched and awaited the worst as Dan went on, "Ay, Sarah's dear Elizabeth and her husband James Jackson, along with their two youngest *bairns* were among those butchered."

Robert sank to his knees, his face in his hands.

"'Tis more, and nasty 'tis. Do ye wanna hear it, *bráthair?*"

"Ye know I must, Dan." His friend looked up, his eyes full of tears, the pain that poured out was so strong that Daniel could barely go on, but he knew that if their places were reversed he would have to know everything. The friends depended on each other for the full truth, wherever it led.

"Well, it would be my wish that ye could keep Sarah from hearin' this most beastly wicked part, but I fear it kenna be done fer long. 'Tis so sorry I be, Rob. Elizabeth's head was smashed in and an arrow was shot through the *bairn* she was nursin'—with the precious wee one left attached ta her breast."

"Sweet Jesus."

"They scalped and hacked her, Robby, and did the same ta the other *bairn* and James. Then they set the Jackson home ablaze."

Overwhelmed, Robert was too disheartened to think or do anything. He just put his head back down and settled like a puddle onto the floor, completely broken.

"The bit of good news, my *bráthair*, 'tis that wee Lizzie lives and be in safe hands just down the trail with Dorrie, our sons, and Albert.

"All Nel could get out of Lizzie was that her folks both screamed fer her ta run and hide, and run she did as she had been trained ta do. She hid in the hollow her Da had dug out under that sprawlin' old oak behind the house. James nary dreamt it would be of any great importance—just figured it would make Elizabeth feel better ta have a safe place ta go ta in case of need. 'Twas there that the neighbor found sweet Lizzie, cowerin' in the hole, chokin' on smoke, and tryin' ta stifle sobs. She dinna seem bruised or bleedin', but was straight-out terrified and in deep distress—poor bairn."

Rob's body rocked and shook as he tried to control himself.

"Nel said that Elizabeth had spoken of her sister Sarah and of us and our friendship often. She knew how close the sisters were and that Sarah and Elizabeth had both recently given birth. She thought the shock of it all might be too much fer the new mother ta bear, so she brought Lizzie ta our place and asked me fer help.

"Dorrie will bring the little lass here as soon as ye think Sarah ken handle it. I be sure that she dinna yet recover from her Ma's death, let alone wee Danny's birth. Rob, I dinna know how she ken take this—or how any of us ken fer that matter."

Robert silently thanked God that his wife and sons were safe, "I hear ye, Dan, I know it will be mighty hard on her. She and Elizabeth have shared a deep bond since childhood, and this will surely scar her heart forever, but my Sarah 'tis some woman. She's very strong, much stronger than she looks. 'Twill take time, but get through this horror she will—and carry on. 'Tis grateful I would be if ye and Dorrie could be here when I tell her though."

"Off ta fetch her I go then, Rob. As scared stiff and exhausted as

Lizzie was, once she felt safe she went out like a candle and was still in a sound sleep when I came here. Albert and the lads will look after her till Dorrie and I get back.

"Nel said that she will come up ta see how Lizzie and the both of ye are later. She and her husband had ta head back ta Cape Neddick. She's such a kind woman and was close ta Elizabeth. We both know how hard this must be fer her."

Dorrie did her best to comfort Sarah, but there was not much anyone could do but hold and try to soothe her. Sarah insisted that the whole thing must be a mistake—that she must rush down to Cape Neddick and make it right. It took some time, but Rob and Dorrie convinced her that she was much too weak and was needed more at home.

It had not sunk in that the damage had been done. Cape Neddick was in ruins, and stronger hands than hers were needed to find and help any survivors, put out the flames, and hope that this nightmare of a disaster was over.

Chapter 55

BROKEN BRANCH

THE YORK area seemed safe for several months, but nearby villages of Kittery and Wells continued to suffer many casualties from intermittent raids. King Philip was killed in a swamp in Rhode Island on August 12, 1676, but this did not put an end to the hostility in Maine. Passionate supporters of King Philip from the Abenaki tribes prolonged the war he had begun, and in the following months several attacks on Casco and Scareborough left a trail of death and those towns in ruins.

By early November 1676, a treaty was negotiated by the Indian Mogg on behalf of his chief, Madockawando. Unfortunately, this treaty like the ones before it, proved to be worthless. By the time the first signs of spring began to appear, the Indians were back at their ploy to wipe out the settlers.

It didn't take long for the madness to strike home. April seventh of 1677 began as a warm fuzzy day—soft cottony clouds floated lazily in a pale blue sky—a welcome break from the blustery winter. The snow had melted sooner than usual and the clement sun hinted that an early spring might be in the cards. Daniel Dill and Robert Junkins sat with Alexander Maxwell at the table in his front window to make plans for the approaching planting season and set out for the fields.

The Cape Neddick massacre had kept them on edge, discouraged and jumpy. The painful blow had demoralized them, and they and their families still reeled from it. Slow to move, they sat a bit longer—Rob and Alex shared a brew while Dan sipped cider that suddenly burst into a spray that spewed over the entire table. His hand flew to his chin, and he cocked his head to hone in on a noisy ruckus that sounded all too familiar. *Let me be wrong*, he hoped.

His first instinct was to keep calm. He didn't want to upset his friends unduly, but his gut lurched and he snapped, "Rob—harken up. Ken that be shootin'? Dinna ye hear it? 'Tis way too many shots ta get a few turkeys. And, I fear those screams and yells are comin' from the direction of yer place."

"What the hell ken be goin' on now," Robert asked, terrified for his family and already half out of his chair. The trio grabbed their muskets and bolted out the door where they bumped into Albert Dexter, who had just finished cleaning up some brush. He asked no questions, dropped his sickle, and joined them as they ran up the hill toward smoke that bellowed into the sky. They half hoped to find a wild grass fire that might be headed for the woods.

What they found was a bloody mess. The field was covered with what remained of unmistakably massacred friends. As he came upon the first body, Daniel called out, "Zounds, Rob, 'tis Andy Rankin. Dinna come here. Yer dear friend has been scalped and 'tis all cut up he be—nasty Injun stuff fer sure."

Rob sat by Alan's mutilated body in disbelief. He still reeled from the Cape Neddick disaster and the loss of Elizabeth and her family. His mind was confused and his thoughts stymied. *How sorry I am ta find ye like this. What animals did this ta ye? I kenna stand it. Oh, Alan—yer slashed ta pieces—how will I ever get ye home?*

The woods seemed eerie as tense eyes searched in every direction for any sign of motion. All was still now, no bird chirped, not a living thing moved, and there wasn't even a hint of a breeze, only dying smoke that rose straight up from grass that smoldered on the edge of the field. On the bank nearby, muskets rested in a neat stack and patiently waited for owners who had felt safe enough to leave them while they hoed the field.

Dorrie and their sons flashed into Daniel's head. Robert could think only of Sarah and their three sons while Alexander surprised himself that his first thought was of Annis. He had taken a shine to Annis Frost, but hadn't realized until now how much she had come to mean to him.

Dan spoke first, echoing everyone's thoughts, "'Tis nary like those savages ta stick around afta they're done their gory work. They musta been in one mad rush ta have left those muskets behind. Just ta be sure, we'd best check ta see if any of our neighbors survive, then we tend ta our own, get help, and come back."

"I've found what's left of John Carmichael and Louie Bean over here. And I think that Isaac Smith fellow. Butchers, sneaky butchers," Albert muttered.

Alexander walked farther down into the field, "John Palmer, and seems 'tis Bill Roans, ta yer right," he offered, "and it appears that two more were hauled off."

"Hold up. 'Tis best ye come, Alex," Daniel cried out from the east end, "I believe 'tis Annis's father, John Frost.

Alex went on his knees and confirmed, "Ahhh . . . 'tis him . . . 'tis John fer sure. *Oh, Annis, I am so sorry.*"

Dan pulled him up by his shoulder, shook him, and stated, "'Tis one thing sure, 'tis nary a soul left alive. Come, *bráthair*, we kenna do a thing ta help 'em now."

"Zounds, that makes about nine friends dead in a field where they were mindin' their own business, just tryin' ta get the soil ready fer the spring plantin'."

Alex decided to state the obvious, "That may well have been us, ye know. We were a breath away from bein' out in the fields this mornin'. Dinna ye see? 'Tis the thistle, Dan—dinna ye know it, Rob? Our work kenna be done."

Robert piped up, "Ye just had ta get that in, dinna ye? Ye nary miss a chance ta whistle the thistle."

In spite of the morbid circumstances, the friends shared glances and raised their eyebrows. A frustrated Alex surrendered, threw up his hands, nodded, and decided that this would probably not be a good time to carry on with more of the thistle's praises. He smugly held his tongue, but he had no doubts when it came to the thistle. *And, then again,* he thought, *How could this happen? 'Tis war all over again—and in our own back yard ta boot. Scotland Parish—my dream—where we settled, built homes and families—where we felt comfortable and safe—invaded and ravaged.*

The Resilient Thistle

Alex was not the only one who was overwhelmed and distraught. He and his stouthearted friends felt betrayed, disillusioned, and resentful.

"Those were all good men, they will be sadly missed," Robert lamented, "Andy Rankin and I went through a lot together at Salmon Falls, and I kenna help but feel guilty. I was the one who encouraged him the most ta settle in Scotland Parish."

"Ay," Alex spoke up, "and he and the rest of them were doin' a great job of makin' it better here. But they came because they wanted ta follow the thistle and their dreams, same as us. They were proud and 'twas was a great thing they did. Ye kenna take that away from them, Rob. They made their own choices and their own way."

That seemed to console Robert somewhat, "Strange 'tis, though," he reasoned, "Isaac Smith dinna even live here—he came ta York on business from Chelsea—he just happened ta stop by Scotland Parish ta visit.

"And Lewis Bean," Dan commented, "Louie was so easy-goin'. He was the only Scotsman who got ta be called *Mister* around these parts. He did better than we did in that regard. We still are naught allowed the respect of the title *Mister*. Neither the Puritans or the Royalists think Scotsmen, prisoners, Negroes, servants, or bondsmen are deservin' of it—Louie was an icebreaker fer us."

Alex tried to get them to move on, "Ye both are right, but let our friends rest we must. 'Tis the livin' we must see ta now. God knows, we are all so tired of all this hate and revenge thing. I thought we had put all that behind us—then these savages strike like ghosts with nary a warning from out of the blue.

"Ye know we couldna agree with ye more, Alex, and we must get back ta our families, break the news, and button down our homes."

Albert Dexter didn't need to be coaxed. He cautiously headed down the hill while Robert and Daniel hurried back to their wives and children. The women were badly shaken up and frightened by the offense and its proximity—especially with the Cape Neddick tragedy still so fresh in their minds.

Alexander didn't return directly to his home, instead he bee-lined it straight up the hill to Brixsome, the handsome Cape Cod style Frost homestead that sat on the front of fifty acres a half mile up from York

Bridge. John Frost had named his new home after Brixham, England, where he had grown up. Sadly, and as gently as he could, Alex broke the sad news of his demise to his family.

The shock of her father's murder had made Alex acutely aware of how dear to him Annis Frost had become, and it broke his heart to see her in such distress. He decided to bring Annis, her mother, and her young brother, Johnny, back with him to his home since it was much stronger and better positioned for safety than the one story more conventionally built Frost house. But it was not easy to convince Annis's mother, Rose, to leave. She was extremely difficult and cranky on a good day, which she conveniently blamed on rheumatism, and she was even more stubborn and cantankerous, although understandably, when she heard of her husband's murder. When Annis finally persuaded her that going to the Maxwell place was temporary, she grudgingly agreed to it—but only once Alex promised to contact her eldest son, Phillip, and convey her request that he come home from the Isle of Shoals to help with the estate.

Chapter 56

DEFENSE

IT HAD been a rough week. The grey on grey sky hung low, obscured the horizon, and trapped the dreary wet weather in place. In spite of it, Robert's new wagon had been busy. He had driven his Sarah, along with Daniel and Dorrie, to York and Cape Neddick and back almost every day to interact with their families and others who had survived the macabre ordeal. They consoled each other, sought comfort, and tried to make sense of the senseless incidents that had caused so much pain.

Once the sad task of the difficult gatherings as well as the latest funerals and burials of Andy and their other murdered neighbors were behind them, the sad trio sat predictably at the table beneath Alex's front window. "Zounds . . . and Zounds again . . . some kind a war, 'tis nary honor nor pride in it. Sneakin' about, murderin' our friends, farmers, fishermen—most especially, wee ones."

Robert was adamant and his dander was up. "As ever was, we must pick up the shattered pieces, if only fer the sake of those dearest ta us. Fer me, I kenna stand ta watch my Sarah feelin' edgy in our own home—bothered about beasts lurkin' about—or worse. We must come up with a plan ta make sure this kenna happen again."

Alex jumped in, "Ay, 'tis a plan we must have, indeed. And if ye recall, Daniel and I are experts at dealin' with sneaky military ways—although worthy ones, I must say! We fought soldiers, nary a woman or *bairns*. 'Twas the best at the cat and mouse game we were when we rode in Leslie's Dragoons, and we know that the only protection against these savages 'tis ta beat 'em at their own game. 'Tis true we are naught the warriors we used ta be, but as much as we learned ta hate war and everythin' about it, 'tis thrown back inta the midst of it we are."

Dan agreed, "We dinna have ta take it lyin' down though, *bráthairs*, 'tis hell, and we got hit straight through our hearts. Now we'll simply have ta figure how ta protect our own, our way. We kenna take on an offensive as we'd wish. 'Tis under English rule we be, and they willna have it—but we sure as hell ken put up the best defense possible. Remember what we declared back in that field? We need ta get doin' fer our families and friends and we know what must be done—so let's be gettin' ta it."

"'Tis wholly right, Dan," Alex confirmed. "Ta begin with our homes must be made safer from attack. We'd best get our arses in gear and make gun ports, portholes, holes big enough ta be able fire a gun through the walls on every side."

"Dorrie will hate it, but our balustrade must come down—much too temptin' and easy fer the renegades ta get ta the roof."

Robert knew Sarah would miss her high porch as well, but he considered the alternative, moved on, and affirmed, "Ay, Dan, my flankers must go also, and we must protect our wells and springs. 'Tis a temptin' target they be."

"Speakin' of water, 'tis sure we must be that the portholes we carve will allow us ta pour water out onta the outside walls—the wetter they are, the safer fer us."

Alexander reminded them, "We built our homes ta last. They are the sturdiest around, and the garrison overhang makes them harder ta climb."

"Ay, and nary a doubt," Robert added, "all the clearin's around the buildin's will have ta be widened ta keep the element of surprise down and any attack at bay. I am sure the ladies will protest that also, but the lofty vines and bushes will have ta go."

"Mahap, 'tis best that ye break that part ta 'em, Alex." Dan grimaced, "Ye know how Sarah has a green thumb and Dorrie loves her tall flowers as well. 'Twill be a shame fer them ta have ta give them up, but better safe than sorry, eh?"

Alex agreed, "And 'tis an example I am glad ta set by startin' at my place."

He frowned, set his jaw, and added, "By gorra, I dinna have ta tell ye that those devious wily foxes aroused my rebellious nature. 'Tis a strong high stockade I'll start puttin' up about my buildin's and spring that will fend off the best of 'em."

"'Tis with ye I am, Alex." Robert was riled up too, "I think some long spears will be handy ta have around—I ken make some up fer all of us. Ye ken be sure that some folks will be lookin' ta us fer refuge so we'll be needin' more room. Fer some time now Sarah and I have been plannin' an addition ta our main house—got it stuck in my mind. I'm naught sure yet how I wanna do it, but I'll figure it out and get goin' on it."

"I mostly agree with both of ye, but I dinna think that I must go that far," Dan contemplated, "My land has more natural protection, though 'tis sure I'll be ta clear it in the weakest spots and take all the other precautions. And Rob, mayhap 'tis a good notion ta build an addition onta the backside of the house. The lads need more room anyway."

Dorrie and Sarah surprised their spouses by not only agreeing with them but also pitching in with practical ideas and help. Alexander was pleased that Annis admired him for not only protecting his homestead but also for his strategic knowledge of warfare—and how thoughtful he had been of her and her family.

"The buzz 'tis that Andy and our other neighbors were killed by Saco Indians. Hard ta tell with so many tribes fired up. We found out the hard way the value of the Madockawando peace treaty. I wonder where and when the next strike will be."

There was no need to wait long for the answer to Dan's question. In early 1678, less than a year later, a small raiding party destroyed two places down near Ferry Neck. Rowland Young's home was one of those burned, but he and his wife managed to escape with their lives. However, the battered, scalped bodies of two men, a mother and four children, were found down the trail—they had not been so lucky.

Naturally upset, Dorrie turned to Daniel, "That attack was not too far from my folks home on Varrell Lane, Dan. What can we do? Don't you think it would be best if they came up here? Daniel shared her concern about her family and went down to the ferry to meet with his father-in-law, William Moore, about at least barricading his home and taking other precautions. Some of William and Dorothy Moore's children had left the nest like Dorrie, but the rest of the family was still young. Dan told him of his and Dorrie's concern for them and invited them to Bass Cove, but William retorted that he and his wife felt confident that they and the ferry were safe since the military support had been increased.

"We thank you and Dorrie for thinking of us, but tell her that we are all fine, and I assure you, in no danger."

This was not the answer Daniel had hoped for, "I guess ye know best. I trust ye, William Moore, and wish ye well, but remember, ye are all welcome at Bass Cove."

They left it at that, but a distraught Daniel shook his head and sputtered to himself as he hoofed it back up the Cider Hill Trail. *Well, as 'tis said, ye ken bring a horse ta water, but ye kenna make him drink. 'Tis better that ye mind yer own business fer once, Daniel MacDhughill— oh, ay, my mistake—I reckon 'tis Daniel Dill in this new world, eh?* He sarcastically mocked himself. *'Tis nasty indeed ta have ta bring such news back ta my sweet Dorrie. 'Tis sure I be that she'll be worried and she'll nary take ta it.*

After this latest raid at Ferry Neck though, things seemed to quiet down and another Indian peace treaty was attempted on April 12, 1678, supposedly bringing the first Indian war to an end.

The brutal hostilities had stormed up and down the Connecticut River Valley—in Massachusetts, in the Plymouth and Rhode Island colonies—and had claimed the lives of hundreds of colonists, many of them women and children.

No one really had much hope that this was an end to the struggle that had become so deeply ingrained in racial and religious conflict. It seemed that the only way it could ever be settled would be by a complete military victory or an Indian conquest.

In Scotland Parish residents carried on. Homes had been made safer, additions completed, stockades and supplies sat in place. All were careful and took precautions, but they were dogged to make the best of a bad situation and act as normal as possible.

A small disruption took place on Cider Hill in early 1679 when

John Pullman pressured Daniel Dill and Alexander Maxwell to get them to sign another petition regarding the Massachusetts control over Maine. They had mulled it over for some time before choosing to side with the king they had fought so hard for back in Scotland. They decided that it would be the right thing to do, but Alexander changed his mind at the last minute. "I am sorry, Dan, but I just dinna care ta do it."

Dorrie had her own opinion and was irate when she found out that her husband had even thought about signing something that she and her family were so adamantly against. They wanted Maine to be free from Massachusetts control.

"Why couldn't you mind your own business, Daniel Dill? I can't understand why on earth you would even think of doing anything for that awful King Charles. Everyone knows he is just a puny weakling who spends his time rolling from whore to whore." She stomped off yelling, "They don't call that tall skinny string bean the *Merry Monarch* for nothing."

Daniel was sharply taken aback, it was unusual for him and Dorrie to exchange words. He tried to ignore his wife's outburst, but he felt bitter old feelings rise up in his throat that were stuck too deeply under his skin to let slide so he scuttled off to Alex's and told him it was a good thing they did not sign the damn petition.

Then, oblivious to his inner knowing that he shouldn't and couldn't drink, he joined in with Alex. They drowned their sorrows in grog and beer. By the time Dan decided to head home they were both quite drunk, and this time a foggy Alex let Dan go, convinced that he would just crash at home and sleep it off. He wished!

Chapter 57

OLD WOUNDS

DORRIE WAS sitting in the sun on the front steps when her wayward husband tottered his way down Cider Hill into their yard. Daniel stopped to barf, then yelled out, still frustrated, "Dorrie, I love ye, but dinna ye ever speak of King Charles in that manner again. I will'na stand fer it, do ye hear? Do ye have any idea of how many good men have suffered and died fer that laird? If ye ever even think of devilin' him like that again, I'll . . . I'll just have ta . . . ta . . . ," his face turned into a shitty grin as he wavered. He looked and felt as sheepish as he possibly could, made a flirty face, lifted an eyebrow, and tried to josh his way out, "I'll have ta paddle ye . . .or somethin' . . . somethin', eh?"

Dorrie knew her husband. Even her poor health had not dimmed the way they loved to banter and tease each other. She realized that this mess had been caused by painful memories he tried so hard to put behind him, and it made her feel sad and sorry for him. She pushed herself up off the step, hugged him, gave him a few friendly whops and was about to order him to get inside and sleep it off.

At the same time, John Card, who was always looking for any reason he could come up with to admonish a Scotsman, was passing by as he often did for one reason or another. When he spied Daniel and saw that he was three sheets to the wind—overheard him shout at his wife and, he thought, threaten to kill her—he counted his blessings, grabbed Dan, struggled to ignore the offensive vomit smell, and arrested him.

Over Dorrie's protests and Dan's feeble tipsy struggles, he subdued his Scotsman and hauled him down to York, where he jailed him for a second offense, and left him there to sober up. This time Alexander, who was under the weather himself, could not save him, and Daniel was not only firmly reprimanded but fined as well.

He took the scolding in stride, paid the fine, left the jail behind him, and headed up the Cider Hill Trail. He was sick and his head pounded as he teetered, half walked and half crawled meekly back toward his home at Bass Cove hoping to make amends.

Just as he got almost to Bass Creek he glanced up and saw Alex Maxwell and Rob Junkins traipsing down the trail, with Alex leaning heavily on Rob for support. Rob had gone down to Alex's and found him sloshed and worried about Dan, so they decided they'd best discover how he'd made out. Once they caught sight of him on the trail, Rob blurted out. "It seems that I kenna let either of ye out of me sight fer a minute. What am I goin' ta do with ye? *Yer whacky in yer head*—both of ye—wallowin' in yer cups like that—disgustin'. Especially ye, Daniel, what ever were ye thinkin'?"

"Stow it, Rob, I be feelin' crappy enough, and regret it I do. 'Tis fer sure, shamed us all I have, and disgraced Scotland Parish. I seem ta have proven that scoundrel, Card's, case fer him. I thought I had ended all of that loathin' from our past, but I let it come over me again. I kenna keep on with it, and my mind 'tis made up ta be done with it, fer all our sakes, and especially Dorrie's. 'Tis right she be—King Charles dinna be worth it—and ye recall how 'twas hate that made the monster, Leighton, push his fine horse too hard in the mud—and got himself wiped out by his own sword. Ye've both been wiser all along. We've a grand life here, and I intend ta honor it and every last Scotsman that we lost by livin' in the cleanest, finest way that I ken."

"'Tis sorry I am as well, old man," Alex confessed. "I know better than ta let ye get sloshed, but I slipped and was lookin' backwards as well. We are both ta blame—and may *mortification* be brought on that blasted Card anyway."

Robert couldn't help but snicker at the mortification word. He covered his mouth, nodded to Alex, attempted a more serious persona and said, "Ye old farts. Dinna worry, I know only too well how ye feel and I hurt as well, we ache fer them every day, but there is nary a way that dwellin' on the past will help anyone. How about we hunker down on that rock by the creek fer a spell and clean ye up a bit before ye face Dorrie."

Once he looked presentable, his two friends tucked him between them, and the three of them hoofed it the rest of the way up the Cider Hill Trail to Bass Cove where Dan was left on his own and the other two made tracks as fast as they could.

The rowdy husband was gratefully relieved as Dorrie waved at him and greeted him with a supportive smile. They embraced, got on with the business of making up, and decided to put the whole thing behind them. That making up blossomed into something unexpected . . . a something they both were more troubled than pleased with, once they found out that Dorrie was pregnant again.

• • •

The last of the multi-hued leaves rattled under foot and a sharp north chill filled the air, typical of a late October day, but by noon an obliging sun enwrapped and warmed all at the gathering where Alexander Maxwell made Annis Frost his wife. They married in a very small ceremony (at Annis's insistence) in front of the Maxwell home.

No one, including himself, had ever thought that this day would come, and Alex had taken some major ribbings from his friends who reminded him of every word he had ever uttered against the institution. He took all the digs in good stride, laughed and teased them back, but when all was said and done, he was very happy with his decision to marry the very quiet and reserved Annis Frost.

Much to Alex's relief, Phillip Frost had moved down from the Isle of Shoals at his mother's request, administered the estate of his late father, and after the wedding, had taken his decrepit mother, Rose, and younger brother, John, back to the now fortified Brixsome homestead. Rose Frost reminded Alex much too much of the aunt who had taken him in as a young lad, and as determined as he was to put up with her for Annis's sake, he was very grateful to Phillip for taking on her care.

Dorrie was heavy with child and hadn't felt well enough to attend the wedding. So her husband made an attempt to report all the details, "Well, Dorrie, ah . . . her dress was . . . ah, simple . . . almost plain, I

The Resilient Thistle

guess . . . ah, well . . . 'twas very sweet she was. Anyway, Annis promised ta fill ye in on everthin' once they are settled in."

"Well, you're right there, I'll get a lot more detail from her. I wanted so much to be there with them, Dan, I had been so looking forward to it."

"Everyone at the ceremony knew that and they sent their love and best wishes."

Dorrie's pregnancy had come less than a year after Willy's early birth, and everyone was concerned for her and the child. She went into labor in the wee hours of the morning, and although the baby was not in a breach position and Dorrie did not go into a coma, the birth proved to be nearly as difficult as their son Johnny's had been. Once more, the doctor took Daniel aside, read him the riot act, and warned him even more emphatically this time that another pregnancy could very likely prove fatal to Dorrie, and probably the child as well.

A chastised Daniel sat by his wife's bed until she finally opened her eyes. She seemed stronger than he had expected. Rather that moan and groan, Dorrie chose to weakly quip to her relieved husband, "You know, I'm getting to be quite the expert at this baby thing."

Dan kissed her and held her hand tighter while the midwife placed the babe in her frail arms. She smiled as she looked down on her newborn son, "A fourth son, Daniel Dill. Aren't we the lucky ones? He looks so pale and fragile, but I know he's as tough as can be, just like you. I want to call this little lad *Daniel II* after his Da. I think he already has your stubborn ways, not to mention your good looks!"

"Naw, Dorrie, he ken do better."

She laughed, why Dan was actually blushing! "He could never do better. I insist, Dan. we'll call him Danny so he won't have to deal with *Junior*. By the way, you old Snowhead, I love you dearly!"

"And I love ye, my sweet Dorrie. I am so thankful that ye've come through this so well. Danny he will be then. But nary more ken there be, Dorrie, do ye hear me? I be blamed fer puttin' ye through all of this, ye know, eh? Nary a person in the world would ever believe what a wild temptress ye be."

His wife gave him a brazen glance and pointed out, "I can't remember hearing any complaints in that area, but of course, my dear—whatever you say—no more."

Daniel took the doctor's warning very seriously, and as soon as Dorrie started to feel better, made arrangements to sleep in the loft. But a frail Dorrie blocked the way. She stood in front of him, took his head in her hands, and gave him a longing look so deep it seemed to penetrate into his soul. "Aw, Dorrie, dinna make this harder than 'tis fer me. Ye know now, 'tis fer the best. I kenna take the chance of losin' ye."

But no matter how much he insisted, Dorrie would not leave Dan's bed. She threatened to follow him into the loft or the barn if need be. "Don't fret, my dearest," she consoled him, "I know I'll be fine as long as we can be together."

It took some time, but she got back on her feet and only sighed or leaned on nearby furniture when her husband was out or not looking. She kept her home immaculate and her smile as bright as ever. Daniel pretended to believe her façade, but he was very aware of how her health had failed, and he was gravely concerned.

His thoughts and prayers merged, *'twas a mad tomcat I was, Mora. Just a nothin'—livin' empty in the past—til she brought me back ta bein' a husband and Da once more. Ye know I love her dearly and I thank ye fer sendin' her ta me.*

• • •

Robert Junkins, true to his plan, added twenty acres to his original land on March 24th, 1680, and another thirty-two acres in the same year.

Another Petition to the King was signed that year, but Daniel Dill refused to take part. He had resolved that he would never place his great treasures at risk again.

Chapter 58

LEAVE YESTERDAY BEHIND

THE FRAGRANT scent of lilacs and apple blossoms followed Robert Junkins as he meandered down the Cider Hill Trail in June of 1681. He couldn't wait to tell his friend that he had purchased an orchard to add to his growing properties. Dan slapped him on the back and congratulated him on his good business sense. Rob's plan was developing even faster than he had expected.

"How 'tis with yer dear Sarah?"

"She is incredible as always, Dan. She seemed ta come through the nasty Cape Neddick tragedy just fine on the surface, but I know that her heart has cried over the loss of her gentle sister and her family every day since. I have nary seen siblin's so close. 'Tis been good fer her ta have our little niece, Lizzie, about."

"What a sad business, Rob. I know 'tis hard ta deal with. We'll be better off talkin' about land. I guess ye'll be harvestin' more apples than ever now. That should keep ye out of mischief. What are yer plans fer that big barn ye have yer mind on?"

"Storage, another work horse, a couple more hogs, and some sheep, I reckon. I plan ta keep them all inside durin' the winter. Sarah loves ta sew and knit. She'll be glad ta get the wool, plus she cooks lamb and mutton in delicious ways we love. I hear ye've received another grant from the town of York."

"Ay, on the west side of the York River," Dan confirmed. 'Tis a fine piece and I be tickled ta get it."

His tone changed, he bit his lip and dolefully outed that Dorrie had just revealed to him that he would be a father again about the beginning of next year.

"Fer Christ's sake, Dan, kenna ye keep it in yer pants?"

"Ye should know, 'tis nary that easy, my friend. We both know the danger, and we believed we were bein' careful, but nonetheless, Dorrie's in the family way again. Of course, we are pleased, but a bit scared. Anyway 'tis done, and we must deal with it. The lads and I are doin' everythin' we ken ta pamper and care fer her. 'Tis most of her chores we've taken over, and we all make sure she rests and takes it slow. Surprisin'ly, it dinna take much ta convince her, Rob—Dorrie—well—'tis nary well she be."

"Then we'll all be prayin' fer her, Dan."

On a freezing, blustery cold January morning, Dorrie's labor began with a force she had not known before. The doctor had a hard time making it up the icy Cider Hill Trail, but he finally pulled in, frozen to the bone, covered with snow and sputtering, "Stupid bastard." Dan knew without a doubt that the remark was directed at him.

True to the warning, this was the worst birth yet, and Dorrie nearly slipped away several times during the labor. She went in and out of consciousness, but she stubbornly persevered and finally took a turn for the better.

The baby was pint-sized and delicate, but their long-awaited daughter grabbed their hearts the moment she appeared—all wrinkled and red.

Sarah Junkins helped the doctor and midwife with the birth and lit up with pleasure when the infant was proudly named Elizabeth. Dorrie beamed, "In honor of our sisters, Sarah, your beloved Elizabeth Smyth Jackson and my Elizabeth Moore."

Dorrie's health did not bounce back as quickly this time. She had been frail before the birth, but this one had worn her out much more noticeably. Everyone was worried about her, but she insisted that she was just fine and refused to be pampered.

• • •

Alexander Maxwell still loved to be the town crier and on an

The Resilient Thistle

unusually fine day a couple of still frigid months later, he burst into Daniel's great room. Dorrie recognized him without even looking up from her book by the sweet clean smell he always brought in with him nowadays. Annis Frost Maxwell had surprised everyone by how comfortably she had fallen into married life. The only things she had brought from her past at the Brixsome homestead were her spinning wheel and a fancy bath tub that her father had crafted for her. She took great pleasure in making Alex bathe in it once a week. He tried, but he never could convince her of how outlandishly ridiculous that was.

Dorrie had been slow to recover from Elizabeth's birth, but was firm about taking her turn at schooling her sons and the neighbors' children. Johnny, now sixteen, helped with the reading and math. She smiled at the intruder while her son hustled his brothers and the other students to the back room and said, "It's always nice to see you, Alex. If you're looking for Dan, he's out back—we're finished here anyway."

"Thanks, Dorrie. 'Tis good to see ye up and around. Annis sends her love." He smiled over his shoulder as he went outside. "News of *The Great Works*, Dan. I knew ye'd like ta hear that Eliakim Hutchinson of Boston, has taken over former grants—some from Richard Leader and those inherited by Robert Mason—Eliakim 'tis the grandson of Captain John Mason. He will own it all, of course. 'Tis a formal deed ta avoid litigation. He did exempt any pine trees of four and twenty inches in diameter or more. The ones we always said were fit ta make masts fer the ships of kings, eh?"

"'Tis good news, Alex. It could have been a real mess if it got inta the hands of lawyers and that litigation stuff. I'm sure Richard would have been pleased."

"I hope so, Dan. It still pains me ta think of his passin'."

• • •

Not too unusual for the area, a cold spring took its time, but eventually turned into a beautiful summer. The white lilacs down by the bank of the Cove were at their peak. The gentle breeze sent their sweet aroma sailing around the massive old log. The warrior turned family man loved days like this when he could hold his daughter,

Elizabeth—they called her, Beth—sit next to Dorrie and watch while the older boys, Johnny and Joe, played with their younger brothers, Willy and Danny. *This is what 'tis all about*, he affirmed to himself.

Dan was grateful that he had expanded the garrison. The addition was getting a lot of use—Johnny and Joe had each chosen a room and moved all their stuff out there. The rest of the family enjoyed it as well. Dorrie was happy to have the extra room for the young ones to romp and play in, especially on fowl days.

Time moved on, and in June of 1683 Alex brought news of another nature that pleased Daniel, "William Bray has replaced Card as Jailer. He'll be at that post fer at least two years. How do ye like those apples?"

"That appeals ta me indeed, although ye know I be a complete teetotaler now—never really cared fer the stuff anyway."

"Ya, right, Dan—until the next time."

"Ye are wrong there, my friend. I know where my bread's buttered."

A good test came up for Dan when April of 1685 rolled around and Alex and his cologne came in all out of breath with the latest, "News just reached us from England that King Charles the Second is dead. He died on February second—he was fifty-four years of age. It seems 'twas made ta appear that he died from kidney failure, but 'twas actually an apoplectic fit that did him in. His brother, James II of England, the one who they also call, James of Scotland—succeeded him. What do ye think of that?"

"Nary much." Neither of them said another word, and they left it at that.

• • •

A summer, autumn, and another long, cold winter passed. No one even dared hope for a decent summer this year, but by July the sun was back.

Several squirrels raced around annoyed that they couldn't hop on the dearly loved old log where Dorrie and Dan sat to enjoy some pleasant moments as they often had over the years. They watched Johnny, a grown up serious twenty, and Joe, two years younger and nearly as tall, take a now rarer moment to play with their brothers, Willy, seven

The Resilient Thistle

and Danny, six—while Beth, already four, napped on the log cuddled at her mother's side.

"Strange eh, Dorrie? I always reckoned that our Willy would take on the looks of my brave brother, William—but 'tis our young Danny Junior 'tis the spittin' image of him. The lassies best watch out!"

"Just don't ever let him hear you call him *Junior*. Rob's son, Alexander, called him that the other day, and he was quick to inform him that he was not *Junior*, he was *Danny*, and he'd better not forget it. They had a good laugh about it, but young Alex got the message. And, our Joey has now decided that he will only answer to *Joseph*!"

The older boys chuckled quietly as they piggy-backed the giggling younger ones on the grass along the Cove's bank. They played about and laughed until Dan called them over to enjoy the picnic spread he had helped Dorrie prepare for lunch.

Dorrie watched her sons' heads bouncing up and down and commented, "The older two are still nearly as blonde as Willy. Look at them! Don't those heads remind you of dandelions bobbin' in the sun? I'm pleased that Danny looks like your brother, William. It's a nice reminiscence for you. I think that our Willy and Joseph are the image of you, my dear, and Johnny has ways that remind me of my brother, Robert."

"Well, 'tis a relief that at least little Beth looks like ye, the only difference 'tis—she dinna get yer hazel eyes. She got stuck with my blues, which I must say look really fetchin' on her. And she's the only one that has yer beautiful black bouncy tresses. What a fine family ye've given me, Dorrie Dill. I love ye, my dearest."

"Thank you Daniel Dill. I love your part in it. You're a great Da, Snowbird."

"Umm, aw, now dinna start tryin' ta put me under yer spell my, lass. "Tis a lot of years it has takin' me, but I be finally wise ta the beguilin' web ye weave."

"We'll see."

Chapter 59

THE SECOND INDIAN WAR

SCOTLAND PARISH had no concept of what they were in for. Little did they know that they were mere pawns caught up in the broad scheme of an aggressive war.

Relaxing days of enjoyment down where the white lilacs grew were now a memory.

In Europe clashes between England and France had made a renewal of conflict inevitable. Following the overthrow of King James and the rise of Protestants, William and Mary, to the English throne, Louis XIV of France declared war on England. He was firmly convinced that he could replace King William with a Catholic.

This gave the French in Quebec exactly what they had hoped for—the opportunity to copy the European war. The Governor of Quebec swiftly pressured Indian allies to join them and attacks were ordered on English settlements.

This callous decision took on the nature of a Holy war—the Jesuit missionaries aided the cause by convincing the Indians that the English were *heretics* who must not be allowed to rob them of their lands. However, there was no doubt that the offer of forty pounds the priests promised for each scalp they brought back furnished the most incentive.

Maine built up its defenses to shield against random raids. Massachusetts authorities assigned a few units of soldiers to York. Local militia was placed under the command of Job Alcock, and he designated five garrisons in York and the surrounding vicinity. In the York area, in addition to the one he assigned to himself, he commandeered Preble's, Norton's, and Stover's at Cape Neddick. In Scotland Parish he selected Alexander Maxwell's Garrison and notified Daniel Dill that his home had been requisitioned by the authority of Massachusetts to be a fort, and that some soldiers were to be billeted there.

Alcock had come up with a good strategy, but unfortunately, sixty soldiers under the command of Captain John Floyd were withdrawn and posted at Portsmouth. That weakened the York defense.

Alexander and Daniel approved of Alcock's plan and readied their garrisons as directed. Even though Robert had not been given orders, he prepared his garrison to hold and protect his own and other residents. "'Tis somethin' we ken do—fer our own and whoever else needs us."

"Amen ta that, Rob, 'tis best we get to it—build more additions, stock up on plenty of ammunition, food, and beddin'—and we'd best build some out houses, as well."

Against Dorrie's protests, both Johnny and Joseph Dill, now adults of twenty-two and twenty, joined the local militia along with their father, Daniel, and just about every able-bodied male in the neighborhood. Rob Junkins' son, Joseph, was not yet eighteen, but had tagged along on so many patrols that, after many objections from his mother, Sarah, had been allowed to participate when his father did. "He must have inherited that stubborn streak from Sarah's side," Robert determined. "I kenna recall any of my folks havin' traits like that."

"Of course naught—that nary could be, Rob." Dan soberly cajoled, " . . . and we thought Alex was the only saintly one!" All three of them chuckled, eyeballed each other, and shrugged.

The younger Dill and Junkins lads were given *home* duty, which they took very seriously much to Dorrie and Sarah's delight. A fourteen-year-old Alexander Junkins took charge of the unit and took great pleasure in ordering about his younger brother, Daniel Junkins, along with Willy Dill and an eager Danny Dill. The two Danny's took every word young Alex said to heart. Willy tried to march to a different drummer, but had no say in the matter, so he fell in with the others. Little Beth Dill begged constantly to join in, but of course, being merely a girl, she was not allowed—that is until she shed so many tears that the boys finally put her on cook detail to shut her up.

Scituate, Scotland Parish, Cape Neddick, and all the fringes of Wells and York, continued to be easy targets that offered plenty of cover for the sneak tactics that the Indians excelled at. The main towns of York and Wells had been passed by due to their open areas and the impact of the secure garrisons and block houses that guarded the hearts of these townships helped keep the enemy at bay—for a time.

Residents were constantly looking over their shoulders, but the cunning enemy seemed to outfox them in spite of the endless surveillance. In early March of 1689 more devious attacks hit Cape Neddick.

Salmon Falls, where Rob Junkins still had many friends, made a big mistake when it relaxed its vigil. In mid-March the town was set upon by Indians led by French soldiers. They snuck up at the crack of dawn while the inhabitants were still in bed, took over the fort, and murdered about a hundred residents, mostly able-bodied men.

After causing all the destruction they could at Salmon Falls, Quamphegon was next. The French and Indian faction attacked the garrison of Thomas Holmes, where he and some of the escapees from Salmon Falls had holed up.

Once the warning horn finally blared, fourteen men rushed up from the lower part of town and charged the raiders. Holmes helped them as best as he could. He shot at the Indians from his front door in an effort to give others a chance to escape. He was pushed aside as the enemy ran right through the garrison and left the stunned defenders behind. Three more homes were burned, including the parsonage, before they were driven off—just as they were about to hit Spencer's Garrison.

At the height of the Salmon Falls' attack, James Plaisted had been taken prisoner by the Indian Chief, Hope Hood. The Thomas Holmes Garrison had regrouped in spite of being attacked and used for a thoroughfare. Hood sent James with a flag of truce to the garrison to demand its surrender.

Holmes let James Plaisted inside his garrison, but rather than return with his white flag to Chief Hood, he hunkered in and informed Holmes that the enemy of one hundred and fifty strong consisted of half Frenchmen and half Indians. He reported that he had seen ten of the French officers taking part in a wild Indian dance with Chief Hope Hood. Plaisted also said that the Indians had captured his brother, Gooden, and that Chief Hood had sworn to him that his brother would be put to death because he killed two Frenchmen. A distraught Plaisted added that he had also seen eight French ships headed for the York River, where he had heard they planned to launch another huge attack.

When Plaisted did not return with an answer to his flag of truce, the Indians and French hightailed it to the north. That news was relayed to Captain Joe Hammond, the commander of Upper Kittery. He pulled together a troop of about one hundred, and they caught up with the French and Indians at about sunset. The unit put up a tough, but futile fight that cost them about ten men. It all ended when the raiders escaped into the dusk.

Alexander Maxwell received this information from two Dover men who sought shelter at his garrison—he related all this and more to Daniel and Robert. "There seemed ta be nary an end ta the damage they caused. 'Tis a rough one fer all of us. Ye'll all be as distressed as I was ta hear that, in addition ta the horrible carnage at Salmon Falls, *The Great Works* suffered twenty-seven cabins burned, two hundred cattle slaughtered, thirty-four folks massacred and fifty-four women and children carried away. I kenna tell ye how many of our friends were among them. Every homestead above Quamphegan Falls was ravaged and burned.

"'Tis hard ta believe, but in spite of the militia's attempts ta hunt them down, those dern Indians stayed hidden and camped somewhere in the area, where they burned more houses and scalped more folks through spring and inta the summer. Only when the trees stood bare in the fall, leavin' them nary a place ta hide, did they slink off. And even then, they left more ruin behind them all the way up ta Wells."

"What the hell 'tis goin' on? We Scots and most of the York folks want ta help, but the provincial government in Massachusetts keeps snubbin' our offers. I reckon we'll just have ta keep protectin' our own as we've been doin'. When will there be an end ta this?" The rejection had dampened their spirits, but they carried on in spite of it.

Alexander's home was now called the *Maxwell Garrison,* and he had made it into a big business. At the first sound of the alarm horn, as many neighbors as could, hightailed it there, and Alex was always ready to welcome them to his garrison's addition that could now hold over thirty-five people. He had converted his great room into a pub, where he and Annis coddled the frantic neighbors with food and drinks. In spite of the reasons for the business, they enjoyed their roles as host and hostess.

"What do ye reckon, Dan? One minute 'tis prayin' away Alex be and the next he's plyin' his wares and fillin' folks with the devil's brew!"

"'Tis a piece of work, he be alright. Kenna help but love him, eh?"

"True, they threw away the mold when they put him out, 'tis fer sure."

Everyone did their share. The *Junkins Garrison* took in folks as well. Daniel's *fort*, also called, the *Dill Garrison*, already nearly full of soldiers, took in any overflow from the other two.

This outlandish war never failed to confuse. One hundred and twenty reinforcements were sent from Essex, Middlesex, and Suffolk to protect York and Wells. Then in June they were suddenly taken away, even though a young York volunteer had been killed in Kittery.

While the Quebec governor continued to call for more attacks in Canada, the Indians and French carried on with their raids on the coastal towns of Maine—including the outskirts of York. On August twenty-second, during one of these raids on the road between York and Kittery, Robert Young was killed and his wife left for dead. The attackers grabbed and rode off with Phineas Hull's wife, but he hid in a shallow well and waited until he could no longer hear his wife's screams or Indian whoops.

Come September 1690, three Bragdons—along with James Freethy and William Wormwood—were massacred on the Cider Hill Trail, just above Bass Creek. Much to the local patrol's chagrin, the raid had taken place right under their noses, just minutes after they had passed by the creek.

"My God, I was on that patrol, Da," a distraught John Dill exclaimed. "We were all alert and searchin' both sides of the trail the whole time. We never heard a sound or saw a thing out of place. How could we have missed them?"

"They be that good, Johnny, 'tis how. If they dinna be, 'tis gone or dead they'd be long ago. Ye have ta hand it ta 'em, they are experts at this foxy sneakin' about."

"Yer Da's right, Johnny," Alex echoed. "Those shifty devils would put our Dragoons ta shame. We're most grateful they dinna pick ye off."

"I really don't think they care to mess with the militia, though, Da"

"Let's hope yer right, lad."

Although towns were vigilant and watchful the sly attackers continued their hits in Maine as well as further north. They purposely made the butchery more as they attempted to increase the terror and break the will of the settlers to fight on. The Indians would often lay in ambush for days, waiting for a favorable moment to strike.

Their daily raids continued into 1691. By then the isolated people of Cape Neddick had been confined to the Stover Garrison for too long. When encouraged by Richard Hunnewell, a famous Indian fighter, they left their garrison. There was no way to save it without more manpower, so it was closed.

On June twenty-second, forty Indians destroyed an unprotected Cape Neddick. When finished there, they attacked twelve villagers who were trying to load a sloop. Before they skulked away, they burned the abandoned Stover Garrison to the ground. It took a couple of months, but that incident inspired the allocation of twenty soldiers to York.

Rumor had it that Chief Madockawando was unhappy with the small victory at Cape Neddick and had his eyes on bigger fish. It was taken for granted that he meant Boston, but as the weather turned colder, the area braced itself for the unknown.

Chapter 60

CANDLEMAS

ON SEPTEMBER 30, 1691, an Indian raiding party landed their canoes on Sandy Beach in Rye, north of Boston, where the renegades slaughtered twelve colonists, and after they brutally interrogated the dozen survivors, carried them off toward Canada.

Under torture, these battered captives revealed that the Boston military had plans to destroy the Indians' hub at some point during the winter. They disclosed that the army was trained and had stockpiled an ample supply of snowshoes.

Once this news reached the volatile Chief Madockawando, he was infuriated and decided to turn the tables. He didn't ask permission or wait for the French. He and his Abenaki pulled together other tribes that included those from Sillery, Canada, and a base on the headwaters of the Upper Kennebec River.

The hyped-up Indians went on the warpath and headed south in the middle of a snowstorm. For twenty-two days they trekked over rough old land trails, and finally, bewildered and lost, they halted on the night of January 23, 1692.

Beat upon by howling winds, freezing temperatures, and flying snow, over one hundred and fifty warriors led by Chief Madockawando and his lieutenants, Sagamores, Edgeremet, and Moxis, set up their camp at the foot of Mount Agamenticus—a position that gave them a grand view of York Harbor and the surrounding area; although they were not aware of what village it was at the time. They took cover, ate and rested up until a faint haze of light hinted at a calmer morning, and their scouts returned with a plan for attack.

The winter had been even harsher than usual. The snow was especially deep in the woods and drifts several feet high created natural obstructions everywhere. The black night, the raw intensely bitter cold, and the deep snow cover found most of York's nearly five hundred residents peacefully asleep in their own scattered homes rather than in garrisons. A welcome break, they thought, from the months of tedious fretful watchfulness. Who would even think of an Indian attack in such ghastly weather?

• • •

Before the crack of dawn, a young Arthur Bragdon entered the woods to check traps that he had set along the northern limits of York, below Mount Agamenticus. He shivered and his teeth chattered in spite of his warm clothing, but all that was forgotten and his hair started to crawl when he came upon a gigantic pile of Indian snowshoes stacked against a huge icy boulder with many tracks and other imprints around it. When he bent over to inspect further, a sharp prod in the back scared him nearly out of his wits. Not knowing what he would face, he slowly turned and saw—nothing—until he looked down and found the curious golden eyes of a mangy dog staring directly into his.

He stood stiff as a board, not even daring to breathe, but to his relief the animal made no attempt to attack, and though it tried frantically to bark, it could not make a sound—its mouth had been tied shut so that it would not give away the invaders' camp.

Arthur quickly began to retrace his steps through the deep snow and moved faster than he ever thought he could on his snowshoes. With the dog close behind, he made straight for Indian Head, hoping to hide there. The going was too hard, so he changed his mind midstride and went for the river. Snow-covered bushes and rocks slowed him down and the frigid air burned his lungs. Goaded on by fear, he finally spotted what first looked like an odd snow-covered rock, but a closer glance told him it was a boat that had been hauled up onto the river bank. He didn't bother to brush the boat out, just rocked and shook it until it broke loose from its frozen bed, then jumped in and pushed off—snowshoes and all—almost tipping it over. He tried to stay calm as his shaky hands grabbed for the icy oars. His mittens were wet and slippery, and the snowshoes were in his way, so he kicked them off and let them fall into the briny tidal river that had not quite frozen over. He then rowed gruelingly toward the other side knowing that it meant his life. Thankfully, the befuddled dog stayed behind.

At about the same time that Arthur had gone to check his traps, two other York men had ventured out in the cold to cut wood. They were not so lucky—the Indians attacked them, smashed in their heads, scalped, and mutilated them. This gruesome act undoubtedly kept them busy and away from young Bragdon, who by this time had reached the other side of the river.

As soon as he climbed out of the boat, he regretted that he had let his snowshoes go—without them the deep snow was incredibly difficult to plow through. His body sunk in, and every time he tried to haul himself out, the heavy mess stuck to legs that were tougher to pull out with each step he attempted. Sheer terror forced him forward until he spotted the nearest cabin and finally rolled, a human snowball, up to the door where he struggled for breath and banged on it as hard as he could.

Peleg Seavey had heard something that aroused his curiosity enough for him to peek out his cabin door. Thinking that Arthur was his snow covered dog, he opened it and the distraught boy fell into his arms. Once he heard him mutter, "*INJUNS*," he quickly sounded the alarm to warn inhabitants on his side of the river of an attack.

They responded quickly, which ensured the escape of many, while screams and shrieks echoed from across the river as the Indians attacked York, where they murdered, mutilated, ransacked, and burned until the town was left in ashes.

Ironically, the savages then simply headed for Cape Neddick Pond, where, exhausted from their killing rampage, they rested, unmolested, all night. The next morning they regrouped and left thirty warriors behind to cover for them as they slinked off through the forest with their plunder and captives. Confidently, they headed toward Wells and their hideouts in the north.

Alexander Maxwell and Robert Junkins looked up from the pile of heavy snow they had just shoveled and saw a sky full of smoke in the south—toward York. Experience had taught them to expect the worst, so they rushed down to Daniel's fort. As soon as they rounded the bend, they spotted Captain John Floyd's horse drawn sled tethered outside the front door.

A tense Daniel relaxed somewhat at the sight of them, "Buck up, lads, Zounds, 'tis glad I be ta see ye, *bráthairs*. John Floyd has reported a most heinous crime. The savages have struck again, and this time 'tis shoddier than ever. Zounds, the towne of York has been WIPED OUT." The two friends stiffened in their tracks and waited.

"The Captain was one of the first on the scene. He was fresh in from Portsmouth and helped ta bury some of the dead. 'Tis a good friend he be and kind enough ta plow through the snow ta bring Dorrie's sister, Sarah, up ta stay with her."

They both sat down heavily, knowing the worst was yet to come. They waited for Floyd to speak. "I heard scuttlebutt that the Indians planned to attack, but further down, probably Boston. It seems they didn't make it that far south, ended up in back of York.

"By first light, after the storm had quieted, it looks as though their scouts ventured out, came upon the fresh tracks of two woodsmen, and murdered them. They then reported back ta Madockawando who ordered his war party to follow the hapless hunters' snowshoe trail to York, where they did their damnedest—and I mean—their damnedest.

"Three garrisons and I'm not sure how many homes were burned. Women and youngsters were slaughtered or carried off, and any man in sight was murdered, scalped, and mutilated. Infants were torn from their mothers' arms, twirled about the savages' heads, and flung into the fire."

"'Tis so utterly damnable, John. Seems though 'tis more?"

The Captain's face took on an even paler shade as he eyeballed Alex and Robert. "Yes—I'm afraid for Dan's wife, Dorrie, there is. Her father's home was attacked. Her brothers, John and Thomas, were down at the ferry with William and are safe. Just about every house in the area of the Moore home was burned to the ground. As far as we know, the rest of the family survived, 'though it's hard to say how or why. Somehow, Dorrie's young sister, Mary, slipped outside, and when her brother, Willy, chased after her, they were both taken."

Dan took over the story, "What a nightmare, eh? Sarah's in with Dorrie now, and they're in a sorry state. Dorrie's barely over that bad bout with pneumonia. She's frail and she dinnna need this. Would ye tell 'em the rest, John?"

Sobs could be heard from the bedroom as an exhausted Captain Floyd sadly reported, "Makes it all the more ironic. It was such a holy time, the Feast of the Purification of the Virgin Mary—*Candlemas*, as you all know. I heard that the Reverend Shabal Dummer had just given a sermon that day that cautioned his flock to be more vigilant. He was found, scalped, mutilated—lying face down, right outside his home."

Floyd looked wearily into the forlorn faces around him, "Reports are that at least one hundred and fifty wild Abenaki Indians destroyed the center of town and killed or carried off at least one hundred and sixty souls. It was said that the screams were painful to the ears and fearful to the heart."

"I'm afraid that we're only too familiar with that scene, John. Go on."

"Horrible. There's not much left of the town. We buried most of the dead in a shared grave across from the meeting house. We gathered up a few children that were crying and wandering aimlessly about. It came to my mind that Mary and Willy might be among them, but it wasn't to be. The least of it was the loss of horses, cattle, sheep, and pigs that were slaughtered or burned and lay all about."

He gave the grieving men a moment before he pulled a soiled paper from his pocket, "I realize that you're aching to know about the people in the village, so here's some of what I've recorded. Your friend Rowland Young was carried off. One of your neighbors, John Card, the former constable and his wife, Elizabeth, were slaughtered. William Bray, you'll remember he was the jailer after Card, he was shot down near the meeting house. By some chance, his son, Thomas, survived. Nathaniel and Elizabeth Masterson were both killed, and their daughter Abigail captured. Your neighbor, the shoemaker, John Pullman, along with Thomas Payne and his two children, were butchered. John Parsons, the other shoemaker, was slain and his wife taken, but their daughter, Elizabeth, escaped. Richard Millberry is dead, and Henry Millberry's daughter, Dorothy, and his son, Richard, were carried off. What was left of John Cooke and his wife, Elizabeth, was found near the Meeting House, along with the bodies of Philip and Anne Cooper. Their daughter, Mary, gone. Thomas Payne and his wife were murdered and their two kids carried off." Floyd dropped the paper like it was red hot and too heavy to hold, totally drained, he said, "There are more. You can read my notes."

"Zounds, what an atrocious tragedy. Yet another one, Captain. We nary figured that we'd ever be caught up in such sufferin' as this again, eh, *bráthairs*?"

Robert quietly affirmed, "Nay, nary in a million years. Thank ye, John Floyd, fer bringin' us the news. Obviously, we'll have ta crack down even more on protection."

"True, all of us will. That's why I must hurry back. This must not go on. Officials from Massachusetts plan to send us more ammunition, and I hope, more soldiers." Floyd heaved a huge sigh and rubbed his forehead before he expressed his regrets.

"I'm sorry that I had to be the bearer of such tragic news, but you and William Moore are such good friends that I felt you deserved to hear the particulars first hand. And when Will's daughter, Sarah, asked me to take her up here to be with her sister, Dorrie, I made the time to fetch her here. I sincerely hope they can be of comfort to each other. Goodnight, and God bless us all."

Once the door slammed behind the kind Captain, the friends mulled over the sad news and decided to meet at Alex's in the morning to contemplate ways to best deal with this latest disaster. After Rob and Alex set off up the trail, Daniel went into the bedroom to try to comfort his wife and her sister, Sarah. He finally got them quieted down a bit, but he felt helpless to soften their grief. His thoughts strayed to poor John Pullman who had asked him to help repair the ferry. *If he hadn't called on me,* he thought, *I nary would have met Dorrie.*

Dorrie shivered and moaned, "How could this happen, Dan? Why? There was no reason in the world for those Indians to come down on York like this."

"My sweet Dorrie, I love ye more than breathin', and I wish there was an answer fer ye. We know that the Indians were out fer revenge and hungry fer bounties. Yer aware that the goin' price is forty pounds fer a scalp and much more fer hostages. I think they will want ta keep little Mary, Willy and the others all safe so they can sell them. We must be grateful that Willy was nary killed on the spot along with the other men."

That didn't seem to do much to reassure the women, and they both broke into fresh sobs. "Sarah saw it all. So many slaughtered. Oh, dear God, our Mary, Willy, and all the others, out in this dreadful cold. They must be in an awful state. Are they warm? Are they hurt?" A shaken Daniel had no reply. She was so very frail and weak. He feared for her life, and Sarah was just plain out of her mind from the horrific shock.

Four days later, Johnny and Joseph Dill set off with their grandfather, William Moore, as part of recovery parties that went out in response to Indian offers that would allow captives to be retrieved, for a price. Rowland Young was among those ransomed on that trip, but there was no sign of either young Mary or Willy Moore.

Chapter 61

SHOWER OF SORROW

THE RANSOMING of prisoners was not encouraged by the Colony's authorities, but funds raised by private groups and churches redeemed many. So many in fact that the Indians, knowing that loved ones would do just about anything to get their own back, took advantage of the situation and turned it into a lucrative business. Many more innocents were abducted, mainly young women and children since they were more easily managed. Men were killed, mutilated, and their scalps collected. Captives not fortunate enough to be ransomed at the designated sites were shipped to Canada, where they were disbursed to various Indian villages or sold to the Jesuits, who welcomed the challenge to convert them.

York was in a desperate struggle for existence. It was devastated and transformed into an armed camp. In spite of unrelenting harassment, attempts at rebuilding commenced under heavy guard, but provisions were low, even basic resources were hard to come by. It was reported that there was a mere two barrels of pork available to service the whole town. Communities from more protected parts of New England heard of York's distress and did help some by sending contributions of corn and other food supplies for the poor people of York.

Captain John Floyd was placed in charge of the entire York area, and he ordered that all soldiers were to be billeted in garrisons. The Dill Fort took on ten more and several were sent to hold-out homes. This ensured that safety was a priority and gave some reassurance of martial support.

Maxwell's became an important shelter, and most of Alex's *guests* were now strongly encouraged to stay there indefinitely. The well-intentioned but undermanned militia was thinly spread and faced this challenge with limited ammunition as they tried to protect the area's residents. Troops came and went and were now a part of everyday life. No one dared travel any distance from home or the garrisons unarmed, and those that did so took their lives in their hands.

Intermittent raids and abductions continued. About a year after the terrible Candlemas tragedy, Dorrie's young nephew, Charlie Trafton—the son of her sister, Elizabeth—was snatched. This proved to be the last straw; Dorrie's health took a nose dive, and it became obvious just how seriously ill she was.

Daniel sat beside her on the giant feather bed they had shared over the years and held her limp hand in his. She fumbled, until somehow, she managed to place her free hand on top of his and tried to pull him closer with an urgency that surprised him. The tiny hand felt so hot that Dan closed his eyes and bit his lip to hold back tears.

He leaned nearer in an effort to hear her soft, barely discernible voice, "I'm so sorry I couldn't be Mora for you, Daniel Dill."

Her words hit him like a ton of bricks. Daniel was shocked and taken aback, as she resolutely went on, "Oh, yes, I knew all along. There's no denying it. I could feel her in your heart, pushing me out from the start."

"What are ye sayin', Dorrie? Ye nary even hinted about any such thoughts. Had I even suspected such a cloud. I would have eased yer mind long ago." He pulled her up gently onto pillows in their soft bed and cradled her head to his chest. "First of all, Mora would nary push ye out. All she ever wanted was fer me ta be happy, and with ye dear, Dorrie, I believe ye must know that I have been, very much so."

His hand went to his weather-beaten forehead then down to brush her damp, soft hair back from the deathly pale face that was still so beautiful, smooth, and lovely that it cloaked her illness and filled him with regret that he had not shared his feelings for her as well as he thought he had. He looked pensively into the dimmed hazel eyes and told her truly, "Ye have come ta mean more than anythin' ta me, Dorrie. I've told ye so many times now. Surely ye believe me?"

The Resilient Thistle

Feebly, she raised her head slightly, managed a smile, and snuggled closer as Dan went on, "Ay, and ye know how I tried all I knew ta get back ta the Scotland of my youth, but it was nary ta be. 'Tis nary mistakin' it. I still get down in the mouth when I look back at the worst. I had young dreams, and I have memories, some that still haunt me, and I fear always will. Indeed, I sorely miss the old country ta this day. I loved it then and I love it now. I nary wanted ta leave it. But, leave it I did, strongly against my will. And ay, tons of tears have tumbled under that bridge, but ye see me here now, and ye know that I stayed because I found ye."

He sighed as he felt her fever ravaged body begin to relax, "I had lost a family and a country and had a mournful feelin' about my life before ye came into it—ye changed everythin'. The best ta come out of all of this has been ye."

Daniel was overcome with emotion and helplessness. He held back his heartbreak and confessed, "'Tis so sorry I am, Dorrie—I reckon that I've taken things out on ye that I shouldn't have and that I've been an angry bastard from time ta time. The rage I tried so hard ta clamp down inside would boil up from the depths of my soul, and I'd find myself flyin' off the handle, out of control. 'Tis nary a chance ta deny it. There's a lot of ire still in there, my Dorrie, but most of it has faded because ye helped me through it. Ye gave me the love I needed and a second chance fer happiness and a family. Please forgive me if I couldna be what ye wanted me ta be."

Dorrie determinedly moved her hand and placed it over his lips, "Enough already! There's nothing to forgive, my dearest husband. Life takes us where it will—you, of all people—found that out. You are everything I ever dreamed of, there's no doubting that. I'm just so very weary, and I feel so completely useless."

The distraught husband took the flaccid hand in his, shook his head, smiled, kissed it, and held it to him, "Nay, nay, Dorrie—that ye nary could be. Were my days unendin', I could nary thank ye enough fer lovin' me, Dorothy Moore Dill, and thanks be ta God that ye do." He held tighter and joshed, "Ye do still love me, dinna ye?"

There was no way she could help but smile at that, and it seemed to quiet her. Somehow, she managed bit of a teasing glance back, then nodded and feebly clasped his arm once more as she fell off into a gentle sleep. He wiped away the soft tears that wet her dear face and held her for a long time before laying her tenderly back on the bed. Then he lowered his head and prayed as he had not done in years.

During the next few days, Dorrie did seem to perk up and appeared especially peaceful, content, and happy. Those days became a blur as he sat day and night slumped in the old rocker by her side. When she stirred from time to time, she looked over, smiled for him, and gently stroked his hand, but no amount of coaxing could get her to eat or to leave their bed. By mid-March, Daniel yielded to a wretched sadness and knew that she was lost to him. When the end came, unlike Mora's nightmare death from the plague, Dorothy Moore Dill slipped quietly away into the night.

Daniel's son's voice brought him out of his trance, "The taking of Uncle William and Aunt Mary at the Candlemas attack was bad enough," John said, "but Cousin Charlie getting snatched finished her, Da. If they could have been found and returned that might have helped, but there is still no word of their fate, and I wonder if there ever will be. I know that just cinched it for Ma, the constant horrors piled up and were just too much. It was unbearable watching her go downhill, we tried everything we knew to keep her, but there was just no stopping it. Did we miss something? Could we have done more?"

"Nay, Johnny. We all did our best, but 'twas out of our hands."

Alex and Robert silently agreed as they paid their profound respects to the woman who had redeemed their dear friend.

Captain John Floyd sent armed militia to accompany the Dill family and the cortège that followed the wagon containing her remains down the winding Cider Hill Trail to York. A few of the men were on horseback, but most of them walked. All carried cocked muskets and kept a close watch for any possible disturbances from the woods. Dan glanced back at the long procession of family and friends and shuddered. His heart felt sick in a way it had not since he had trod down the trail from Dunbar.

Although it was a challenge to break through the still frozen ground, Dorrie was buried in the old graveyard beside her mother, a resting place that lay near the mass grave that coldly held the victims of the Candlemas massacre. The scant remains of burnt houses scattered around the area were charred reminders of that disastrous night and its life changing consequences.

The hostilities certainly did not let up with the passing of a fair lady. The threat of treachery was always there, and death continued to slip through vigilant patrols.

On August 20, 1694, much to Alexander's dismay, Daniel Livingstone and his grandson left the safety of the Maxwell Garrison and were killed by Indians a short distance away. Patrols were increased, more precautions were taken, but still the savage forays carried on. Hopes for 1695 were dashed when it proved to be just as bad. The area remained an armed camp with few resources.

"'Tis afraid I am that York dinna see the worst of this mess yet."

"What do ye mean, Alex?" Dan couldn't see how things could get much worse.

"The provisional government's declared martial law on all the villages above Boston, and they especially mentioned York. The area is closed. This means that folks are trapped like rats. They kenna move on even if they want to. If they're caught tryin' ta go, they'll be fined or jailed. So, we're ta be human shields ta protect Boston, eh?"

"'Tis surely unfair. Goin' ta make it tough fer a lot of families—especially those who were burned out. We're lucky ta be fairly stocked up and independent here on the hill, but even our supplies kenna last ferever. I fear we're in fer a long haul."

Chapter 62

WHEN IT RAINS, IT POURS

EARLY IN the next spring, Robert Junkins, cautiously, with his carbine in one hand and a cane in the other, made his way down a slushy Cider Hill Trail to pay one of his usual visits to Daniel's fort. However, this visit turned out to be most *unusual*. He took a deep breath in, pulled himself straight, set his jaw and doggedly presented his friend with news he knew would not be welcome.

"'Tis a long way we've come, eh, Daniel? We had a legacy of bitter tears, but we changed that inta hope and its promise of more. We were just stubborn, mule-headed old grunts, but with hard work and the help of Sarah and Dorrie, we were brought back inta the human race."

"Ay, ye got it right there, Rob, 'twas their softness that saved us. They warmed our beds and our hearts. They gave us back a joy of livin' and families we ken be proud of. We have both been blessed, eh, old friend? Ye with yer fair Annie MacNab and Sarah—and me with Mora—then Dorrie—we're so lucky ta have been so dearly loved."

Robert saw an opening that served his needs and jumped into it, "Ay, Dan—'tis so—I echo every word, and 'tis why I want ta make sure that Sarah and my lads know that their futures will be safe after I'm gone. Ye know me pretty well by now, *bráthair*, and I suspect that yer aware that I could be in a lot better shape. Actually, my health has gone ta hell. It frosts my arse ta admit it, but I kenna even make it home from here without pantin' like an old hound dog. I kenna even go out on patrol any more—ken hardly even get out of my own way.

'Tis most aggravatin', Dan."

"'Tis more than sorry I be, Robert Jonkings. What ken I do ta help ye?"

"All's bein' done that ken be, but thank ye, Daniel MacDhughill. My Sarah's doin' the best she ken fer me with her fussin', great cookin' and all, in spite of all the wild goin's on from this ugly war and its confines, but I have ta face the fact that I'm nary gonna get any younger or healthier, so a couple of days ago I made out my will."

Dan was obviously stunned, "What? Are ye daft, *bráthair*? Yer nary goin' anywhere. Yer needed here more'n ever now. Ye kenna even think of such a thing."

"Now, calm down, ye old hothead. 'Tis nary such a bad thing—ye might even give it some thought yerself. Anyway, 'tis already done—I just wanted ye ta know. I've named my son, Joseph, as executor of course, he bein' the eldest—and he has reluctantly agreed. I haven't mentioned it ta Sarah yet because she'd most likely react the same way you just have!

"I constantly count my blessin's, Dan. I've done what I set out ta do here and much more. I consider myself the luckiest man on earth, and I will leave it at that. I was born in Scotland and I'll die in Scotland, and truth be told, I'll die a happy man."

Dan sat speechless and sulked until Rob changed the subject, "How's about we cast a line? Let's go see if we can catch some of those wily trout. I have a cravin' fer some—ye know how tasty my Sarah cooks those slippery buggers."

Daniel was profoundly shaken, but he bit his tongue, forced himself to butt out, and the two friends rambled cautiously off to the Cove and their favorite fishing spot.

Well into the next year, 1697, York continued to be a devastated shell of a town. Displaced residents remained in the garrisons, could not relocate, and were still under martial law. The Indian war front remained surprisingly quiet—until May of 1698—when Enoch Hutchins was scalped and mutilated as he worked in his field with his three young sons. His wife, Mary, and daughter, Sarah, eleven, watched out the window, helpless and in terror. Sarah tried frantically to rush out the door, but her mother held her back, musket in hand, expecting the savages to rush the house at any minute. That did not happen. The Indians grabbed the young boys, Ben, Jon, and Samuel, then disappeared into the woods and were gone.

While his older brothers seemed to prefer the bachelor lifestyle, Daniel and Dorrie's youngest son, Danny, married Elizabeth Foss, daughter of John and Mary Chadbourne Foss on November 8, 1698, in a quiet ceremony performed at her home.

On a much sadder note, less than a year later Robert Junkins was gone. He died peacefully on December 3, 1699, in the garrison home he was so proud of in Scotland Parish, surrounded by his beloved family. The gentle, but spunky warrior just missed making it to December 24 and his seventy-eighth birthday.

The loss tugged at Daniel's and Alex's hearts—they were crushed and grief stricken. With tear-filled eyes, Alex reminisced, "God, wasn't it only yesterday that Rob blurted out on the *Unity*, 'I was born on December 24, 1620, in Careston, Angus, Scotland'? And then—the dam broke and he let us inta his life."

Dan rubbed his head and wondered, "How many lifetimes ago was that anyway?"

Rob's burial plot was bordered by three hard rock maple trees that represented the Holy Trinity in the Scottish tradition. They had been carefully selected and transplanted by his son, Joseph, and his friend, Danny Dill shortly after Robert had made his will.

Rob's widow, Sarah, lovingly performed another Scottish funeral rite as her husband had requested. She carefully placed a small wooden bowl containing soil and salt on his chest. She bit her lip to help keep her composure as the memory flooded back of his nearness and warmth, while he explained the ritual to her and what he wanted her to do.

"I'd like the soil ta come from our garden," he had whispered as he sat with his arm around her on a bench near the roses, "'Tis ta signify that my body will become one with the earth and the salt will symbolize my soul, which will live on. Think fondly of me when ye do this, my darlin', Sarah, and remember that I will love ye forever."

With a heart that was heavy, but full of a love shared, she caressed his cold cheek and kissed him gently—then the lid was slowly lowered on a life well lived.

Bagpipes wailed as the Scotland militia escorted Robert's

The Resilient Thistle

impressive cortège from the Junkins' Garrison to his final resting place on a beautiful rise that overlooked the scenic marsh. That rise was now covered with snow and ice, but Joseph Junkins and Danny Dill volunteered for the task and had doggedly broken through the frozen ground to prepare the grave while Alexander and Daniel Junkins axed and shoveled until they cleared a vast space around it.

Family and friends stood firmly in the bitter cold throughout the poignant service to pay their respects and say their last farewells. After the final lingering tones of the bagpipes faded, Annis Maxwell, who had volunteered to stay with Sarah for a few days, left for the Junkins' Garrison along with Robert's three sons. Daniel Dill and Alexander Maxwell walked slowly and silently up the Cider Hill Trail to the Maxwell Garrison where they sat at their usual table by the front window and began their lament.

"Two down, old friend," Alex commented. "Dear God, how we'll miss him."

"Ay, the best of the best," Dan added, ". . . and two ta go. I ken say it now, Alex, I always tried ta put up a good front, but I nary thought we stood the chance of a snowball in hell of endin' up anything but dead along that march of sorrows."

"We all had our doubts, Dan, but 'twas the thistle that got us through, ye know that dinna ye?"

He was saved from delivering a bitter answer when Micum MacIntyre's tall frame loomed over the table. Dan and Alex nodded at Robert's empty chair in unison, and the three of them sat quietly with their memories until evening fell gently over Scotland Parish—far, far away—from Netherside and Balbinney Careston, Angus, Scotland . . .

where, there once lived a lad . . . .

Chapter 63

PICKING UP THE PIECES

THE SITUATION between England and France seemed fairly stable, and after the death of their leader, Madockawando, and some of his chief sachems, yet another peace treaty with the English was signed at Mare Point (now New Brunswick). Perhaps the Indians had finally begun to realize that they had been used as pawns by the French to advance their own ambitions.

No one in Maine or its territories believed it for a moment. They'd seen savagery firsthand after too many such treaties had been broken. The new century found folks still discouraged and under the same heavy dark cloud.

The *Act to Prevent the Deserting of the Frontier* that included York and eleven other villages was still in effect. This heartless law that made it illegal for residents to leave the area continued to confine York's citizens. They felt trapped, used, and hopeless—and the town's morale sank even lower.

On the other hand, Scotland Parish was dug in and determined to carry on as normally as possible. Daniel Dill accepted a land grant that he suspected could be his last. At about the same time, following in his father's footsteps, his son, Danny, received a grant of seventeen acres along the York River, not far from his father's fort—a site he knew that his friend Alexander Junkins had taken an interest in for some time, so with everyone in agreement, as soon as the paperwork was completed, the land was transferred to Robert's second son.

Things moved forward at *The Great Works* also. James Stackpole inherited from Spencer and Joy a residence at Wise's Gateway that he turned into a boarding house and pub with a license to sell beer, cider, rum, provisions, and horse meat.

Eliakim Hutchinson sold all his lands and mill at *The Great Works* to John Plaisted. Plaisted in turn sold one third of his lands to John Hill. John Hill married Mary Frost, daughter of Major Charles Frost and built a house across the road from the Hill Garrison where he joined neighbors John Wilcox, Basil Parker and George Leader.

On September ninth of the same year, 1700, Danny Dill's young wife, Elizabeth, safely gave birth to a daughter. The proud grandfather, Daniel Dill, was very touched when they named the child Dorrie.

Not long after that, Daniel Dill, took his son, John, aside and sat him down, "Ye know, Johnny, that my dear friend Robert Junkins was a very practical man, and when he made arrangements fer his family in the event of his death, I rebuked him. When he suggested I should do the same, I told him he was daft.

"But, Johnny, he was right, as he usually was, and—since I'm nary quite as bright eyed and bushy tailed as I used ta be . . . ," he winked at his son and they both laughed before he went on, "I have decided ta prepare my way by makin' my will, and as my eldest, I would like ye ta be the executor. The arrangement would be that I could stay on here fer the rest of my days, but everythin' I have would be left ta ye except fer what I'd like ye ta write down fer me now."

Johnny had been taken off guard, but he took the pad and pen his father handed him and started to write. "I want ta leave yer brother Joseph five shillings, William three, and Danny two. Not that they need it, of course. My God, Joseph is thirty-two now, Willy's twenty-two, and Danny is a grown man of twenty-one with a family. We both know they are doin' well, but I do believe they will be honored ta be thought of. I want ta leave dear Beth four shillings—she may need them since she is nary strong and lacks a means of support. Of course, I know that ye will take good care of her. Well, what do ye think, Johnny?"

It was a lot to take in, but after serious thought, John reminded his father, "That's fine, Da, but I guess I should mention one thing. As you know, I have hoped for some time now to make Sarah Hutchins my wife, but since her father's murder and her brothers' capture, she and her mother won't budge—they still won't let go of the possibility that the lads will return to the home they were stolen from. In case that she will one day agree to marry me though, I would want to bring her here to live with us."

"Nothin' would make me happier, son."

"As far as you settling your affairs, well I learned long ago not to argue with you. If that's your wish, then I think it is grand and fitting. Naturally, I will always take good care of Elizabeth for as long as she should need it. And thank you, Da."

Dan pulled back his chair and stretched himself as tall as he could. His silver hair slipped out of its rawhide clasp and fell in wisps about a weather-beaten, but still attractive, face that held blue eyes that had retained their lively sparkle and belied his seventy-five years.

"'Tis done then. Write it up and I'll make my mark on it—then tuck it away and we will speak nary more of it—except, of course, I might want ta mention it ta that rascal, Alexander Maxwell!"

King William of Orange died in 1702 and his sister-in-law, Anne, rose to the throne of England. Queen Anne made it her first priority to rekindle the war between England and France. As soon as the news got to Canada, that was all they needed—several hundred French and Indians under their new leader, Bomazeen, celebrated by luring Joseph Dudley and his party to an attempted peace parley, where they murdered them. The third Indian war was underway—in less than three months nearly five hundred Indians and French kicked off attacks from Casco to Wells, where their vicious onslaughts raised havoc, stole many lives, and carted off numerous hostages.

However, things had been quiet further south. In York orders remained in effect that all residents be sequestered in garrisons in that town—and in the Maxwell Garrison or the Dill Fort in Scotland Parish—but since the general feeling of late had been that the hostilities had burned themselves out with this last push, vigilance turned into carelessness and not all conformed to this ridged ordinance.

This proved to be an error with costly results. As twilight waned in October of 1703, a raiding party set upon and burned a home that sat just north of Bass Creek in Scotland Parish. The home belonged

The Resilient Thistle

to Arthur Bragdon, the very Arthur Bragdon that had escaped the Indians at the Candlemas attack. The now, *Captain* Arthur Bragdon, was out on patrol and had no idea that his wife and three children had left the safety of the garrison for a respite to clean the house and entertain the widow Hannah Parsons and her daughter, Esther, who had not long ago escaped the Well's attacks.

Arthur Bragdon had incredibly eluded death once more, but his wife, Sarah, and two of his children were slaughtered while his daughter, Abiel, along with the Widow Parsons and Esther, screamed desperately as they were carried off into the night.

Now, grief stricken by the loss of his family, Arthur organized many searches for Abiel, the Widow Parsons and Esther, all to no avail. He vowed vengeance against the radical Jesuit priest, Sebastian Rasle, who, in cahoots with the Governor of Canada, had been at the root of the war's horribly harsh deeds since its onset.

Daniel Dill Sr. had learned to trust his instincts and had never let up on his vigil against ambushes, he insisted that his family stay in the Dill Fort. Sarah Junkins' three sons did the same for their garrison. Danny Dill, his Elizabeth, and infant Dorrie, took his father's advice and moved from their adjacent home back into the fort.

Danny's Elizabeth had to admit that she felt safer there, but she put her foot down when it came to doing everything for everyone. She successfully drafted John, Willy, Joseph, her husband, Danny Jr., and Daniel Sr. to dig in and help her and Beth with the chores. That made life a lot easier and better for all, plus she was a great cook and everyone was more than pleased with the tasty improvements in the food.

Infants know nothing of war and mayhem, so in his own good time another grandchild arrived for Daniel, this time a son, John Dill, was born on November 8, 1703, to young Danny and his wife, Elizabeth. "We'll simply have to call him John, Lizzy. My brother has dibs on Johnny. He tried, but he never could shake it."

Young John was followed two years later by a brother who was born on February 2, 1705, to the prolific Danny and Elizabeth Foss Dill. Much to his grandfather's surprise and delight, they named this wee one *Daniel the Third*.

Hopes that Indian attacks had petered out were dashed once again when the third Indian War escalated and more lives were snuffed out as devastation and destruction continued. York and Kittery were hit again. Then the Indians old favorite—what was left of Cape Neddick—suffered with more massacres and ruthless abductions.

Richard Leader's daughter, Elizabeth, who lived in Lower Kittery was killed on May 4, 1705—her husband, John Howell, escaped because he was at work. Elizabeth's sister, Ann, and her husband, Samuel Clarke, who lived just over the bridge in Portsmouth, also escaped.

This news fell hard on Alexander Maxwell. Thoughts of his friend, Richard, came flooding back, and he knew how brokenhearted his friend would have been at this loss.

Ironically, in that same year, Daniel's eldest son, Johnny, still in hopes of making Sarah Hutchins his wife, continued to prosper and added another land grant in Scotland Parish to his holdings and assured his father that he would apply for more when he could, to increase the family holdings.

Just two months later, Annis Maxwell died suddenly from a heart attack. This tragedy on top of the sad news that related to Richard Leader's family, prompted a forlorn and traumatized Alexander Maxwell to make a most serious visit to his old comrade and friend, Daniel Dill.

"With Annis gone, Dan, and me with nary an heir ta carry on fer me. I've decided ta follow the examples ye and Robert set and have made a record of my worldly goods and designated what I want done with them, once I depart this wonderful Scotland."

"Oh, Zounds . . . dinna tell me . . . ken it be . . . another one?"

"Ay, 'tis the way it goes, ye old gizzard, so listen up. Ta begin with, I've sold the garrison, pub and all, ta Micum MacIntyre. He made me a good offer, and I've accepted. 'Tis only right, he's lived next ta it fer so long now, and he loved it from the moment he saw it, just as I did. Ye remember how I was taken by the spot those many years ago? And I can stay on fer as long as I wish, of course.

"I could tell that ideas ta improve it already raced through Mic's head. He mentioned that he wanted ta make his giant garden even bigger, and that he'd like ta make the property inta less of a stockade and more of a home again, once that's possible, if ever. Who knows when the dern Indians will ever be done with it. 'Tis so fed up with it, I am. Surely we've had more than enough of other people's wars."

"Ay, Alex, seems 'tis nary an end ta it, though. Ye just reckon 'tis over and another pops up, worse than the last. 'Tis nary the legacy we wished ta pass on, eh? Dinna get me started down that road. I dinna travel it too well if ye recall!"

Alexander cracked himself up, "Right ye are, Dan. 'Twould nary be good fer me ta drive ye ta drink . . . again . . . and 'tis a crummy miserable drunk ye make, by the by!"

"Hold on now, 'tis nary a thing ta josh about—ye ireful old critter. Ye know plain enough—'tis sarsaparilla I drink these days—and fancy it I do—so there." Dan decided he'd leave it at that, grinned, gave an *I surrender* shrug and brought Alex back to the subject, "Well, ah hum . . . um . . . back ta Micum . . . ye know what's best fer ye, Alex."

"Ay, I'm set on it, and in any case, I ken use the money from the sale of the garrison ta improve the small meetin' house we all enjoy. Ye know I love how it stands on that land I bought from Thomas Moulton years ago. I'm bequeathin' the buildin', the land 'tis on, and another piece that surrounds it at Gallows Point, ta the Reverend Moody with the understandin' that he will build a proper church and parsonage there as soon as 'tis possible. Seein' as he already lives there and 'tis pastor of the meetin' house, it all should fall inta place.

"'Tis in honor of the thistle I'm doin' it, Daniel, and our homeland, and alright, ye heathen . . ." He could tell by the smirk on Daniel's face that he was about to tell Alex what he could do with his thistle, so he admitted. " . . . ah, might be 'tis partly fer selfish reasons as well. But, mind me, yer descendants as well as John MacKinney's, Robert Junkins' and more, will all remember our roots, the thistle, and hopefully, some of the stories from our homeland too.

"'Tis the end of the line fer me as far as heirs go, but I'll have the church, and long after I'm gone I'll still be a part of it. All a slice of my dream, ye know—a church fer our new Scotland."

"Amen, Alex. I admire ye fer it. 'Tis wonderful."

"Just like the minutes on Prior Castell's clock, eh? Tick tock, tick tock, if 'tis nary one thing 'tis another. We're fadin' away, Dan. First there was a throng of us, now practically none. 'Tis pretty humblin', eh? Well, we kenna change any of it. 'Tis nary an enemy we two ken stand together against now, nary a new world ta conquer—and if there was it wouldna do us a bit of good! We gave it hell, though, dinna we, *bráthair?*"

"Ye ken bet yer bippy we did, *bráthair!*"

Chapter 64

FALLING LEAVES

ALEXANDER MAXWELL did not just fade away into the sunset as he feared he might. Two years later he was still enjoying life at his garrison and pub, where he continued to live, under the agreement he had made with Micum MacIntyre. However, early in the muddy spring of 1707, a distraught and concerned Danny Dill came bounding through the Dill Fort's front entrance. "Alexander Maxwell needs help, Da. Albert Dexter ran down the hill yelling at the top of his lungs for you to come. Any Injun within fifty miles could of heard and shot him dead. Anyway, Alex is asking for you—he's in a bad way; he slipped and took a terrible tumble from his garrison roof."

Daniel and his sons rushed up to the garrison and separated Alex from the ladder, bare bushes, and dirt, while a frustrated Daniel lashed out at him, "Alex, what in heaven's name were ye thinkin' of? What the hell were ye doing up on that roof in this wet slippery weather? In case it dinna grip ye yet, we're nary the lads we once were, ye know. We're both cozyin' up ta eighty, we'd be smart ta stay off from roofs even on dry days," Dan muttered on as they carried Alex inside to his bed. "Ye old pain in the arse, and besides, yer nary well a featherweight, ye know. Ye'd do better ta walk."

"Whoa there, Daniel, takes one ta know one as they say. Yer a crotchety pain in the arse yerself. Now, ye look here—ye know that the roof only leaks when it rains. How else could I find where it needed fixin'?" He had a hard time croaking that out, but he wanted to make light of his foolishness.

A piece of rusty iron that had been half buried in the mud was firmly wedged in his foot and blood oozed from all around it. In addition, he had bruises everywhere and his left arm was broken.

He was well cared for, and at first it seemed that his luck would hold and he would recover just fine, but infection was fast to set in. Before long it had spread up his leg—the dreaded blood poisoning.

Every time the wound was cleaned and wrapped in a new bandage, he would say the same thing, "Dern it all, Dan, look at all that pus. Dinna that foot just remind ye of John MacKinney's ugly ever weepin' leg?"

"I have ta admit—it might a bit, Alex. Good news 'tis, John carried that leg around fer a good many years. Ye wouldna want him ta show ye up now, would ye?"

"Good try, Dan, ye always were a cockeyed optimist. I ken handle the foot, but between the blood poisonin' and the pneumonia, 'tis draggin' me down.

"Dinna seem too long ago, we counted—*two down—two ta go*—from right in this very house. Well, it looks as though it will soon be three down, old friend. And, before ye know it, our tough old row on that *Trail of Sorrows* will have faded inta history. 'Tis been a whale of a ride, though, eh, Daniel MacDhughill?"

"Indeed, Alexander Maxwell. And ye have been more resilient than any thistle could ever be, my *bráthair*—and I mean *bráthair* in the most profound way. It was yer faith that kept us all goin'. Why we had ta go through such hell 'tis a danged mystery, but the four of us shared a bond that very few ever know, and in spite of all the pain, 'tis the love and friendship that will be what I always treasure.

"Ye probably dinna realize it, but I owe ye more than I ken say. Ye know I hate ta admit it, but ye've been right all along—and, I suppose—ay, Alex—the thistle.

"Faith is different fer each of us, 'tis fer sure. But it had ta be somethin' or someone unbelievably outstandin' that got us all this way. If 'tis any rhyme or reason ta it, I'd like ta be shown. Anyway, I came ta cheer ye up, old man, and here ye've broken my heart. Thanks fer bringin' a reluctant, ornery Scotsman along with ye on yer adventure. What an amazin' satisfaction 'tis. We're all proud of ye, Alex."

"I could nary have done it without ye, Dan. My God, I know more dead people than live ones now. That must be a sign that 'tis time ta move on! Mullin' over things, I've found that I dinna have many regrets, but I do feel badly that I picked on my aunt and Alex Mankaneer so much, even though they did deserve it, ye understand."

The two had a quiet laugh and went on to relive many more tales. Alex's stomach ached so from laughing that he asked Dan to help him sit on the side of the bed, and as Dan moved him he noticed that, although the years had taken their toll and even though he was well over seventy, remnants of his friend's magnificent physique remained. Something else remained also—still standing out, knotted and twisted on the now scrawny back were the scars and welts that had been engraved forever by the unfair whip scourging he had suffered at the hands of George Leader at *The Great Works*. Dan squirmed, *and ta think that the arrogant old bastard still lives comfortably there. Damn.*

"You will make sure I am buried near that old oak tree up by my meetin' house, eh, dear *bráthair*? And Dan, it must be a very small and quiet ceremony, and I want it to be held in what one day will be the Scotland Parish churchyard, no cortège. Remember, no big ceremony. Be sure the Reverend Moody refrains from one of his long, soul-perturbin' (as Rob would say, eh?) sermons. Just a short, cheerful remembrance—I beg ye, lad."

"Consider it done, my *bráthair*; ye know I will honor yer wishes."

"I go in peace with a heart full of love and hope for a better world, Dan—and ye'd best remember John MacKinney's threat . . . *Dinna grieve fer me bráthairs, I've had the best of both worlds and ye helped me through it all. Smile when ye think of me, or I'll be back ta get ye.*

"So, Danny, that goes double fer me, and dinna ye think I willna hold ye to it."

"I'll nary count ye out yet, but if I'm about when the time comes, Alexander Maxwell, it will be as ye wish, although I must say this dinna sound much like the pompous arse I know and love."

"I know 'tis jibin' me ye are, Dan, but a lot of truth 'tis said in jest. Indeed I have changed, and fer the better I hope. And while we're on the subject, I've noticed how much ye've improved over the years as well, old friend."

"Ye've got me as usual. Ay, and of course, 'twas Dorrie that did it fer me. She took in a blustery, rough, poor excuse fer a man and gave me back my life. It took me too long ta realize that lovin' her dinna take a thing away from my dear Mora."

They were silent for a spell, until Daniel went on, "Well, Alexander Maxwell, I suppose ye'll want the Trinity trees, the wooden bowl with the dirt and salt thing too?"

"Ye've got it, old man. A bagpiper, and a thistle engraved on my stone ta wave its lovely head over me. How else would I go out?"

That settled, Dan smiled and swiftly steered the conversation to, "We've had some great old times, eh, my friend? And some we'd as soon ferget as well. I'll nary ferget the look on yer face that terrible day when Rob Jonkings was sold and thrown in that wagon. We thought he was lost to us forever dinna we?"

Alex nodded his head and returned the smile. Daniel was quick to move on to other things and offered, "How's about we go down ta the old fishin' spot tomorrow? 'Tis been a spell since we've had a good old bullshite session."

"I'd like that Dan, 'tis a great idea. Let's do it. We ken sit on that old log, the one we all love where the river slips up inta the Cove."

"Ay—where the white lilacs grow. 'Tis about my favorite place." Pleasant memories flew into Dan's head.

• • •

The lilacs didn't have the slightest intention of putting blooms out so early, but new fresh grass and other young green growth had pushed up through the cold ground and filled the sunny spring day with a wholesome soft aroma.

Young Danny Dill and Alexander Junkins helped them down to the river's edge, propped Alexander Maxwell's leg up, tucked his blanket about him, and left him and Daniel sitting on the old oak log with a lunch basket and fishing gear. Danny assured them that they would be back to get them before sundown.

Daniel's heart sank as he sat there with Alexander just as he had with Robert Junkins back when Rob had broken it to him that he had put his affairs in order. With immense effort, he pushed those memories aside, put on a smile (a good facade), baited the hooks, and got them both settled in to wait for *the big one*.

The fishin' turned out to be just sittin', of course, but it was grand as the time-tested friends drifted back to days of their youth—the glory and the gore. By the time the boys returned for them, they found them still sitting there, leaning on each other sound asleep, and it took considerable shaking to wake them and get them home.

The recurring pneumonia finally overcame Alexander Maxwell, and when he died in October, Daniel Dill kept his promise. With the Reverend Moody's help, he saw to it that Alex was buried quietly on the north side of Gallows Point, in the manner he wished—just below the old oak tree, surrounded by the Trinity maples, stone with thistle engraved on it—bagpiper and all—in the beautiful meadow he loved, just across from Robert Junkins' Garrison off the Cider Hill Trail.

Chapter 65

ABOVE THE CHAOS

THE TOWN of York notified Massachusetts in 1705 that most residents were unable to pay back taxes as a result of being required to live in garrisons while their own homes and lands deteriorated. They were damned if they did and damned if they didn't—seemed to be caught between a rock and a hard place. Homesteads couldn't be worked and residents were not allowed to even attempt to improve their fate elsewhere since the colony prohibited them from leaving town while Indian troubles continued. Daniel's son, William, was disappointed and frustrated to find himself one of those caught up in the cauldron. He wanted badly to pursue a fishing career with the O'Hara's in Gloucester, but he was told that he couldn't leave. No one was allowed to go. On top of it, his position in the militia made him even more valuable to the area.

Life in York and surrounding areas was nothing like it had been in the old days—before the Candlemas attack. Improvement was slow and its struggle for existence was arduous. While most of the population remained confined in the garrisons, the Indians continued their sniping, and although the town and area were somewhat protected by troops, there were still many causalities and extensive loss of life.

Scotland Parish did fare better, even though its progress was tied directly to York's. Although Daniel had slowed down a lot and his health was failing, he still enjoyed watching his sons establish good lives for themselves in spite of all the area difficulties. He loved to encourage them and constantly tried to insert positive things into their lives.

Horses were more plentiful and cheaper now, so he purchased a huge sturdy workhorse to help with the farming, and to his family's delight, he traded some of his animals for two geldings, a gentle mare to pull Beth's wagon, and another old plug to help with the general work and provide entertainment for his grandchildren. This investment worked its magic. The whole family loved the horses. What's more, their care required building an addition to the big barn, a task everyone enjoyed digging in and helping with, and one that kept more somber thoughts at bay.

On July 16, 1708, young Danny Dill's wife, Elizabeth, gave birth to a fourth child, a daughter they called Dorcas. Danny assured his father that it was a well-respected old name, but Daniel made it known that it was not to his liking. "Too bad, Da, Lizzie loves it and that's good enough for me." Lucky for Elizabeth, she was young and strong and took childbearing in stride. A good thing because she and her husband both wanted a large family.

• • •

Since the murder of Enoch Hutchins in 1698, his widow, Mary, refused all attempts to get her to leave their home in Kittery. No amount of cajoling or threats could budge her—and Sarah would not leave her mother alone. The women clung to the hope that sons, Ben, Jon, and Sammy would somehow get back home.

Johnny Dill was part of a patrol that made regular visits to the Hutchins homestead to ensure their safety. It was there he had met and fallen in love with Sarah Hutchins, but as the years passed, he and Sarah had all but given up on a life together.

That all changed when Sarah's brother, Samuel Hutchins, now seventeen, was discovered and redeemed. By pure chance, one of many search parties that had traveled to Quebec to pay ransom for the return of a relative, found Sammy and paid for his freedom as well. Information from Sam led to the discovery of where Benjamin was being held, and he was ransomed also—then unbelievably, the third Hutchins' son, Jonathan, made his own way home. The happy reunions were wonderful; however, there were a lot of adjustments to be made and big expenses to be paid—but once Ben Hutchins finally took over the family responsibilities, Johnny Dill wasted no time. He made a formal proposal to Sarah, and they married in January 1709.

"And about time, too," Daniel chided, "Yer older than I was when I married yer mother. How old are ye, anyway—forty-three, eh? Indeed, yer old enough ta be a grandfather. Good gravy, yer brother, Danny has been married fer nearly nine years, has four kids, and ye ken be sure he's workin' on more."

Johnny laughed, "Well, at least I'm way ahead of Joseph, although I must say he has his eye on Elizabeth Tripe. There's no reason for him to drag his feet. I've told him many times it's obvious that she cares for him—but God only knows when he'll get around to courtin' her. It's just too bad that Willy wasn't allowed to spread his wings and try fishin'. He would so love to give it a go."

"I know he would, Johnny, but he'll find his way—fer now though, the militia needs every man it ken get. Ye know that I'm just jibin' ye about Sarah—I realize how long ye and she had ta wait. I be so happy fer both of ye. 'Tis a tear it brings ta my eye. Yer wife is a lovely woman and yer lucky ta have her—after all, 'tis well known that there's a definite shortage of lassies around here!"

Johnny, who was used to his father's joshing, gave it right back to him, "Da—you are one ornery old rascal—just as Alexander Maxwell often told me."

The Dills enthusiastically welcomed Sarah into the family. She obviously returned Johnny's feelings, was cheerful, helped Elizabeth and Beth keep the garrison clean and shiny as Dorrie had, and added another good cook to the fort.

Barely nine months after the wedding, Johnny and his wife, Sarah Hutchins Dill, happily welcomed a daughter on October 17, 1709. They named her Mary Dorrie Dill, after her two grandmothers.

As his father had predicted, his son, Danny Jr. was at it again—Lizzie gave birth to another son, Joseph Dill, on January 14, 1710.

Just about that time Robert and Sarah Junkins' eldest son, Joseph, married Abigail Ingersoll, and in October, they were blessed with a son, Joseph Junkins Jr.

Dan Sr. exclaimed, "'Tis a lot of Joseph's, eh? How will we ever keep 'em straight? We'll be needin' nicknames galore!" It seemed that the Dills and the Junkins had turned a corner—and good things were happening for them again.

Chapter 66

FICKLE FATE

AND INDEED, all did seem well. Scotland Parish remained buttoned up. The Junkins and Maxwell (now MacIntyre) Garrisons and the Dill Fort looked and were very formidable. The basic design of each had grown considerably, and their many add-ons provided safe shelter for ten to twenty, sometimes thirty-five or more plus various numbers of soldiers, in addition to the families who now lived there permanently.

Robert Junkins' widow, Sarah, had firm support from her sons, Joseph, and wife, Abigail; Alexander and wife, Katherine; and Daniel and his wife, Eleanor. A great comfort to Sarah, they kept order and kept a constant vigil at the Junkins' Garrison.

Micum MacIntyre remarried, had a family, and ran his garrison efficiently, as Alexander Maxwell had hoped, including the pub. He made sure that all was in constant readiness and even added more "booby traps" to ward off invasion.

The Dill Fort carried on in a similar manner. Daniel Sr.'s eldest son, Johnny—now married to the love of his life, Sarah Hutchins—was basically in charge since Daniel was, as he said, *no longer a spring chicken*—although he still managed lighter duties and put up a very good facade of being in charge. Sons Joseph and Willy had really wanted to move on, but still could not because of the *Act to Prevent the Deserting of the Frontier* that prohibited residents from leaving the area for any reason. Daughter Beth's health had never been good, but she was well enough to enjoy cooking and sewing and she helped Sarah and Danny's wife Lizzie, in any way she could. Life under the constant threat of attack was confining and far from ideal. Food and supplies continued to be sparse, but all made the best of it. No Indians or French ever attacked any of the three dwellings. However, any resident who ventured outside the fortresses took their lives in their hands and were fair game for sly bounty hunting savages who suddenly seemed to appear from out of thin air.

April 6, 1711, Danny Dill kissed his wife, Lizzie, checked in on his ailing father just after lunch, and jokingly asked, "And how are you this fine day? Feel like some fresh fish for supper tonight, Da? Joe Junkins and I are headed down to the fishin' hole. Wanna come, Da? Johnny? Willy? How about you, Joe? Anyone?"

"Sounds like a great plan to me," Johnny goaded, "but us workin' Dill's have already started re-roofin' the barn—want to get it done before it rains."

Joe Junkins rubbed his head and said, "Pay him no mind, Danny—my brothers begged off too, and I almost didn't come myself. Abby had a bad spell with the mornin' sickness, but as the day wore on, she bounced back, kissed me, and said she would love some fresh fish—and you can bet that my Ma, Alex, and Daniel agreed!"

"Abigail must be gettin' anxious. When is the new wee one due, Joe?"

"Not for a few months yet. I'm bettin' it will be another son. Abby said she's glad she'll be welcomin' our child before the hot weather settles in."

"Well, that should make it just about right. As you know, my Sarah's due next month. We're very ready! In the meantime, we all love fish. Let's see what you and Danny can catch. Just in case you get lucky, I'll tell Sarah to have the fire hot and the pans ready. Some fried potatoes and corn bread would slide down real good with 'em."

"Deal," Sarah Dill, heavy with child, called out from the kitchen. "He's hinting at that because it's his favorite meal. He's lucky we all enjoy it too! We'd love it if you would join us, Joe Junkins."

"Thanks, Sarah, but I've already told Abigail to keep the fire stoked and her pans ready to go as soon as she sees me comin' up the path with a bunch of fish."

"Another time then. Enjoy and stay safe."

"Oh, ya. It's a perfect day for it. Those slippery little devils are just starved and waitin' for us. Your mouths are goin' to start waterin' the minute you see the bunch we're goin' to haul in," Danny crowed. "And we're even goin' to clean 'em for ya!"

Joe Junkins made a droll face. He wasn't so keen on the cleaning part, but he shook his head in agreement, and the two friends headed down the path.

The sun was high, but the afternoon was still brisk as they sauntered jauntily down to the favorite spot by the Cove. Danny Dill Jr. and Joseph Junkins gulped in the fresh invigorating air and exhaled frosty clouds that hung like smoke about their heads.

They hopped over spotty areas of snow that lingered in crags and crannies all the way down to where the faithful lilac bush stood stiff and bare—only the hearty evergreen trees retained any color. The friends settled in on the old oak log, joked around, and were surprised when they started to catch fish straightaway. "I guess we'll show your Da we mean business," Joseph grinned.

"You know how I love to make the old man happy," Danny smiled back.

The Cove had always been a protected and safe place where the families enjoyed its peaceful beauty and plentiful fish. Not so safe on this day. A raiding war party of five brightly painted Abenaki had silently ventured down the York River and decided to hide their canoes just past the entrance to the Cove.

They chose a wooded spot by a clump of Cedar trees where they decided to relax for the rest of the day. They settled in and waited for the tide to rise and for darkness that would protect them while they slipped down the busier part of the river. If they hadn't heard Danny and Joseph laughing, they never would have found them.

Once they spotted the two men, a couple of the Indians quickly took advantage of the situation and fell on the unsuspecting friends stealthily from behind.

A heavy first blow swiped Danny on the side of his head. Caught off guard and dazed, he dropped his fishing rod and fell forward. The Indian buck wasted no time and quickly stripped his prey of boots and clothes.

Danny grunted, began to stir, and reached for his musket, but a wiry fist grabbed him by his golden hair and righted him halfway up. The hand moved up, firmly grasped his throat, and crushed it forcefully, while the other hand chopped viciously at his hair, scalp, and skull with a war axe. This was the young Indian's first kill, and he was not good at it, Danny Dill struggled in a vain attempt to deflect the blows and fight off his assailant, but his life ended abruptly once the blade hacked deeply into his brain.

At the same time, a second savage struck Joseph in the back, crushed the wind out of him, knocked him on the head and stripped him. This Indian proceeded to do a much more careful and neater job as he sliced Joe's full, handsome hair from his head, held the scalp up, took a step back, and looked with satisfaction at his coup before he released Joseph and threw him down beside Danny's body.

The naked bodies were kicked, then hurriedly wacked with tomahawks. Believing that the two were dead, the warriors tucked away the fresh scalps, scooped up the men's muskets, clothing, and boots, shared a quiet but happy hoot as they grabbed the freshly caught fish, returned to their jubilant companions, and paddled speedily and stealthily upriver rather than heading south as they had planned.

By early twilight, blood had congealed over Joseph's eyes, and when he somehow stirred and tried to rub them open he quickly found that his right arm wouldn't work. As he finally managed to squint out a look, he knew at once what had happened. His first thoughts were of Abby, *Abby—oh, God*. A bit more aware, he croaked out, "Danny, are you alright? Are they gone?" He peered over at Danny's slumped body and realized from its odd angle that his friend was beyond all help.

A thousand teeth seemed to be chewing at his head and the pain was so bad that he couldn't feel the wounds the tomahawk had opened on his body. Blood was everywhere. He didn't know if he could move and wasn't about to try. He figured that if he wasn't dead yet, he was on his way. Then something stronger than him took over.

Fear, not for himself but for his family overwhelmed him, "Must warn the others," he moaned, and from somewhere within he gathered enough strength to pull himself halfway erect and slowly and very painfully forced his way toward the Dill Fort.

It was Albert Dexter who caught sight of him trying to crawl up the path. He rang his panic bell and cried out for help. Terrified, everyone ran out of the Dill Fort to face the horrible bloody sight of what could only be Joseph Junkins.

Johnny Dill's scream followed Sarah's as they all headed down the path to help Joe—and at the same time glanced hopefully past him for signs of Danny. They looked fearfully at each other when he did not appear.

Aghast at the gory sight, Sarah retched, then steadied herself, retied her apron tightly about her swollen body and held the injured head as strongly and gently as the jostling would allow, while Albert Dexter and Willy Dill carefully carried Joe into the fort.

Once they had helped Albert and Willy lift Joseph Junkins into waiting arms, Johnny and Joseph Dill took off for the Cove in search of Danny. They were appalled to find their brother's blood-soaked battered body sprawled over the old oak log.

Joseph Dill immediately vomited onto the ground as Johnny looked hopefully for signs of life. His brother's stiff cold body dismissed that wish quickly, and he clenched his jaw, shook his head, and glanced over at Joseph, who wiped his mouth with snow, fought off more nausea, and returned the painful sad look in John's eyes.

"I don't understand how Danny and Joe could have been ambushed . . . especially here in this hidden dear place . . . so protected . . . so safe. How did those rotten skunks find them?"

"Joseph, I don't know. And I've no idea how we are goin' to break this news to Lizzie, to Abby, or to the Junkins family. What can we do? What about Da?"

"Let's get our brother home first, Johnny, and deal with all that later."

Chapter 67

PLAY THE PIPES SLOWLY

ONCE JOSEPH Junkins was safely in the fort, Sarah Dill asked Beth to bring a water basin and rags, while Albert and Willy tried to make him as comfortable as possible. Beth brought the water, but barely managed to hand it to Willy before she gagged and ran from the room. Willy swallowed hard and helped Sarah as she gently blotted up as much blood as possible from the many gashes that covered his body, but even such an easy touch conveyed too much pain to do much good. In addition to his bloody head, Joe was so badly wounded that no one could even imagine how he had managed to move, let alone get to the fort alive.

 Albert mounted his horse and took off up the trail to the Junkins' garrison to fetch Abby and Sarah Junkins. Once the initial shock of the unthinkable sunk in, Sarah requested that her son Daniel Junkins take charge of the garrison, then tried and failed to get Joseph's very pregnant and distraught wife, Abby, to stay home with the rest of the family and her ten-month-old son, Joseph, Jr. Abby started to panic.

 Albert Dexter took charge of the situation, and with Alexander Junkins' help, they hoisted Abby up onto his horse and gave her firm instructions to hold tightly to the horse's mane. Albert took hold of the reins and guided his horse and priceless package off to the Dill's. Sarah and her son Alexander followed them down the hill, also on foot.

 Abigail Junkins, made every effort to contain herself, but it was a losing battle. She kicked the old horse to try to speed it up, but it was insulted and just stopped. Albert coaxed, "That won't help, Abby. Be brave. We'll get you there as soon as we can." She settled down a bit and held on. All she wanted was to be at Joe's side.

Albert tried to prepare her for what she was about to face. When she slid off the horse she started to freak out again, but somehow a firm calm overcame her. She entered the Dill Fort strong and determined to face the atrocious scene she knew she must if she was going to be of any comfort to her hideously mutilated husband.

Joe tried to smile at his wife as she held his hand, and he slowly related the story while fading in and out of consciousness. "Take me home, Abby," he begged, "I have a great need to go home. Please, let's go home."

Micum MacIntyre, along with his sons and Joseph Dill, searched the Cove and area. The only sign left by the Indians was the dent their canoes had made in the Cove's bank. They were long gone—no one had seen or heard anything.

The sun was starting to set by the time the MacIntyre's returned to the Dill Fort. They took one look at Joseph Junkins and shook their heads. Abby and Sarah Junkins pleaded with them to help Alexander grant his brother's wish and get him home. A makeshift stretcher was hastily put together on which they carefully laid his pain-wracked body and carried him as gently as possible up the hill to the Junkins' Garrison.

Robert Junkins' firstborn, beloved son, Joseph, made a valiant attempt at life, but no matter how hard his loved ones tried, there was no way to relieve his pain or save him. He gave up the ghost after ten hours of pure misery.

Meanwhile, Danny Jr.'s widow, Elizabeth Foss Dill, was trying to deal with her own tragedy. Her husband's body had been wrapped in a quilt and placed on a table in the fort's great room. Lizzie was confused and disoriented, but she still insisted in caring for what was left of her husband herself. She tearfully wrapped his destroyed head again and again and wiped the wounds on his body over and over. Finally she relented and asked Johnny to help her dress his brother in his favorite shirt and Sunday best.

Willy took Danny Jr.'s five small children, the youngest of whom, little Joseph Dill, was not quite a year old, to their bedroom in the Dill Fort where Johnny's wife, Sarah, and his sister, Beth, tried to quiet and comfort them.

Lizzie Dill sat rigidly and unmovable beside her husband's body. Willy stayed with her while his brothers, Johnny and Joseph, continued with the many tasks that waited, including the funeral arrangements. They were still at it when the sun rose.

• • •

Daniel Dill Sr. had just recovered from a recent bout with pneumonia and was still frail and weak. After his son, Danny, and Joseph Junkins had headed for the Cove to go fishing, he decided to sit out on the back porch and enjoy his favorite river view.

Johnny's wife, Sarah, wrapped him warmly. He teased her, then reminded her to be sure to wake him as soon as the fish were ready. When no fish ever came and the afternoon turned colder, he figured the fish were slow to bite. He yawned, realized that he was tired, and decided he'd take a nap before supper. He had Sarah help him to his bed where he quickly fell into a deep sleep. His good ear was buried in the pillow, so he never heard Albert Dexter's panic call or any of the scurries that followed.

Once things had quieted down somewhat, Johnny looked in on his father and was relieved to see him sleeping peacefully. He decided to let him rest as long as he could. Once Joseph returned they'd all decide on when to tell him of the tragedy. Judging from the way he usually slept, he reasoned that he'd probably be just fine until morning, so he reported back to Sarah and returned to the responsibilities at hand.

Sometime in the tranquil hours after midnight, Daniel awoke abruptly from his sound sleep. He felt shaken and agitated. Something fearful nagged at his head. He wasn't sure what it was, but it had his attention. He was prickly and uneasy.

Beth sat with Lizzie while Johnny, Sarah, Joseph and Willy huddled in the great room, still in shock. They were exhausted and struggled to cope with the terrible loss of Danny and Joe Junkins—none of them noticed when Daniel quietly slipped out the back of the fort and slowly wobbled down the path to the Cove.

The old oak log was still swathed in Danny's and Joseph's blood, but the old soldier didn't seem to notice as he dragged himself up onto it, stiffened his back, and sat up as straight as he could. He had on only his thin nightshirt, but did not feel the cold wet of the night or the blustery wind that tugged at his still full head of pure white hair.

He sat silently for a long time, looking up at a sky that held no moon or stars, until—suddenly—it seemed bright as day. The glow moved toward him and he gazed into it.

"I see ye there," he whispered, "I see ye all . . . Ma . . . Da." He smiled and said, "Mora and Ellie . . . Duncan? . . . Dorrie! . . .

"Zounds, Rob Jonkings—yer a sight fer sore eyes—what be ye doin' here?

"I see ye all," he repeated, "plain as day. What's goin' on? How ken this be? And my dear brother, Willy—'tis so wonderful ta see ye, . . . but what's my son, Danny, doin' here with ye? Zounds, ye could be twins. How come yer here, lad?"

Their blonde heads glowed brightly in the shimmery light, but Daniel was not afraid. Rather he was overcome by happiness and a peace he had never known.

Danny reached out, "We've come for you, Da. Take my hand. Come ride with us. You're just fine, Da, and we all love you."

Daniel's face lit up, he smiled, reached over and clasped the beloved hand. Suddenly he was on a horse—and as they turned to ride off—he thought he caught just a flash of a giant kilt. He smiled and waved as John MacKinney, Robert Jonkings, and Alexander Maxwell joined them, and they charged off into the radiance.

• • •

No one missed Daniel until first light when his son Johnny, who hadn't slept, checked his bed. He panicked and ran into the great room, thinking his father might have wandered in there. Then he thought, *My God, he must have thought he'd tease Danny about no fish—or he's gone to the Cove to look for him. I have to find him.*

But his father was nowhere to be found in the fort, so John gathered his brothers and they went searching for him. The three of them found him—his stiff body somehow still sitting upright on the old log, his face frozen in a contented smile.

His son Joseph was overcome and could not speak.

"Strange, Johnny," Willy lamented, "he looks so peaceful. Look at that smile."

Their hearts sank, and they wilted like trounced dogs, still numb from the horrible loss of their brother Danny and Joseph Junkins. The surviving Dill sons stood there like fence posts—until Johnny finally found his voice and said, "I don't know how, but it seems that somehow, the shock of Danny's murder must have gotten through to him and finished him. Our father has come to the end of a long journey. God, grant you peace, Da." He glanced at his brothers and said, "God help us—let's take him home."

• • •

Joseph Junkins was buried next to his father, Robert, within the Trinity of maple trees he and Danny Dill had helped transplant. At Sarah Junkins' insistence, Daniel Dill and his son Danny were laid to rest nearby on the same rise overlooking the marsh and river.

Once the service was over, the cortège had disbursed and all was still—only the Dills and Junkins stood and stared at the three caskets until Sarah Junkins finally moved, kissed her daughter-in-law, Abby, and her sons, Alex and Daniel, and put her arm around Johnny Dill, "We'll miss them and the pain will never go away, but it's time for us to move on as they would wish and leave them to a well earned rest."

"We'll try, Aunt Sarah, God help us, we'll try.

"Farewell dearest Danny and Joe. And as for you, Da and Rob Junkins, this is it," Johnny sighed, "the end of an era. And what a legacy you proud noble warriors have left. You ran the whole gauntlet with raw unyieldin' courage and sheer heart."

"True, Johnny—and no one will ever know how they did it.

"Stubborn, cantankerous, incredible, wonderful—Scotsmen."

> Who truly knows what lies in the hearts of men
> or what they can endure and accomplish.

EPILOGUE

...AND—LIFE GOES ON...

The Boston News Letter of April 9, 1711, carried the story:

Piscataqua, (York) April 6th

```
    On Tuesday last five of the skulking Indian Enemy
killed two men about Scotland Garrison at York, viz.
Daniel Dill and Joseph Jenkins (Junkins), the last
whereof they also stript and scalpt and after the enemy
withdrew, they supposing him dead, Jenkins arose and
marched to the Garrison, and gave an account of the
action, and lived but about ten hours afterward.
```

• • •

A second child—a son, Enoch Daniel Dill—named for both grandfathers—Daniel Dill Senior and Enoch Hutchins—was born to Johnny and Sarah Hutchins Dill on May 26, 1711, barely a month after his uncle Danny Dill's slaughter.

On June 16, 1711, just a bit over two months after her husband's brutal murder, Joseph Junkins' widow, the former Abigail Ingersoll, gave birth to son, John, who joined his older brother, Joseph Junkins Junior.

The garrisons continued to be a refuge for residents, and when a count was taken later in 1711 it was found that they sheltered about 540 souls. Very prominent among these safe havens were the Robert Junkins and Alexander Maxwell (MacIntyre) Garrisons and the Daniel Dill Fort.

Dorrie Moore Dill's brother, Thomas Moore, traveled to all the Indian outposts he heard of. No news of little Mary or Willy was ever found, and sadly it was the same for many others.

The Indian Wars didn't just go away after 1711, and Scotland, York, and especially Cape Neddick continued to feel the brunt of burnings, massacres, and abductions, including the slaughter of livestock, until England and France made peace once more and signed the ratification of the Treaty of Utrecht on March 30, 1713.

Another Indian peace treaty soon ensued, and it seemed that the Third Indian War was over. The next ten years were comparatively peaceful. However, four more such wars were to follow, and the conflicts and hostilities eventually turned into the 1745–1761 war against Canada.

Captain Arthur Bragdon led an offensive attack that ended the life of the radical Jesuit priest, Sebastian Rasle, who in cahoots with the Governor of Canada, had been at the root of the war's horrible deeds since its onset.

When Robert Junkins' widow, Sarah Smyth Junkins, died on March 20, 1718, her son, Alexander, inherited the Junkins Garrison in his late older brother, Joseph's, place.

The Junkins family continued to live in Scotland Parish for many years. A direct descendant of Robert Junkins—Alan Junkins and his wife, Nancy—currently live in a home Alan created on property adjacent to the cellar hole of the garrison built by Cromwell's *Scottish Rebel Prisoner-of-War*, Robert Junkins in the 1600s.

The proud Junkins Garrison deteriorated over the years and eventually surrendered to a fire ignited by lightning. Alan and Nancy, with the help of their grandchildren, are constantly excavating and researching the Junkins Garrison's history as well as that of Scotland Parish and the surrounding areas.

The MacIntyre Garrison (originally Maxwell Garrison) still stands, silent and empty, on Cider Hill Road in Scotland, York, Maine. Its additions are long gone, but the main garrison house on its beautiful lot overlooking the marsh and river has been kept up and restored by the MacIntyre family, some of whom still reside in York, Maine.

The meeting house at Gallows Point that Alexander Maxwell had such high hopes for survived for many years but now is no more and never became the church Alexander had hoped for. The Reverend Moody went on to become quite a character—giving sermons from behind a mask, always marching to his own drummer.

No remnants have yet been found of the Dill Fort, but Daniel Dill's legacy was carried on by Mary Dorrie Dill, Johnny and Sarah Hutchins Dill's daughter, and their son, Enoch Dill—and by Danny Dill's' children: Mary Dill Carey, Dorothy Dill Lambert, John Dill, Daniel Dill III, Dorcas Dill Allen, and Joseph Dill. The author's family descends from Johnny's son, Enoch.

The Dill families eventually moved out of Scotland Parish, but reminders of their lives there exist in the *York Historical Society*, town records, and with distant relatives who live in the area.

Beautiful Bass Cove now boasts a development of modern houses. Scotland Parish still stands in all its beauty as part of York. The histories of the Scotsmen who founded her can be found with a little research. The well stocked *York Historical Society* and town records hold an abundance of intriguing information and has a *Junkins' Room* where the original cradle made by Robert Junkins is on display.

The towns of Unity, Berwick, and Salmon Falls still stand and welcome visitors. The twenty saws of *The Great Works* are long gone, but pieces of their history can still be found in local museums and with the many descendants of Cromwell's *Scots Rebel Prisoners* who still live in these lovely areas. The *South Berwick Historical Society*, housed in the *Old Counting House,* has loads of information. There is a *Great Works High School* and the *Chadbourne House* still stands near the gorge where the saws once worked.

• • •

About the block of fancy green marble in the Durham Cathedral floor that was said to hold healing powers from Saint Cuthbert—back in 1827—while alterations were being completed on the eastern end of the Durham Cathedral, the stone tomb of Saint Cuthbert was opened and a 1,300-year-old coffin made of oak was discovered that held a complete skeleton dressed in garments of linen and silk. Other relics were recovered, and among them were a small gold cross and an ivory comb.

Prior Thomas Castell's magnificent clock with the proud thistle on top has undergone many repairs and updates, but it still stands and can keep time in the south transept, under the stained glass Te Deum window.

Some of the graffiti the Scot prisoners etched into the stone walls of the Cathedral may still be observed, as well as the Nevilles' battered coffins.

The tragic dilemma of the Scottish prisoners-of-war confined at Durham and transported on the *Unity* as cargo to the *new world* was appalling, but it was not nearly as ill-starred as what befell those left behind in the Durham Cathedral. Half of these men and boys died in the filth from contagious diseases within a few months after the one hundred and fifty Highlanders landed in Boston.

Of the Scotsmen who remained in the Cathedral and managed to stay alive until the spring of 1651—five hundred were sold to Marshall Turenne for service in the French army, where they were forced to continue the fight against the Spanish—side by side with a troop of English soldiers that had been sent over by Cromwell. Very little is known of their fate or that of those sent to Virginia or the West Indies.

• • •

Overall, approximately 1,700 Scottish prisoners-of-war died of malnutrition, disease, and cold after being force-marched about one hundred and twenty miles from the battle ground in Dunbar, Scotland to imprisonment in the Durham Cathedral in Northeast England.

In 1946, laborers found bones while digging a ditch on the north side of the Cathedral. These bones led from the Cathedral's north door to under the music school. What or whose bones had been found was not verified at the time.

The beautiful Cathedral continued to be restored and updated over the years and was designated as a World Heritage Site by UNESCO in 1987.

What was suspected in 1946 was confirmed in November 2013, while construction was underway to add a new café in the Durham University's Palace Green Library. Durham University archaeologists were present when human remains were discovered, and the bones were unearthed by researchers from the University.

The tangled bones of at least seventeen and likely twenty-eight persons were removed from two deep pits. The extensive tests and historical evidence confirmed that the remains were those of Scottish soldiers from the Battle of Dunbar who had been incarcerated in the Durham Cathedral in 1650.

A commemorative plaque was placed on the Cathedral wall in a germane ceremony conducted in 2017 and an arrangement was made for the sad bones to be reburied at the Elvet Hill Road Cemetery in Durham City, close to where the remains were originally found. The bones of other Scotsmen who died in Durham Cathedral still lie buried in Cathedral grounds.

LIFE AND MAN—AMAZING—MIND BOGGLING!

ACKNOWLEDGMENTS

My daughter, Catherine Gemmiti—an amazing woman, contributor and editor of *The Resilient Thistle*, author, song writer, and researcher. Joyful thanks for joining me on this adventure!

Kevin McKinney, who, on a search of his own, took the time to help us with ours.

Alan and Nancy Junkins—Alan is a direct descendant of Robert (Jonkings) Junkins. His sharing of Robert's history, and much more, was vital to the revival of this story of Daniel, Robert, and Alexander—bráthairs, comrades, neighbors, and friends from almost four hundred years ago. And thanks for the friendship we descendants of Robert and Daniel share now.

Virginia and Dexter Spiller—The York Historical Society, York, Maine. Virginia is a walking encyclopedia of information, knows exactly where it all is, and played a vital role in the research for *The Resilient Thistle*. Among numerous other valuable research items, Virginia introduced us to the remarkable, *History of York, Maine*, by Charles Edward Banks. And, thank you to Patricia FitzGerald, Librarian, for permission to use this valuable record of the past.

The Palm Harbor Writers Group for being there when *The Resilient Thistle* was a foundling.

Mark Newhouse and Louis Emond—thank you for the thoughtful support and constructive advice.

The Creative Writers' Groups in The Villages, Florida.

Greg and Cindy Sharp, Sea Hill Press, Leesburg, Florida.

Special thanks to friends, relatives, and readers, for the encouragement along the way.

Printed in Germany
by Amazon Distribution
GmbH, Leipzig